Death Runner

A Jake Smith Mystery

by
H. David Whalen

Chapter 1

The farmland night sky is ablaze with orange glowing light and the stink of burning wood. It is shortly before five o'clock Good Friday, April ninth, nineteen seventy-one. The closest neighbor, a half-mile away, makes an emergency call to the Morrow fire department.

The elderly farmer couldn't sleep, the stench consuming his nostrils, and arthritic legs pounding him awake. He rolls out of bed earlier than normal and struggles to pull on his overalls. It was a tough night and a rougher morning. Days like this he grieves having lived alone since his wife passed years prior.

He makes his way to the front door following the beam of the flashlight clenched in his fist. He snatches his favorite sweat-stained straw hat off the rack, and he steps onto the front porch. The man takes one painfully slow step at a time down the four stairs and starts across the yard towards the barn. An old hound dog drags behind. Looking around, he sees the radiant western sky above his overgrown orchard.

Alone on the moonless dark road in a timeworn Ford pickup he misses, by mere seconds, the marina-blue Chevelle SS screaming past along the dirt road and sliding onto the main paved thoroughfare. It thunders, lights off, into the pitch-black horizon. The near-deft farmer might have heard the car if he remembered to put in his hearing aids.

The neighbor arrives at the disaster a good half-hour before the rural volunteer firefighters show up. The home has been an uncontrolled inferno for well over an hour. There isn't much they can do, outside of preventing the adjacent trees and overgrown dead-grass from spreading the flames.

Chief Jeff Gaulin gets on his radio and calls for assistance from the larger Lincoln City fire station. Morrow's outdated small tender is already halfway through its main tank as Lincoln's large Mack pumper pulls onto the scene and helps spray water on the lost home. An hour later all left is charred ember studded framing sporadically standing. Everything else is a smoldering heap of low flames and ash. Finally, both engines soak the remaining cinders and standby to let the mass fizzle out on its own. All left is a waiting game; it is going to be a long day.

As the sun peeks over the eastern hills, an A1 fire investigation team shows up called in from Fayetteville, the largest city in Washington County. Henry Mitchell is the lead man with thirty years' experience, while his partner has been working with him for the last seven. They survey the destruction.

Gaulin approaches the team. "Good morning, gentlemen."

"Morning Jeff," Mitchell reciprocates, "doesn't look like we can get started for a while." He turns to his partner and suggests they go for eggs and toast. "We'll see you later, Chief."

Just before noon, the investigators are back. They stand around catching up with various acquaintances for another hour. Gaulin explains that the first man on the scene was Charles Stone and points in the direction of the neighboring farm. He returned home just after sun up.

The two-man team drives over to talk with Charlie. The farmer tells them he hasn't seen the young family for a while and prays they are all right. Other than that he knows not what happened.

Back on the scene, the investigators suit up in their Velocity Nomex protective gear. They start shifting through the edge debris, before working their way into the depths of the destroyed structure.

Mitchell is where he believes should be a back bedroom. Carefully he scrapes away malodourous rubble uncovering a tiny-charcoaled encrusted foot. Continuing meticulously on, a small body

4

becomes unearthed. The fragile burnt lump cannot be more than a year old if that.

"I got something here!" his partner bellows.

"There is a baby over here," Mitchell returns.

Both men head to their vehicle. They need relief from the scorching ash piles. Between them, they guzzle a gallon of water. Mitchell radios to have a coroner come to the area.

The men return to their gruesome task. Just before dark, they finally finish. The two distorted blackened bodies are all they recover.

Chapter 2

She was born Elizabeth Marie Jacobs in nineteen fifty-three in Kansas City, Missouri. Her single twenty-five-year-old mother worked whoring the streets of the shantytown on the city outskirts.

After Liz's birth, it took more than a year for the Housing Authority to approve her mother's application and move them into a tiny studio apartment within the inner-city slums.

The streetwalker left her baby girl with a neighbor every night. The baby cried constantly until four years of age. The babysitter and her alcoholic husband violently tried to stop the crying; only making it worse. Enduring the unruly child as long as they could, the couple finally called it quits on their unstable marriage. The man moved to St. Louis and the woman went to live with her father in Chicago.

Without someone to watch over her young child, Liz's mother would leave the infant girl alone in her crib while standing on the corner or working close-at-hand bars. Nightly she brought home a variety of men. Most were vicious leaving her mother in a constant bruised and battered state. The only way she made it through each night was staying high snorting cocaine. Any money she made went to drugs. The neglected child was extremely thin and hungry day after day.

The same week the child turned six years old, her mother moved a man into their one-room apartment. Liz was left on her own to get herself to first grade and home again. Her mother slept while the sun was up and the unkempt man worked the day shift at the local Harley-Davidson factory.

The boyfriend rode his motorcycle to work every morning before six and returned drunk late every afternoon.

After a couple of months, the man started molesting Elizabeth as soon as her mother hit the streets. The drugged out whore either didn't believe the young girl's horrific stories or wanted the dirty man worse than her daughter. The abuse lasted two years until her third-grade teacher got involved.

One afternoon Mrs.Cobb asked the withdrawn waif to stay after school. Elizabeth sat quietly in her dirty torn dress, head down refusing to look at the teacher. Mrs. Cobb gently held Liz's hand and questioned her about her home life. After more than an hour with very little response, the teacher let her go home.

Thankfully Mrs. Cobb didn't give up. She knew it would take time and determined to save the girl. She started keeping Elizabeth late many days a week. After a month, the young girl broke down. She cried uncontrollably and sobbed out her home-life abuse tale. The teacher promised her it would stop that day. She took the girl to the office and phoned the police.

Immediately a detective team showed up accompanied an older woman social worker. While the officers questioned the teacher, the social worker talked with Elizabeth. She was good at her job and it didn't take long before Elizabeth told the whole awful story; every prod and poke in appalling graphic detail. The dumbfounded woman excused herself, leaving a detective to watch over the child, and went to the washroom. Even though her life was child abuse cases, she balled uncontrollably loud, worse than a colic newborn. This was the worst case of molestation she ever heard in her twenty-nine-year career.

Another half hour later they loaded the child into their car and went to Children's Mercy Hospital.

Liz was examined and questioned for hours. As soon as reports were finalized the detectives went to Liz's house looking for the molester.

It was a dark blustery evening and the place is empty. Liz's mother was gone in search of drugs and money and when Elizabeth hadn't shown up from school, the man strapped his meager belongings to the back sissy bar on his older Harley Panhead and hit the wet pavement west to California.

Elizabeth Jacobs is placed in a children's home and eventually into the foster care system. She never saw her mother or the evil man again.

Going from home to home growing up, Liz never lived in one place that wasn't marginally better than her mother's filthy apartment. Liz's abuse didn't stop as promised and continued off and on her whole childhood in one home or another. On her sixteenth birthday, Liz ran away.

She went looking for her mother, but couldn't find a trace the woman ever lived. It was unknown to her that her mother had overdosed on coke and passed away shortly after she lost her daughter eight years earlier.

Chapter 3

A man sits in his pickup for a half hour watching customers come and go from the QuicMart gas station on South School Avenue. It is after eleven-thirty Saturday night in nineteen sixty-nine.

Finally, there is a break in the foot traffic. He quickly pulls down his ski mask and runs into the small store carrying an old WWII Walther-P38, 9mm semi-automatic pistol. His father had brought the German military gun back from the European Theater in nineteen forty-five.

At the age of eleven, twelve years earlier, Kenneth Walker's old man beat him for the last time. Young Ken went into the garage, pulled the P38 and a box of shells from an old water damaged cardboard box filled with war memorabilia that his father kept. He loaded the magazine with eight bullets.

The son returned to the house where his father dozed on the couch, too drunk on vodka to stay lucid. They were alone in the house, his mother working late at a market. Ken stood over his father for the longest time with tears streaming down his face. Hatred at a final point consumed his mind and his courage built to killing level.

The young boy shoved the barrel hard into the man's forehead.

Barely opening his blurry eyes, "What the hell are you doing?" screamed the dazed man.

Without a word, Ken pulled the trigger and exploded his father's brains all over the living room wall.

Splattered with blood he ran to the kitchen and wrapped the weapon in tin foil before burying the package behind a shrub in the backyard.

The blast shattered the still spring air and a neighbor immediately phoned the police. By the time the child returned to the living room, sirens were heard screaming up the street.

Ken spent the next ten years in juvenile hall before being released at the age of twenty-one. He spent the following year wandering the streets of Fayetteville looking for work. Unable to find a job he started selling marijuana and other illegal drugs for a local dealer on the campus of the University of Arkansas.

Desperate to get into the drug business on his own, this night Ken went to his old childhood home and snuck into the backyard digging up the ancient Walther.

"Get your hands up!" shrieks the robber.

The terrified young male convenience store clerk quickly complies, "Please don't shoot. You can take anything you want!"

"Empty the register into a bag! No sudden moves or I'll blow your head off!" speaking from experience.

Grabbing the brown paper bag containing two hundred and thirty dollars, the thief runs from the store and hastily drives away. A mile up the road, Ken turns right on Twenty-fourth Street and drives up the small mountain mound to the local country club where he sits in the parking lot counting his take.

"He thinks, "At this rate, I'll need to hit two or three more places."

After hearing the sirens blaring past down South School Avenue, Ken leaves the lot, following the short curvy road down to the main thorofare. He drives north to the smaller town of Springdale and robs another station.

Using the same modus operandi he pushes on, west to the town of Lincoln for his last robbery of the night.

Back in his half-way house, he counts the bills; five hundred and eighty-seven dollars. It's enough to make a buy and get his own product to sell.

Randal Brown isn't pleased with his protégé going out on his own but concedes the white population of the university to him. Ken Walker is the newest drug dealer in Northwest Arkansas.

One night, a few weeks later, Ken wanders into a strip club and sees Lulu Love teasing a pole on center stage. Her long blonde hair flips from side to side to the steady beat of Creedence Clearwater Revival's *Bad Moon Rising*.

Over the next few months, Ken visits Kats often to memorialize the alluring young woman. During each visit, he stuffs every dollar bill he can muster into her bright pink g-string. Lulu never gives him a second thought.

Chapter 4

Living on the streets, after running away from her last foster home, isn't a step up for Elizabeth Jacobs. She survives scrounging garbage at night and hiding in dark corners during the days. She steals everything she can get her hands on and sells the bounty to pimps and drug dealers.

In 'sixty-eight she meets a group of hippies staying in Budd Park and a young man they call Moonrock. Liz moves into his old VW microbus with him. The couple tries to survive making and selling paper flowers on street corners.

Eventually, they leave the group and moved south to Bentonville, Arkansas. Neither could find work and they can't afford food or gas. The pair spent their days panhandling and their evenings arguing. They are there only a couple of weeks before they started physically fighting.

Liz gets up early on the morning after a fisticuff. She is bruised and sore from his beating. Elizabeth walks to the highway and sticks out her thumb. The first car to come along, a late-model Pontiac, picks her up.

"Good morning, Beautiful. Where you headed?"

"Not sure. I just know I can't find work here and need to try somewhere else."

"You're in luck. I own a little business in Fayetteville and always looking for help."

"What can I do?"

"Don't worry your pretty little head about it. I'll teach you everything you need to know. First, we'll stop and get you some food. My name's Denny. What's yours?"

"Elizabeth."

He pulls into a local diner in Rogers. Denny has a soda and Liz scarfs down a burger, fries, chocolate shake and two pieces of strawberry pie. Her wide periwinkle-blue eyes sparkling with delight.

Denny explains that as soon as they get to Fayetteville they will stop by his business and she can take a shower and clean up. He assures her sure she'll love the other girls and be able to borrow pants and a clean top. After which they will go shopping and he'll buy her new outfits both for work and play.

Liz tells the stranger that she doesn't have a place to stay. Denny again assures her she has nothing to worry about. He owns a small apartment complex where most of his employees live and she can bunk up with another girl until a unit becomes available. He also offers insurance and other benefits that she can choose from and he deducts from weekly pay. He goes on telling her that the first week he'll get her to a dentist to fix her teeth and a doctor for a complete checkup, all at his expense. The second week she can start work.

Liz was so excited at her first job she overlooks asking what's entailed.

A half hour after leaving the café they pulled into the parking lot of Kats. Liz exclaims, "Oh you own a bar?"

"Well yes. It specializes in men's delight. Your pay is minimum but all the girls live off their tips which are where all the real money is made. You could easily pull down five hundred or more a week. It all depends on what services you offer. It's like you'll be self-employed. The sky is the limit!"

"Services?"

"Let me show you around and introduce you to the other girls. Then we can sit down and talk. You never have to do anything you don't want to do! It's fun and easy work."

Kats is closed this early. As soon as Denny and Liz slip into the bar, she sees the stage and glistening chrome pole. Behind the bar is a young woman washing glasses. An older gentleman is stocking bottles of liquor on a shelf in front a mirrored wall. All of sudden a large reflective-tiled ball on the ceiling starts to spin spewing colored light beams around the dim room, and a voice from beyond shatters the quiet scene, "Good morning. Boss. What have you got there?"

Turning around she notices the DJ booth elevated in the back corner where a young man is testing sound and broadcasting equipment. He waves at the new girl, "I'm Ethan."

Liz's waves back. She turns to Denny, "What kind of bar is this?"

"Let me introduce you," ignoring her question.

They approach the bar, "This is Grace, one of our bartenders."

Grace looks over the filthy ragged young girl. She nods without speaking and turns her back on Liz starting to wipe down the back counter with a dirty dishrag.

Denny makes an excuse for her rudeness, "She hectic before opening. You'll like her when you get to know her," wrinkling his nose.

"Milt, come over here."

The older man walks over, "Hi, I'm Milton but everyone calls me Milt."

"Hi, Milt."

"All right then, let's go to the office. I'll introduce you to my wife and the three of us can chat."

Liz follows Denny through the clothes strewn ladies' dressing room into a large walnut paneled office. There is a giant floor-safe standing in the corner, with a couple of rifles leaning against it, and two desks with a well-dressed beached-blonde sitting behind one. The glass wall looks into the barroom through a one-way mirror. Liz has never seen a one-way mirror and surprised that Denny and his wife spy on everything that takes place on the floor. She also notes a closed-circuit system screen on the corner of his desk picturing the dressing room.

14

"Meet my wife Charlotte," Denny's opened hand outstretched toward the sitting lady.

The three sit down for their talk. They discuss the dancing and money and benefits. Liz is hesitant with taking her clothes off in front of strange jeering men. Charlotte tries to calm Liz down saying she's in charge of the girls and watches out for them. Charlotte also reinforces the fact that nobody ever has to have sex with a patron and only dance untouched. But she also states most girls make the majority of their income servicing the clientele. She tells Liz her stage name is Lulu Love.

After an hour of convincing Liz and Denny's wife go the dressing room where Liz meets Madison, the first dancer to arrive. She's twenty-one, a few years older than Liz, and extremely friendly. Madison lends Liz clean clothes and shows her where to shower and clean up.

After shopping with Charlotte they return to Kats. Her new boss asks Madison if Liz can stay with her for a while until an apartment comes open.

Elizabeth spends the rest of the day and evening watching. After Madison's shift ends the two girls go home to her apartment together.

Chapter 5

Powell Tucker is eighteen years old in nineteen sixty-nine, and a freshman at the University of Arkansas. He attended an early summer orientation weekend with his father, Newton Tucker, Lieutenant Governor of Arkansas.

The father and son arrived midday, a few hours before the Friday night orientation party. Newton took his son to Kappa Sigma's fraternity house and introduced him around. He had been a member and president many years earlier. Powell immediately accepted as a pledge for the coming semester.

As the father and son team are leaving, the current student ruler slaps Powell on the back, winking, "We'll see you at Rush Week, Brother."

Being young and naive Powell asked his father what the guy meant. He's told it's just a little harmless initiation ritual; nothing to worry about.

Powell arrives at school a week before the semester starts. He needs to move into his dorm room and plans to get acquainted with his new fraternity brothers. As soon as he's settled he heads to the frat house.

He receives a chilly reception from the few early members settling in and is invited to leave immediately. Going down the outside steps of the old two-story home Powell runs into Jackson DeFrey, the fraternity's president, whom he had made a few weeks earlier, "Powell Tucker, right."

"That's right."

"Where are you going? Come on in and meet the boys."

"Well, I already met a couple…they asked me to leave."

"Nonsense. Did you tell them who you are?"

"Didn't have a chance to."

DeFrey puts his arm around the new man and escorts him back inside. He introduces Powell around and the freshman is immediately welcomed by most. The head student leads him to the kitchen and pours a couple of beers into large red plastic cups from the ever-present keg, for himself. They go back to the living room and DeFrey sits in the regal seat that's there just for him. Powell wiggles onto the couch between two other brothers.

"Not yet young man!" DeFrey's bouncing his bent index finger up and down pointing to the floor. Powell glances around the room and everyone in attendance has bouncing fingers. He moves to his assigned seat.

Tucker starts to say something. DeFrey is wagging his index finger, "No! No! Only when you're spoken to first." Again all the brothers are following suit with the gesture. It's going to be a learning curve for the outspoken new student.

The group chatters away with stories of last year's Rush Week; all laughing and each adding to every tale of woe. Powell sits quietly for three hours. His buttocks are numb and feet tingling, but every time he tries to stand or shift positions, the finger-wagging and head shaking starts up again.

Finally, Jackson stands and announces everyone is going to the Grub Shack for a burger and brew. The group cheers and jumps to their feet including Powell.

"Sorry, this is a fraternity outing. Please sit back down. You can leave *after* we're gone," patronizing Jackson.

Twenty minutes later the group saunters out the door and Powell stands and stretches his legs, wondering what he getting himself into.

Chapter 6

Liz's life as a stripper and sometimes prostitute is neither a happy time or a sad time. It's more commonplace to see her dancing at Kats than anywhere else. Her life is nothing more than a day-to-day existence. She and Madison become the best of friends. Seven months after moving to Fayetteville Elizabeth is still sleeping on Madison's couch.

Her prostitution amounts to quick blowjobs in the alley behind the strip club. Liz despises men and refuses to get into bed with any of them. To get through each day dancing and servicing clients Liz has taken to smoking weed and taking capsules of Seconal, commonly called reds. The prescription drug is a barbiturate which took in higher than recommended doses results in a high stupor, poor judgment, and slow uncertain reflexes. Liz starts taking the illegal drugs thanks to Madison's prodding and supplying. It's the only way Liz survives each night.

All the girls have to split the extra money with *their* ~~they're~~ boss and Liz only pockets ten dollars an act. Cash is always tight and she struggles to make ends meet.

One freezing dripping night Lulu Love leaves work at three in the morning. She stands outside the front door of the club bundled up in her light summer-coat contemplating how to get home. She doesn't look forward to walking the nine blocks to the apartment. A semi-attractive young man appears from nowhere.

"Hi, I'm Ken, but my friends call me Squirrel."

"Not interested. Leave me alone!" recognizing the patron and assuming the fellow is looking for a date.

"Want to buy some smoke or something to warm you up?"

18

Liz figures she could use a little something for the cold wet walk home, "How much for two reds?"

"For you, Sweetheart, five each."

Liz forks over ten ones and handed two red pills.

"Why don't we go to Lou's for a cup of coffee. You look like you need someone to talk to."

"I don't think so."

"Come on. Biz is slow tonight," looking up at the angry leaking sky, "besides I have a warm dry car. One cup and I'll drop you off anywhere you want."

She looks over the skinny guy. His chocolate-brown wet hair plastered against his head, with bangs trailing streams of water down his face. But those magical hazelnut eyes are too much to resist. Liz follows Squirrel to his car. They race over to Lou's All Night Diner.

Sitting in a worn-out green booth they stare at each other shivering while waiting for the coffee.

"Look at us," the young man comments, "a couple of drowning squirrels without any nuts." Both break into laughter.

The pair sits enjoying each others company for a couple of hours over the hot beverages and burgers followed by a slice of stale apple pie each. The rains stop as the sun rises. Liz looks out the picture window next to them, "It's getting light. I really need to get home and go to sleep."

True to his word, Squirrel reluctantly stands, "All right but I need to see you again. Can we have dinner and catch a movie?"

"I'm off on Mondays. Would that be alright?"

"Elizabeth anytime is right for me."

After their first date, the following week, they become inseparable and spend every opportunity together. Four months later they are again at Lou's sharing an early morning breakfast in the dark. Liz is quiet and not herself. Squirrel is scared it's over and waiting for the hammer to drop.

"What's going on, Elizabeth?" he can't stand it any longer.

After a long moment staring into his intense haunting eyes…those eyes. "Ken, I'm pregnant," anticipating he'll run like a squirrel fleeing a trap.

"That's wonderful. Let's get married!"

Stunned by the jolt, "Married? Are you sure?"

"Of course. We'll go to the justice of the peace this morning." He braids a small band from his unused napkin and places it on the third finger of her left hand. Laughing the pair make plans for their future.

By nine-thirty, they're husband and wife. Early afternoon they find a large run-down house, out in the country. The drug dealer hands over a month's rent and deposit. Rushing back to Liz's apartment the pair grabs her limited belongings.

Her husband waits in the car while Liz goes into Kats and tells Madison she married and moved out. Madison squeezes her tight and long, "I'm so happy for you. Does he have a brother?" Both enjoy the hysterical moment.

Liz heads to the office to quit. Denny's furious. Charlotte is outwardly calm, "Lulu, you can't just walk out. You're revered here by all of us and our customers."

Liz is crying. There is no way she's staying, besides she'll be showing before long and couldn't work anyway.

The boss woman continues, "Honey, we both happy for you. Why don't you take some time off? Babies are expensive and you'll need as much money as you can make. After giving birth, get into shape and come back, even if it's just a couple of days a week. You're always welcome here." She ends, "Good luck Elizabeth, and keep in touch with us."

That's is exactly what happens. After baby Emily is brought into this world Liz returns to Kats three nights a week.

Chapter 7

The start of classes and the beginning of Rush Week for the new students entering UOA starts the last Monday in August following the summer orientation. Powell Tucker meets his nerdy roommate, Phillip Ward, the week before. Phil is attending for the education and not interested in joining a fraternity.

The bookish student disgusts Powell. He can't understand anyone refusing to be humiliated by the older bullies of Kappa Sigma. They aren't going to be friends.

Kappa Sigma holds a Sunday evening event for the twenty-three new pledge candidates, outlining their requirements for membership.

After the national rules, President Jackson DeFrey launches into the four unofficial rules of their chapter. First and foremost a candidate must be from an upper social and economic family. The fraternity is not a welfare department. And no rednecks. Second, every first-year member must contribute twenty-five percent of all monies received, family support or work income to the fraternity. This is used primarily for parties. Third, each student must possess the mental fortitude to be accepted into the secret Society Of the Dagger after two years as a regular member. Lastly, all members must be straight with no exceptions. Any member discovered otherwise will be subjected to SOD's wrath!

"Any questions?" DeFrey asks the floor sitting pukes.

"When can we move into the frat house?" Tucker speaks up.

"Pukes don't ever talk first! Sit quiet, heads lowered. Never, never make eye contact with anyone! If you have a question raise your hand. If a brother is interested in what you have to say, he will call on you!" DeFrey asks, "Anyone care what this Puke has to say?" No Brother cared.

"Any other questions?" Not one puke raised a hand.

"Gentleman, go to your dorms and make your toga. You'll be wearing this every day and night for the week. Don't remove it unless a Brother requests you to. Let the games begin!"

Every Kappa Sigma member walks by Powell and slaps the back of his head, "Dumb ass! Where did we find such a stupid child? What shit-hole did you crawl out of!" and similar comments.

"We adhere to a strict Code of Silence. If I hear of anyone repeating a word from this House, SOD will bury you!" glaring at each floor sitting student one at a time. "We'll see you *pukes* tomorrow. Now get the hell out of here!" Jackson ends the meeting.

Back in his room, Phil asks how the meeting went and Powell refuses to comment or even look at his roommate. He tears the sheet off his bed and configures it around his body as a makeshift toga, before laying on the bare mattress and staring at the ceiling until he falls asleep.

Monday morning Powell heads to his first class. He walks by a couple frat members who each slap the back of his head, "You're too dumb to make Kappa Sigma, Puke!" and "What makes you think you're Kappa material?" respectively.

Tucker keeps his head lowered and quietly walks on.

"Hey Puke, did I dismiss you?"

Powell returns and stands solemnly before them, staring at their shoes.

"Drop and give me twenty!"

Powell falls to the dirty cement and struggles under his loose fitting sheet to accomplish the task. A small group of students stops to watch and add their unruly comments. After they let him go, the freshman continues to class. Along the way, other students stare or laugh at his wardrobe and submissive behavior.

Chapter 8

Powell Tucker enters room 2254 in the Old Main Building. It's a large theater-style auditorium with two hundred seats slanted upward from the stage. He scans the room. Phil Ward, his roommate, is sitting front row center. Looking further over the scattered students he spies two sheet-draped pledges close to the last top row. Powell climbs the stairs and takes a seat next to them. The three exchange nods but refrains from verbal acknowledgments.

At precisely nine o'clock a suited man sporting short-cropped hair and salt and pepper stubble along his chin line walks across the stage to the center podium. The room immediately goes deadly silent.

The man slowly looks over the newest crop of students, "My name is Professor Jachimiak and this is Polisci 101. Anyone in the wrong class should leave now." No one moves. "Good." Continuing on with fiery green eyes, "You!" Pointing, "Ninth row, third seat, adorned in your bed sheet, stand up." Small giggles cover the room as the man gets to his feet.

"Name!"

"Powell Tucker, Sir."

"Mr. Tucker, this is a serious class, you should get out of bed before attending." More laughs.

"Yes, Sir. I take this class *very* seriously. I'm planning to follow in my father's footsteps and pursue a career in state government," hoping to bait the professor into questioning his lineage, and affording the opportunity to impress his classmates.

"Mr. Tucker, dreaming is one thing, achieving is another. I would hope your aspirations would exceed any of your relatives. Please sit down."

Embarrassment blankets his face as he plops into his sit.

"Mr. Tucker, one more thing."

Powell jumps back to his feet, "Yes Sir?"

"Do you support or oppose the Viet Nam insurgency?"

Powell thinks, "This is a trick question. If I support the war I'm nothing more than a status quo want-a-be politician and if I oppose, how could I have a hope of joining my father's regime?" He answers, "There are good reasons supporting both sides. If we continue…"

Interrupting, "Thank you, Mr. Tucker, spoken like a true politician. Please take your seat."

Relieved, Powell sits back down.

Professor Jachimiak resumes his two-hour lecture and assigns reading the first three chapters of the text before the following Wednesday class. The students are dismissed. As they're shuffling past the stage, "Mr. Tucker, Can I see you for a minute?"

Powell stands next to the raised platform with the Devil glaring down. When the room is empty except for the older professor and young student, "Mr. Tucker, you seem like an ambitious fellow. There is no doubt you could be the Lieutenant Governor one day." He obviously knows who Powell's father is. "Have you ever heard of SDS?"

"No, I can't say I have."

"Students for a Democratic Society. They have a chapter on campus. I suggest you check them out. That'll be all for today." The professor turns on walks across the stage to a far exit door.

Chapter 9

By four-thirty, after a full day of humiliation, he's on his way to the frat house. Without a word or eye contact, Powell takes his place on the floor next to the first arriving pledge.

A beer drinking brother pipes up, "Maybe there is hope for that dumb-ass puke. He can at least tell time!" The house fills with rowdy laughter coupled with added comments about Powell's aptitude.

By five-ten twenty pukes are on the floor. Three others don't show having decided frat life isn't for them.

"Pukes, take off your togas!" an unknown Brother instructs.

One anxious young kid jumps to his feet and tears off his bed sheet.

"Who told you to stand? And why are you wearing underwear?"

"I…I thought you wanted me to."

"Hell no!" yells DeFrey. "Anyone who can't follow simple instructions isn't ever going to be Kappa Sigma! Get the *hell* out of here!"

With tears trickling down his face, the young man grabs his sheet and runs to the door. The nineteen left are frantically squirming around the floor pulling off their togas. Each is handed a bottle of baby oil and instructed to cover their bodies while being warned not to get a drop on the floor. One nervous kid manages to spill his bottle.

DeFrey pulls a toothbrush from his back pocket. He coughs up a large glob of mucus and spits it into his free hand. After coating the toothbrush, he hands it to the offending pledge, "Get that crap off my floor. Then clean this house from top to bottom. And don't let me catch you off your knees!"

Turning to the others, he points at the front door, "All right pukes, to the flagpole!"

The group of slippery young lads runs naked to the front yard. Most are covering their private parts with their hands. A group of sorority sisters already line the sidewalk. All are laughing and pointing with the exception of their pledges, who stare at the ground.

"Gentlemen reach for the stars!"

Every pledge follows the command. The girl cheerleaders jeer and scream in delight.

"Puke Tucker you're up first. Climb the pole!"

Powell gets about halfway up the dry pole before sliding back to earth. No other puke makes it as far up as the pole keeps getting slicker and slicker with every attempt.

After the last try, the sorority ringleader announces, "Girls, it's your turn. Strip to your underwear and show them how it's done!"

One male pledge takes a peek and is caught.

"You just washed out, Puke!" shouts a brother.

The embarrassed young man starts for the house to retrieve his sheet.

"Not so fast. You're never entering my house again, Puke!"

"I'm just getting my toga," through dry sobs.

"I own that sheet now! Get out of here before I have the rest of these pukes take care of you!"

The kid runs off as fast as his legs can move. As soon as he hits the cement sidewalk he slips and cracks his head to everyone's glee.

"Get him Pukes!"

The kid jumps to his feet and disappears between the buildings.

The rest of the week is similar, classes during the day, new tortures every night.

The pledges endure "Running The Gauntlet", maneuvering through two rows of brothers while being punched and brutalized, "Assuming The Position", being paddled until they can't sit down. "Dinner Time", swallowing raw eggs and Tobasco sauce sprinkled with live red fire ants. Every night new and worse activities are thought up. The list never ends until the Saturday night's finale, the Toga Tromp.

The first ceremony is in the front yard, de-robbing and burning of the puke's togas in a large bonfire. At the end of the night before activities, the pledges were told to wear shorts under their togas for the party.

The frat house fills with men and women, liquor and marijuana. Unkown to Powell hard drugs are secretly being consumed upstairs in individual rooms.

The remainder of the night the barely covered pledges serve liquor, food, weed and anything requested. Between the serving tasks, they clean vomit and spilled food and drinks with toothbrushes, pick up empty containers and trash with their mouths and all other demeaning janitorial tasks the brothers can think up.

Living through the last party night of Rush Week, the six remaining pledges attend the Sunday evening induction ceremony. Powell finally accepted as a full Kappa Sigma Brother.

Chapter 10

In December, a week before Christmas, Ken Walker strolls into Kappa Sigma's frat house. It is the evening after the last day of finals before winter break. Friday, the next day, most students head home for the holidays. The frat house's annual Santa Basha has the house packed with drunk and stoned students.

"Hey Squirrel, we need to talk!" Jackson DeFrey screams above the throbbing beats of Led Zepplin's *Whole Lotta Love* with the dancing students shrieking out-of-tune sing-alongs.

The drug dealer fights through the throng to DeFrey, "What's up, man?"

"Let's step into the backyard."

Outside there is a large circle of boys and girls passing joints around. In a dark corner, a few young men are sharing a hashish pipe. An upstairs bedroom contains the cocaine snorters and throughout the house, a few students are taking tabs of LSD.

"You need more Mary Jane?" Squirrel asks.

"Got plenty, but I do need Blow."

"Don't have any right now."

"Make a run!" and DeFrey walks off.

Squirrel heads for his Chevelle and roars down the street to the nearest Circle K. He goes to the outside pay phone and calls his former boss, who he uses as his supplier. Randal Brown conceded the UOA campus territory to Walker but retains the BAD members and their friends.

He makes an arrangement to pick up half-dozen eight balls of cocaine, all his source has in stock. Squirrel pays Randal one-hundred-twenty dollars for the twenty-one grams. He drives over to a small neighborhood market, he frequents and buys a pound box of powdered sugar. The man takes his money and leaves the box sitting on the counter. Squirrel has to ask for a paper bag.

"Hey, Mike, I need to take a leak!" grabbing his purchase.

"You want me to hold it?" the clerk shakes his head, "You know where it is, man."

Once inside the small dirty one-head room, the dealer locks the door. He opens the powdered sugar and pours a quarter of the box into the paper bag. After ripping off a top flap, he throws the opened container with the rest of the sugar into the trash. Squirrel then does a line of coke before adding the rest to the bag and vigorously shakes the concoction, cutting the drug by more than one-to-one. He pulls a box of plastic sandwiches bags from beneath his coat, where he had stashed it after stealing them off a market shelf. Pulling out fifteen bags from the twenty-four pack he again discards the extras.

The dealer forms a make-shift scoop from the cardboard flap. He scoops the white powder into the fifteen clear baggies. After a few adjustments between bags, he's satisfied they're all close to equal and ties the top of each into a knot.

He stuffs two jacket pockets with the baggies and heads to his car and back to the party.

"Jeez, what took you so long?' Jackson spots Squirrel.

Ignoring the comment, "I got fifteen eightballs, who wants one?" glancing around the crowded room.

"Let's go upstairs."

Once in DeFrey's bedroom, the negotiations begin.

"How much do you have?"

"Fifty-five grams. Like I said fifteen eightballs."

"How much?"

"Thirty."

"It was twenty last week!"

"That's when there was availability. This is the last in the county for a month. My guy ripped me off but I knew you needed it and paid! Do you want one or not?"

"One, I want them all. But at twenty-five!"

Knowing he only paid nine after the cut, "Crap, I can't-do that!"

"You're not only doing it but you throwing in twenty-five joints for *free*!"

"No way, man!"

"Bad idea…let me get a couple friends up here! You're leaving without the powder. It's your choice if the cash goes or not!" Adding, "And then you're eighty-sixed, we'll buy from Brown."

Doing some quick math in his head, Squirrel decides two-fifty-five in his pocket for an hour's work and continued business will have to suffice. Thinking, "Besides I really don't have an option."

"Ok! Ok, man! It's Christmas, this time only!"

DeFrey exchanges the cash and for the fifteen baggies, "Where's the weed?"

"I'll have to get it out of my car." Squirrel heads downstairs and isn't planning to return with the freebie. He figures by the time everyone's back from holiday, Jackson won't remember their deal.

On the front porch, Powell Tucker stops him, "I need some stuff."

"Follow me, man !"

Walking down the paint worn creaky front steps, Squirrel asks, "What are you looking for?"

"A couple of joints."

"I thought you didn't use?"

"If I'm getting any tonight, she wants to smoke a little."

"I can sell you a nickel bag, but you'll have to roll your own."

"Where do I get the papers."

"Ask DeFrey, he's a regular shopkeeper."

Chapter 11

"Chief, your new officer from San Diego is here," Secretary Margret calls Chief Parson through the open door.

It is the second week in February, more than a year before the farmhouse fire. Detective Jake Smith, let go from the San Diego Police Department moved to Fayetteville, Arkansas to start a new job as a patrol officer. Smith didn't want to live to close to his job and found a nice rental east of Springdale on an arm of Beaver Lake, a half-hour drive northeast.

"Show him in," Parson responds.

"Good morning, Chief," Jake Smith, hand extended.

"Glad you made it, Smith." Parson does not stand or accept his outstretched hand. "Have a seat. I'll just be a minute, and then I introduce you around," as he goes back to handwriting on a yellow legal pad.

"All right, let's get to work." The chief stands, and Jake follows him to his secretary's desk. "Margret, can you type this up and put a copy in everyone's box?" setting down the sheet ripped from his pad.

"I'll do it right now, Sir."

The pair walks down one floor to a front office. They pass a few personnel on the way and Smith's not introduced to any of them. Without knocking Parson enters with Smith trailing. "Conner, this is Smith from California."

"Good morning, Conner," Smith again extends a hand.

Without standing, or accepting the shake, "Lieutenant Evans, if you don't mind."

"Of course, Lieutenant," but was thinking, "Lieutenant Prick is more apropos."

"I'll leave you two to get at it then." Chief Parson leaves.

Conner Evans ignores Smith and continues reading a report. Jake remains standing and glances around the office. It's hospital-white and the only thing on the walls is a cork bulletin board with a couple of notes pinned to it. Looking over Evan's desk, there are no personal items seen, no family pictures, knickknacks, or even a tarantula embed globe paperweight.

Smith is thinking to himself, "Where's the Southern hospitably I've heard about?" after meeting the first two bulldogs.

Finally, the lieutenant stands "Come with me!"

"I'll be the dog's tail!"

Evans glares at him trying to figure out what he means. Smith's twinkling blue eyes and soft smile mask the sarcasm.

They walk into the locker room, "Officer Clarke, here's your new partner." Evans pivots and leaves.

"We'll get together soon, Lieutenant," Smith cannot resist calling at his back.

"Senior Patrol Officer Kelson Clarke," the much younger officer states.

"Jake Smith," he answers sans sticking out a hand. Even the much larger San Diego department is not as particular in hierarchal formality as this hog-waller town.

Kelson gets Smith indoctrinated with the procedures of acquiring a uniform, badge, gun, and other amenities of the job. "After you're finished, go to lunch at noon and we'll hit the streets when you get back!"

"Great, where can I get a two-martini lunch?"

"Have you found a church yet?"

"Haven't been looking, should I be?"

"Only if you want to live here!" it is Kel's turn to smile. "Welcome to the Bible-belt, Smith."

After finding a small deli, a block away and eating half his hoagie sandwich while downing two cups of coffee, Smith returns to the station ready to work.

Clarke is standing next to a squad car in the east parking lot as Smith walks up. The patrol officer tosses him the keys, "You're driving," and gets into the passenger seat.

The team spends the afternoon cursing town, the old historic downtown section, the University of Arkansas, surrounded by lower-income residents and bars, and the subdivisions of the East and West ends before finishing their shift in the large luxurious neighborhoods of the South section.

Arriving back at the station, "We're on the late shift the rest of the week through the weekend. I'll meet you here a little after nine tomorrow night, and we'll do some real police work," Clarke informs the new man.

"Where can I get my schedule?" Officer Smith, inquirers.

"I'll give it to you tomorrow. You can just plan on working every night, from ten to seven."

No goodbye, or see you later or want to get a beer. Both men head for their respective cars and leave the area.

Smith is a half-block away when he remembers to turn around and go back to the station to change into his civvies. He has not had on a real uniform for more than eight years.

Chapter 12

The first training month with Officer Clarke is a real treat for Smith.
The squad car chit-chat is all business. Kel is not a coffee drinker
and ignores any requests from Jake to make a quick unscheduled
stop. Moreover, Smith gets the butt of the work.

When they pull over a speeder, Kel waits in the vehicle, unless
he needs to stretch his legs. Kids are pushing each other on the
sidewalk and Smith has to break it up. He only received one
accidental punch in the cheek. One domestic disturbance left Smith
wrestling with the drunken brute on the front lawn, while Officer
Clarke, calmed down the gorgeous young Hispanic woman inside
the home. Of course, it is always Smith's assignment to write the
reports. Clarke figures he needs the practice.

By the end of the month, there is no doubt in his mind, that he
should have moved anywhere but Arkansas. Everyone talks in a
slow Southern drawl, drive oversized domestic brand pickups that
feature back-window gun racks, and barbeque every night. Smith
doesn't fit the mold. The rest of the Fayetteville department boasts a
close camaraderie.

Kel and Jake become cordial, as close to friends as possible, but
there is a barrier between them that Smith cannot understand. What
not one person mentioned is everyone in the department has a cousin
passed up for his hiring.

His long-term friend from San Diego, Harrison Knight, who was
instrumental in his hiring, has retreated to job-security within the
departmental ranks. Harrison barely speaks to Smith on the job,
though they usually work different shifts and don't see each other
often. When the new officer has a rare day shift, Smith runs in Harry
at the morning coffee pot. They talk, if the room is empty, and are

becoming friends again. They even meet for an after-work libation now and again.

One afternoon in late May, Smith spills coffee all over his uniform and swings by the station to change his shirt. When he enters the locker room Officer Clarke and Detective Quarrie are standing in the back corner. "Don't let that ever happen again!" forcefully voices the detective to his subordinate.

Both startled men look up at Smith. Their conversation ceases immediately and the room became deadly quiet. They stared at the intruder the whole time he changes. Upon finishing, Smith nods to the men and goes back to work.

Walking past the detective room, Smith sticks his head in. The room is vacant except for Knight sitting at his desk. Jake steps over, "Hey Harry, how's it hanging?"

"Hi, Jake, what's up?"

"Nothing just headed back to the streets." All alone, Jake mentions, "I've noticed Quarrie and Clarke are pretty tight?"

"Yeah, that's weird huh? For a long time, they hated each other."

"Oh yeah. I never noticed either way."

"Well that's was before your time. It's only been the last year they resolved whatever problems they had."

"I'm off at six, want to get a beer?"

"Can't tonight, Judy's got plans. We'll do it soon though."

"Great! Have fun. Give Judy and the kids my love."

Smith hits the streets. His curiosity is on high alert and mind racing over the freak run in and Harrison's insight.

Over the next few weeks, he notices slight nods of acknowledgments though no conversations between Quarrie and Clarke. "They're obviously still friends but something's amiss," Jake thinks to himself.

Early one morning Jake is having trouble sleeping and heads to work well before his shift starts. He stops for coffee at the Waffle House in Springdale. Two cars are in the lot and he recognizes

35

Clarke's immediately. Smith flicks his lights off wondering "What is Clarke doing up here and why so early?" He pulls around the to the side of the building and parks in the dark unnoticed. He slyly walks to the edge of the building and peers around the corner through the restaurant's front picture window.

Inside he spots Quarrie and Clarke taking over coffee, thinking, "And Clarke told me he doesn't drink coffee!" He watches. When they finish, Clarke sides a thick envelope across the table. Quickly Quarrie conceals it in an inside coat pocket. The men stand, shake hands and head for the door.

Officer Smith rapidly retreats to his compact Datsun pickup and slumps down in the driver's seat. He bends his rearview mirror down as far as it goes and watches. Clarke's vehicle passes his field of vision. No other car is seen for five minutes. "Quarrie must have gone left to the highway," he reasons.

Smith goes into the empty restaurant and orders a coffee to go. He fumbles with his wallet and jokes with the cashier, "I can't do a thing before coffee."

"I know what you mean. I'm worse than that." They laugh together.

"Hey, two cars were pulling out as I came in. I think I know one of them from high school back during the war…the Civil War that is."

"Laughing again, "Ah come on you not that old, it was probably the First World War."

Enough fun, Smith gets to the point, "Do you know them?"

"Nah, they come in…maybe once a month." She adds, "Oh, one time the young guy came in wearing a cop uniform. He sat around, maybe an hour. The other guy never showed and he left."

"I better hit it. My name is Jake, just moved to town. I'll catch you later."

"Nice to meet you, Jake, I'm Sherry. Have a good day!"

Jake starts investigating his workmates on the sly. He's spending less time sleeping and every free minute watching and taking pictures.

Within three weeks he's snapped photographs of Clarke talking and receiving envelopes from a huge Black man, a skinny white dude, and numerous corner markets.

Smith starts hitting a different bar every night. He never was a real drinker and lucky if he finishes nursing a single beer. Late one night he's in the College Club when the large dark-skinned man rambles into the room. Smith sits on a corner stool at the end of the counter and watches. It's not long before the man hits the head and Smith follows him in. He approaches and tells the man they need to talk. Not mincing words Smith lets him know that if he wants to keep dealing a weekly donation is in order.

"I'm not paying another cop for anything!" And the big man storms out, not only from the restroom but also the establishment.

Smith follows him to the corner Circle K and watches as the guy makes an angry phone call. He's too far away in the shadows and can't hear a word but he sure he knows who's on the other end. As soon as the man steps into the light Smith clicks a picture.

At work, he looks up every drug bust for the past year and goes to the evidence room with a bogus retrieval slip to check a box on a mugging case. Left alone to search, Jake examines all the evidence boxes on the drug cases. Two of the ten are missing drugs or money or both.

Officer Smith goes to the detective's room and asks Harrison if they can talk in private. Stepping to the outside sidewalk, Smith explains his extracurricular activities to his friend. He asks Harry to look into who had access to the missing evidence.

"Jake, what do you think you're doing?"

"My job."

"Your job doesn't include spying on your co-workers!"

Jake shows the detective his picture of the drug dealer and asks if Harrison knows the man.

"Everyone knows Randal Brown."

Knight disbelieves his friend and tells him he's mistaken, and not politely. After persisting, Jake convinces him to at least check the evidence log and see who's requested the cases in question.

Two days later Harrison meets Jake for an after-hours beer at Sal's Bar, the local cop hangout. After a couple of beers and Jake's beratement from the other off-duties, they walk to the parking lot together; Harrison has to get home and Jake isn't welcome inside alone.

"Jake,…Quarrie requested access to your boxes." Thinking, he goes on, "You might have something, but I'm out of the loop! You're on your own. I can't be involved in ratting out brothers and I advise you do the same. Everyone has something to hide and an in-depth investigation into the department is above my pay grade!"

"Harry…" hesitantly, "you're clean aren't you?"

"Of course! I just can't afford to be ostracised with you! And you'd better be damn sure you want this!"

Chapter 13

Harrison Knight started with the San Diego Police Department, as a patrol officer in late nineteen fifty-seven. He served four years in Navy with the last two stationed at the Coronado Naval Station across the bay from the city.

He loved the area and decided to stay rather than going back home to Lincoln, after his discharge. His short Naval career consisted primarily as a Shore Patrolman. And he was a natural for the local police department.

The younger Knight met Cadet Jake Smith in the Police Academy. They rented an apartment and bunked together through the four-month training program. The academy was a stressful rigorous course and both men excelled in the program. Once on the job, they continued to be roommates.

Harrison was more ambitious however Jake had more intellect. Ambition won out and Knight was on the fast track to detective level. He should have been promoted in another year or so, but during his third year on the force, Knight's mother contracted cancer. His father's Alzheimer's progressed faster than the doctors anticipated and his old man wasn't capable of taking care of his wife. Harrison Knight left the SDPD and moved back home.

Even with Harrison gone, it took Smith seven years as a patrolman before receiving a promotion to detective grade.

Knight's mother passed away six weeks after his return. And his father a year after that. Harrison sold the family home and rebought in a Fayetteville suburb. He applied for the police department and was accepted.

As a street officer, Harrison met Judy Gilcrease. They had a whirlwind romance and were married three months later. Their first child was born ten months after the wedding and their second and third years later.

Jake and Harrison remained friends through Christmas cards and occasional phone conversations.

The last time they had face-to-face contact was when Harrison flew to San Diego to be Jake's best man. Judy and their son stayed behind.

When Smith was fired from SDPD, he contacted his friend and flew to Arkansas. Harrison, now a detective, was instrumental in Smith's hiring at the Fayetteville Police Department.

Chapter 14

Two days after snapping Brown's picture Smith is on patrol. He's concentrating on the vehicle in front and doesn't notice the old rusted out Ford sedan shadowing him.

He pulls up behind the vehicle stopped at a four-way and notices one of the brake light's is out. As the car pulls away, Officer Smith flicks on the reds and pulls it over. It's an attractive blonde student from UOA and the officer gives her a fix-it ticket for the nonworking light. After the pissed woman pulls from the curb, Smith sits in his squad car filling in the report.

All of sudden there is a loud screeching of slammed brakes. He looks over and down the double-barrel of a shotgun.

BLAM! BLAM! Two quick rounds fired off. Smith is already ducking into the passenger seat but his shoulder is above window level and absorbs numerous pellets. Blood's immediately gushing. He grabs the radio screaming, "OFFICER DOWN! OFFICER DOWN! SHOTS FIRED! CORNER OF COLLEGE AND BAXTER!" He reaches over and flips on his siren. Tires squeal and the Ford shoots down the street!

Minutes later sirens are heard from every direction. And soon two officers are on scene with more en route.

Officer Smith is taken by ambulance to Washington Regional. He's wheeled into emergency and examined. Nothing is life-threatening. Dr. Yei spends the next hour picking shot out of his arm and shoulder with long stainless steel forceps. A nurse enters and bandages his wounds while the doctor tells him he was extremely lucky to be alive. And he has to spend the night in a room for observation. Doctor Yei wants to make sure no blood clots form and no infections start.

Three hours following admission, Officer Smith is wheeled into room 302 and put into bed number one. He's missed the dinner hour but a young Candy Stripper finds him a sandwich and coffee.

Chief Parson enters his room halfway through his tuna sandwich, "Jake, how are you doing?"

"Anxious to get out there and find these two lowlifes."

"We already have every officer looking for the car you described and Knight and Overstreet are in charge of the investigation. We're getting these two! You're a blessed man, Jake. I hate to think what could have happened!"

"Thanks, Chief, but I'm kinda taking this personal."

"Jake, you're off the next week and that's not a suggestion!" He asks, "Do you think this was a random cop shooting...you know just an unfortunate opportune situation, or is there a reason someone would be targeting you?"

"No reason anyone would be after me. It could have been any man in that location at that particular time."

Harrison Knight comes into the room, "Chief! Jake! Good to see you on this side of the dirt, Buddy."

"I'll leave you two alone. Jake, we'll be in touch all week and not at the office!" Parson excuses himself.

Before the door completely closes, "Is this due to the matter you're looking into?"

"I would think so." Jake motions Harry in close and whispers, "I approached Brown two nights ago and demanded protection money. He told he's already paying. He immediately found a pay phone and made a call! And here I lay!"

"Crap, I didn't think they would go this far."

The friends chat for a while before Knight has to get going. He tells Jake he'll pick him up in the morning and drive him home.

Not ten minutes later Detective Quarrie stops by. "Good God Jake, I'm glad to see you alive."

"Yeah, it was a close one."

"You can't be too careful who you talk to. You should stick to vehicle situations!" barely auditable.

"What are you saying!"

"Well, heard you're harassing some people in town and I'm just saying…better leave the detective stuff to us. We're running an investigation on these guys and will have them soon."

"You're right, Otis, I've certainly learned my lesson. Hey thanks for stopping by, but I really need to get some sleep. We'll catch up tomorrow." Smith shouldn't have winked at the detective.

"Yeah, we'll catch up. You can mark your calendar on that!"

Chapter 15

Smith's laying bored in his hospital bed the morning after being shot. He's sore and shoulder throbbing. Even so, he can't wait to be released and has summoned the nurse numerous times to check on his paperwork. Each time he's told as soon as the doctor sees him, they'll let him go.

He just received his second cup of coffee, "Good morning Officer Smith," an attractive red-head is standing in the open doorway.

"Don't just linger there, bring in my release forms."

"I'm Alexis Dench of the Northwest Arkansas Times. I'd like to ask you a few questions?"

"Great, a reporter," thinks Smith. "Well, Mrs. Dench, I don't believe I have anything of interest for your rag."

"Ms. Dench. You can call me Alex. My readers are interested anytime a law enforcement officer is hurt in the line of duty. We have a very supportive citizenry here. I don't believe we had the pleasure of meeting. Are you new to our little community?"

"I have been in your blessed community a good month now," grinning.

"This isn't a dead community, but very much alive and thriving." Alex feels insulted and on the defense. Smith's obviously a facetious man. She continues undeterred, "Only a month? It's only fair that you give us a chance! Where are you from?"

"America's Finest City!"

"Which is?"

"San Diego, home of the sun!"

"I've never been. Born and raised right here in Fayetteville. Never traveled much and not very far."

"A sheltered Southern Belle, hey?"

"You can say that," slightly embarrassed and turning a light shade of pink.

Smith doesn't overlook and comments, "A little color does you good. You should visit Southern Cal."

Turning a shade darker and changing the subject, "Can you tell me how you got shot, Officer?"

"Call me Jake. A man pulled a trigger."

"Did you see him?"

"Two cold-blues over a barrel."

"So you can't identify the shooter?"

"That is correct."

"Mr. Smi...er, Jake, this doesn't have to be difficult. I just want the community to know your story. Maybe someone will come forward."

"I like difficult!" sarcastically joking.

"Obviously! Where were you when the incident happened?"

"In my cruiser."

"Which was where?"

"College Avenue just off Baxter."

"See how easy this can be," her turn to smirk.

"Excuse me, I need to examine Mr. Smith," Doctor Yei enters the room.

Alex waits by the nurse's station. Fifteen minutes later the doctor walks up to the counter, "Nurse, you can release Mr. Smith."

The reporter waits impatiently until Jake finally emerges from his room cradling a stack of papers and a prescription bottle of a medicinal morphine derivative.

"Mr. Smith, I was hoping to buy you breakfast and hear your story."

Smith hadn't noticed her, "Alex, you're still here?"

"We can go to Lou's and then I'll give you a ride home."

"Jake!" Knight is too loud for a hospital and every orderly on the floor shushes him.

"Here's my ride. We can talk later, Alexis." She doesn't overlook Jake using her full first name and likes it.

Knight comes upon them, "Ms. Dench." he nods.

"Detective Knight," she reciprocates. "Jake and I are on our way to breakfast if you'll excuse us?"

Harrison looks at his friend and winks. "Looks like you're in good hands, buddy. I'll get back to work."

Jake looks over the attractive reporter, "I'll catch up with you later, Harry."

At the diner Jake orders the country special, steak & eggs; he's starving after refusing the hospital cottage cheese and fruit cup.

The reporter and policeman chat away for hours. Smith tells her a condensed puffed up story of his life and the current shooting. Dench follows suit with her own inflated adventures. Alex finally drops him off at the police station.

After pursuing what has and has not been discovered on his shooting investigation, Knight takes his friend home.

The next morning with his coffee Jake reads the front page story:

OFFICER SURVIVES SHOOTING

Fayetteville Police Officer, Jacob Smith was shot late Wednesday afternoon on the corner of College Avenue and Baxter Lane. The two shotgun blasts shattered his left shoulder. Officer Smith spent the night in recovery at Washington Regional.

After his release, Thursday morning Officer Smith will be confined for weeks of recovery on heavy medication.

Jacob Smith is a recent transplant to our area from San Diego, California. He served a distinguished and a decorated seventeen-year career with the San Diego

Police Department, before his good friend Detective
Harrison Knight of FVPD, convinced Smith to relocate
to our fair city.

Officer Smith moved to Fayetteville less than one month
ago. He was immediately accepted as one of ours and
quickly claimed friends and respect within the department.
After such a short tenure Officer Smith has already proven
himself in all areas of law enforcement.

Detective Harrison Knight is leading Officer Smith's
shooting investigation. He states they have viable leads,
and promises to have the suspects in custody soon.

Officer Smith will be in our thoughts and we pray for a
full speedy recovery!
Alexis Dench, Reporting

Smith smiles at the article. He knows departmental ribbing is on
the horizon now that the world knows his name is Jacob.

Chapter 16

Another week later, Smith is feeling well enough to get back on the job. He's written a lengthy report outlining everything he has and enclosed in a large manilla envelope complete with the clandestine pictures.

He doesn't sign the report or leave his name on anything. Jake goes into the station in the middle of the night and sits in his truck outside the front glass doors. As soon as the duty officer steps away from his desk he hastily enters the building and heads upstairs and tries to slip the envelope under Chief Parson's office door. It's too thick. Smith looks around the outer office. He's desperate to drop and run. He pulls out Margret's chair and lays it on the seat and pushes it back under her desk.

As he tries to sneak back out, the duty officer runs into him in the lower hallway, "Officer Smith, what are you doing here at this time of night?"

"Evening, Matt. I couldn't sleep and headed out for a cup of Joe. It was pretty embarrassing, when I went to pay for it, I didn't have my wallet. I figure I must have left it in my locker and came to check," chuckling.

"Did you find it."

"Yeah," and he happily holds it up. "Have a good rest of the night. I'm going home and try and get a little shut-eye. I'll be back on duty tomorrow. See ya."

By eight-thirty that morning, Chief Parson is sitting at his desk, door closed, reading Smith's report and examining the pictures. He has Margret call senior Detective Knight to his office.

"Close the door Knight and take a seat."

Harrison does as told and never utters a word. He sits quietly while watching his boss look over pictures. Eventually, Parson hands him the photos, "When did you take these?"

Knight studies the pictures. Smith told him about them, but it's the first time he actually saw them. They are sharp and leaves no doubt as to what is happening. "I didn't take these."

Parson hands him the report. Detective Knight carefully reads every word. "Who wrote this? It's really damning."

"This isn't you?"

"No Sir. This is the first I've heard any of this." Harrison fabricates.

Parson hands over the evidence room log, "You sure…Officer Olson told me you checked one of the files listed?"

"I was checking one of my cases." Knight continues lying, "I must have marked the wrong number."

"Look, Harrison, this is serious, I know you don't want to jeopardize your reputation within the force, but *we* can't overlook the facts. I'll handle it from here and keep you out of it…if I can. Tell me what you know and how you discovered the indiscretions!"

"You know I would if I had anything. I'm in the dark here, Chief. I'll help you with anything you need me to do."

Obviously unhappy, "Work in the office today! We'll talk later!"

As soon as Knight leaves, Parson runs the situation through his mind. "Margret, get Officer Matt Williams on the horn!"

"Morning," groggy and half asleep.

"Good morning, Williams."

"Chief?"

"Who was here last night, Matt?"

"The regulars were in and out all night. Nothing out of the ordinary."

"You're absolutely positive?"

"Yes."

"Sorry to wake you, Officer." Hanging up. "Margret get me a list of everyone on duty last night."

The phone rings, "I'll get it, Margret. You just get me the list."

"Chief Parson." Picking up the phone.

"Williams here. Sorry I wasn't with it a minute ago. I just remembered, Officer Smith stopped by to pick up his wallet around three-thirty."

"Thanks, Matt. Get some sleep. I'll try not to bother you the rest of the day." Click.

Parson's leary of alerting anyone else who might be connected and waits for his secretary to return.

When she's back and handing over the names, "Margret, see if Smith's in the building! I just received a message from his doctor."

A few minutes later, "He's patrolling on the westside, Sir"

"We better get him in here! It might be important."

"Yes, Sir!"

Another hour and Smith saunters in, "Good morning, Chief."

"How's the arm, Jake."

"Still pretty sore." He quickly adds, "I ninety-nine percent, a hundred by this afternoon," with a little grin.

"Shut the door and take a seat."

Smith complies.

"Jake, I know what you have done! You should have talked to me first."

"I haven't heard, did they get the guys who shot me?" trying desperately to get off-subject.

"No, but I see you did."

"I did?" surprised.

Parson pushes the thick manila envelope across the desk.

Jake stares at it without touching it. Finally, "What's that?"

"You tell me!"

"Uh…copies of all the tickets I wrote since getting here?" in an odious attitude.

"Jake, we're not playing here!"

"No, Sir…ahh, I mean, Yes Sir."

"You orchestrated a complete investigation on your own. Kevin Rogers, the county DA will be here in an hour. I need to know who else is involved before we make any arrests. Jake, we need your cooperation on this. Am I clear?"

"Crystal!" relinquishing defeat. He doesn't have a choice but to be involved, "I worked on this for a while…the rest of your team is tight as far as I know."

"Thank goodness! Get a cup of coffee and wait in Margret's office. Don't talk to *anyone*. When Kevin and I are ready, I'll call you. Also, close *her* hallway door."

"Thanks, Chief. I'll hang loose." As walks to the break room, everyone greets him, "Good morning, *evil twin*," or "*little progenitor*," and similar biblical references to his given name. All in good natured fun, of course.

Chapter 17

"Smith, we're ready!" Parson stands at his door after a two-hour meeting with the District Attorney.

Smith enters the office. "Jake, meet Kevin Rogers."

"Jake Smith, nice to meet you, Mr. Rogers."

"Please call me Kevin. Have a seat."

It's an intense closed-door session. The DA explains the evidence Smith collected is a good start, but it all circumstantial. He needs something conclusive.

"Kevin, I'm not sure I follow. We have pictures, a paper trail, and Randal Brown's admission of making protection payments."

"Let's me go through what we really have. First, your picture of two friends having coffee and one handing an envelope to the other. We don't know what is in the envelope; it could have been a birthday card."

"Too thick for a card."

"It's just an example. It could have been any stack of papers. Next a picture of Officer Clarke talking to Brown and receiving an envelope which we also don't know the contents. We only assume it's cash but there again could be anything. See what I'm getting at?"

"What about the missing evidence Quarrie checked out?"

"We know he was in the room with the missing money and drugs, but we don't know if it was already gone or someone else took it later."

"I talked with Brown and he told me he was paying protection to the police, and Clarke is seen receiving the envelope!"

"Yes, but as I said we don't know what the envelope contains. Brown could have been paying off another officer and just handing

Clarke information. Brown could be Clarke's informant for all we know."

"The point is what you've done is good, now we just need one piece of hard evidence to get one of them to break. I'm afraid if we jump-the-creek a lawyer can get them off." DA Rogers states.

"I understand. Chief do you have any ideas?" Smith asks.

"I do," answering. "If we can catch two participants during an act, we have them. Or we need to find a third party witness we can leverage."

"I'm on it, Chief!" jumping to his feet.

"Hold on, Tiger!" Parson continues, "I'm assuming you can't function at full speed yet so you're taking another week off as far as anyone will know. You and Knight will spend the week watching." Confidently, "We'll get someone!"

"If we're done here, I need to get back to my office?" the DA breaks in.

"We should have something by the end of the week, Kevin." Parson stands as Kevin Rogers leaves.

The Chief calls Lieutenant Evans and lets him know Smith will be out another week. Also that he wants Detective Knight to go to San Diego for a few days to check Smith's background and see if there's a connection to the shooting.

Off the line, "I'll have Knight rent a cabin at the Colonial Court in Prairie Grove. You guys can bunk together. Check out a department vehicle and I'll have your car towed to impound for storage."

Smith thinks before voicing, "Isn't that a little suspicious? Why would *I* need an unmarked?"

"Don't worry, I'll cover it. You go there and wait. I'll send Knight down and you guys figure out how to handle the surveillance between you."

Chapter 18

Smith is sitting down the street from the Colonial Motor Court. Knight pulls in and rents a place. As he is walking to the door, Smith parks beside Harrison's vehicle, "Hey, Harry!"

"Hi, Jacob," with a grin a wide as the Pacific. "Boy did you dive in head first!"

Smiling, "Yeah, but it was only a matter of time before someone caught on. So Evans bought it that I'm still out another week for medical reasons."

"Oh yeah. That was feasible."

"What's Evans story anyway?"

"Well, the word is he grew up on the streets of Brooklyn. A tough kid always in fights. Apparently, when he was seventeen or something, he hurt a man severely in a mugging gone bad and flew the coop ending up here. He's never married, hates Fayetteville and has always wanted to go back to the City but can't. He's a bitter man. Why the interest?"

"Nothing. He's just as cold and flat as a sheet of ice."

They settle in and work out a schedule to observe their targets. Smith is concentrating on Clarke and Harrison on Brown.

By the third night of surveillance, Knight is sitting in his car outside of the College Club. He followed Brown there and calls Jake to confirm his location.

In the meantime, Jake tailed Officer Clarke to his suburban home and is sitting down the block in the dark. A couple of hours later, he's ready to call it a night on Clarke and head over to join Harrison when the officer appears at the door wearing street clothes. The suspect gets in his car and drives towards town.

Smith fires up his car and takes off to the College Club. He's on the radio to Knight, "Clarke's on the move. I'm betting to your location. Can you conceal yourself in the alley and get a picture if there is a handoff?" figuring they wouldn't do business inside the bar or meet on the street.

"Will do!" the radio goes silent.

After racing to the lounge, Smith is coming in from the east and a car is approaching from the west. Smith slows to a crawl. The oncoming car turns into the alley and Smith quickly parks. He runs to the head of the alley and peers around the corner. Clarke's car stops behind the bar and the red brake lights go off.

Many minutes later the back bar door swings open and the giant Brown steps into the dim washing light from an upper window at the far end of the lane.

As soon as the door slaps shut, Clarke steps from his car. The small glow of his dome light extinguishes seconds later. And the two men stand face to face.

Without a word, Brown hands over an envelope. A brilliant flash instantly illuminates the alley.

"What the hell?" yells Clarke.

Smith draws his weapon as he's running down the passageway repeatedly screaming, "POLICE! GET ON THE GROUND! POLICE! GET ON THE GROUND!"

From where the flash originated, Knight pulls his service revolver from his shoulder holster and steps from the shadows."POLICE, FREEZE!"

Smith shoves the barrel of his pistol into Brown's forehead, "ON THE GROUND!" though he's secretly hoping for a revenge opportunity.

Knight's gun trained on Clarke, "Better do as he says, Officer."

Both men are handcuffed and Knight retrieves his vehicle and pulls it down the alley. The prisoners are loaded in the back seat and the two officers slide into the front. They'll pick-up Smith's department car later.

Once at the station, Brown is deposited in a cell and Clarke moved to an interrogation room. He cools for an hour while Knight calls the Chief.

A half-hour later Parson, Knight, Smith and DA Rogers meet in the Chief's office. They formulate their questioning plan and head to Clarke's waiting room.

Parson and Rogers go into the adjacent observation chamber and Knight and Smith the interview room.

"What the hell's going on?" demands Clarke.

"Calm down Officer, "We have a couple of questions." Harrison in control.

An hour after hour drags on. Clarks's tight lips slowly loosen as each picture is set in front of him at the appropriate time and Smith teases him with tidbits of information he has.

By midnight Clarke's quietly sobbing and demanding an attorney. DA Rogers steps into the room. "Officer Clarke, I'm District Attorney Kevin Rogers." Without return acknowledgment, he continues, "I know you just asked for an attorney, but before we go there, I have a proposition for you."

Clarke sluggishly looks up from his drained face but doesn't open his mouth.

"Officer, as you can see, you and Quarrie are going to prison for a long time. How do you think your wife and children will handle this? Can they stand up to ridicule and humiliation for *your* crimes?" Letting it sink in for a few moments, "I want to offer you a deal. If you don't accept it, that's your choice, but I'm sure Quarrie will! Whoever cooperates first has a chance at reduced prison time. You have to make a decision right now!"

After many moments of silence, "You're making a mistake, Officer!" the DA is stepping towards the exit.

"What do you want?" mumbles Clarke.

"Everyone and I mean *everyone* involved. And you will have to testify against them. Am I clear?"

"Y…yes," hesitantly searching his mind for options.

"You're making the right choice for your family, Kelson," confirms Rogers.

"Time to start talking," Knight interjects. "Who's in this with you guys?"

"It's only me and Quarrie."

Smith takes a whack, "Come on Kel, we have *all* the evidence and more photos. This is your one chance!"

His dripping red eyes look up at his former trainee, "And…and Evans. That's all I swear."

Parson and Knight are shocked and can't hide the obvious. Smith is beaming with delight and his friend now understands why he was asking about Evans.

"Shit, you didn't have the Lieutenant, did you?" Clarke whimpers, visually upset after observing the two surprised faces.

Parson out of his normal low-key persona is staring at Knight and Smith in disbelief.

"You did the right thing, Officer," reflects the DA, "We would have found out any way you know."

Clarke makes a written statement and list containing Brown and a couple others including all markets and owners forced to make payments.

"Smith please escort Officer Clarke to a holding cell. Knight put a team together to pick up Evans and Quarrie. Kevin, how long for search warrants for all their homes, vehicles and other properties?"

The four men split up to carry out their assignments.

A couple hours later, Evans and Quarrie are sitting in cells while their houses are being torn apart.

Six hours after that Kelson Clarke is led from his cell to the detective's squad room. As Smith escorts him past the other cells, Evans hollers, "You're a dead man, Clarke!"

After more paperwork, Officer Clarke is released under house arrest. He walks to the impound yard and retrieves his car. Kel drives to the police station's glass double front doors. He sits there for over an hour before taking his personal revolver from the glove box and puts it to his head. Firing the .32 caliber Colt, the compartment instantly blankets in blood and brain matter.

Sergent Abraham McGill is promoted to Lieutenant replacing Evans. And Matt Williams is promoted to Sergeant, and Gerod Hollis promoted to Detective along with other department shake-ups. Smith remains a patrol officer.

A few weeks later Brown is released by the court on a technicality, and back selling street-corner pharmaceuticals.

The stolen get-away Ford from Smith's attempted assassination is found, but the hitmen never caught.

Over the next several months Quarrie and Evans are sentenced to four and six years respectably in Tucker State Prison in Dudley Lake Township, an hour south of Little Rock.

The prison was built on the site of the old Tucker cotton plantation. Coincidentally the acreage was family owned by the Tuckers for generations ending when the father of the state's current Lieutenant Governor sold the land to the State.

Chapter 19

It's early the morning after Clarke's suicide and a long night interviewing the disgraced men. Smith and Knight are leaving headquarters, both exhausted officers are heading to their homes for much need sleep.

As soon as they breach the front door, "Good morning, Officers."

"Crap!" Knight reflects spotting Times reporter Alex Dench. He turns to Smith, "She's your girlfriend, you talk to her. I'm going home!"

"Hi, Alex," Smith manages a fatigued smile.

"Breakfast, Jake?"

A deep sigh coupled with furled brow look, "Sure, why not."

"I'll meet you Lou's."

Smith is too tired to eat and orders his seventh black coffee. "Can we make this quick?"

"Of course, Jake. Tell me about Officer Clarke's suicide."

"Not much to tell. He was caught red-handed and thought he could save face for his family, I imagine."

"Red-handed doing what?" she questions.

"You'll have to find out from Parson."

"Does it have to do with you being shot?"

Smith tries a smoke screen, "It's just a low-level white-collar crime."

"In my experience, an embarrassment for a white collar crime rarely constitutes suicide. What aren't you telling me, Jake?"

"It's not a simple embarrassment. It's a career ending...and obviously, a life-ending crime.

"Criminals are present in every walk-of-life, why would officers be above that level of morality?'

"We want people to trust our judgments and respect our decisions. Being caught a criminal does neither to promote that image. He joined the wrong side under the pretense of a law enforcer. You can never outlive that disgrace, especially after swearing to the oath"

"God's or man's oath?"

"Alex, I'm too tired to play games. Do you have any specific questions?'

"What is Clarke's crime? Is anyone else is involved?"

"I'm not at liberty to comment on any of that. Parson's will undoubtedly hold a press conference later today."

"Jake, please level with me off-the-record, of course."

Smith sits quietly reflecting on his previous experiences with TV reporter Virginia Small in San Diego. "What exactly do you mean by *off-the-record*?"

"It means, as you well know, anything you tell me is in strict confidence and I won't repeat a word until Parson confirms it."

"Then what good is it. Just wait for the press conference!"

"With a little forehand knowledge, I'll be able to look for collaborating information and ask the right questions to Parson. This is big and I'm contemplating outside media descending upon us. For FPD and our community's sake, I would like to contain the story as much as I can and publish the truth."

Too tired to think straight Smith reluctantly divulges part of the story. Later, on his way home, he realizes he has once again fallen prey to a pretty reporter's tricks and regrets saying anything.

Next day the Times front-page story reflects two of his secret disclosures along with Parson's limited statements. Smith is summoned to his boss' office and verbally reprimanded. Only because he broke the case, a written reprimand is not inserted in his file.

Dench already is at her desk writing follow-up outlines, when she is buzzed, "Alex, Officer Smith is on the line."

"Hi, Jake," picking up.

"You betrayed me!"

"That's not true! I only disclosed what Parson or others stated or eluded to."

"What about the fact that Clarke used his personal Colt and Lieutenant Evans is the ringleader. Parson only said that other higher up personnel are being looked at!"

"Clarke's wife told me he owned the gun and Evans is the logical choice since Parson isn't looking at himself!"

"Logical choice doesn't dismiss other choices. It could be anyone from a sergeant to the Mayor!"

"Are you saying the mayor is involved?"

"Hell no! It's just an example! You better not print any of that crap!" Smith slams down the phone. To himself, "Damn, I'm a slow learner!"

Chapter 20

Early evening of May fourth, nineteen-seventy, the day thirteen Kent State student protesters are shot by the National Guard in Ohio, Powell Tucker is walking past the Administration Building. On the steps is a group of SDS students led by a man shouting into a bullhorn. Most of the crowd's right arms raised, fists shaking and many bouncing protest signs as high as they can reach. More students fill the parking lot and grass strips leading to the building. They're soaking in every spewed word. Tucker stops to see what all the commotion is about.

The rhetoric coming from the yelling leader lambasts the government, President Nixon, and the invasion of Cambodia. Powell is swept up by the excitement of students screaming and applauding.

The riled crowd is getting dangerously out of hand. An innocent student walks by and yells, "You idiots don't know what you're talking about!" Instantly a group of young men led by Tucker surrounds his roommate and beat him. Laying in a fetal position trying to protect his body, Phillip Ward is kicked into unconsciousness.

Officer Smith and the rest of the force scream to the scene, lights flashing, sirens piercing the darkness. They observe students shattering the glass doors and infiltrating the building.

Paramedics run to the unconscious lad and throw him into the back of an ambulance.

Soon the police have the structure surrounded. They're fighting back the angry mob as bullhorns volley back and forth between the officer-in-charge and the student leader hanging out a third story window.

Just before sunup, the Arkansas National Guard arrives on the scene. The majority of students have calmed and sitting in a large conglomeration, arms locked and refusing to disperse. Inside the building is a smaller, yet just as a determined sit-in. At the sight of the government militia, the students return to an uncontrollable screaming horde.

Tear gas is thrown sporadically at the crowd. Even the local police are unprepared and have to retreat upwind from the clouds of choking gas.

Many students are dragged off and thrown into paddy wagons and hauled off to jail. Smith interferes with one arrest, questioning a shorter-haired conservatively dressed young male student, "Do you know the man wearing a brown corduroy jacket? He was standing over there, away from the crowd observing," as he points.

"Get lost, Pig!"

The guardsman continues hauling the student away.

Smith talks to numerous people and eventually discovers the man's name is Jachimaik.

Three hours later the crowds are again manageable and the Guard storms the building.

The riot lasted more than twelve hours. Fayetteville's jail is overfull with protestors and the two hospitals have standing room only with the injured waiting for turns at treatment. The Administration Building suffers a million and a half dollars of damage.

Dean Vagger arrives and starts compiling a list of students for expulsion. It's going to cost Newton Tucker a considerably larger than normal contribution to keep his son in school.

Powell Tucker decides it's time for him to get further involved and after his release, he returns to his dorm excited to attend the next SDS meeting and start his political career.

Even if it's not the *right* side, it's not the wrong side!

Chapter 21

Reporter Dench is interviewing a group of National Guard when she sees Officer Smith sitting alone, writing notes on a pad.

She bolts from the group. Lifting the yellow crime scene tape, Alex scoots under and runs to Smith's bench, plopping down beside him. They haven't talked for a couple of weeks. She hopes Jake is over their little misunderstanding. "It's good to see you, Jake."

He looks up not realizing he had company. "I have nothing to say."

"Jake, I'm sorry I broke your confidence. I overlooked finding collaborating statements. I'll triple check everything you tell me in the future. Please forgive me!" offering the sweetest demure smile she can conjure up.

Smith looks into her lovely apologetic eyes, "If I can't trust you we have nothing to talk about!"

"Jake, you *can* trust me! I made a stupid mistake. It'll never ever happen again!"

Melting into her apology, "What can I do for you today?"

"What caused this riot?"

"Well, it's a result of the dead and wounded students at Kent State."

"What does that have to do with UOA?"

"Anti-war demonstrations reflect on everyone in the country. UOA isn't below the fold on this one," speaking in newspaper terms.

"I know the country is on edge. It's understandable watching caskets of our young coming home every night on the evening news, but violence met by violence doesn't justify these actions."

"Everything our government does against the will of the people justifies reaction at all levels. Students are doing whatever they can."

"They can vote and have their voices heard."

"That's long-term solution and a crap shoot. The war must be stopped today!"

"Now you're sounding like a radical reformist."

"I agree with the young people of this nation, just not their solution."

"What should they be doing?"

"I have no idea, it's above my pay grade."

"Is beating unarmed protestors above your pay grade?" trying to trap him.

"I never beat anyone! And only defended myself when I had to!" Smith is again pissed at the reporter.

"Jake, I didn't mean you personally. I'm referring to "you" as a whole," trying to cover her misspeak. "It seems too many are getting hurt or arrested for voicing their opinions…you know, exercising their First Amendment rights." Dench making a feeble attempt to agree with Smith.

You must know Professor Jachimiak!" Smith unwilling to concede. "All talk, no action! He tries to get everyone else to do his dirty work while sitting in his gilded cage."

"So you're saying, Jachimiak is behind this?"

Hand holding his shaking head, "Damn it, Dench," he raises his head and stares into her eyes, "you know I did *NOT* say that!" Smith clomps off as mad as he's ever been.

The next morning's story reflects Smith' philosophy on the state of the country, without using his name.

Parson isn't fooled and once again reprimands his officer. He tells Smith that if he can't keep his mouth shut he'll be relieved of duty. After dismissal, the Chief retrieves Smith file. He pulls out the note he made at the time of Smith's first offense. Parson writes a written report including both incidents and inserts into the officer's permanent record.

"Apparently the First Amendment doesn't apply to policemen," thinks Smith. He's defiant in defending his rights though he vows to refrain from ever voicing them to Parson or Dench!

Unfortunately, Smith needs his job more than his freedoms.

Chapter 22

Powell Tucker is just starting his sophomore year at the University of Arkansas. After a year of dorm life, he is allowed to reside in the frat house. He rushes to move in two weeks before the start of the fall nineteen-seventy semester. He's the first brother to arrive at school and has the house to himself for the next three days.

On his second day, Powell is walking from the kitchen, in his underwear, carrying a fresh cup of coffee. It's already after ten in the morning. He's startled by a tall gorgeous blonde wearing short cut-off jeans and a tight white see-through sheer blouse standing in the middle of the room.

Jumping out of his skin, he drops the mug of hot fluid, screaming, "CRAP!" It shatters on the well-worn hardwood floor, splashing liquid and leaving trivial burnt patches on his bare legs.

No reaction to the dancing man trying to quickly wipe his lower extremities, the goddess grins, "Good morning."

Finally under control, "You the hell are *you?*"

"You should try a little congeniality," looking over the guy's firm tan muscular body and two-day growth below his messy blonde hair, thinking, "He's more beautiful than me!"

Powell had spent the summer lifting weights under the hot Arkansas sun in the backyard of his parent's Hot Springs home.

"I'm Powell," moving in for a handshake but praying for a hug.

"Cheryl Thompson. I'm president of the Alpha Delta Pi. We're your sister sorority." As soon as he's close enough, his wish comes true as she throws her arms around the young Adonis and squeezes her large bosom into his lightly haired chest.

Powell refusing to let go, Cheryl finally pushes him off.

"Would you like a cup of coffee or a soda?" the pleased student asks.

"Coffee would be great. I like mine in the cup."

Returning with their drinks, Cheryl's already perched on the sofa. Powell hands her a mug and retreats to the Kappa Sigma president's throne. He plops down trying to increase his stature to her level.

"You shouldn't be sitting there," Cheryl observes.

"It's alright. It'll be mine soon enough," the arrogant grinning student chimes up.

She sits quietly drinking her beverage and soaking in the view. Powell talks non-stop trying to impress her with every nuisance he can rapidly come up with. Eventually, Powell takes a breath and Cheryl seizes the opportunity, "I must be going. Some girls are arriving today and I have to be there. Thanks for the coffee."

"Wait…maybe we can get a beer or burger tonight?" he'll work out the details of his underage drinking status later. On the other hand, Cheryl is a couple years older and of age.

"I'll see. It depends on who shows and what they want to do."

She stands to leave and Powell glides to her expecting another hug. She sticks out her hand, "It's nice to meet you. If I don't see you before we'll all be attending your Togo Tromp." She leaves the disappointed man standing alone in the empty room.

Powell runs to the kitchen phone and starts looking for Squirrel's number. He's desperate for two services; first, a fake ID and second a couple of joints…just in case.

Chapter 23

Saturday evening the Kappa Sigma frat house is full of drunken brothers planning Rush Week activities. Powell Tucker pulls out his list. The previous week while alone in the house he wrote down all the actives from the previous year and added a few he heard about and came up with a couple originals.

He stands and calls for attention. When all's quiet he reads the list item by item. Each verbalized entry is met with cheers and applause. Finally, he gets to his three submittals; dog collars to lead pukes around by, lipstick signs scrawled across every pledge's chest and a stripper at the toga party to sexually embarrass the underwear-clad young men.

The students discuss and whittle down the list to the important ones that meet the demeaning criteria required and will fit into the busy week's schedule. Powell's proudest entry, sexual embarrassment, got cut by Presidential Executive Order.

Edward Wright is older than most and certainly more mature than all. He spent four years in the Army with two tours in Vietnam before discharge, followed by three more years employed as a factory worker. Wanting more from life Ed enrolled in UOA under the VA Bill college program. Now he is a twenty-eight year old senior and the current president of Kappa Sigma. His word is law!

Powell hasn't seen Cheryl since their mid-morning meeting. He can't shake her from his dreams and has been by the sorority house a few times, but there was always too much activity going on to barge in. He's expectant that they'll run into each other during Rush Week or at the very least she'll be at the Togo Tromp.

The following evening is the annual pledge orientation. There are twenty-nine pukes vying for Kappa Sigma membership this year.

They need to cut the list to eight. The fun begins at their first meeting.

The brothers decide the first order of business will be dog collars. The Pukes will have to wear them continuously for the week, while the members will carry leashes. At every opportunity, a brother will hook up a pledge and parade them around the campus like a Westminster Kennel Club Show, forcing their captives to jump small bushes and sit on command.

The plan is to start with a parade at this orientation. During the first hour, each pledge will strip to their shorts and members, will spend an hour dragging them around through each sorority house, before returning and memorizing the rules.

After the week of mortification, nine pledges are left for the final night of humiliation. The fraternity has one more to cut to make. It's a toss-up between two, but by the end of the evening, one will be gone!

The Togo Tromp is well underway when Cheryl Thompson and her Alpha Delta Pi entourage walk into the house. Most of the girls are wearing Stolas, a couple had on homemade Palla cloaks, and of course, their pledges were adorned in the homeliest floor-length dresses to be found.

Powell Tucker has been watching the door for an hour and as soon as they enter, he makes a bee-line for Cheryl. "Madame President, what are you drinking this evening?" bowing low.

"Nothing presently," patting his lowered head. "Kind Sir, fetch me a Screwdriver?"

Powell almost wrenches his back as pops up quicker than a jack-in-the-box knocking Cheryl's hand away. The girls start giggling at his bumbling mistake. It's probably the first time of his life he turned beet-red and rapidly ran to the kitchen bar.

With a Screwdriver in one hand and a gin and tonic in the other Powell studies the room looking for the goddess of his dreams.

When she's not visible he starts asking around. Eventually, a plain girl in a long dress tells him their queen went to the backyard.

He fights his way through the swarm of partygoers guzzling the gin and spilling most of the Screwdriver. Pukes, toothbrushes out, immediately scrubbing the wet floor behind him.

Powell stands on the raised porch eyeing the crowd. There she is! He spots Cheryl talking with Ed Wright and a group of his frat brothers. He makes his way over.

Interrupting Ed's joke, "Here's your drink, Cheryl."

She's already holding a full glass of the orange and vodka beverage. Looking at his meager offering she starts laughing, "Peasant, if that's all you can carry you'll be running all night long."

"Powell, why don't you find a nondrinker to entertain. We're busy here!" Ed brushes him off.

It's the second time in as many encounters with the beauty, that Powell's face is covered in scarlet. He slinks away from the hooting group. Discarding the glass containing an inch of liquid into a patch of dead grass, he heads back inside.

Thinking there isn't enough booze in the county to rebuild his esteem, Powell makes his way upstairs to the coke room.

Three students are laying lines of the white magical powder with a Master Card and snorting them through a rolled up twenty off a small mirror laid on a dresser. He loudly proclaims, "My turn!" and pushes an unknown nerd aside.

It's the first time Powell ever tried blow and he likes it. He returns to the room three more times that night and spends the rest of the party avoiding the girl he previously idealized.

Chapter 24

Sunday morning he's down from the cocaine high and laying wide awake fully clothed on top on his bed. He's depressed and angry over his humiliation of the previous night's affair. He's on edge and his nerves a wreck. Powell Tucker is craving more white powder.

The disheveled student makes his way to the kitchen for a cup of coffee. No other brothers are up yet and there isn't any of the brewed beverage made. He resigns to make a pot. Rather than the regular two scoops, Powell fills the brewing funnel to the brim. He overlooks putting in the paper filter. The thick mole-taupe liquid is wrought with grounds. It's undrinkable sludge. Powell downs too quick mugs full.

He moves to the wall-mounted phone and finds Squirrel's number scribbled on a small piece of torn paper pinned to the corkboard conveniently located next to the unit. He dials.

After an eternity of rings a sleepy voice answers. He asks the female if Squirrel's there. The handset slams down in his ear. He redials and receives a busy signal.

Powell leaves the house and aimlessly wanders the grounds of the university. Eventually, he ends up standing on the sidewalk in front of the Alpha Delta Pi Sorority's abode. It's not even seven–thirty yet and the place is quieter than a church on Monday morning.

After standing for too long, he walks away. On his way back to the frat house he passes the Student Union and spies a phone pay. As he climbs the front steps two Black Americans for Democracy members emerge, "What are you doing here?" is asked.

"I just need to use the pay phone." Reaching into his empty pockets, "Can I borrow a dime?"

"Look Soda Cracker, you're not welcome here," the triple XXX sized BAD's President, forcefully states.

"This is an emergency!" back at him.

"Go to a hospital!"

"Not that kind!"

"There is no other kind. Get off our porch!"

"Look, I have nothing against your kind, I just need to score a little."

"Our kind is gonna beat your kinds' ass!" the second member threatens.

Powell holds both his hands in front of his chest. He backs down the stairs and runs for the inner safety of his current dwelling.

He sneaks upstairs into the previous night's coke room. Two frat boys are sound asleep. One snoring louder than a steam locomotive. Powell quietly moves to the dresser. Glancing back at the snoozers before slowly opening draws and searching for baggies of blow. None was to be found. Powells licks his right index finger and wipes the small mirror picking up any residue left from the party night and smears his gums after which he makes his way back to his room.

Late that afternoon he's back on the phone. This time Squirrel picks up. Powell makes an arrangement to meet him at the Grub Shack sandwich shop a block from UOA and purchase a couple of eight balls.

By the end of the week, Powell Tucker is a full-fledged addict!

Chapter 25

Five Black Americans are shot, and clubbed by the Klu Klux Klan in Earle, Arkansas, just across the border from Memphis. None one killed. It was seven months after Jake Smith arrived in Fayetteville and went to work as a patrol officer.

The violence quickly spread to student protests on the campus of the University of Arkansas in Fayetteville. Coupled with the ongoing Vietnam War demonstrations, now escalates BAD members fighting for civil rights. Officer Smith, hastily taken off street patrol, assigned to the University campus.

Tuesday, mid-morning, Smith is standing in front of the Student Union Building, the offices of BAD, sucking down the last couple of swallows of his cold coffee. On the porch atop of the wide concrete steps, five dark-skinned students stand to converse and ignore the growing crowd of white kids gathering on the grass across the wide cement walkway shouting racial slurs and derogatory ethnic remarks.

A few girls are sitting at a table behind the assemblage. Two are hastily making signs on poster board with fat black-tipped makers. The majority of signs read "Back to the trees Boogies", "Go Back to Africa" and such, while others refer to stopping the Vietnam War and the illegal invasion of Cambodia. Taped to the Student Union building are two large white butcher paper banners, "All Men *ARE* Created Equal" and "Black and White Together." The Black movement is certainly more congenial to uniting than the opposition group.

Smith realizing he is in the middle of escalating trouble calls for backup. Before help arrives, he witnesses a tall good-looking young student throwing a rock at the small gaggle on the porch. That starts the riot.

The BAD members retreat into the building. The screaming protesters throw everything they can get their hands on as the crowd moves on the building. Officer Smith is smashed on the right side of his rib cage with a full soda can and on the forehead with a rock, causing blood to gush down his face. He runs for safety around the corner of the building and gets on the radio calling for riot gear and every on and off-duty cop brought in.

Sirens permeate the air as units start arriving. An officer runs to assist Smith and assure him everyone from all agencies within a hundred miles is on their way.

Two students light makeshift torches and try to start the building on fire. Another male student throws a flaming molotov cocktail through one of the shattered first-floor windows. It is a killing-mind frenzy. The militant mob is rapidly increasing beyond manageable proportions.

The small contingent of police tries to form a line between the militants and the Student Union Hall. Police are beating young people with their batons; students are fighting back with a barrage of rocks and everything within their grasp. There are wounded and battered participants on both sides. Broken arms and bleeding heads are rampant. Police bullhorns scream unheard instructions to disperse and return to class.

For the next two hours, more and more officers keep infusing the scene. Many hours later, the rioting subsides and the area is empty sans police officers.

Chapter 26

Patrol Officer Jake Smith assigned permanent duty on the University of Arkansas campus following the September riots. He always allocated the worst or most mundane tasks his Lieutenant could invoke. Jake is just happy to be off the night shift.

Early that summer, Harrison had a difficult murder investigation and consulted Jake on the sly. The seasoned detective actually solved the crime for his friend though Smith's name never mentioned and Knight received all the credit. No matter the size of a department, politics always come into play.

At his new post at UOA, Smith is wandering the campus looking for the man who threw the first rock and started the unchecked fiasco. He wanders into the cafeteria for a fresh cup of coffee during the lunch rush. At a window table sits the good-looking student, he is searching for, with another guy and three girls.

Smith wanders by their table, stopping, "Hi, I'm Officer Smith. I noticed a couple of you at the demonstration yesterday. I might appear to be the enemy, but I'm actually against the war and think you guys are making a difference. Keep up the good work. But try to keep it peaceful." He starts away.

The blonde leader pipes up, "I'm Powell. Glad you're on our side. We are members of Students for a Democratic Society and resigned to stop the war injustice."

Smith's back, "I didn't know this campus had an SDS group."

"Oh yeah, we're fighting for equality."

"Well, I have to get back to my rounds. Maybe we can discuss your mission sometime?" As Smith walks away from the group he thinks, "What a load of crap. The riot certainly wasn't about equality or unity."

The officer heads to the school office. He needs to find the political science professors and find out who this Powell guy really is.

"Professor Bartosz Jachimiak is head of the department. You can find his office on Campus Drive in the Old Main building."

Smith makes his way over while searching his mind for the familiar name. He finds the third-floor office of Professor Jachimiak. The man isn't in but an office hours schedule is posted on the door along with a sign-up sheet for appointments. He writes his name on the first open time, four-fifty that afternoon.

At the selected time Smith is standing in the hall waiting his turn. By the time a brunette-headed female student is leaving Jachimiak's office there are two others standing and talking demonstration plans a few feet from the officer. The girl ignores the uniformed man and tells the other two, "He'll see the next appointment."

Smith enters the office and takes a seat across the desk from the professor.

"Good afternoon, Officer. What can I do for you?"

"Good afternoon, Professor. I'm looking for a little information on one of your students named Powell. He's a tall handsome blonde kid."

"Oh, I'm very familiar with Powell Tucker. He's a great student, smart and ambitious; a real up and comer. Keep your eye on him. One day he'll be governor and maybe even president."

"Or more likely in prison!" Smith thinks. "I've heard the name Tucker. Isn't there a Tucker in the state capital?"

"You're very astute, Officer. That's his father. He's Arkansas', Lieutenant Governor."

Smith doesn't miss interpreting the degrading remark. He already dislikes the sanctimonious man. "So I understand he's involved with the campus SDS organization?"

"Powell's on the fast track. By next year he'll be running it. Is there a problem with that group. They're all bright young people with futures leading this country...when the time comes of course."

"You seem to know a lot about them?"

"SDS? I'm their faculty advisor...unofficially of course."

"I met Powell earlier today and he seems to be a sharp kid. I just thought you might guide him a little to keep his demonstrations peaceful."

"He's certainly not a violent person. As I said he's very ambitious and wouldn't do anything to jeopardize his future."

Smith stands, "I better leave you to your important forthcoming leaders. Thank you for your time, Professor." His turn at a little dig. "Oh, one other question. Do you have a student with messy mid-length brown hair who hangs around with Powell?"

Smirking, "That could anyone, Officer. Powell is extremely popular and a lot of students look up to him and hang around."

Smith leaves thinking he needs to keep an eye on that man. Professor Bartosz Jachimiak might think he's the self-appointed faculty advisor for Students for a Democratic Society, though that won't last if I have anything to do with it."

Chapter 27

Dench finds Smith on patrol around the University of Arkansas campus. They've become a little more than working associates and developed a casual friendship, having long dinner's and philosophical banter back and forth. Smith is definitely a left-wing cop and Dench a conservative right-wing Christian. They enjoy their time together, but neither willing to concede on any political stance.

"Jake, I need your input on this latest situation!"

"Alex, I can't be in your paper on any side of a racial issue!"

"Is that what this riot is about?"

"No comment," determined not to be trapped again.

"Jake, this could be your moment to arise as a leader for what you believe!"

"No comment."

"We both know you're an opinionated supporter of the anti-war movement."

"This isn't anti-war. And I've learned to keep my opinions to myself!"

"Not over dinner last week." Dench is grinning from ear to ear.

Not responding to the last comment, "If you really want the truth you should talk with Terrence Wilson…" after thinking, "and maybe Powell Tucker."

"Who are they?"

"Wilson is president of BAD and Tucker, he's an up and comer," repeating Jachimiak's bombast.

"I have heard of BAD, but what is SDS?" another test trap.

"You should spend more time on campus."

"And what's with this Tucker guy?"

"A white kid born with a silver spoon. His father is the Lieutenant Governor."

"So you think I'll get the straight scoop from both sides?"

"No! There is no straight scoop! You'll receive two bias opinions and then you have to formulate your own! This isn't a cut and dry issue. People in this country have been socialized into one side or the other for generations."

"Jake, what do you think I should report on?" acting demure and needy.

"Just the facts. No op-ed opinions or false conclusions. Just the facts and do not stray from those. If I were you, I would stay as far away from reasoning the confrontation as you possibly can. It's for your own safety."

"Thanks, Jake. Your advice is well appreciated. It'll be a short article on facts alone and the readers can form their own opinions". Wearing a sly grin, "I certainly don't want to feed the flys."

Chapter 28

Three days after the attack on BAD's headquarters Kappa Sigma Brothers are sitting around the house. It's Friday evening and the beer is flowing.

Brother Andrew, who was inducted the same year as Powell, speaks up, "We gotta get revenge on BAD!"

"Yeah," Powell interjects. "I had a run-in with that giant loud mouth President a couple weeks back. He threatened to kill me!" reflecting on his begging for a dime incident.

Ed Wright, this year's leader, stands and quiets the jeering group, "Let's not get jumpy. What happened Powell?"

He lies, "I was walking to class and this ahole won't move over for me. The bastard walked right into me knocking me down. Then he proceeds to tell *ME* to get off *HIS* campus or I'm a dead man!"

"We aren't going to put up with that!" Andrew proclaims.

All the brothers start chanting, "Death to BAD! Death to BAD!"

Ed's back is against the wall, "ALL RIGHT, calm down! I'm calling a special meeting of SOD."

Everyone is dead quiet waiting further instructions. "Now!" Wright stands and heads for the door. Before stepping out he turns, "Powell, you're with me!"

Nine senior brothers jump to their feet and leave the room.

The ten SOD members assemble in a basement room of Founder's Hall a half hour later. All are dressed in heavy dark-burgundy monk style robes, faces concealed in the shadows of their hoods and standing in a tight candle-lit circle. Powell is the only one out of costume and stands quietly against the back wall.

Looking over the assemblage, "This meeting of the Society Of the Dagger is now in session. Sergeant of Arms, roll call, please!"

Powell having previously taken European History realizes everyone is named after an ancient knife.

The next twenty minutes pass with the traditional start of meeting pomposity. Finally, "Guest Pugio, please step to the inner circle."

"Sure thing, Ed."

"SILENCE! Never use names!"

"Sorry," Powell squeaks out.

He squeezes between two unrecognizable figures into the middle of the circle. Powell repeats his previous lie. "Revenge! Revenge!" mantra starts softly and continues to rise in volume.

The Dagger-King Baslard raises his open-palm hands high over his head. The room becomes quiet. "Battle gear!" Everyone sheds their robes. They're all dressed head to toe in black. Going around the circle each member dons a black balaclava. Within the dim flicking circle, only the whites of their eyes pop out.

Baslard next command, "Onward Dagger Legion!"

A column of SOD members follows their leader upstairs to the grass and reassembles under a large old Oak Tree eager for the plan.

"We'll storm their headquarters and find out where BAD's president resides. From there we'll make a little social call to his den and correct this problem." He goes on to outline the complete plan, ending with, "No further oral communication between SOD members from here forward." Baslard looks over his band of thugs, "ONWARD WARRIORS!" swinging his raised right forearm from the elbow in a forward motion.

The column sneaks through the black night hiding from tree to tree, building to building and arrive at Performing Arts Center. Baselard and two other members peek around the corner of the edifice at the Student Union Building. All dark and quiet.

Baselard leads his platoon across the grass and positions against the south wall of the enemy fortress. He whispers to the second man in line, "Find a way in. Pass it on." His message goes from ear to ear until reaching Powell tagging along at the end of the line.

The team spreads out trying every window and door on the first level. All are locked tighter than a chastity belt.

"Guest Pugio, find me a large rock. We're going in!" the King proclaims.

Powell's back in a flash with a larger than fist-sized rock. The group follows their leader to a concealed basement entry.

"Rock!" Baselard holds his right hand out behind him as he's peering through the window into the basement darkness. Powell deposits the rock into his hand. Baslard shatters the window and reaches inside unlocking and opening the door. Quickly everyone scurries into the safety of the dark basement. Powell the last one through closes the door behind him.

They stand in muteness for two full minutes, waiting, listening.

"Flashlights on!" commands the leader. "Everyone back here in ten. Commence!"

The group scatters, mostly in pairs. Pugio tails King Baslard and Knight Dirk, second-in-command.

Right on time, they regroup in the designated spot. Only one brother isn't back yet. "Has anyone seen Serf Sica?" Baslard asks.

Just then a light is seen flashing from around the corner followed by the missing member. "Glad you could join us Serf." the King comments.

"I got it!" Sica hands over a member's list with phone numbers and addresses.

Scanning the list, "Here we go…Wilson, Terrance (President), Rm 406, Walker Hall."

The group stealthily slithers back across campus to the location, close to where they started their operation from.

Dirk tries the ground level front door of the four-story building. It's unlocked.

Slow and silent the SOD members make their way up the stairs to the top floor. They find room 406. Moving with extreme caution Baslard peeks in. There are four beds in the room; three have sleeping bodies. The fourth is empty.

"Serf Sogdian, tape," barely above an undertone.

Sogdian, the only one wearing a backpack, removes it and hands out six rolls of gun-metal gray duct tape.

"You three take the bed on the left. You three, the right bed, and the rest of us will do the big guy!" whispers Baslard.

They enter and quickly follow orders. Each BAD member's mouth is taped by one Dagger, while the other two hog-tie the arms and legs together, securing with many wraps of tape. The five, four SOD's and Powell have a tough time securing the large man. He fights back ferociously knocking two to the floor. Powell gets punched hard in the face.

The two jump back to their feet and back into the melee. After the giant is finally secure leaving all arms scratched and bleeding. Powell's face is red and swelling; his left eye is swollen shut. And King Baslard's neck is bright red from taking a two-handed choke. All are gasping out of breath.

They pull Wilson to his feet and lead him down the hall to the stairwell. He's clothed in a t-shirt and boxer shorts. Wilson isn't going easy. He spins his body into anyone close and kicking constantly. The fight continues up the stairs leading to the rooftop. On the top rung, Wilson manages to knock Tucker over sending him tumbling to the bottom. Tucker lays in the doorway battered and dazed.

Once out in the night air, Wilson's finally too weak to fight back.The mob pushes him to the edge half-wall. His midnight-black pupils as large a charger plate. The eye-whites bulging from their sockets. His body trembling beyond control. Sweat pouring from every pore.

All members have a hand on the large man while the Dagger King makes an impromptu verdict, "We are gathered here in the name of justice. I find you, Terrence Wilson guilty of the crimes you're accused. You are hereby sentenced to death!"

The plan is to hang Wilson by his feet over the side of the building, scaring the crap out of him before hauling him back to safety and running off.

SOD struggles to get him sitting on the ledge, back to the spread out campus. They start to push him over with two students grabbing each leg. Wilson gyrates out of control.

The grips aren't strong enough to hold the squirming overweight body. His bare sweat soaked legs slip free. Terrence Wilson falls fifty feet to the hard short Autumn grass below breaking his neck. The president of BAD dies instantly.

Ed Wright goes ballistic, "Why the hell did you drop him!"

"W...we didn't mean to. He was just too slippery to hold."

Knight Dirk screams, "Let's get the hell out of here!"

"Meet back at the room!" yells Baslard at the fleeing students.

At the base of the stairs, SOD members are jumping over Tucker who is just coming to and not comprehending what's is happening.

Baslard, the last man down helps Powell to his feet and they follow the others back to the Founder Hall's basement room.

Each SOD member is instructed to keep quiet and never discuss tonight's activities with anyone. "This will test of our blood oath to the limits, men!" King Baslard, polls his members. Each, in turn, swears to secrecy.

"Pugio, are you Ok?"

"I'm good!"

"Knight Dirk, gather all robes and head gear...and the backpack. Take them to the furnaces in the maintenance hall and burn them. Stay there and make sure the job gets done. Serf Sogdian help him. And return to the house as fast as you can."

Chapter 29

The body lay crumpled in an all but recognizable mound of flesh. Black blood-soaked grass surrounds the twisted lump.

Donna Pearl is hurrying through the dark morning to her part-time job in the school's administration building when she trips over Terrence Wilson's lifeless blob.

Straining her barely awake eyes, she sees two dead orbs staring back from the dark mass. Donna's screams could be heard for blocks throughout the large campus. The few students up at this hour include Professor Jachimiak's student Teacher Assistant. They are all running towards Pearl's shrieks. The male TA helps Donna to her feet and they join the small group staring at the formless figure.

"Who is it?" an attendee questions no one in particular.

The TA leans over and touches the object. It topples flat on the dew covered ground. "Is that Terrence?"

"Terrence who?" the unknown voice asks.

"Terrence Wilson, President of BAD."

"Oh my God!" yelps Donna and she runs to call the police.

Within minutes two Fayetteville squad cars light up the area. One officer is on his radio while the other is pushing the group back.

An unmarked car screams onto the scene. Knight was headed to the office early, anticipating a jump on his day's work, when he heard the call over his radio. The detective immediately takes charge, "Officer, tape off the area! Don't let anyone near the body!"

He retreats to the second patrolman and student cluster. Three girls are crying, the TA and a male are standing to the side in shock. "Who found the body?"

Through uncontrollable sobs, "I...I..." Donna raising a small shaking hand.

"Mike, can you take the other's statements. I want to talk to her," gesturing towards the hand-up student.

"Let's step over here." Knight gently takes the girl's arm and leads her under the porch light of Walker Hall. "What is your name?"

"D…Donna Pearl."

"Can you tell me what happened?"

"I…I was going to work early…and…I needed to finish last week's entries before Monday…when I tr…tripped on Terrence." Donna starts shaking and squealing through unmanageable emotional spasms.

"What's Terrence's last name?"

She barely can speak, "Wilson."

The sun is breaking the eastern horizon. It will be daylight in twenty minutes. The small student group is growing with lookie-loos.

Jake Smith is sitting in his dark kitchen, sipping coffee, watching the moon's swaying reflections off Beaver Lake. His ever-present police scanner crackles to life, "All units in the vicinity of UOA respond to a body in the Walker Hall area. Ahh, south of Maple and west, off Campus Drive."

"I guess codes aren't important when I'm off duty!" Smith reflects out loud. He's been chastised numerous time for not using the secret police codes over the radio. He gulps the last inch of coffee and pours himself another cup, before stepping to the porch and lighting a Marlboro. Since last Monday's attack on the Administration Building, Smith's new campus priority schedule has him off on weekends. He plans on enjoying his Saturday relaxing.

Before eight AM Smith phone is ringing. He continues to read the morning Times on the back deck disregarding the annoyance.

By the fourth call in as many minutes, Jake methodically refolds the newspaper. It looks like it was never opened. He even slips the rubber band back around holding it as one unit and lays on the outdoor table for later. He strolls to the kitchen and seizes another coffee. It's not even half a cup. Jake starts to reloads his drip coffee maker for a second brewing.

The loud ringing interrupts his thoughts again. He watches the small glass percolator top bubble with light brown liquid. The exasperating phone noise doesn't let up. Infuriated, he picks up the handset, "Good morning."

"Hi Jake, Sergeant Williams here."

"Hey Matt, what's up!"

"There's been a murder at UOA! Knight is requesting your presence. How soon can you be there?"

"Patch me through. I'll see what he needs."

"He needs you at the scene, Walker Hall!"

"Yeah…well…I guess I can traipse by for a minute or two." Jake doesn't wait for a reply and hangs up. He glances at his coffee pot, it's still perking away but nowhere close to finishing. He turns off the burner and heads for his pickup.

"Morning, Sherry."

"Hey, Jake. Large black to go?"

"You know it's so!" Smith stopping by the Waffle House on 112.

Eventually, Jake Smith is approaching the campus. He doesn't know where Walker Hall is and drives around until he spots the lights and activity. He pulls up Campus Drive and parks his piss-yellow compact truck in the middle of the street behind a flashing unit.

Grabbing his large to-go foam cup he wanders around checking out the area. Jake spots Harrison talking with Overstreet next to a mountain shaped white sheet.

"Morn'n Harry, Don."

"Hi, Jake. Glad you could make it." Jake's trying to figure out if his friend is being sarcastic for him taking his time or if he's really glad he's there.

"You know, anything for the force!" Jake definitely sarcastic.

88

"We got a real can of worms here!" Overstreet, tired of the chit-chat.

"Wormfood I can see, but probably not worth canning," Jake's on a roll.

"This is a real problem, Jake." Knight takes over. "Students attack and try to burn the Administration Building. Now a student leader is dead…murdered! We're going to have our own Nam right on campus."

"White or Black leader?"

"Terrence Wilson, BAD's President!"

"Crap! Those damn white kids can't keep it in their pants!" Smith reflects. "How did they kill him…assuming he was killed and they did it."

Overstreet whips back the sheet. Smith sees the duct taped wrists. The head twisted past the maximum rotation point and almost completely backward on the shoulders.

"Jake I'm going to need reports on everyone you talked to on campus the past week. And anyone you think could be involved. You're our boots on the ground!"

Chapter 30

Jake Smith goes to breakfast at Denny's on the highway at the south end of town. He fearful of running into Dench if he went to Lou's Diner.

He sits nursing his fifth coffee of the morning. It's even a lot for him and his nerves are trembling. He waiting for his runny eggs and burnt bacon.

A geriatric gentleman sits on the stool next to him. "Aye, whippa snappa, you cola?" Yer shacka like Elvis."

"No cola…too much coffee."

"No cola? *Cola*! *Cola*!" The fellow wraps his arms around his chest and shakes like he is shivering. To much coffa. That's new one." The old gent trying to laugh between coughs and spewing mucus.

"Too much tobacca…" laughs Smith.

Under control many minutes later, "Haven't see ya around here."

"New in town."

"Ata so? You hear about the killa at the school this morna?"

Smith looks at him and decides he doesn't need this, "No I missed that."

"I use ta janita there, ya know?"

"No! I didn't know that." Smith can hardly wait for his food and signals for a refill.

The waitress nods an acknowledgment. By the time she pours another cup, Smith's food is up and she brings everything in one trip.

"That's right."

"How long ago was that?"

"Couple of three years ago. Gota sick, see. Hadda give up my apartment and move ina the home."

"From all the tobacco?" Smith smiles.

"Thera strange boys in that school."

"What do you mean by strange boys?"

"I spy on them meet'n up in the basement. All hooded and wearin Halloween costumes. And speak'n in tongues and such."

"That must have been frightening." Smith believes the old man senile and fantasizing. He shovels in the last two forkfuls of eggs with the remainder of his toast. Smith mumbles through his overstuffed mouth, "I have to get going. It was nice chatting." Smith drops a ten on the counter and is moving for the door.

"Yes, nice chat. Next time I'll bring the pictures."

Smith's bolts back like a rocket. Looking under his furled brow, "What did say?"

"I'll bring the pictures."

"What pictures?"

"The ones I took of the kid's dressa up."

"How many pictures do you have?"

"Don't know. A couple shoe boxes full. I'd taka since '51 or '52."

Smith sits back on his stool. "When you're finished your breakfast, I'll give you a ride home and you can show me your photos."

"Ride? Live next door. In home, like I said."

Smith and his new friend walk over to the Tender Care Convalescent Home. The front door is locked and Smith rings the bell. A voice comes over a speaker, "Yes?"

"I'm bringing one of your residences back from his outing."

Smith hears a small whirring noise and a click, "Please come in."

The pair approaches the front desk. "Barnaby! Where have you been? How did you escape this time?" The homely blonde with dark roots responds forcefully but not loudly upon viewing the older gentleman.

Barnaby gives the woman a sly grin. He has a few more tricks up his sleeve.

"Where did you find him?"

"He found me," Smith answers.

"Thank you for bringing him home. I'll take him from here, Mr. ?" she stands offering a handshake.

"Smith. Call me Jake," accepting the greeting. "Barnaby has some things to show me. If you can point me to his room?"

"I'm Kathy. I'll show you the way."

The three navigate the rest home and find Barnaby's room at the far end of the East Wing. "Thank you, Kathy. Barnaby and I are just going visit for a few minutes. I'll check with you when I leave."

The receptionist isn't sure about the new stranger taking an interest in old Barnaby. And she stands not knowing whether to leave them alone or not.

"We'll be fine, Kathy," Smith gently pushes her arm towards the open door. As soon as she clears the frame Smith shuts the door behind her.

Kathy stands in the hallway trying to eavesdrop. A PRN nurse walks by pushing a cart full of prescription medicine neatly arranged in small disposable paper cups. She asks the receptionist if she lost something. Kathy responds that there is a stranger in with Barnaby and she's not sure why they closed the door on her. And maybe the nurse could make up an excuse to enter and check things out.

They barge into the room without knocking. Smith looks up from the chair he's sitting in. Barnaby ignores the intrusion and starts pulling out pictures from one of the two boxes and laying them on the small desk.

The nurse turns light pink in embarrassment. She's thinking the men are probably family and looking over a few old snapshots, "Sorry, I have the wrong room," glancing at the label on the pill bottle she is carrying.

After the two women leave, Smith spends a long time carefully looking through every black and white photograph. He looks at Barnaby, "How did you get these?"

"I like photographs. Used have my own darkroom. I made a special padded bag to hold my camera with the lens sticking out and stuck it through a small hole I cut in the wall from the closet in the next room. They never heard the camera go off. It's why some's pretty dark and hard to see. Had to try to time when candlelight was available. Used low light Tri-X film."

"You did a wonderful job!" Smith shows the man his badge and explains he is investigating the crime. "Do you think these students are involved in the murder?"

"No'a these guys, but same group." Back to adding an "a" and dropping last letters of words.

"What group is that?"

"It's Kappa Siga sometha. They's have club…SOD!"

"What's wrong?"

"Wrona…not son-of-a-bitch, *SOD*, Society Of ta Dagga."

"Society Of the Dagger?" Smith wonders what that's all about. "You've been a great help, Barnaby. Can I borrow these? I'll bring them back when I'm finished."

"Of course. Wanna help the police."

Smith leaves and stops by the reception's desk, "Thanks, Kathy. I'll be back."

"Are you a relative of Barnaby?"

"No, just met him. I'm a police officer." He shows her his badge. "He has some information on a case I investigating."

"You know, Barnaby talks a lot, but he's very intelligent. His dementia affects his short-term memory and after the stroke, he developed some speech problems. He tends to drop the last letters of words and add an "a", but he remembers the past very well. Did he tell you he was an Engineering Professor at UOA?"

"He said he was a janitor there."

"That was only after he started getting sick and couldn't remember students names. I heard he would get mixed up in the middle of a lecture and start to talk about his childhood."

"Thanks, Kathy, I'm sure we'll meet again."

Chapter 31

Smith calls Detective Knight's private line. It goes directly to his answering machine. He reasons Knight and Overstreet are still on scene. He drives to the campus.

The area is stilled taped off. The body is gone. Police are guarding; students are everywhere. Some carrying signs, others hanging banners from windows. Two groups are standing, one on each side of the street screaming racial slurs and threats back and forth.

Smith walks over to an officer, "Doesn't look like a good situation?"

"It can explode any second. National Guard has been mobilized and put on standby."

"Have you seen Knight?"

"He and Overstreet went to see Dean Vagger a while ago. Haven't seen them since."

Smith thanks him and starts strolling along the edge of the tape eyeing the crowd. He looking for any recognizable Kappa Sigma boys. They're usually front and center.

He notices two standing, conversing. Smith approaches, "Hi guys. Andrew, isn't it?"

"What do you want, Pig?"

"Where's the rest of your club?" the uniformed man asks.

"Do I look like their mother?"

"I always thought you were a little too effeminate," The officer grinning from ear to ear.

The other member speaks up, "Get lost, Oinker. We don't know anything!"

"Now you want to be honest?" laughing, Smith walks away towards the Administration Building.

Getting close, he sees Knight and Overstreet coming down the steps. Smith waves and Overstreet notices him. He turns to his partner, "Your idiot shadow's back."

Knight glances around and notices the waving Smith. "He's a good man. You need to give him a break, Don."

The three come together in middle ground. "What's up, Jake?" Knight asks.

Looking around, "Let's sit on that bench," pointing.

"You can tell us your bogus theory here," Overstreet commands, as Smith walks away.

Knight follows his friend and disgusted Overstreet follows his partner.

Smith and Knight sit on the bench, Overstreet stands to lord over the subordinate.

Smith pulls six of Barnaby's photos from his top pocket and hands them to Harrison. Knight carefully looks them over, "What are these?"

"Pictures of SOD members. I think SOD committed your murder."

"What is SOD...a bunch of farmer kids?" Overstreet belittles. "This is a waste of time. Harry, we got work to do!" He takes a couple of steps away. Knight doesn't move.

"Tell me what's going on, Jake."

"SOD is a secret offshoot of *Krappa* Sigma; Society Of the Dagger. They meet in the basement of Founders Hall. I found a janitor that's been photographing them for twenty years. Most of the photos are unrecognizable. These six are the best."

"So you think these are our murderers?" Knight interrupts.

"No. These are all previous members. I don't have current pictures. But the group is still active."

"When did you get these, Jake?"

96

Not responding to the question, "I could only find two Krappa members at the scene today. Where do you think the rest of them are?"

"That might be the question of the day!"Knight's joining Smith's team.

Overstreet stayed within earshot of the conversation and now returns taking the photos from Knight and studying them. "These don't mean anything!"

"Let's make a visit!" Knight stands.

The three make their way to Kappa Sigma House. Smith reaches for the doorknob. Overstreet immediately knocks his hand away.

"We're doing this by the book. If they don't invite us in, we can't enter without a search warrant! And we certainly don't have anything to constitute that!"

"He's right!" as Knight rings the bell.

An unfamiliar frat brother opens the door a crack, and looks over the trio, "Well, well, who left the pen open?"

He tries to close the door, but Smith's foot is holding it open.

"Move your foot, Piggie!" yells the kid.

Ed Wright opens the door further, "What can we do for you, Officers?" He's wearing a white turtleneck sweater.

Smith observes the pow-wow breaking up. Powell's walking, back turned, up the stairs. Professor Jamimiak is sitting on the couch. Other members are all heading to the kitchen. Two slip into the bathroom and quickly shut the door behind them.

"We have a couple of questions for you!" Overstreet demands.

Smith speaks up, "Actually we just want to discuss the potentially violent activity that seems to be appearing all over campus and would like to solicit your help to try and calm down the students before anything erupts."

"Invite Officer Smith and his friends in, Edward," the professor speaks up.

Write follows the order and fully opens the door.

"What do you expect my boys to do Officer Smith?"

"Professor, we both know your word goes a long way with students. I was hoping we could show a little solidarity here…maybe stand together on the administration steps and you can give a speech on how peace and cooperation are the best actions."

Laughing, "You give me too much credit. Besides, my joining your side would escalate your problem, certainly not the opposite."

"It's a little warm in here, wouldn't you say?" Knight addressing the student leader, who keeps massaging his neck.

"I'm fighting a touch of the flu and trying to stay warm," Edward responds.

"What about the rest of your gang? They're not at the rally, is everyone sick?"

"The semester is in full swing, no one can afford to start missing classes now. It's better to be safe than sorry," smiles Wright.

"Is it? Where were you boys last night?"

"Right here, staying warm."

"That's not what Andr…one of your friends said." Smith tries a little lie to set him off balance but refrains from spelling out a squealer. It doesn't go unnoticed and everyone starts quietly wondering about Brother Andrew's loyalty.

"Ed, tell us about the Society Of the Dagger!" Knight commands.

Wright's stunned look doesn't go unnoticed.

"It's a private group dedicated to preserving justice through the First Amendment. A very noble and peaceful organization that has been conducting good works on this campus since the Second World War." Jachimiak delivers his canned speech, prepared for just such an occasion.

"Don't you mean the Second Amendment, Professor?" Smith tries a little misdirection,

"These law abiding citizens don't perpetuate the use of firearms, though they certainly agree with our Constitution in totality."

"I was referring to the "security of a free White State" part," Smith's feeble attempt to trap the man.

"Officer Smith, we both know, or I would hope you're bright enough to know *white* or any color is not mentioned in the Second Amendment." He goes on to quote the Amendment for Smith's benefit, "A well-regulated Militia, being necessary to the security of a Free State, the right of the people to keep and bear Arms, shall not be infringed." Jachimiak looks directly at Smith, "The Amendment simply supports the reason to bear arms."

"I was just paraphrasing as to how some people might interpret it," Smith displays a small grin.

"It would help if you know what you're talking about…"

Knight jumps into the fray, "Professor, we're not here for your class lessons. We need to talk to Powell Tucker and the other students retreating from your little meeting!"

"I'm afraid I don't understand what you mean. I solely stopped by to speak with Mr. Wright and offer my next year's TA position to him."

"Edward, can we see your neck now?" Overstreet bluntly asks.

Wright stupidly pulls down his turtleneck while faking a cough, "It's red and inflamed. This sickness is killing me. I need to go back to bed," coughing again.

"It looks like hand marks to me!"

"Of course. They're mine from constant rubbing."

Knight tosses Wright an ashtray. He catches it in his right hand.

"You're right-handed and there's definitely a left-hand print on your neck!"

"When my right hand is tired, I use my left. Are we done here?"

There's a sudden bright flash as Overstreet removes a small pocket camera and snaps a picture.

"This interview is over!" screams Jachimiak. "Where's Officer Smith?"

In the excitement, Smith snuck off and went upstairs. He finds Powell Tucker hiding behind a shower curtain.

Everyone turns to the commotion on the stairs. Tucker loudly proclaiming, "You're finished, Smith. My Father will bury you!" as Smith is holding the handcuffed Powell by the arm as he maneuvers the student down the staircase.

"What's the meaning of this?" demands the professor.

"Mr. Tucker's coming to the station for a little talk!"

"Don't say a word, Powell!"

"Call my father," and Powell rattles off a phone number.

At the station, the son of the Lieutenant Governor follows the advice and refrains from uttering a single word. Knight photographs the young man's face and arm wounds.

Powell's put in a holding cell. An hour later, Chief Parson walks into the detective's room and tells Knight he just got off the phone with the state's attorney general and to release Tucker. Under protest from Knight, Overstreet, and Smith, the chief is unbending. He tells the trio to keep digging, but at this time they don't have enough evidence to hold the student.

The beaming Tucker holds up his cuffed hands.

Chapter 32

Jake Smith is off again Sunday morning. He makes a pot of coffee and saunters to the edge of the lake to enjoy a cup and a smoke in the morning solitude while planning his day.

First, stop by Lowes to pick up a sink washer kit. He needs to install a new O-ring and stop the constant dripping from the kitchen spigot. He is not a motived man and this, like other mundane chores, he has procrastinated long enough. It has been leaking since he moved in almost eight months earlier. Next stop is Harp's food store for a few groceries.

While Jake moseys through the huge home box store towards the plumbing aisle, he notices a stack of Hibachis. The display proudly sports a $1.99 sale price. He decides to barbecue a steak for dinner. He grabs an empty nearby shopping cart and throws in a grill, and a bag of charcoal complete with a can of lighter fluid.

"EXCUSE ME, Sir! That is *MY* cart!"

"Sorry, I thought it was left by someone."

"Yes, me! I was down the aisle picking up a bag of fertilizer."

Jake noticed her struggling with a large twenty-five-pound bag. Rather than assisting her, "Oh, you're a gardener?"

"Can I just have *my* cart, please?"

"Well possession is nine-tenths of the law!" smiling and patting the cart handle.

"Well, I never…"

Jake interrupts her, "Let me give you a hand." He grabs the bag from her and plops it into the cart with his Hibachi.

Sighing, "That's a relief!"

"What else are we picking up today?"

"*WE* are not picking up anything else. Will you kindly remove your stuff from my cart?"

"I just need to grab a washer kit from plumbing. As he starts to push the cart away, "Oh, by the way, my name is Jake."

Hustling to catch up, "I'm Maggie. You're obviously not from around here."

"Sure I am. I moved here from California eight months ago. I'm a police officer in Fayetteville."

Maggie, an attractive middle-aged light-brunette with blonde highlights is about the same age as Jake, maybe a year or two older. Her attractive blue eyes highlighted by crows-feet are the only marks on her perfect skin. "I thought policemen had better manners than this?"

"Let me barbecue you a steak tonight and make it up to you?"

"Californians are a little too aggressive for my tastes. I will pass."

"Maybe another time then?" Jake stops, in front of a pegboard display of faucet fixes, "Damn, there's a lot of choices. I should have looked to see what kind I have!"

"Just grab the universal kit. I need to pick up a small garden rake," as Maggie spins and starts for the garden tool department.

Jake snatches a washer assortment package and hurries to catch her, "Hey, wait up! You're going to need our cart!"

Maggie stops and turns, and glares at him, before pivoting and continuing on. Secretly she's enjoying the fun.

They eventually make the checkout line. Jake tries to pay for her purchases as well as his. She flat out refuses. They banter back and forth as the line behind them backs up blocking the main aisle before the disgusted male cashier finally calls for additional employees to open.

In the end, Maggie agrees to a cup of rescissory coffee. The pair loads their purchases into their respective vehicles and walks down the block to a local coffee shop. They laugh and talk for a couple of hours before Jake convinces Maggie to come to his place that evening for the cookout.

Chapter 33

It's six weeks later and most of UOA students have calmed down and back in class. The ones still protesting are the members of BAD seeking justice for their murdered president. The case of Terrence Wilson has stalled. All Kappa Sigma Brothers are tight-lipped and no collaborating evidence is found. Knight and Overstreet are frustrated at every turn with State Government interference. Smith spends a lot of time on his campus duty trying to appease BAD members with, "The investigation is ongoing and we're close to an arrest."

Halloween night, Saturday, nineteen seventy, arrives. All Fayetteville officers are on duty. Officer Smith is cruising UOA's campus just before midnight. He slowly drives past Kappa Sigma's frat house on North Lindell Avenue. The large party of costumed students is spilling all over the front yard.

He spies Powell and Wright talking with a group of girls. Both men flip off the officer. Smith takes the long way around the block and parks in the ministry lot on the corner two doors down from the frat house.

He sneaks up behind a large Oak tree from whence he can view the backyard of the party. The kids are engrossed in their own activities and fail to notice the prying eyes. Ten minutes or so later, Wright and his group make their way into the area. They connect with the huge hodgepodge circle of smokers passing around numerous overfilled joints of weed called "bombers" and are quickly offered a hit. The five newcomers all partake of the illegal smoke.

Smith goes back to his patrol car and writes in his pad. It's the first time he's ever witnessed Powell or Wright doing drugs. His radio snaps to life, "A group of six or seven juveniles is breaking car antennas in the area of Cleveland Street and Whitham Avenue."

Smith responds, "I'm three blocks from there, I'm on my way."

He drives down Cleveland and turns onto Whitham. All's quiet not a soul in sight. Smith stops at the head of Taylor street and turns his lights off. Shorty a group emerges to a front yard at the far end of the street. The officer throws his vehicle into reverse before turning down the street.

The gang is standing on the sidewalk and as Smith gets close he flicks his overhead "reds" on and off. The surprised gang scatters. Kids are running through yards in every direction. Around the corner on West Douglas, he spots two jetting across the street into a UOA parking lot. Smith flicks on the roof mount light bar and floors the gas. He squeals his tires as he bounces into the lot.

The faster kid is close to crossing the next street and getting lost within the safety of the campus buildings. The other chunky kid is twenty-five yards behind. Smith turns on his siren.

The exhausted kid stops, bending over trying to catch his breath. The office slams on his brakes skidding to a stop. He turns his siren off and exits the car, yelling, "Get on the ground!"

Smith approaches the prone juvenile and snaps on the cuffs. He instructs the kid to get up and walk to his car.

"What's your name son?"

"Jeremy Trask."

"How old are you, Jeremy?"

"Fourteen."

"Well, Jeremy looks like you've been a busy boy tonight."

"I haven't done anything, man!"

"Where do you live?"

"Over on Taylor."

"Is that the house you guys were standing in front of?"

"Yeah."

"You're in a lot of trouble Jeremy. I have a couple people that specifically saw you breaking car antennas." The officer lies.

Proceeding to cry, "I was just with them, but I didn't do anything."

Smith stares at the sobbing youth. The boy leaning over the car hood doesn't look up.

After minutes of silence, "Jeremy, I think I can help you get out of this."

No response. Smith continues, "Stand up." He takes off the cuffs and turns the boy around. "I know you guys hang around Kappa Sigma. I've seen you talking to Powell Tucker and Edward Wright," another far from the truth statement met without a response.

"If you want to go home tonight you better talk to me, son, else you're going to juvy. Are we clear?"

Looking down and inaudible, "Yes."

"What did you say?"

"Yes, Sir."

"Good. Now, what do you kids need to talk to them about?"

"Ahh…they gave us part of a joint once."

"Let's go!"

"Where are you taking me?"

"Juvy! I thought we were going, to be honest with each other?"

Tears rolling again, "Please don't take me there. I'll be honest."

"Last chance. What do you do over there?"

"Some of the older guys buy weed once in a while. I DON'T. I never even tried it!"

"That's good, son. You don't want to get mixed up with drugs." Smith hands Jeremy his business card, "If you ever need me, call and I'll help you. Get out of here!" Smith knows he'll be squeezing the kid for info when the time comes.

Jeremy quickly takes off running in the direction of his home.

Returning to his vehicle, Smith gets on the radio, "Car 215 reporting in. All's quiet in the Cleveland area. No juveniles present. Returning to patrol. 10-4"

Smith certainly doesn't believe the kid is as innocent as he portrays.

Chapter 34

"Smith, get over to the Trask house! Some woman just called and they need to see you immediately. She won't talk to anyone but you!" Detective Knight is radioing Officer Smith on UOA's campus.

"That's an extra big 10-4. Hugs and kisses, Detective." Smith, never surrendering an inch, walks to his patrol car and drives to the Trask home.

After identifying himself, the woman invites Officer Smith in. Jeremy is sitting on the living room sofa. His head is down and eyes bloodshot from leaking.

The woman takes an overstuffed green flowered fabric chair and Smith sits on the matching couch next to the adolescence youth. He rests a hand on the boy's thigh, "What's going on Jeremy?"

The lad starts sobbing again.

"Tell the Officer, Jeremy."

"I…we were on the campus…you know…the night the Black guy was killed."

"You were there!" shocked by the admission.

"Tell the Officer everything you told me." Mrs. Trask interjects.

"Yeah…ther…there was four of us." Smith sits silent and Jeremy continues, "We were just hanging out you know…nobody was smoking….weed. We saw a line of guys running from behind a building."

"Did you recognize them?' Smith asks.

"No, they were all black."

"Black? You mean African American?"

"No…well I don't know. They were dressed in black clothes and black ski masks." After a long moment of silence, "Except Powell."

"Powell Tucker?"

"Yeah…I think that's his last name."

"What did you do then?"

"Followed. They broke a window and went into a building."

"Walker Hall?"

"I don't know. We hung around for a while and were just about to leave when they came out. We followed them again and they went in another building across the campus. We waited and soon there was a fight on the roof. We couldn't see anything…it was real dark."

A longer than normal break, "Tell him, Jeremy."

"Th…they dropped a guy off the roof. We split real fast."

"Could you see the unmasked guy?"

"You mean Powell…no, I didn't see him. It was so dark I only saw figures moving around."

Turning to mom, "Mrs. Trask I need you and Jeremy to come to the station and tell this story to the investigating detectives."

"I figured. We're ready now."

Smith transports the pair to the station and turns them over to Knight, before going to the high school with other officers and bringing in Jeremy's three friends.

At the station, Smith sits with the three additional youths until their parents arrive.

In the end, two of Jeremy's friends tell the same story, almost word for word. The third's father would let him talk without a lawyer present.

All available officers descend on UOA. Smith follows Knight and Overstreet into the administration building. They receive a list Kappa Sigma members and which classes their currently attending. The whole fraternity rounded up and arrested.

Chapter 35

Alex Dench and her photographer show up at UOA, following the police caravan. She did not understand what is going down from the frantic buzzing on her police scanner but knew it had to be big.

Arriving she witnesses a large contingent of police vehicles arranging throughout the campus. Alex views Smith following an unmarked car and tails them to the Administration Building.

It's a mystery to what the operation is. Everything appears normal. There are no visible student gatherings anywhere. Alex and her photographer stand in the building reception area questioning Donna Pearl. The part-time student worker doesn't know anything and is as mystified as the reporter is.

Three men come off the stairs and Alex is on them like a lizard on a fly, "Officer Smith, can you tell us what is happening?" her tape recorder microphone shoved into his face.

"Sorry, Ms. Dench this is police business. Please stay back!" he responds.

"If you interfere in any capacity, you're going to jail with the rest of them!" Overstreet threatens.

"The rest of who? How many people are you looking for? Is this about the Terrence Wilson murder? Are they white students? Boys or girls? Or both? Any faculty personnel?" she machine-guns questions while trying to stay up with the departing men. No response received.

The photographer is snapping as fast as he can. He runs in front of the troop and gets headshots of each officer and group shots of them marching towards him. The officers display blank emotionless expressions. Every picture could double as a mug shot.

Alex glances across Garland Avenue and stops to watch four officers drag three male students, including Edward Wright from Kappa Sigma's house. She jets to catch up with her group who has already entered the Sam M. Walton building in the College of Business section.

She stands in the entrance foyer trying to decide which way they went when she hears yelling down the right-hand hall. Alex runs in the direction of the ruckus. Her photographer is standing at an open door clicking photos as fast as he can.

Peering inside, Alex watches the Lieutenant Governor's son arrested without incident inside the student jeering room. Powell Tucker is paraded passed, his t-shirt pulled up over his head. She turns to her companion, "I trust you got face photos during the arrest?"

"You bet I did!"

Outside Knight and Overstreet manhandle Powell towards their car. Smith strides off in another direction.

The reporter quickly decides they have enough Powell pictures, "Come on, we need to see what Smith is up to!"

Running after Jake, "Is there more arrests, Officer?"

The cameraman catches up.

Smith suddenly stops in his tracks and turns to the reporter. He leans in so close the photographer can't hear, "Alex, stay close at hand, this is going to be better than Powell!"

Alex can hardly contain her excitement. Beaming at her companion, "Stay close, it's getting better." Ignoring Smith's secret offering. Again, they are on Smith's heels. Smith finds a free officer, "Come with me, Jim!"

They observe the arrest of Professor Jachimiak from the front of his packed auditorium and being lead from the building. The rooms buzzing with confusion and the camera's film-advance lever is ratcheting and aperture clicking faster than humanly possible.

The reporter takes time for a couple of quick student interviews, after which, Dench, and her assistant speed to the police station. The duty officer stops the duo and doesn't allow them past the front desk. She steps to pay phone and calls her editor, "Hold the deadline as long as you can. I have a huge story and need all the time I can get!" After the man questions, she explains Tucker and Jachimiak's arrests coupled with a huge unknown number of students.

They stand, sit, and pace for hours. Smith eventually comes down. There's nothing more for him to do and he is going home.

"Jake, can you make a comment?"

"Sorry, Alex can't say anything at this time. Go and write your story! Chief Parson will hold an official press conference sometime tomorrow. You'll be notified."

"What is the professor being held on?"

The officer refrains from voicing, "Collusion, harboring fugitives, obstruction of justice, and a litany of other offenses.

Chapter 36

Smith has been evading Alexis Dench's since he met Maggie. They only talked business over the phone or at chance encounters and never shared a meal together. Jake is avoiding the inevitable.

Officer Smith is on standard patrol at the university. Dench is there at the same time interviewing students and faculty for the following morning's edition, a follow-up on the arrests of Professor Jachimiak and the complete Kappa Sigma Fraternity membership.

It's an unusually warm Fall day and Alexis heads to the cafeteria for a cold drink. After purchasing a large sweet iced-tea, she stands to look over the tables for her next victim. She spies Officer Smith sitting alone with a cup of coffee and staring out a window. Alex walks over and takes the seat opposite him.

Jake looks up. His eyes are bloodshot and he looks a mess.

"Are you are right, Jake."

"Sure, why wouldn't I be?"

"You look like you haven't slept in a month?"

"It's not that bad…I have had my hands full with the Wilson murder and yesterday's arrests. Sorry I haven't had time to return your call."

"Call! Jake, it has been three weeks. I made at least a dozen calls!"

"I know…sorry."

"What's going on?"

"Work's been tough and I've been really busy…," looking down he quietly mumbles, "and I met someone."

"You met someone? You mean a woman?"

"Yes, we've been spending a bit of time together…as my schedule permits," trying to minimize the relationship.

"I'm happy for you," she fibs. "You know we were never an item. Hell, we couldn't even see eye to eye on a single subject."

"It wasn't really like that, I miss our talks."

"Goodbye, Jake," she stands and bolts through the door before the tears start cascading beyond control.

The following day Jake Smith reads the morning feature on the campus arrests. It is his day off work.

Rereading the feature numerous times, he throws the paper in the trash. It is the first article Dench has written since meeting him that there was no mention of his involvement.

Sadly, Jake takes his mug and goes to the lakeshore for a smoke. He likes Alex. Undoubtedly, more than he should and now realizes she might feel the same. He stands chain-smoking and skipping the occasional stone across the lake surface. "I really screwed the pooch on this one. How stupid can I be?" he thinks followed by a day of self-loathing.

Maggie calls late in the afternoon and invites him out to dinner. Jake makes an excuse that Knight just phoned him and they have to get together and go over a case. His girlfriend tells him he still has to eat and maybe Knight and he can get together after dinner or better yet, she and he can have a late night rendezvous at the Comfort Inn.

Smith sticks to his story and declines all suggestions.

Chapter 37

Even though the following day is Veteran's Day, a school holiday, Dean Vagger stops by Kappa Sigma house.

The living room is full of arguing students. When he walks in unannounced, the room becomes as quiet as a rabbit. "Where's Edward Wright?"

"He's still in jail. I don't think he'll ever get out."

"Who are you son?"

"Albert Loafer, Sir"

"How long have you been at UOA, Albert?"

"This is my third year, Sir."

"I see. How many are still in jail?"

"Not sure, Sir. We figure nine or ten, Sir."

"How can you not be sure? Don't you know your own members and who is missing?"

"Yes, Sir, but rumor has it that Powell Tucker was released to his father's custody."

"I see." Vagger thinks before speaking again, "Who's the acting president now?"

"We don't have one, Sir. That's kind of what we're discussing, Sir." Meekly adding, "All our senior members are in custody."

"Well Gentlemen, Kappa Sigma is officially closed. You have one week to find new living quarters!" Vagger leaves to let the students figure out their predicament.

"What can we do?" a brother asks his the beleaguered group.

"We need to call our Board of Directors," Albert suggests obviously taking charge.

"What can they do?"

"Don't know, but it's their job to intervene on our behalf."

Loafer makes the call. Being a holiday, Albert is forced to leave a message. The chairman returns to them a few hours later. The acting leader explains the situation. The man on the other end promises to look into the state of affairs.

The next morning Dean Vagger and Chairman Klucke meet. After a long discussion, the visitor convinces Vagger that it is unfair to punish the underclassmen for the offenses, no matter how egregious, if they weren't involved. They agree that most Kappa Sigma members are at the University for the sole purpose of obtaining an education, and do not deserve the unwitting stigma.

The only concession Klucke makes is to let Dean Vagger suspend the fraternity for two months and install a president of his choosing to straighten the mess out and make sure the remaining members are on track. If his man reports anything, what so ever negative, Kappa Sigma will be closed and banned for all eternity from UOA.

The men shake on it and the chairman reports the good news to the waiting members at the house. Of course, they all agree to whatever circumstances are set and promise to earn the respect they need to stay.

Monday morning at seven AM, Dean Vagger and an older student walk into the house. Members are running in every direction getting ready for class.

The dean, yells, "Everyone just *stop*! I want all members assembled here in ten minutes!"

The two men sit, one in the "King's Chair" and Vagger in an opposing chair.

Not more than three minutes later, every member is standing in the room. Some half-asleep and will not understand a thing Dean Vagger states.

"Gentlemen, meet your new Fraternity President, Johnathon Yates." The new student leader sits defiantly and doesn't acknowledge any greeting addressed to him. Vagger continues, "He is the word of God as far as this house goes. Gentlemen, you have exactly two months to prove yourselves before I close you down for good!" Dean Vagger gets to his feet and marches out.

Jonathon stands, "Gentlemen, you heard the drill! I am keeping this place open! Any Brother, not having a three-point-o-grade point average or above by the end of this semester is out! That is four weeks, Gentlemen! If it's too late for you PACK UP AND GET OUT THIS WEEKEND!"

The new King walks out and goes to class leaving the group to process on their own.

Chapter 38

For two months the Jake and Maggie affair has been heating up, despite the fact Maggie is a devout Methodist and attends services numerous times a week. Actually, she is the church secretary, with a small office adjoining Minister Laymann's, and is at the offices almost daily.

Jake is a C&E Christian; meaning he goes to services on Chrismas and Easter when he can. Most times he's working, either at the police department or in front of his TV watching a game. He has only attended a handful of times in the last several years.

Their relationship is blossoming and they get along fabulously. It would be perfect if Maggie would lay off the constant Bible-thumping and conversion techniques annoying Jake to no end.

Maggie decides to introduce her boyfriend to her three grown boys. The youngest one lives in the area and works for Walmart in Springdale. The other two are driving in and spending the weekend. The oldest from Little Rock where he is an assistant attorney for the State, and the middle boy, from Springfield, Missouri, works as a high school math teacher. Thanksgiving is the perfect setup and she invites Jake to the family dinner.

Smith arrives at Maggies West Skelton Drive home just after three-thirty. The large four-bedroom custom home was built on three acres by her former husband. Before he suddenly passed from a heart attack at age forty-two, he had been a general contractor and built many nicer homes throughout North West Arkansas. Maggie was left very well to do.

In the two months since Jake and Maggie started seeing each other, this is the first time he ever went to her home. He stops on the side of the road looking down the long driveway, trying to see the large house behind the numerous trees and perfectly shaped large shrubs. Jake checks the address and his written directions to make sure he's at the right place. He had no idea Maggie has money and is hesitant on whether or not to even go in. He has been trying to quit smoking, but this is too much and he pulls the nearly full pack of Marlboros from his glove box and lights up.

After more than ten minutes, Jake decides he has no choice. His quandary continues at the spread of vehicles already there. In the dirt beside the three car garage is a dust-covered one-ton dually Ford pickup truck with door magnetics advertising Harvey's Construction and Custom Built Homes. In the opened garage, beside Maggie's brand new silver curb-side fastback Toyota Celica sits an older sky-blue Mercedes-Benz convertible Cabriolet in immaculate condition. It appears it hasn't been driven for a while. In front of the garage is a new model jet-black Chevrolet Monte Carlo with a bright-red Camaro convertible sitting next.

Behind the Camaro sits an older white Ford Falcon Futura, and next to it is the preacher's new pearl-white Cadillac Eldorado Brougham featuring it's brushed stainless steel roof. Jake pulls his dirty-yellow Datsun pickup into the dirt next to the construction truck. Besides the jacked-up Ford, his compact import looks like a kiddie car. Jake's pleased he at least changed out of his new Levis and pocket T-shirt into slacks, a button-down shirt, and loafers.

He stands at the large double oak doors and rings the bell. Minister Laymann opens after a couple of seconds, "Jake, it's nice to see you again," shaking his hand vigorously. "You really need to get to church more often."

"I'm trying though my schedule is rotten these days." Jake fibs.

"Well, we all have to make time to praise the Lord. Maybe I can speak with Jim and see what can be done," referring to Chief James Parson.

"Thanks, but I would rather you didn't."

"Come on in. Everyone is anxious to meet you!"

"Oh great!" thinks Smith.

"You remember my wife, Angel?"

"Of course. How are you Mrs. Laymann?"

"Fine Jake. We sure did miss you at service this morning."

"Sorry, I was planning on getting there, but I didn't get off until five and didn't hear my alarm," another lie.

Maggie comes over and plants a soft kiss on Jake's cheek, "Let me introduce you to my sons and their families."

After meeting Adam, Benjamin, Caleb and their wives and four children, it doesn't go unnoticed to Smith that the men are all named after Biblical characters and in alphabetical order from oldest to youngest. The children don't make much of an impression though they are all extremely polite and well groomed. The seven-year boy, David, and a five-year-old girl, Mary, belong to Benjamin and his wife. And Adam also has a five-year-old daughter, Sarah. The youngest, Caleb, and his current girlfriend thankfully don't have children. "They need to hurry before the Bible runs out of names!" Jake smiles to himself.

After all the introductions Maggie tells Jake to take her seat as she needs to go to the kitchen and check on dinner. The Layman's immediately stand and excuse themselves. They must be on their way; they have two more stops before going home to their own meal.

The minister, again enthusiastically shaking Jake's sweaty hand, "I expect to see you with Maggie this Sunday."

After another lame work-schedule lie, the minister and his wife leave. Jake moves into the kitchen to see Maggie. They embrace and share a passionate lip-lock.

"Ahem," Jake and Maggie quickly separate, embarrassed. Adam's wife Martha is standing in the kitchen doorway, "I just wanted to give you a hand, Mom."

"I'll check on the roast. Maybe you can put together the salad for me."

"What can I do?" Jake asks.

"Nothing. Go and get to know my sons. I'll call you when it's time to eat," beaming from ear to ear.

Jake has a good time conversing with the group. All Maggie's sons are bright and personable men.

When finding out Adam works at the capitol, he asked if the attorney had ever met Newton Tucker. Adam acknowledges he had once. He went on to tell Jake that Newton was an arrogant individual and though he couldn't put his finger on it, Adam just got a bad vibe and would avoid ever crossing that man. Jake mentioned he knew his son, Powell from the SDS association. Adam was unfamiliar with him.

After dinner's Christian dominated conversation, Jake's uneasy in the environment and in a hurry to get home and crack a beer and have a smoke or two. He doesn't perceive an easy exit plan and endures a long evening.

Smith finally escapes hours later.

Chapter 39

Powell's finally back at the school Sunday evening following the Thanksgiving break. Arrest and murderer rumors have dwarfed his dope fiend reputation across campus. His frat brothers give him a wide berth and avoid him at all costs. Powell's cocaine addiction has escalated beyond manageable proportions. He's failing most of his classes due to absentee status. Depression has overtaken his life.

In the afternoon of December first, Johnathon Yates corners him in the frat house kitchen. Jon asks the other two brothers to give them the room.

"What's up?" asks the underweight Powell. His dead eyes staring above heavy dark bags.

Jon's frank and doesn't mince words, "You've become an embarrassment to this house. We've taken a vote and you're out…*TODAY*!"

"Who needs this bullshit house!" Powell turns and heads upstairs to pack his clothes. The rest of his prized belongings, an autographed Mickel Lolich baseball from the winning game of the 'sixty-eight World Series, a framed original eight by ten black and white photograph taken ringside at the rematch between Mohamad Ali and Sonny Liston, signed by both Ali and Howard Cosell, along with other one-of-a-kind sports memorabilia his father had acquired for him during his high school sports days, were long gone. Squirrel's hole now looks like a sport's Hall of Fame Museum. Powell's cherry-red convertible Mustang, a high school graduation gift, is also gone. He grabs his single brown bag of clothes and leaves the house for good.

Powell knows the five thousand dollar Master Card his father gave him for emergency money is maxed and his bank account empty. His father's thousand-dollar monthly allowance, deposited on the first, won't clear for a couple of days. Walking across campus he stops a young girl and panhandles a buck in change and walks to an outside pay phone and calls his mother.

"Hi Mom, are are you doing?"

"Powell, are you *alright*?" concerned as her son only left her house a couple days before.

"Everything is great here. All my professors understand I was railroaded by the cops and are letting me make up my missed work," he fantasizes.

"We're anxious to have the family home for Christmas, Dear. Your sister is driving up from Austin. William can't come but she's bringing the kids.

"Wonderful, I can't wait. Listen, Mom, I'm a little short right now and was wondering if you could wire me something to get through?"

"Of course Darling. How much do you need?"

"I was thinking twenty-five. I want to buy next semester's books early and get a head start on reading."

"I'll go to the Western Union now and wire it."

"Thanks, Mom. I have to get back at the books, finals are in three weeks. See you over the Holidays. Love Ya," hanging up. Powell heads to pick up the money.

He asks for the twenty-five hundred in twenty dollar bills and pockets the cash. At the corner market next door, the Tucker boy calls Squirrel and tells him to come over to the Razorback Motel on North College Avenue.

He walks the two miles and checks in for a week.

Chapter 40

Finals start December fourteenth. Powell manages to make it to each of his five three-hour finals. He does a line of dope for clarity before each test.

He's confident he aces every exam, even though on the political science essay test he walked out after the first page and ignored the remaining seven pages. Powell rationalizes the stand-in professor won't chance to fail the Lieutenant Governor's son.

Friday morning Powell goes from office to office of each one of his teachers. The hallways are crowded with groups of students crammed beside every door trying desperately to read their grades taped to the walls. Powell elbows his way to the front of each throng. He failed every class!

The distraught man heads to the quad and sits on a cement bench. He's there only seconds when a female student approaches.

"How are you doing, Powell?" Cheryl asks.

"Why would you care?"

"I thought we might talk," as she sits down beside him.

"We have nothing to talk about." Powell stands to leave.

"I'm sorry you feel that way. Dean Vagger asked me to find you. He wants to see you in his office."

Without another word, Powell ambles off toward the Administration Building.

After he spends more than a half-hour waiting on the bench, "Dean Vagger will see you now." Powell stands and enters the inner shrine.

There isn't any small talk and Vagger gets to the point, "Powell you're suspended from this institution."

The disgraced student, head lowered, shows no reaction.

"Son, let me give you a little advice. You need help. Go see Mrs. Dower in counseling. She can set you up in a drug rehabilitation program. Get yourself clean! There aren't any options here."

"Yes Sir, "he meekly answers.

"You won't be allowed back for a full year. However, *do not* put it off. The drugs are killing you." He goes on, "You started here so positive with such a bright future. Mr.Tucker, this is your life, there are no rehearsals or rewrites. Don't blow it!"

"Yes, Sir. Did you call my father?"

"Not yet. I expect you to tell him. Are you going home for Christmas?"

"I'm trying to get there."

"I know a student who's doing really well since going through the program. She lives in Little Rock and I am sure she can help you get home. She has been an inspiration for many people in this institution. I will speak to her. What's your number?"

"I...I don't have a phone."

"How can I reach you?"

"I'll have to call you."

"Do it this afternoon before it's too late. I will call her now. Good luck Powell."

He leaves and walks back to the dirty apartment room he is sharing with Ethan Eastman. His roommate already left for work at Kats as their DJ. Powell does a line before walking to the bus station and boarding for Hot Springs.

Chapter 41

It's late afternoon and the sun is setting by the time Powell gets off the bus in his hometown. He finds a public pay phone and calls his parent's home.

As soon as she arrived from Austin after eight hours on the road, Nikki called her husband to let him know she made it safely. William wasn't home from work yet and she was expecting his call. Powell's older sister answers the phone.

"Hi Sis, looks like you made it?"

"Powell, please don't tell me you're not coming."

"I'm here…in Hot Springs! I'm at the bus depot and hoping you can pick me up?"

"What in the world are you doing riding a *bus*? Where's your Mustang?" Nikki prods.

"It's kind of a long story. I'll explain when you get here. Don't tell Dad, Ok?"

"Dad's not here yet, but probably stuck traffic on the highway. Gladis is making fried chicken and dumplings for dinner. If I remember that's your favorite."

"You know it is!" Powell adds, "I'll wait for you by the front door. You don't have to park, I'll just jump in!"

"See you in a few, Brother."

On the way back to the house Powell explains to Nikki that three frat brothers stole his car one night and went joyriding while drunk. The driver lost control and ran into a tree. When she asks if he called the police, Powell continues the untruth telling her that just isn't done to brothers, and besides, there wasn't that much damage and the car is in the shop. All the fraternity chipped in and his car will be ready by the time he returns.

As soon as the pair enters the house, the father is surprised to see both his children, "Powell, I didn't expect to see you. Where's your car?"

His son relates the same tall tale he told his sister. Their old man doesn't buy it and promises to call Dean Vagger first thing Monday morning. Powell quickly interjects that the school is closed until after the first and nobody's working administration for three weeks. The dad tells his son he'll drive him back to school after the holiday and get to the bottom of it.

Powell's mother pipes up, "Powell you've gotten so much skinnier, are you sick."

"No Mother, I'm fine just not eating much lately, too much time studying. That's what's important right now."

Thankfully Gladis interrupts, "Dinner is served."

All through the break, Newton's on his son about the car and his eating and what's really going on. The day after Christmas, Powell gets up early and sneaks out of the home. He leaves a note on the refrigerator stating he has to get back to get a jump on his studies for the start of the next semester. A high school buddy meets him at the end of their long tree lined driveway and takes him to the bus station.

Newton's steaming after reading the note. The women of the house are more concerned about Powell's well-being.

The Tuckers plan to spend the day visiting close friends. Newton dresses in a suit sans tie while Mrs. Tucker puts on a festive dress. She goes to her jewelry box for a Christmas broach and her favorite solitaire diamond necklace her mother gave her for her sixteenth birthday.

As soon as she opens her jewelry box it's obvious her fifteen-thousand-dollar, diamond encrusted, Van Cleef & Arpels necklace is gone. Newton presented it to her for their thirtieth anniversary the year before. Normally the necklace is kept in their safe deposit box at the bank, but she wore to Dale Bumpers private celebratory party at the downtown Capital Hotel after winning the governorship in November. She just hadn't gotten around to returning it to their box.

Newton runs to his Bently and heads to Fayetteville.

Chapter 42

Jake Smith bumps into Alexis Dench at Lou's. It is four days before Christmas. UOA still on break, and he's scheduled an afternoon city-patrol shift. Driving past the café and he notices her car in the lot. Jake pulls a U-turn and goes into the establishment.

He sees Alex sitting alone in a booth and goes over, "Good morning Alex. May I join you?" Before she can speak, Jakes sits down.

"Hi Jake, it's been awhile," cordial, but not overly joyed to see him.

"Yes, it has." Jake jumps in with both feet, "Alex, I sorry for the way our last meeting ended. I miss you and thought maybe we could get together for dinner? You know…a real date?"

"How's Maggie Harvey?" scowling at his invitation.

"You know Maggie?"

"Of course, I know her! I know most people in this town. So you two broke up and I'm the rebounder?"

Stuttering awkwardly, "It…it's not like that." Silent for an uncomfortable length of time. "Alex, I made a mistake. You're who I really want to be with."

"How's it like?" she's got him right where she wants him.

"Alexis, can you give me a chance? I'll do anything to be your friend again."

"Friend?"

"Y…you know what I mean."

"I know exactly what you mean, Jake Smith," interrupting his incommodious apology. She stands to leave.

"Please talk to me, Alexis," Smith begs.

"You have two minutes!" She doesn't sit back down, rather folds her arms and scowls.

"I've never been a ladies man...what I mean...I just don't have time for more than one...let me rephrase, I've always been a one-woman man. I never cheated on my wife when I was married ...and I've only had one long-term relationship after." Smith fabricates about not cheating on his wife before she found out and divorced him. "It ended badly when she cheated on me," trying the woe-is-me card. "That's when I moved here," wearing a pitiful, scorned man look. "I wanted to be with you, but couldn't do that to Maggie...or you. I just was at a loss on what to do."

"Let's make this crystal clear! Did you break up with her or the other way around?"

"Maggie? I ended it!" Smith continuing the lies. Maggie and he are still seeing each other and as hot and heavy as ever.

"You know this is a small town, rife with gossip and that's not the story I hear!" she tries to pin Jake down, "How was your Thanksgiving, you know with the whole Harvey clan! Did you break it off over turkey?"

Smith had overlooked the fact the Alex and Maggie attend the same church, "N...no. It was after that."

"During desert?"

"No...I mean after Thanksgiving."

"When then?"

"I...I can't lie to you. We haven't been seeing each other, and haven't officially broken up...I'm trying to tell her...you know gently but haven't had the opportunity...since we haven't seen each other," the lies don't stop. "I'm doing it today, I promise!"

Alex is really mad. Enough of his lies, she stomps down the aisle.

Jake throws a twenty on the table to pay her bill and bolts after her. He catches up just as she turns on her ignition. "Alex, please? I really miss you! I begging for a chance to prove myself to you!"

130

"You're going to miss me more!" and starts in reverse.

One last ditch hail Mary, "Alexis please listen! I need you and I know you feel the same about me!"

Alex stares into Jake's electric-brown eyes and his pitiful scrunched face, "Smith, you have one chance!" She hits the gas and races out of the lot.

The gawkers on the sidewalk start applauding.

Now Smith has a problem, Maggie's in Little Rock staying with her eldest boy and his family for Christmas. She'll be back New Year's Eve morning and expects to ring in the new year with her boyfriend.

Smith sits at his kitchen table the following morning, pondering how to break up with Maggie and get Alexis to give him a chance.

Jake calls Alex and is again untruthful swearing the deed is done. His feeble plan is to keep Alexis busy and away from church until he can really fulfill his promise to her. Jake asks Alexis to dinner for Christmas Eve."

Alexis suggests they get together that evening. She hasn't had a serious relationship since her failed marriage right out of high school, subsequently plunging herself into college and after, her career.

She spend's the day fantasizing the *Alexis and Jake* romance novel with its fairytale ending.

Chapter 43

Newton Tucker arrives at the Fayetteville bus terminal a good hour and a half before Powell is scheduled to arrive. Since Powell's express ticket was dated for a January nine-twentieth service and he bailed early, he had to buy a new local ticket which stops at every wide spot along the road between Hot Springs and Fayetteville.

Powell emerges from the bus happy to be home and away from the Family Inquisition. He's flabbergasted to see his father pacing the sidewalk. The older man is beet-red in anger. Without so much as a greeting, "Where the hell is Mom's diamond necklace?"

"It's good to see you too, Dad," trying to act nonchalant. "What are you talking about?"

"Your Mother's Van Cleef & Arpels anniversary necklace is gone and you're the only one who would do that. HAND IT OVER!" he screams.

"Father, I would never steal from you!" reassuring. "Maybe she just misplaced it."

"It's not MISPLACED!"

"Well, I certainly don't have it!" Powell has no luggage and carrying a solitary paper bag with the only extra set of clothes he owns. He hands over the bag, "Take a look. I have nothing to hide."

Newton rummages through the sack and finds nothing but dirty underwear and clothes. "Empty your pockets!"

Now his son is in trouble, "You don't trust me, Father?"

"I certainly don't! You've changed too much this semester. And I don't believe your hogwash car story either! Nobody has their car stolen and refuses to report it!" Father repeats, "Now empty your pockets."

"I don't believe your bullcrap." Powell pulls the wad of bills from his front jean pocket, "This is all the money I own."

His father quickly counts a hundred and twenty-four twenties. "Why are you carrying all this cash on you? This should be in the bank." Without waiting, "What's in your other pockets?"

"Nothing, they're empty."

"Powell, I see the bulge."

He relents and pulls out a few loose bills and some change…and a small baggie half-full of white power, "That isn't mine. A brother asked me to bring it back from down south."

The older man pats his son's remaining pockets. They're empty. He misses the flat pawn stub. "Which brother?"

"It doesn't matter."

"The hell it doesn't! I'm turning him in! Is it the same guy who you say stole your car?"

"Yes. But I have it under control. I'm trying to help the guy get straight."

"Get straight by buying him more drugs?"

Powell's too strung out to get his lies straight.

"I hope you know what you're doing, Son" Newton turns to his car. "It's not ending here!"

As soon as he's back home, Mrs. Tucker and he tear the house apart. The necklace is definitely gone and he calls the police.

Chapter 44

Two Hot Springs detectives show up in the late afternoon at the Newton home to investigate the theft.

While they were waiting for the officers to arrive, "What did Powell tell you, Honey?" Mrs. Tucker asks.

"Said he knows nothing about it, but I'm not buying it. He had twenty-five hundred in cash on him and a bag of cocaine."

"Drugs? No not our son."

"I'm afraid so. I'm calling the school right after New Year and getting to the bottom of this."

The doorbell chimes.

The family and officers sit in their living room. Newton share's his insurance information declaring the insured value and hands over a copy of an insurance picture of the Van Cleef & Arpels necklace. He's asked if he called his agent yet, and tells he doesn't have the man's home phone number but would call first thing Monday morning.

The lead detective questions if they have any idea who did the crime. Newton tells the men that the house has been full of company for ten days and the necklace was present at the start of their visitor's arrivals. And an outsider could not have gotten past the security system.

Newton, Mrs. Tucker, and Nikki are all questioned separately. At this point, the officers don't suspect Nikki. She is too protective of her brother, now their prime suspect.

They're not sure if Mr. and Mrs. Tucker could be running an insurance scam. They doubt it but will look into it, after Powell.

Each asked about other visitors and repair men or any other people in the house during the time. Mrs. Tucker tells them their cook Gladis and her twice-a-week cleaning lady were the only outsiders in the home. The man questioning her takes down their information.

As the detectives stand at the front door to leave, the lead, again asks Newton about his son. The man mentions that Powell was there for a few days, though he doesn't think he's involved.

The detectives thank them for their time and state they'll get right on the investigation. The lead states they'll start with pawn shops first. Mr. Tucker suggests starting with any around the downtown bus terminal. When asked why he answers, "Just a hunch."

Chapter 45

Monday morning Detective Davidson and his partner show up for work at the Hot Springs Police Station. After grabbing a coffee and moving to their respective desks, their Lieutenant comes over and asks where they're at on two cases in progress. Davidson tells the boss they have a new jewelry theft to work on first.

The lieutenant lets them know in unequivocal terms that jewelry doesn't trump rape and to stay on their current caseload first. Davidson explains the Lieutenant Governor was robbed of a fifteen-thousand-dollar necklace and that State position takes precedence. He's told to spend the day on the necklace and report back to him before he clocks out. At that time a determination on which case takes priority for the rest of the week will be made.

Constructing a game plan on where to start looking for the Tucker necklace, The lead tells his partner to start calling pawn shops while he goes downtown to the bus depot area to personally checks out Newton's hunch.

A block before the station Davidson sees the first pawn shop. He continues on and parks in an unauthorized spot in the depot lot and hurries to the sidewalk in front of the terminal.

Standing, he looks up and down the street. There is a pawnbroker directly across, one on the same side at the corner and one in the next block that is visible. He heads to the closest establishment. It doesn't open until nine-thirty. He checks his watch and has a half hour to wait.

He moves on to the next shop.

"Good morning." He shows his badge, "Did you receive any new pawns Saturday morning?"

"Saturdays are always busy. And the day after Christmas is busier yet. Everbody's trying to turn unwanted gifts into cash."

The detective pulls out the necklace photo, "How about this item?"

"Nope, I certainly would remember that!"

Looking at the camera high in the corner monitoring the transaction counter, "Can I look at Saturday's tape?"

The man has nothing to hide and quickly agrees. Davidson thanks him and tells him he'll be back to view the tape, before heading to the next store, where it goes about the same way.

Back on the sidewalk, he checks his watch. It's almost ten and he goes back to the now open first stop.

After the introduction and first question, the owner says that he has never seen the jewelry in question. Davidson asks to view Saturday's tape and told, not without a search warrant.

The detective reaches over the counter and picks up the phone.

"Hey, you can't-do that!"

"Either I call in a search warrant or you're closing and we're going downtown. Either way, you're not leaving my sight. What's it going to be?"

"All right, all right. I have the necklace, but I was going to call you guys this morning!" he admits and lies.

"Get it and let's view the tape."

Davidson follows the owner to his backroom office safe. The owner retrieves the necklace and they watch the transaction.

The tape is blurry and snowy showing a man wearing a baseball cap pawning the jewelry. Davidson pulls out the photo he obtained from the father. It's hard to tell but sure looks like it could be Powell Tucker.

The detective impounds the necklace and the tape and goes to the station to pick up his partner. They head to the Tucker mansion.

Sitting alone with Newton in the study, doors closed, Davidson tells the man they have the necklace and a suspect. The homeowner turns on his VCR and pushes in the tape. The three men view it.

"Oh my God, I knew it was him!"

"The tape isn't conclusive. How can you be sure?" Davidson's partner questions.

"I know my son. I know his gait, his posture, his mannerisms…it's him."

"I'll call Fayetteville and have him picked up!" Davidson states.

"No detective. You recovered my property, I'll take care of my son."

Chapter 46

The morning after the detectives tell Newton they have his necklace, he gets on his phone and calls the Kappa Sigma fraternity house.

"Hello."

"Powell Tucker, please."

"Who is this?"

"His Father!"

"Oh, Mr. Tucker, Powell's not here."

"When do you expect him back?"

"Ah,…he doesn't live here anymore."

"Where the hell does he live?"

"Sorry, Sir, I don't know."

"Who's the president?"

After pondering the question, "Mr. Nixon?"

"Of the fraternity, stupid!" Newton's disgusted.

"Oh, sorry Sir. That would be Jon Yates."

"Put him on!"

"He's asleep. He drove all night and didn't get in until six o'clock this morning."

This kid's too dumb to be Kappa Sigma, "Well what do you think I should do, call back?" sarcastically.

"Noon would be a good time to try."

"GET HIS ASS OUT OF BED NOW!"

Less than two minutes later, "Good morning, Mr. Tucker." Jon's wide awake answering the call.

"Good morning, Jon." Trying a little sweetness. "I just inquiring as to what's going on with my son?"

After a little polite back and forth, Johnathon Yates levels with the Lieutenant Governor; Powell has a drug problem and was kicked out of Kappa Sigma, also he's been suspended from school. Jon's thanked for his cooperation and Newton promises to send a donation to his former fraternity.

Newton phones UOA's administration. A student worker tell's him that nobody will be back in the office until the following Monday, after New Year's, and that she doesn't know anything pertaining to his son.

Newton's next call is to his best friend, formerly his campaign manager and currently his Chief of Staff.

"Good morning Billy, are you alone?"

Newton hear's a muffled, "This is private. Please close the door."

A few moments later, "What's up, Newt?"

"I need a little discreet investigation work. Do you know anyone?"

"Oh Newt, is it Julie?"

"My wife's not the problem," laughing at Billy's assumption. He silently waits.

When nothing more is divulged, Billy knows not to ask what the real problem is. "Sure, we used two PI's during your campaign."

"Better give me both."

Newton copies down the info and calls the first name. The woman tells him that he will have to come into their Little Rock offices and get set up with an associate investigator. Also, they guarantee their services, she's sure they can assist with any needs he has.

Newton dials the second number. "English Investigations, Art of Secrecy, please leave your name and number and I'll get back with you."

Newton does not leave a message. He drives to a local service station and uses an outside pay phone and calls back English Investigations to leave a voice message.

"English Investigations, Art of Secrecy," a man with an English accent answers the phone."

"Mr. English?" surprised someone picked up.

"Speaking."

I'm looking for an investigator. I was referred to you by a former client of yours."

"Very good. What type of service are you seeking?" Very few people have his number and almost any former client is a good recommendation.

"First, let's get to your abilities and background," Newton suggests.

The intrigued PI loves covert operations, "Very good, Old Chap, I am rather quite qualified for any type of work. I was trained MI6. It was quite cracking work indeed. After a twenty-year career, I recently moved across the pond and took up in Little Rock starting my own business. Secrecy and discretion are my specialties."

"When can we meet? My name is …"

The investigator breaks in, "No names on the blower! Where are you located?"

"I'm up in Hot Springs. Ah…at a gas station pay-phone."

"I will meet you at the waterfall in Garvan Woodland Gardens at..." looking at his watch, "four hours, that will be six o'clock. Are you familiar with the area?" Thinking, *a payphone*, this is my type of client."

"I'll be there. How well I know you?"

"You won't, I'll find you, Bob's your uncle."

Chapter 47

Newton Tucker drives his Cadillac to Garvan Woodland Gardens. He leaves his estate as the sun is setting forty-five minutes early for his meeting. It's barely light as he parks in the empty lot and walks to the ground's map enclosed behind plexiglass in a large wooden covered visitors plaza.

The Lieutenant Governor finds the waterfall and the trails that lead to it. He looks around at paths leading off in all directions and returns to the map making sure he takes the right route before starting out.

He hears falling water splashing on rocks, and steps off the path and stands quietly hidden within a clump of natural grown Cottonwood Trees. Twenty minutes later he's cloaked in complete darkness. Unknown to him an unseen obscure dressed man has been watching the whole procedure from across the falls.

By six-thirty Newton is chilly and offended by the no-show. He emerges from his seclusion and starts on the path back to his car. He follows the dirt trail's detour around a huge old oak.

A few steps up the trail, "'Ello Gov'nor." In his native Cockney accent.

Startled, Newton spins, looking at the stranger wearing a black turtleneck below his black blazer leaning casually against the back side of the massive tree.

Confused and unsure what to say, "I'm not the Governor."

"I know exactly who you are Mr. Tucker," The accent gone. "Shall we take a stroll to the lake?"

On the five minute walk, Arthur English further briefs his new client on his background. After graduating Oxford at age twenty-four the year before Hilter invaded Poland and started WWII, the British

Army recruited him into their intelligence division. He operated in Europe until the war ended in '45 and was again recruited, this time into MI6.

Art worked out of Century House at 100 Westminister Bridge Road in London. Even though the brass plaque bolted to the front of the twenty-two story complex read, "Minimax Fire Extinguisher Company" it was the British Secret Service Headquarters. During his tenure, he added fluent Russian and German to his repertoire of English, French, and Spanish. He ended his brief summary, "I was a foreign spy for twenty years. I recently moved to Little Rock and opened my own business as I previously mentioned over the telephone."

The men stand on the shore of Lake Hamiton watching the low Harvest moon's reflection rippling off the water.

"Well, Mr. Tucker, what can I do for you?"

Newton explains the situation with his son and the necklace. He also tells the PI of Powell's suspension and drug addiction. "I don't know where my son is living or how he's acquiring funds to feed his habit. I want you to go to Fayetteville and find him and how this fiasco all happened."

"I would be happy to accommodate. My fees…"

"I don't care what it costs. I want you in Fayetteville by morning, understood?"

"I will be there by midnight. How do I communicate with you?" the mysterious man asks.

"Don't know, you can't call me at work or home!"

Do you have someone I can leave a message with?"

Thinking about it, "Call William Masse." Tucker gives the PI Billy's private number.

"I will simply say, Operation Waterfall, nothing else; Operation Waterfall and hang up. I will meet you at the waterfall six hours later. Day or night does not matter."

"Thanks, Mr. English." Shaking his hand.

Walking away, the former spy turns, "Call me Art." and evaporates into the darkness.

Chapter 48

Arthur English arrives in Fayetteville and checks into the downtown Mountain Inn fourteen blocks from the University of Arkansas. It's after midnight.

He's up at six and after a light breakfast and reading the Times newspaper in the hotel café, Art decides to drive around and learn the lay of the land, before heading over to the fraternity house.

By mid-morning, Art heads to Kappa Sigma. He parks his nondescript white sixty-nine Chevrolet 108 panel van on a side street and walks around the corner five blocks to the house.

It's after ten and without knocking he enters the dwelling. A mass of young men is bustling around trying to ready for a day at the lake. They ignore him assuming he's someone father looking for a son. Arthur wanders the house upstairs and down getting the feel for the place before returning to the front room and grabbing the arm of an unsuspecting student.

"Ease up there, Bloke!"

"Let me go!" jerking his arm unable to free the vice-like-grip. "What the hell do you want?"

"Only a wee chat, Andrew."

"I'm busy! Who the hell are you?" now terrified and screaming. The rest of the boys stop and stare at the intruder.

"Very good. Now I have your attention. I looking for Powell Tucker."

"Powell who?" the captive still squirming.

The grip gets tighter, beyond bearable. "Do not lie to me, son."

"Just let me go and I'll tell you where to find him."

"It does not work quite that way, Mate. You tell me where to find him and I will release you."

"I…I don't know where he lives, but he hangs around Bud's Beer and Kats."

"Better not faff and get on with it." Releasing his grip. "Stay handy, Andrew, we may have a few more bits and bobs to cover. Cheerio." Art strolls out the front door.

"How the hell did he know me?" screams the kid. Of course, the seasoned operator grabbed someone who had been identified by name while he inspected the house.

Mr. English looks at his watch and decides to check the administration offices and see what he can learn.

The building is almost empty, but there's a student sitting at a reception desk. He approaches and asks, "Where is everyone at?"

The girl tells him is still Christmas break and she's only there fielding questions from early arriving students. She knows who Powell Tucker is but not an acquaintance and doesn't know his activities.

"Very well, Lass." Not ready to give up, "Working whilst the toff is still on holiday, you must be a good student."

"I need to work to pay for school. It's not a choice."

"Still it takes a lot of gumption."

"Yes, I do need to graduate at any costs if I ever want a life."

"I am always impressed when young people have a direction in life." He removes a fifty dollar bill from his wallet and sets it on the counter, "I hope this will help you out."

"I can't accept that."

"Of course you can, Dear. It is for your education." The PI turns and steps towards the door.

"Thank you. I certainly can use it."

Arthur knows now is his opportunity. He goes back to the counter and leans in close, "Say you could help straight away with a tiny favor?"

"I told you I don't know Powell Tucker," suspiciously eyeing the man.

"I understand. It is just that his mother has not heard from him over the holidays and is worried sick. I am sure you called your mother for Christmas?"

"She lives in Fort Smith. I drove down for two days."

"You are truly a lovely daughter. My name is Steven George." He extends his hand.

Gently shaking it, "Nice to meet you, Mr. George. I'm Donna."

Without letting go he gently rolls her hand over to lay loosely on top of his and gives her a sad forlorn look deep into her eyes, "I just had a wee epiphany. Maybe you could take a peek at Powell's file and let me know where he resides?"

Hesitantly looking around before returning to his soft sky-blue eyes, "I guess that wouldn't hurt. I'll be right back."

Returning to her post she tells the man that there isn't any address listed. He thanks her and starts to leave.

"But…" the girl states.

He swirls around.

"Dean Vagger had a note saying he referred him to another student for help. A girl named Debbie and her phone number."

Arthur takes the offered information and wishes the student well in her schooling. He lays another fifty on the counter and finally leaves.

Walking back to his van he spies a payphone and calls Debbie. Luckily she is back from Little Rock. The PI again uses his alias Steven George and states he's an old friend of the Tucker family and is on his way to Hot Springs but would like to see Powell on his way through town. They chat for awhile. Debbie finally says that she has never officially met Powell and doesn't know where he lives.

English finds Bud's Beer joint and once again parks blocks away and walks the final leg to his destination. No one knows or admits to knowing Powell Tucker.

He tries Kats.

Chapter 49

Maggie Harvey comes home a day earlier than planned. It's early afternoon and she anxiously phones Jake's home. Of course, he's working and she's disappointed when the answering machine picks up. Maggie leaves a gleeful upbeat message for Jake to phone her ASAP.

Maggie sits next to her phone all evening and no return call from Jake. She's concerned and before going to bed calls the station. The front desk officer informs her Officer Smith got off duty at four o'clock and isn't scheduled to return until New Year's Day.

Smith spent the night with Alex and doesn't get the message until the following midday, New Year's Eve. After listening to Maggie's euphoric message, Smith musters up the nerve and picks up the phone. Maggie answers before the first ring ends, "Hello, Jake?"

"Hello, Maggie."

Hearing Jake demure quiet voice, "What's wrong Honey?"

"Maggie, I'm sorry but I have to work tonight."

Boldly, "Jake, I've been doing a lot of thinking…you should quit that job and move in with me. I have plenty of resources and thought we could start up Harvey's Construction again. Caleb can work with us too. It's perfect."

Smith is floored at the suggestion. It certainly isn't going as planned.

"Honey, are you still there?"

"Yes, I'm here." More silence, "Maggie, I love my position and *really* don't want to leave it. I was born to be a cop." Silence on both ends, "Maggie I also have been thinking…with my job and lousy hours…I can't give you the time you deserve and…"

148

Interrupting, "Jake, are you breaking up with me?" confused and puddling up.

"Of course not!" the spineless man replies, though thinks, "Crap, I should have just said it!"

Going on, "We both know how hard it has been to spend time together. Maybe we should...should take a break. You really deserve someone that can meet...err give you the time and attention you warrant."

"Honey, we can't-do this over the phone. Instead of going to the church party tonight, we'll spend a quiet evening here and figure out how we're going to make this work."

Thinking quickly on his feet, "This is just what I'm talking about, I can't get out of duty tonight." Smith's has lied more in the past two weeks than his entire life.

"That's alright, Honey, just come over whenever you can. I'll wait up for you."

"It could an all-nighter. I won't be in any condition to talk."

"Why don't you come over now before your shift?"

"Doesn't this woman ever give up," Smith thinks to himself. "Maggie I already worked all night and need to get a couple hours sleep."

"The man at the station told me you were off at four yesterday." Now wondering what's really going on. Maggie's not prepared to let her boyfriend go!

"How am I going to get out of this trap?" in his mind. "Four? That's right. Four was the end of my shift, but I had to help Harrison on a case the rest of the night."

"Can't the detective and his partner work on their own cases. How did they manage before you came here?"

"Sorry Maggie, I'm exhausted and need sleep. We'll have to talk after the holidays. See you soon." Smith quickly hangs up.

He retreats to the lake to spend the rest of the afternoon trying to solve his two girlfriend problem.

Chapter 50

English stands before the second-floor door knocking within the run-down apartment building. When no one answers, he picks the lock and enters.

The stench immediately penetrates his nostrils. The filthy one room unit smells of stale urine and vomit. There is a makeshift kitchen table with two old wooden chairs. The rough plywood top littered with white powder and an overfilled ashtray containing cigarette and Doobie butts. Along the back wall is a kid crashed on a vinyl blow-up mattress. Along the adjacent wall are another kid and mattress. Arthur steps to the closest one and kicks the half-full air mattress. The underwear-clad kid rolls over, "What the hell are you doing?"

"Powell Tucker?"

"Who are you?"

"Are you Powell Tucker?" Art repeats.

"No man, he's over there," as he rolls over.

The air mattress shakes like an earthquake as it's kicked again, "Take a walk, Mate!"

Rolling back over, the man looks up at the well-built athletic giant, "Leave me alone!" he mumbles.

"I am not asking! Pull on your trousers and hit the road or I will toss your ass into the cold the way it is!" The strange bully yanks the man to his feet.

"Ok…ok, man. I just need to take a leak."

"Locate a bush!" and he shoves the guy hard across the small room into the door.

"What's going on?" Powell looks up through blurry eyes.

As the man crosses to Powell the other guy runs over and grabs his pants and t-shirt before flying into the hallway.

"We need a chat, Powell."

"I got nothing to say to you!"

Art grabs Powell and roughly pulls him to his feet. He throws him across the room at the table, "Sit down!"

Powell sits quietly shaking, head down. He's afraid his drug bill has escalated to enforcement level. "I'll get the cash today. My father is wiring me the money."

"Newton is not in a charitable mood these days."

"You know my Father?" surprised.

"I know you! Drug addict, ostracized by your brothers, kicked out of school, stealing from your Mum. You have no secrets from me!"

"I hit a rough patch…but I'm getting clean."

"You are damn right there." Art tells the kid to dress, before vise-gripping his arm and walking him out.

On the way to the van, Powell's asking where they're going, who he works for and other needed questions. The PI stays silent.

In the van while driving to an unknown location, Powell doesn't have to ask, the information flows freely, "Your parents have put up with your shenanigans long enough. This is your one and only chance!"

The pair rides along in silence for three hours heading southeast. Powell assumes an encounter with his father is pending. His mind is racing; he needs cover stories for getting kicked out of school, taking cocaine and most important, stealing his mother's necklace.

Eventually, the van pulls onto a narrow paved way outside of Little Rock. Past the old-stone wall lined driveway, there is a monument sign standing in front of the refurbished white-pillared mansion, its black cut-out letters proudly reading, "PILLAR POINT RECOVERY CENTER."

"You're taking me to rehab?"

"And Newton said you were not bright."

"Look I don't need rehab, I told you I'm clean."

"Your supplier, please. Name, address and telephone number!"

"I don't know, Ethan takes care of that."

"Cut the crap, Powell; name, address, phone."

Powell gives up the only name he knows, Squirrel and the phone number. English writes down the information.

They head inside and Arthur English switches immediately back to his native accent. After the introductions and Powell's objection to the necessity of treatment, he is admitted.

Powell questions the length of his stay and told the standard program is six weeks though some stretch longer. He'll be there for as long as it takes.

Two large white-uniformed male orderlies are called and escort Tucker through a locked door and deep into the secure facility.

Chapter 51

Smith, dressed in a pale-yellow button down dress shirt covered by a peacock-blue pull-over sweater and wearing dark navy-blue slacks and black loafers. He grabs a medium-blue sports coat and heads for Alex's place.

He doesn't use his key and rings the bell. Alexis opens the door wearing a slinky backless vermilion dress. Her low-slung neckline adorns a perfect size string of pearls above just the appropriate amount of cleavage showing from her ample bosom. Her shoulder length cabernet sauvignon-colored impeccably curled hair sports lighter-red salmon highlights running through. Alexis' light-blush eyeshadow, lipstick and matching nails accenting. Finally on her feet were deep-red Jack Rogers sling back high-heels with see-thru peep toes completing the total look.

"My God, you're beautiful!" exclaims Jake.

"You don't look half-bake yourself, Mr. Smith," their eyes twinkling across the threshold. "Would you like a quick nip before we head over?"

"I would like more than that!"

"Calm down, Jake. We'll ring in the New Year later."

"I guess I'll settle for a Scotch then."

"Wonderful choice, Mr. Smith."

Jake leans in for a huge hug. "Don't mess me up, Jake. You'll have to be satisfied with a kiss on the cheek for the time being."

Smith is off work but on-call for the evening. Most of UOA's students are still out of town and won't be back at school for another week. Jake prays it'll be a quiet evening in Fayetteville, but he won't be able to drink or relax. Spending time with Alex is his reward.

They sit and enjoy their drinks. Smith explains it'll be the only alcohol he has that evening due to his on-call status. Alex is disappointed but doesn't show it.

"Let me grab my wrap and we should be off."

"We don't have to go you know."

Laughing, "Jake, I didn't do all this *just* for you." Of course, she actually did, knowing Maggie's back in town and thinking, "It's not the time to ask if she's called?" Nothing is spoiling this magic night.

Smith drives as slow as possible to Knight's home and the New Year's Eve party. He doesn't want to share his vision with any gawking person on the planet.

The street is full and blaring music permeates the air. Jake is resigned to park in an alley blocks away and the couple saunter to the party.

Smith opens the door without knocking and follows his date inside. The house and backyard are filled with neighbors and friends. Most of the department officers are working, but all off-duty personnel, higher-ups, secretaries and support staff are in attendance.

Judy notices them coming through the door and hurries over, "WOW! The King and Queen have arrived!" looking over the gorgeous couple.

"Happy New Year's, Judy." Smith leans over and pecks her cheek.

"You guys just raised the bar for this place," she laughs. "Harrison's in the backyard guarding the keg. Alexis, come with me and I'll introduce you around."

Smith goes into the yard and finds Harrison conversing with Chief Parson and a couple of others.

"Jake, I'm glad you made it." Looking around, "Did Maggie come with you?"

"Hi, Harry, Chief." Ignoring Knight's question. "Do you have any soft drinks?"

"I think there's a couple in the ice chest. You'll have to dig past the beer!"

Smith looks around for the ice chest. Knight continues his soliloquy directed at Parson. Bored, the chief excuses himself, "If you'll excuse me for a moment I have to speak to Smith." And he happily heads off to freedom.

"Jake, I'm glad you're following the guidelines regarding drinking while on-call."

"Wouldn't have it any other way."

"I see Alexis Dench…" looking through the open sliding glass patio door, "Is she with you?"

"Yes, I didn't want to show up empty-handed and she didn't have plans tonight."

"I sure I don't have to caution you, again, about being careful with that reporter. She's ambitious and never misses a comment."

"Yes, Sir. We agreed, *NO* business tonight. You'll never have to worry about my big mouth again!"

Touching his shoulder, "I sure I won't! I better find my wife and see how she's doing." Glancing at his watch, "We have to make an appearance at the Mayor's party. If I don't see you before we sneak off, have a Happy New Year, Jake."

"Thanks, Chief, same to you and your misses."

Jake wanders around making small talk to various people from work. He's talking to the chief's secretary and her husband when he receives a tap on the shoulder. And turns to see Alex standing, beaming in her full glory.

Jake can't control himself. He leans over and steals a quick kiss on her lips, "Are you having fun?"

"It's a great party. I know almost everyone. It's time you and I go to the living room and dance the night away!"

"I thought you'd never ask!" beaming with pride as he notices people ogling her. As they walk across the yard and through the house, a man after man pats his shoulder. Some wink and others just nod in approval. Smith's grinning like a twelve-year-old on his first date.

Alex and Jake dance to every song for an hour. They're joined on the floor for a few songs, but mostly alone. Guys keep trying to cut-in, but Alex rebuffs them with, "Maybe the next song." Nobody tries twice.

Just before midnight Harrison runs into the house and snaps off the stereo, "It just came over the radio, there's a gang fight at Kats! Someone reported shots fired. Anyone on call, get down there NOW!"

Smith looks at Alex, his face drained, "Sorry, I have to go. Harrison will take you home anytime you're ready. It's all arranged. But please stay and have a good time. I'll call you as soon as I can." He even surprises himself, "I love you, Alexis." as his softly kisses her forehead.

She throws her arms around Jake and whispers in his ear, "I love you too, Jake. Be careful out there and hurry home to me."

Smith is the only one to run from the residence. He's out of breath by the time he reaches his truck. After a few short gasps, he removes his coat and sweater and reaches into the glove box for his department-issued revolver and extra bullets.

Fifteen minutes later Officer Smith parks next to the alley behind the strip club.

Chapter 52

Private Investigator Art English drives to his Little Rock office. He phones Bill Masse. As soon as Newton's Chief of Staff answers he states, "Operation Waterfall," and hangs up.

He checks his watch and knows he has to be at the Garvan waterfall by eleven o'clock that night. He punches his answering machine and listens to the messages, writing down two names and numbers. He makes the calls and arranges one meeting for after the first of the year. He makes another personal call to a lady friend and arranges to meet for dinner two hours later at Café de Paree.

After a leisurely meal, Art excuses himself for the three plus hour drive to the waterfall, promising to call her over the coming weekend. He strolls to his discreet beige sedan and hits the highway.

Newton's already present when the PI approaches, "Mr. Tucker it's good to see you again."

"Art, what did you find out?" punching to the reason they're standing in the cold.

"I admitted Powell into Pillar Point. He'll be there until he's drug-free."

"Good. Good. That was quick! What now?"

"When your son is discharged he'll be Mr. Clean. You should probably let him stay at home for a few months to keep an eye on him. He can start looking for a school to transfer to. You don't want him back in the Fayetteville environment."

"Right. OK is that it then?"

"I'm going back to Fayetteville to find the dealer. He'll understand that he's never going to sell to your son again. That should do it unless you have something else."

"I think we're good for now! Do you have a bill?"

"Don't believe in leaving a paper trail. Three days work plus expenses…six thousand cash will cover it." English hands Newton a plain white business-size card that only has a twelve digit number written on it. "If you can make a straight deposit into my account at Farm Bank, we can avoid another face to face." He adds, "Remember deposit cash, no checks or transfer. No trails! And destroy that card when you're finished."

Chapter 53

The street in front of Kat's holds three police cars and cops hiding behind them from sporadic gunfire emitting from within the club.

Officer Jake Smith hugs the red-brick wall as he sidles along the sidewalk to the front corner of the building. He squats and peers around the corner. Right in front of the club door is half a dozen Harley choppers angled back wheel against the curb, front pointing down the street. He stands and slowly makes his way towards the front door. He stops beside a window. It's normally painted over with a fluorescent-pink sign advertising hot topless women. Tonight the frame is empty. A few pink shards remain along the edges of the shot out the window.

Smith quickly bobs his head taking a glance inside. It too dark to see more than shadows. A thunderous bang rings out. A bullet whistles by his fast retreating face missing by an inch as more glass pieces explode from the frame. He's not far enough out of range and a fragment embeds in his face below his temple. Smith tugs out the jagged piece and wipes the blood on his sleeve.

Not one police answering shot is fired. Everyone's on strict "hold your fire" orders. The negotiator in charge doesn't know how many, if any, innocent patrons are still inside or even alive.

The bullhorn again sparks to life with the same unheard message, "Inside, hold your fire! Hold your fire! We need to talk!"

Smith looks in the direction and the voice. He sees his lieutenant and another officer waving frantically at him to move back. He doesn't want to chance another glance and retreats the way he came.

Back around the corner, Jake resurveys the scene. "It looks like the front is covered," Smith mumbles to himself. He hears additional sirens wailing their way. He understands the backup units are for the currently unattended perimeter. He heads back to the alley.

Again barely sticking his head out he looks down. It's almost pitch black and he can't see anything. Smith shakes his head, thinking, "It's now or never!" Quickly he runs bent over to the closest trash can and squats behind listening. Not a sound can be heard except for the repeated bullhorn message from around front and the answering shots.

Another glance and he is on the move again. Smith melts into a dark recessed doorway and waits. Nothing. Twenty more feet and he's concealed behind a large green commercial dumpster gasping for breath. He jumps out of his skin at the sound of a scurrying rat.

Another peek. He can make out Kat's back door across and thirty feet or so down the alley. A faint light seeps under the bottom crack. Smith takes two steps, from his safe-position, towards the door. Gun drew, safety off and cocked with a bead on the door. Midway through the next slow deliberate step, the door blasts open breaking the alley silence with a loud bang as it swings wide and crashes into the adjoining wall.

A large overweight Black man stumbles to his stomach on the cold dirty cracked asphalt. Smith plants his raised foot and doesn't move another muscle. A police unit screams to a stop at the alley head from whence Smith started. It's headlights and spotlight illuminates Smith's figure.

The prone man looks up at the lights. He cries out at the silhouette, "Please help me!"

A tall stringy-haired, bearded man steps into the door frame laughing, "Nobody can help you!" He levels the shotgun at his helpless victim. The alley explodes in an ear-splitting crack as Officer Smith drops the biker. Immediately bullets are flying past Smith from behind. He dives for cover, now on the opposite side of the dumpster, "Shit, now the cops *and* the perps are shooting at me!" Plink! Whiz! The police bullets ricochet the steel container.

Another biker appears in the doorway. Not seeing Smith crouched in the dark, he raises a rifle and returns fire at the distance officer. One bullet unbelievably makes contact and the uniform crumples to the ground.

Smith aims and fires three rapid shots. The second outlaw drops.

The large man is trying to belly crawl to safety screaming, "Help me! Help me!"

The next police unit enters the far end of the breezeway. Smith is again lit up. He hurriedly stands and frantically waves his badge high in the beams. A moment later, the squad car headlights flick off then on and off. The alley goes black. Smith believes that whoever is in the police unit understood. He reloads his weapon and cautiously approaches the down man, never letting his eyes drift from the doorway.

A few steps later, Smith bolts across the alley to the back wall of the Kats building. A face appears and disappears from the doorframe. Smith bolts to the fat man, firing two shots at the doorway. He struggles to get the man on his feet. The face is briefly seen again, and Smith fires twice more.

Careworn from handling the heavy overweight man they make it back against the wall. The grateful man looks Smith in the eyes. He blinks hard and stares, "Officer Smith?" Looking at his blood flowing face, "Did you get shot?"

"I should have let them kill you, Brown!" recognizing the drug dealer he thinks responsible for the hit on him.

"Smith!" a whisper is heard.

Looking over, Smith sees Sergeant Williams against the wall on the other side of the doorway and nods.

"Lay down, Brown!" Smith softly commands. As soon as Brown's down, Smith yells as loud as he can, "Police! Come out with your hands up!

Two filthy men jump into the alley firing wildly in Smith's direction. Smith is firing back as he dives to the asphalt. None of his shots make contact. His buddy on the opposite side starts firing. One biker is hit in the arm and the other in the mid-back area.

It's a miracle Smith wasn't hit, notwithstanding him missing his fellow officer.

The arm wounded biker darts back inside. The other lay motionless on top of one of his dead buddies.

Smith again wipes the dirty blood mixed sweat from his face wound onto his other sleeve. He points at the open door. Both officers creep towards each other. Through silent hand signals, they agreed to make a move. Smith nods and squats on one knee looking down the hall into the club. His counterpart stands behind him feet wide apart, cradling his gun two-handed.

A gang member inside sees the men in the light emitting down the hallway. He drops his weapon and raises his hands, "Don't shoot! We give up! Don't Shoot!"

"Get everyone where we can see them! Hands up!" Smith screams.

Three men bunch together, guns drop and hands rise, "This is all of us! Don't shoot!"

Smith and Williams slowly work their way down the hall. Williams gets on his walkie-talkie and calls the front units, "It appears under control. Three men down, three other's surrendered. Proceed entry with caution. It might be an ambush. Repeat, PROCEED ENTRY WITH CAUTION!"

Smith get to the barroom entrance and looks around. Bodies are strewn everywhere. The only ones standing are the three bikers. Smith yells, "CLEAR!"

The front door crashes open and police stream into the room. Smith steps in still holding his gun in ready position, he sweeps it across the room prepared to drop anything that jiggles.

Six uniforms storm the standing men and throw them to the floor handcuffing each. "Someone, find the lights!" a voice rings out.

Over the next twenty minutes of chaos, emergency technicians set up a triage area and administer aid to the less severely wounded while waiting for the ambulances' return. Some of the critical ones already loaded and on their way to Washington Regional.

An officer escorts a doctor who happened to be in the outside crowd through the door. He starts checking bodies and shouting orders, "This one NOW! Gone! Gone! Hold, on this man! Gone! This woman needs blood!" He assesses every laying body. Finishing, the man following him and taking notes reports to the officer-in-charge; three patrons and one dancer dead, twelve wounded, five critical. Smith breaks in, "Someone needs to check a downed officer at the south end of the alley!"

The back alley results in two dead bikers, one critical and the officer with a bullet lodged in his leg. The gravely wounded outlaw eventually arrives at the hospital, DOA.

"Help us!" a voice is heard through the shattered one-way picture window. Two uniforms jump into the office. Money and drugs are scattered over the room. The floor safe is wide open. "Over here."

The officers round the far large wooden desk. Under it, they find Denny and Charlotte Daniels huddled together shaking uncontrollably. Denny's cheek is spread down the middle and blood pours on his wife. Tears streaming down both faces.

Smith, visibly shaken, needs air and walks into the street.

"Jake! Jake!" Alexis Dench bends under the yellow police barrier tape and runs to her lover before anyone can stop her. They melt into each other's arms for the longest time.

Chapter 54

After drilling Smith for facts, the reporter leaves him at the Kats'
scene and hurries to the office. She'll be up all night and most of the
next day writing her story. Likewise so will the police and other
officials staying on scene trying to figure out what took place; the
how, why, and what of the dead and living. Processing the crime
scene will last days before tackling the investigation.

Alexis takes short power-naps between downing pots of black
coffee. By seven in the evening on New Year's Day, she's satisfied
and turns her articles into her editor. She's anxious to get home, shed
her destroyed dress, scrub her makeup-streaked face and collapse.

The new dress she bought just for Smith's benefit is ruined with
dried blood from her love's leaking face.

The stories are published the following morning. First and
foremost it includes a full-column of her boyfriend's heroic and life-
saving bravery coupled with a complimentary picture.

The next article covers the six bikers taking over the bar. Alex's
first draft;

> *The melee started as a brawl between the*
> *Belial Biker Motorcycle Gang and a group*
> *of local men when the leader of the*
> *outlaws jumped on stage and grabbed a*
> *dancer's breasts.*
>
> *As the locals were winning the fight the*
> *gang leader pulled a gun and opened fired,*
> *killing the first two men.*
>
> *Everyone but the outlaws hit the floor. As*
> *the customers and employees were covered*
> *by the gun-toting man, the five remaining*

bikers robbed everyone else. They discovered
three concealed pistols.

Two members immediately shot out the office
mirrored window and climbed inside. Denny and
Charlotte Daniels, Kats owners, already hidden
beneath their desks, are pulled out. Charlotte
opened the safe while her husband was brutalized
and face slashed. Standing alongside the safe,
they found a rifle and a twelve gauge shotgun.
Inside the steel safe, they came across another
pistol. The pair stacked Charlotte's desk with
bundles of hundred dollar bills and baggies of
drugs.

Nine ear-splitting shots erupted from the bar
area. Apparently, they missed one guy's boot
buried pistol during their robbery. Milton Renner,
an older age employee, pulled the gun and
unloaded it at the leader. He missed every shot
and died instantly in a barrage of return fire.

The two men ransacking the office jumped back
into the bar area, knocking the money and drugs
to the floor. Their thick black motorcycle boots
broke the bags of drugs open in the chaos. White
powder and one-hundred dollars bills were scattered
in their wake.

Not wanting to be left out both men join in and
started shooting the prone hostages, resulting in
numerous dead and wounded. The final tally is
unknown at this time.

When Officer Smith and his partner entered the
establishment through the back door the gang was
all but out of ammunition and surrendered.

After hours of rewrites and tweaking, finding each appropriate adjective for maximum impact and clarity, She turns in the best story of her career.

Alex's other piece, a nineteen-seventy year events highlight story that she had been working on for weeks ends up buried in Section C.

The reporter keeps the Times front page full of updates for days, and every week through the speedy trial until the three surviving outlaw bikers are convicted and receive the death penalty.

Kats reopens three weeks after the massacre.

Chapter 55

The following Monday, January fourth, after a weekend of relaxation at his lady friend's house, English returns to Fayetteville to find Squirrel.

Arriving around noon he checks into the Cosmopolitan feeding his habit of never staying at the same hotel twice.

Art leaves his room right after checking in and goes to Kappa Sigma. He needs someone to settle Squirrel's where about. Of course, he walks right in unannounced.

It's the first day of spring classes at the University of Arkansas and the front room is empty. He makes his way to the kitchen cork bulletin board and looks over the pinned notes. He finds one written with "S" and a phone number. Art pulls his scribbled note from his wallet and compares the number. As expected, it's the same number Powell had told him. There's little doubt he supplies the house and more than just Powell Tucker.

The PI heads upstairs and briefly opens room doors and glances in. Typical messes; nothing out of the ordinary, nothing in place. At the final room on the left at the end of the hall, he peers in and sees a small mirror on the dresser holding a single-edged razor blade. He enters the room and starts a search. In a bottom dresser drawer, he finds a baggie of cocaine.

The front door slams! Art shoves the drugs into his pocket and heads downstairs. He finds a man in the kitchen staring into the open frig.

"Ello, Mate, would you happen to have a toad-in-the-hole in there?"

"The startled student glances around the room, "Who are you?"

"A friend of the fraternity. I have a couple of questions."

"I'm busy," the young man states. "I don't have any answers!"

"That would be a clanger, Mate. They are easy questions. Let us start with who stays in the room is at the end of the hall on the left?"

"I'm not telling you anything!"

"Cheeky monkey, eh?"

Art takes three steps forward and without notice throws his palm-open right hand into the guy's throat. His thumb and forefinger straddling the student's Adams Apple. "Not worth buggering up for I would say?"

"What the hell? You're hurting me...let go!"

"You are not hurt at this point! Who resides in the room?"

"S...Sam." the student stutters

"And who might Sam's roommate be?"

"I...I am."

"Better chinwag about your bloke Squirrel?"

"Don't know what you're talking about."

Pulling the clear sandwich bag of coke from his pocket with his left hand, Art wiggles in front of the scared man's eyes, "I think you are familiar with Squirrel?"

"No...no...what's that?"

"Very well then, I am sorry to spoil your day." Art releases the neck and wipes down the front of the kid's shirt. "We'll have a little wait on the chesterfield."

"Wait for what?"

"The bobbies. I am sure they have questions also, Mate."

"Who are you?"

"A concerned friend. Let's go into the other room for the time being."

"Th..there's no reason to call the police. I...I'm sure I can help you."

Art gets everything he can from the student, which is barely enough to start. The kid only knows Squirrel's number and that he saw him at Kats a couple of times. The PI also gets the directions to the club.

English drives to the strip club. It's mid-afternoon and the place is sparse with customers. He saunters to the bar and orders a draft. Sitting he sips the beer. The barmaid stands a few feet away washing glasses. Art starts a casual conversation.

"How long have you been barkeeping, Lass?"

"Too long. I'm saving up to go to college."

"You should begin with morning lessons. Before you know it you will be complete. An education is the only thing you keep the rest of your life."

"You sound like a teacher."

Laughing, "Hardly not. I was just like you. Worked to go to school, but never made it." He was building a bond sharing like-experiences.

"What do you do now?"

"Give it a try?"

Grace looks him over, "Salesman?"

"That is quite right. One stop here tomorrow and I am off for another six months."

"What do you sell?"

"I hock packaging. I have been calling on Tyson for two years. Every time I ask they give me bugger all," more laughing.

Grace joins in with a small giggle. I kinda know what you mean. I've asking for raise for a year."

"That should be motivation enough to go to school."

"Yeah." Both continue laughing.

"I will have another pint."

When she brings his drink he lays a second twenty on the counter, "Keep the change."

"Thanks, What's your name?"

"Eugene McKenzie."

"Eugene? So if I yell Hey U! I'm talking to you!" Both can't contain their giddiness. "I'm Grace."

"It's certainly nice to meet you, Grace." After a slow sip, Art raises his right palm-up hand, He wiggles his fingers it in a come hither beckoning. Grace to moves in closer. He glances over his shoulder before leaning over the bar and looking Grace in the eyes, "Do you know where I can get any marijuana?"

Laughing and standing up, "You don't have to worry around here. It's no secret everybody smokes." Grace adds, "This is a college town and you are in a strip club!"

"Sorry, I did not want to act divvy or have you nicked."

"No worry. Tell you what, I go on break in a few. Have another drink and we'll go to the alley and get high."

The PI didn't expect this invitation, "I would rather purchase a little taste for later in the privy of my room."

"I'll just give you a couple of doobies."

Now it's getting more complicated. Art didn't really want drugs just the drug dealer. "I can not accept it from you. You have to save your money for school. If you can just set me up, I am happy to purchase *you* a couple for your trouble."

"I like the way you think, U. Lulu should be here in a half hour."

"Who is Lulu? A girl supplier?"

"Lu? Hell no. Her husband. They call him Squirrel." After a moment of silence, "If she's working, he'll be here."

Not more than twenty minutes later Lulu Love walks through the front door.

"Hey Lu, come here," the barmaid notices the stripper and calls her over.

"What's up, Grace?"

"U is looking for a little weed. Is Ken with you?"

Art makes a mental note of Squirrel's first name.

"Nah, he had to go to Fort Smith. Can't help you, Dude," addressing the stranger, before going to the girl's dressing room.

"Thanks for trying, Grace. I will see you later." English walks into the men's head. A few moments later he steps back into the bar. Grace is busy with a customer and he slinks into the dressing room. Lulu is the only person there.

He approaches her, "When do you figure your husband will be available? I am looking for a little heroin to take back to Powell. I have to leave in the morning, and need to sow it up tonight."

"Who are you? You a cop?"

Laughing, "Just a poor man in need!"

"I don't know you…and I don't know anything about drugs." Lulu stares the man down.

"Do tease me, Lass. Let us start with your full name?"

"Lulu Love."

"Very good, now do not make me turn you into a mutter!" English pulls out a knife and sticks the point against her throat. "Do not make any gormless moves!"

"I…I won't. I don't want any trouble," she whispers.

"You *are* a smart tart. Let's get at your real name?"

Still quietly, "Liz Walker."

"Very good, where does Liz Walker and Ken Walker live?"

"Morrow."

"Address?"

Her home doesn't have a physical address, but she gives the stranger directions to their farmhouse.

"We will be seeing you soon Mrs. Love." He gives her his best teeth showing grin and leaves.

Chapter 56

Private Investigator Arthur English strolls back into Kats a little after nine PM. Lulu Love is on stage pole-dancing to an unruly mob of jeering men. Grace sees Eugene immediately and smiles. She looks at the back left corner of the club and slightly nods her head.

Art glances to his right and sees a ruffled-hair skinny man sitting alone in a large booth. He turns his head back to Grace and nods thanks. He walks to the booth and sits down.

"Ello Squirrel. It is nice to finally meet you."

"I don't know you and don't want to!"

"I am sure your Liz mentioned me. I am just looking to purchase a little treat for Mr.Tucker."

"Powell, I know. Where is he?"

"I am afraid he is stuck in Little Rock at present. That is why I'm here."

"You look like a cop!"

Laughing, "And you look like a drug dealer, Chap." Adding, "If I were a bobby we would not be sitting here playing games."

A lengthy hard stare, "I'm out of product. You'll have to find someone else!"

"You were out of product this morning, but after you day's jaunty you're flush again." Art bluffs.

"You don't know what I did today!"

"Oh I do, your misses filled me right in. She trusts me."

"She told me what you did to her!"

Another long stare, and English states, "Meet up in the alley in ten minutes, Mate!"

The PI saunters out the front door and makes his way to the back of the club. The alley is typical, dirty and filled with trash cans. He spots a large stack of empty cardboard beer cases and figures it's Kats, So he walks over and waits.

Twenty minutes later, the back door to the club opens and Squirrel walks into the dark alley.

Without warning the man grabs Squirrel by the neck and slams him high into the cement-block wall, feet dangling.

"I…I knew you were a cop!"

"I told you, Chap, I am not the police! But I am a friend of Powell." After a prolonged look through the dealer's eyes, he goes on, "My friend is clean now. You are never going to sell him any drugs again. You understand, Mate?"

"Sure, man. No skin off my back."

"I do not believe you are taking me seriously." He reaches into the dealer's pocket and extracts a full bag of blow, "What is this worth?"

"Th…three, four thousand."

The PI turns the baggie upside down and shakes the contents to the ground. The gentle breeze flowing through the alley scatters the white powder.

"What the ****!"

"Just a little reminder of our chat. Now, if we have an understanding, you better naff off."

"You're dead, man!"

Art throws a mean punch into the dealer's gut and crumples the guy to the filthy asphalt.

"You better smarten up quick, Mate. I won't be the one on the other side of the turf!" he tells the man lying in a fetal position rocking back and forth. And he places a well-designed kick to the man's lower back.

"Are we clear, *now*?"

Squirrel whimpers a painful, "Yes."

"Was that a *yes*!"

"YES, I UNDERSTAND!" loud and clear.

Back at the Cosmopolitan, Arthur English calls William Masse's private number. It's long after everyone has gone home for the day. He leaves a message, "Operation Waterfall concluded. No further contact."

Chapter 57

Pillar Point's first two weeks are hard for Powell Tucker. The first week he spends in solitary withdrawals in a hospital-style room. He wretches, shivers and sweats constantly. When he shook too hard and pulled out the dripping IV or the monitoring feeds, a male nurse shows up to reconnect him. The same monster brings him uneaten meals three times a day.

By the third day, he is starting to regain control of his mental facilities and allowed to bathroom alone. The uncontrollable shaking stops though he still sweats through the nights.

On the seventh day, Powell's moved into the general population.

Week two starts the rehabilitation process. The regimental schedule requires raising at seven AM, followed by breakfast and an hour of self-reflection. Later are individual meetings with counselors and psychiatrists. After lunch is two-hour groups. Another hour of reflection, and a little free time before dinner. The evening time is spent in the rec room, socializing with fellow patients, playing board games or watching television. Everyone's in their rooms by the nine o'clock lights out.

Powell doesn't play well with others and consistently refuses to participate with his personal problems, but does offer snide, obnoxious remarks. After all, he is Powell Tucker, son of the Lieutenant Governor Newton Tucker, student extraordinaire, changer of the old guard system and certainly not a drug rehabilitation patient. He refuses to let these incompetent fools break him down!

By the end of the month, he made one friend. A shy young girl who has been at Pillar Point close to six months. She is scheduled to go home on the first day of February.

The day arrives. While her parents are in the office waiting for their daughter, she's saying goodbye to her friend. They promise to hook up after his release.

She advises Powell, "If you want to get out of here you got to play their games. The longer you fight them the longer you stay. It's simple math." She winks at her friend, "I'll see you soon," and places a quick peck on his cheek before following a nurse down the hall.

Powell thinks hard about her advice and decides she is right. He does everything he can to appear the perfect, unpretentious patient. The condescending staff isn't fooled by a sudden change in attitude.

By the middle of February, Powell asks about getting out. Dr. Yakiniku tells him it's a long treatment and she's hoping to release him by Mother's Day. Maybe she shouldn't have been so brutally honest.

Late into the night, Powell's up. He gently removes his roommate's pillow from under the sleeping man's head. Laying both pillows, his and his roommates lengthwise along his bed, he covers them and arranges to look as though there's a sleeping body. Earlier at lights out, he stuffed the door latch bore with a torn part of a napkin preventing the latch from locking.

He silently opens the door and peeks out. All clear, he sneaks through the halls. Powell belly-crawls past the picture window of the nurse's station where a nurse, nurse practitioner, and guard are chatting the night away.

He makes his way into the rec room containing an emergency exit. He knows he can't slam through and get away before the alarm alerts an escapee. Powell studies the aluminum opening bar and the magnetic contacts at the top of the door. Even if he could find the wires, breaking the connection would also set the alarm off. "There has to be a way to fail the power system to the building," he rationalizes. He'll need to escape before the emergency generator kicks in. The office door opens and he hears laughing in the hall.

176

He runs to the doorless room entry and glimpses around the frame. The three personnel are walking together in the opposite direction towards the wardrooms to check patients.

It's now or never. He runs silently to the slowing self-closing office door and slips in unnoticed. Quickly scouring the room he spots a pair of blunt-end bandage removal scissor-handles sticking out of a pen cup. Seizing the shearing instrument, Powell cuts a small length of telephone cable from the desktop phone. He grabs the Bic lighter and a handful of loose vendor machine change, laying beside a pack of Kools.

He sneaks a peek out the door. The three are in front of the last two rooms peering through the small door windows. Powell moves stealthy back to the rec room.

Rapidly Powell strips both ends of the cable. He carries a chair under a ceiling mounted fire sprinkler and climbs onto it. Lighting the Bic he holds it as high as he can. He's getting desperate as the voices are coming closer. Suddenly the siren deafens the ward and water sprays from every head.

He hastily jumps from the chair and moves to an electrical outlet. He jams each end of his stripped wire into different horizontal slots. The electrical system shorts and the building darkens. He's out the emergency exit in a flash and forcing the slow hydraulic door closed as hard as he can push. It slowly gives way and closes at the exact same instant the generator relights the building. The statue slowly grins when no different alarm signal activates.

Powell Tucker runs through the dark forest, tripping over fallen logs and thick underbrush. At the edge of the woods, legs and arms dripping deep red liquid, he hears screaming sirens coming up the highway. He crouches in the dark listening until they pass. Then he makes his way down the road to a service station. Using his ill-gotten change he calls a high school buddy that had moved to Little Rock right out of high school.

He stands in the shadow of the building for twenty minutes, after which, Powell is picked up and driven to his friend's apartment.

The next day Powell borrows five-hundred dollars and hitchhikes to Fayetteville.

Chapter 58

The following morning, Valentine's Day, Powell wakes up at seven as he's accustomed to. He's on his air mattress across from his roommate Ethan's empty pad. He got in late the night before. His last hitched ride dropped him off at the far end of the city and he walked the last four hours to his apartment.

By late afternoon Ethan still hasn't come home. Powell's bored; he spent the day walking, sitting and laying down within the one room apartment. Back to sitting in a wobbly wooden chair at the makeshift table, his brain goes to auto-pilot. After an hour of mind games playing God and Devil, he gives in and goes to the corner market to phone Squirrel.

The insipid drug dealer is home sick with the flu. His temperature is one hundred-point-four and he's not leaving his couch. It's Liz's night off from Kats and she's home pumping her husband full of chicken soup.

Powell begs for a delivery. After haggling, they settle on two bills for two eightballs of blow, four times the going street price of twenty-five dollars per.

Ken tells Liz she has to make the delivery. She flat out refuses, "I have to watch you and take care of baby Emily. You're too sick if she needs you."

"You'll be there and back in an hour. We're four times on this one. You can take my SS."

"Only if I get half to do whatever I want with!"

"Half the sale or half the profit?"

"Profit!" not knowing the difference or realizing she just took a twenty-five percent hit on her share.

Liz finds the dingy upstairs apartment and knocks. The door flies open, "Lulu Love!" shocked not to see Squirrel. "Come on in, Darl'n."

"I'm not stepping a foot in that garbage dump."

Looking up and down the inside hallway, Powell leans in closer and whispers, "We can't-do a deal in the hallway. The nosey manager has spies everywhere."

"Crap!" Liz steps inside.

"Have a seat. I'll dig up the cash." She's unaware he locked the door when he closed it.

"I'll stand!"

Lifting the corner of his blow-up mattress, "Let's see…I paying double…that's a hundred."

Liz is assuming he's talking a hundred each. She pulls the drugs from her purse and lays two baggies on the table.

Powell walks over and hands her one bill.

"What's this bullcrap. It's a hundred each!"

"I'll tell you what, Darlin', one bill for the drugs and one bill for the sex!"

She grabs the two baggies and tries to open the door. Spinning around, "Let me out of here, you perverted bastar…"

She hasn't finished by the time Powell latches onto her small shoulders and drags her across the room, throwing her onto his mattress. The mattress is all but out of air and she hits the floor hard hammering her head. Blood starts oozing and matting her hair. Powell's on her like a dog on a steak.

Liz is flailing her small thin arms wildly at the laughing man, "Come on Lulu, a little quickie for old Powell. I know you're into me. I see the way you look at me when you're dancing."

"Get your ass off me. Ken's gonna kill you!"

"Squirrel doesn't have to know. I'm sure you other clients are your little secret."

"I don't have any *clients*!" she screams. Her useless swings only teasing the man.

"You do what you think's best. I'm certainly going to." As he rips her blouse wide open, buttons flying. He grabs her bra and pushed it up to her neck. "Ohhhh…just like I remember."

He undoes both their jeans and forces himself inside her.

Still laying under the dead weight of the man's body after he's finished, Liz tries to push him off.

"Hold on, Honey." Powell reaches under the mattress and produces the second hundred. "This one's yours. You earned it." Laughing he stands and rebuttons his Levi 501s. "Better get going before you're missed, Darl'n."

Powells at the table laying a line as Liz grabs the other hundred and runs through the now unlocked door.

"See you soon, Baby," Powell laughs as she's halfway down the hall.

She drives to Madison's apartment. Her friend is at work, but Liz still has a key. After showering and cleaning her wounded head, she borrows a clean t-shirt and drives home.

"That took longer than I expected?" Ken questions as Liz walks across the living room.

She throws the two bills at him, "I stopped to see Madison for a minute."

Chapter 59

Two solitude weeks of loathing after her attack, Liz is getting ready to go to work. Ken's asleep on the old couch. She goes to their bedroom and find's his wallet in his top dresser drawer. Standing silently and looking back at the door, she's satisfied he's dead to the world and she rummages through his forbidden billfold.

She finds and removes the tiny slip of paper pushed deep behind his driver's license and copy's the name and number written on it, before putting everything back as found.

Liz goes into the other room and gently shakes her husband, "Ken? Ken?"

Dazed and still half asleep, "Huh. Hun, what do you what?"

"I'm going to work. Did you want me to drop Emily off?"

"Ahhh, I'm heading in later, I'll do it."

"Thanks, Dear. Have a good evening." Liz kisses Ken's forehead and leaves.

On her way into Fayetteville, Liz stops in Prairie Grove for gas. While the car is filling, she gets on the phone and calls the stolen number.

"Lo."

"Mr.Brown?"

"Who dis?"

"I'm Ke...uh, Squirrel's wife."

"Wasup, Ms. Squirrel?"

"Squirrel asked me to call you and see if I can pick up some heroin?"

"H? Wass he wants with that?"

"I think he has a buyer. Can you tell me how it comes and the price?"

"Fiteen a ten dose."

"So that's fifteen hundred for a hundred grams?" trying to understand.

"Undred megs! I don't av da much."

"How long would it take you to acquire it?"

"Ah, four mayba fit days."

"That's great! Don't tell Squirrel, this is between you and me, understand?"Adding, "I also need syringes."

"I'ss understand. Undred megs and two sticks. Hows I hook you?"

"How will it come?" not understanding the quantity.

"Ah, bundles."

"What's a bundle?"

Ten little squares. Like chocolates," grinning.

"Chocolates? You mean brown squares?" sounding distressed.

"Fo sho."

"I...I was with a girl once and she snorted a white powder and said it was horse."

"Yous wants powder? Whites or chocolate?"

"You can get white powder?" her mood picking up.

"Four Benjamins up."

Starting to sob, "I don't have that much."

"Chill the grill. I'll hook you up and catch you lata. I gotta bounce."

"When you get it let me know at Kats. Ask for Lulu. I'll see you in a week, Mr. Brown! You a lifesaver." Liz hangs up and smiles for the first time since Powell raped her.

During the coming week Lulu's at work every day. Even on her days off, she hangs around. She needs to come up fifteen hundred dollars and plans on robbing her boss.

She knows there are cameras everywhere except the office. While Denny and Charlotte are working, which is every day, the safe is frequently left open. She straightens out a wire coat hanger and places a large piece of duct tape on one end. The tape flaps out from each side of the hanger by a full two inches. She carefully sets the makeshift device upright in the corner of her locker. Now it's a waiting game.

Later in the week, Denny goes to Bentonville for business. Liz is just hanging out in the dressing room pretending to construct a new costume. It's late morning and Grace is tending bar. Madison is the only dancer and on stage. Charlotte steps from the office, "Lu, you're here early?"

"Hi, Miss Charlotte. I making a couple adjustments on my new outfit for tonight."

"It's always nice to see an ambitious young lady. Keep up the good work!" as she steps into the ladies room.

Without hesitation, Liz gets her coat hanger and tape contraption from her locker. She reaches the taped-end high covering the camera lens. Slowly rotating the hanger, Liz gets one end of the tape to hold. She rotates back until the other end adheres. She leaves the hanger dangling and runs into the office. The safe's open and there is money all over Charlotte's desk where she's counting yesterday's take.

Liz grabs a stack of bills from the safe, rubber-banded together and shoves them down her pants. She heading for the exit when she hears the toilet flush and bathroom door open. She freezes. Liz can't let Charlotte see her leave the office. She looks frantically around and moves to Denny's desk.

The door opens, "Lu, what are you doing in here?" the boss demands.

"There are only small safety pins in the dressing room and I was hoping you or Denny had a large one?"

"You're in luck, I have one." Charlotte goes to her desk and opens the shallow top drawer. Searching through the mess, "Here it is. I thought it was bigger. Will this do?" holding up the found pin.

"That's perfect." Liz accepts it and heads back to her outfit.

"Lu! Please shut the door behind you."

Liz steps back and closes the door with a, "Thank you Miss Charlotte."

Quickly she goes to her hanging rod and pulls the tape off the lens. She discards the sticky piece and returns the shaft to her locker. Liz takes the top and shorts she was playing with and pins them together just as Charlotte opens her door.

"Miss Charlotte, what do think?" holding up her outfit.

"Very nice. Have you seen anyone wandering around back here?"

"No, I've been alone since I got here. What's the matter?"

"Not sure. The cameras are always so sharp and clear, but I just checked Denny's screen and that camera is so blurry, I can hardly make out the room," pointing to the corner unit.

"Haven't seen anyone."

"Probably getting old or something. I'll have Ethan take a look." She returns to her room closing the door behind her.

Liz retrieves the hanger from her locker and shoves it down her pants.

As she's walking stiffly across the barroom, Madison yells at her, "Lu, are you hurt?"

Lost in thought and started by the call, Lu stops and turns, "I'm fine, why?"

"Sorry, I just thought you were limping a little."

"No. No problems. I'll see you in a couple of hours." Liz walks out as fluid as she can with the coat hanger jabbing into her calf.

She drives to Madison's apartment and lets her self in. After counting the two thousand dollars in hundred dollar bills, she put five hundred in her purse and the remaining she hides under the bathroom sink inside a box of rat poison.

Chapter 60

A few days later, Liz walks into Kats and Madison instantly runs up to her, "The big guy was in here looking for you. He wants you to call him," and she hands her a cocktail napkin.

"Thanks," looking at the number. Scrawled across the napkin are "RB" and a number.

She goes to the ladies dressing room and using the phone dials the number.

"Lo."

"Mr. Brown?"

"Is me."

This is Squirrel's wife. Do you have my package?"

"I'ss gots it."

"Where can we meet?"

"Youz has my money?"

"Yes."

"There's a Waffles place on one-twelve."

"That's perfect. I get off work at three this morning, is that too late?"

"I'lls be in the park'ns lot." CLICK.

"Everything all right?" Madison enters the room concerned for Liz.

"Perfect!" Hey, I'm not on for a half hour. I have to run out for a sec. if I'm a little late can you cover me?"

"Of course, Honey. Are you sure you're Ok?"

"Everything's great. I'll see you in a few."

Liz hustles to her VW bug and drives to Madison's apartment and recovers her stash of money.

The rest of the evening drags on for Lulu Love. She's anxious for her meeting.

At three-ten Liz pulls into the Waffle House parking lot. She sits in her car peering through the large front windows. An only patron is a Black fellow sitting at a table eating. It has to be Randal Brown. She heads inside.

The huge man doesn't look up at the sound of the doorbell and continues devouring the largest stack of waffles Liz has ever seen.

She walks over, "Mr. Brown?"

The man glances up. Still stuffing in giant bites of his breakfast, he's unable to speak and nods at the empty chair across the table from him. Liz takes the seat and sits quietly until his finishes.

He leans back and chugs the full glass of milk. After setting the glass down the man pats his giant chest and a loud obnoxious burp exits his mouth. "Yous gots the grip?"

"Oh yes."

"I'ss arounds ta back," as he stands and steps toward the exit. He turns back to the still sitting woman, "Yous com'n?"

Liz jumps up and follows. Outside he looks over her car, the only one in the empty lot, "Drives in back!"

Liz takes her car around and parks next to Mr. Browns midnight Cadillac. She reaches under the seat and pulls out the rubber banded brick of hundreds and scoots to his vehicle's open driver's window.

"Pulls in!"

Liz climbs into the passenger seat and hands over the cash. The giant slowly counts every bill. He looks at her and nods, then makes a small pointing gesture at the glove compartment. She opens it and takes the bag of smack and two syringes. She asks Mr. Brown how to take the drug.

"Da's lot of powders. Yous only takes a line, before nap'n."

She asks how much a line should be and he holds up his thumb and forefinger a quarter-inch apart. Liz asks about shooting the drug and he explains the procedure. She thanks him and leaves.

Two days later Liz is off. She's sitting on their couch watching TV. The shower turns off. A few minutes more and her husband comes to her and gives her a big kiss, "I'm going to work. It'll be a late night. Don't wait up."

As soon as his Chevelle thunders down the street, she jumps up and goes to the bedroom to change. Liz puts on a tight high-cropped T and extremely short cut-off Levis exposing her navel and half her butt. She retreats to the bathroom and does her makeup and puts her hair in a ponytail. She gathers up baby Emily with a diaper bag and change of clothes. While her car is warming up she runs back inside for a tablespoon and disposable lighter. She almost forgets the items.

On her way into Fayetteville Liz drops her little girl off at the baby sitter's and tells the older woman she'll be back in a couple hours.

Thirty-minutes later she's sitting in her bug outside of Powell's apartment block. It's mid-evening on Friday night. Minutes of watching with nobody coming or going she sneaks quietly upstairs. With her ear to Powell's front door, she listens for voices. None are heard. She did hear someone turn a faucet on and off. Liz hopes it's Powell and Ethan's at work. She knocks softly.

"Well, well, Darl'n. What a surprise?" Powell answers the door. He's only wearing a pair of jeans, and barefoot.

"Can I come in? I have a little treat for you," patting her purse.

He looks her up and down, "By all means, Darl'n."

Liz enters and goes the makeshift table, "My husband's busy tonight and I thought we might get stoned." She lays a small baggie of white powder on the table.

A wide grin blankets his face, "Now that's my girl." He bends over and tries to kiss her.

"Don't rush me. I have to get in the mood," gently pushing him back.

Liz pulls the broken piece of window pane close and shakes some powder on it. She pulls Charlotte's business card from her purse and makes two perfect extra thick lines of powder. The woman then pulls a dollar bill from her jeans and rolls it into a tube and hands it to the anxious man.

Thinking the white powder is coke, Powell snorts a line. It's so big it takes him two inhalations. "Damn, that's good. Your turn," offering Liz the bill.

"Hold on, I need to clean up a little first," winking and walking to the bathroom.

She closes and locks the door before putting her ear to it. She hears Powell walking around and the air mattress squeaking as he straightens his blanket.

"You ready?" the euphoric young man yells.

"Not quite. You can have the other line, I've got plenty."

He looks at the table. "Well, if you insist, Honey."

She flushes the toilet and turns on the hot-water sink tap. When the rushing water turns hot, she puts in the stopper letting the water partially fill the basin. Smiling, she puts down the toilet seat and lays out the full bag of drugs, syringes, and her tablespoon and lighter. Scooping a half spoonful of smack, she lays the handle resting on the bag of dope careful not to spill any. She rummages through her purse and finds her eye drops. Liz sucks some hot water from the sink into the eye dropper and puts a few drops on the powder. She gets the lighter and slowly lifts the spoon and puts the flame underneath. Soon the water and powder are bubbling as one. She sucks the liquid into the first syringe and repeats the process filling the second.

Elizabeth slowly opens the door and peeks at Powell. He's laying on his vinyl mattress, smiling, eyes closed. Liz takes a soft step forward. The floor squeaks, his eyes pop open. She stands perfectly still watching, waiting. Within seconds, his lids slowly shut as he dozes off again.

Liz makes her way to the foot of the mattress and kneels down, laying one syringe on the floor and retaining the other within her clasped fist. Gently, using her left forefinger and thumb, she spreads his big toe from the next. She pushes in the syringe and squeezes the plunger until not a drop is left. Powell doesn't move a muscle. Still, she watches him closely. Satisfied he is out cold, Liz repeats with the second tube full of liquid heroin.

She goes to the bathroom to prepare the next treatment. While filling the syringes, Liz hears Powell vomiting violently. When all is quiet, she returns and double-doses him again.

The procedure goes on for almost an hour before her baggie is completely empty. Powell never opens his eyes but tries to throw up a couple of times early on.

By the time the entire bag of smack injected, Powell Tucker, is lying comatose.

Liz cleans everything in the bathroom and off the kitchen table. She looks back a Powell; his body makes a final uncontrolled violent jerk.

The murderess drives through the countryside, discarding Charlotte's card, the tablespoon, and other evidence along the way. Elizabeth Walker picks up her daughter and goes home.

Chapter 61

"Car 215 proceed to School House Apartments. A man is reporting his roommate is 10-45D."

"10-45D?" repeating.

"Dead body! Smith, you need to learn your codes!"

"That's a big 10-4," sarcastically back. Patrol Officer Jake Smith flicks on his light bar and hits the gas. Excitement surges through his veins. A fresh body is right in his wheelhouse. It'only five-thirty and the sun hasn't risen yet.

He parks kitty-corner across the apartment driveway. Leaving his red lights flashing, Officer Smith rushes to the outside doors. A man and woman are milling around, "Where's the body?"

The apartment manager answers, "Upstairs 206."

Taking off he pushes through double doors and takes the stairs two at a time, Smith hits the upper hallway and draws his gun.

Halfway down the vestibule, a young man is sobbing against the wall.

"Put your hands where I can see them," the officer yells.

The man turns his head and slowly raises his hands.

Smith approaches, "Who are you?"

"Ethan Eastman."

"What's going on, Ethan?"

"I came home from work and found my roommate dead!"

"Where do you work?"

"I'm the DJ at Kats."

"Who's your roommate?"

"Powell Tucker."

"How did he die?"

"Don't know."

"Sit tight!"

Smith pushes the cracked door wide open and peers into the room. A naked man's body is lying motionless on a plastic pad against the far wall. He steps into the room and looks around. Nothing appears out of place however the room's almost bare. It smells worse than a locker room after a game. He holsters his weapon approaches the body. Bending over, careful to avoid the dried vomit, he puts two fingers against the ice-cold throat and checks for a pulse.

Standing the officer pulls his walkie-talkie from his belt and calls it in, "Officer Smith here. Dead body confirmed. I need a detective and the coroner."

"Officer please use appropriate codes."

"****," as he pulls out his pocket code guide.

"Please refrain from inappropriate language over the air!"

"Look I need a…" still checking his guide, "reporting a 10-55," meaning coroner case.

"10-4, Stay on scene Officer!"

"Will do…uh 10-4." Not releasing the broadcast button quick enough, "What a ******* idiot!" goes over the air. It'll be his third reprimand since joining the department.

Within minutes Detectives Harrison Knight and Donald Overstreet are on the scene. Each take turns checking for a pulse, before joining Smith.

"What do we have here, Jake?" his friend asks.

"Did you happen to bring me a cup of Joe?" looking at Overstreet holding a steaming paper cup.

"Knock off the crap, Smith." Overstreet chimes in.

"Crap?…no *coffee*!"

"Tell us what you have!" Harrison repeats.

"Ethan, out there" pointing to the door, "is Powell Tucker's roommate" now pointing at the body, "and he found him a few minutes ago when he came home from work."

"Where does he work?"

"Kats. It'll be easy to check his alibi."

"Thanks, Smith!" Overstreet sarcastically."Go canvas the neighbors!"

Smith sulks out. He doesn't find a single neighbor, though only two answer his pounding, which was home on that Friday evening. Neither heard or knows anything, other than the pair were very quiet, no parties or visitors ever seen or heard.

Keith Klint pulls his black coroner's wagon into the parking lot. He acknowledges Officer Smith standing outside the building entrance enjoying a Marlboro. Smith flicks his smoke into a dirt-patch along the edge of the parking lot and follows him back upstairs.

The crime scene investigator arrived shortly after Knight and Overstreet. And when Klint and Smith enter, they notice only three yellow tent markers indicating something found; one on the table, one by the vomit and one seen through the open bathroom door sitting on the sink.

The coroner goes straight to the body. Knight and Overstreet join him and Smith starts a conversation with the investigator.

"Looks like you found something?" motioning at the table.

"Not much.There's a trace of white substance around that indented knot in the plywood. I suspect it's coke."

"A couple of druggies live here, huh?"

"Yeah probably, a little more powder behind the toilet."

"And the vomit?"

"OD most likely. Nothing else here."

Klint interrupts, "Smith, can you help me bring my gurney up?"

"And the body down?" grinning.

"Of course."

After loading Powell's corpse into the back of the wagon, "Keith, any chance I can get a peek at the autopsy?" Smith questions.

Glancing around in the bright daylight for big ears, "Jake, I'm doing it as soon as I get back. You know this guy is the Lieutenant Governor's son?"

"Sure, I talked to him. You know before."

The coroner glimpses at his watch, "Swing by around two and I'll see what I can do."

"Thanks, Doc," Smith puts his hand on the man's shoulder before heading to his patrol car.

Chapter 62

Knight and Overstreet start the Tucker investigation. They sit at their desks mid-Saturday morning before receiving the autopsy report. One detective is scribbling everything known, each fact on a different note page. The other is listing all the players in the same configuration.

Exhausting their brains they move to step two. Knight heads to the coffee room for a couple of refills while Overstreet steps to the large wall-sized cork board and starts to pin names, written on separate notepad sheets. Knight returns, setting a mug down on his partner's desk and slinks into his chair to sip his and watch his teammate.

Powell Tucker, Drug Dealer, Ethan Eastman, Kappa Sigma, his list is small. He moves back and stares at the four names. Knight goes to the board and adds his know facts below each name; "Lieutenant Governor's son" and "drug overdose" below Powell Tucker. A large question mark under Drug Dealer and "roommate" beneath Ethan Eastman. The final slip goes under Kappa Sigma; "Powell former member – from Eastman".

Back at their desks. Overstreet picks up the phone and calls the morgue, "Doc, how's the autopsy on Tucker coming?"

"Just finishing my report. You should have it in an hour."

Hanging up, "An hour. Let's bring in Eastman!" Overstreet.

They go to Kats, knowing the man can't be in the apartment.

It's too early and the strip club is locked. Nobodys around and they decide to visit Kappa Sigma.

The pair of detectives drives to the frat house They stand at the door looking at each other. Knight shrugs his shoulders, "Let's go in."

They enter without knocking. A few students are milling around the room. One is sitting in a regal chair reading a physics textbook. He glances up, "Can I help you?"

Showing their badges, "Detective Knight and this is my partner Detective Overstreet.

The student stands. "Johnathon Yates. I'm the fraternity president."

"Johnathon, we're investigating Powell Tucker's death and would like to ask you a couple of questions."

"Tucker's dead? How? Where?"

"Did you know Powell?"

"I've only been with Kappa Sigma since December and never met him."

"December? And you're the president?" Overstreet questions.

"Well, yes. It's kind of a long story. Basically, Kappa Sigma was suspended and I was installed to straighten out the house."

"Knight understands, "Suspended over the Wilson murder?"

"That's right."

"Is there anyone here who was around during that time?"

"Oh sure, I don't who's here right now, most of the guys headed to Eureka Springs for the day."

Overstreet, "I'm sure you guys discussed it. What do you think happened?"

Yates, "What I was told is Tucker's dad got him off on probation. Wright is spending the next forty in prison and Professor Jachimiak got five years."

"We're aware of the story," Knight states. "Why do you think Tucker only received probation?"

"The way I understand it, Tucker was there but left unconscious on the floor below and had no knowledge or involvement in the actual murder. He got a deal for fingering the others."

"Who can we talk to that was here at the time?" they're already familiar with the Wilson outcome.

"Albert Loafer or Samuel Simmons would be your best bet. Oh, and try Cheryl Thompson over at Alpha Delta Pi. I heard Powell had a thing for her."

"Thanks for your help Johnathon. Good luck with Kappa Sigma." One more thing, Knight almost forgot why they're there, "Who sells drugs on campus?"

"I wouldn't know. I'm not into that scene."

Outside, Knight checks the time. "Let's stop by the morgue on the way back to the office. Did you know Tucker flipped?"

"No. That was never disclosed and his records were sealed."

"So Powell ratted out his brothers. That's a lot of motive for revenge!"

"It certainly is *if* Tucker hadn't OD'd."

At the morgue, they're told Kleint has gone to lunch but informed his report was already couriered over.

Returning to the office, Overstreet makes and adds a couple more notes to the board. "Anything in the autopsy?"

"Oh yeah, Powell was murdered with heroin!" Knight exclaims.

"Heroin? Well, overdose is still the cause of death. I doubt the dealer will be charged with murder."

"No! I mean intentionally *murdered*! Premeditated Captial Murder!" The men share and discuss the autopsy in depth.

Knight stands wiping his face, "I'll be right back. Going to pull the Wilson file."

Knight returns and adds mug shots of Professor Jachimiak, Edward Wright and Randal Brown to the board. Looking at the three pictures, "Jachimiak has money and friends, but he'll be out in a couple of years with good behavior. But now Wright was instrumental in the Wilson murder and the only brother to flip was Powell Tucker. You know how tight frat bothers can be?" he states, "And Brown could be our dealer."

"That seems like a lot of supposition! We might be jumping the gun here. Tucker could have shot his own foot," Overstreet surmises.

"Impossible! There were thirty-five injections. Tucker couldn't have been conscious that long."

"How does someone commit capital murder with heroin? I think the best bet would be man-two," meaning involuntary or voluntary manslaughter. "Look, maybe a couple of guys were partying and Tucker passes out and they think it would be fun to get him higher."

"I don't believe this is a simple party trick gone wrong," Knight's diligent. "A couple of extra hits is one thing, but he was injected thirty-five times, hidden between his toes! Somebody wanted that kid dead!"

"Holy moly!" Overstreet flabbergast and finally understanding.

Chapter 63

Late that same afternoon a man enters the Fayetteville Police station, "I need to see Chief Parson, *now!*"

"And who should I say is here?"

"Newton Tucker."

"Yes, Sir," the desk sergeant responds and picks up the inter-office phone.

The Lieutenant Governor had been notified of his son's death and flown into Fayetteville by private jet.

Jake Smith enters the foyer for his late shift.

"Officer Smith, can you escort Mr. Tucker to the Chief's office?"

"Sure thing Sarg. Please follow me."

On the way upstairs, Jake introduces himself and offers his condolences. He mentions he knew Powell and they talked on numerous occasions about the student activity at the university. He also mentions how well his son was thought of by Professor Jachimiak. He didn't mention that the professor was serving time and is trying to bait the man for more information. Adding, "Too bad he started using cocaine."

"You know he was in rehab."

"No. I haven't seen him for a couple of months." Smith caught off guard.

"He checked in at Pillar Point down by Little Rock."

Arriving at the office, Newton shakes Smith's hand, "Can we talk later, Detective?" assuming Smith, still in his street clothes, is higher up the food chain than he actually is.

"Of course, Sir."

Newton is shown directly into the inner office.

199

"How did my son die?" without introducing himself and jumping straight into the pertinent discussion.

"Please have a seat, Mr. Tucker. I'm Chief Parson."

Without another word, remaining on his feet, Newton stares at the man.

"I have the autopsy report and apparently your son overdosed on heroin."

Still glaring, "Heroin? He had a little cocaine problem but nothing more than that!"

"When was the last time you talked with Powell?"

"He was home for Christmas. He never mentioned he had left school. Probably because Kappa kicked him out."

"So you knew he was using?"

"Of course. I had him in rehabilitation at the Pillar Point Recovery Center."

"And he was released?"

"No, he left before he was well. On his own, I might add."

"Mr. Tucker, your son had an inordinate amount of heroin in his system and there isn't any evidence that he was a perpetual user." After a moment of thought, "We think some else might have injected him."

"Are you saying someone killed my son?"

"We're looking into that possibility. But it still could have been an accidental overdose."

"*How do you figure that?*"

"Well, he and a friend could have been shooting together…you know, helping each other out and it got out of hand."

"Out of hand? What the hell does that mean?"

"When we find who he was with. The friend will probably be charged with second-degree manslaughter. It carries a thirty-year maximum sentence."

"Thirty! So he could be out in fifteen? That's not good enough!"

"Here again Mr. Tucker. I only speculate on possibilities. We will find out what happened."

"I'll be at Mountain House. Have Detective Smith keep me informed!" Newton exits before the surprised Parson can answer.

"Margret, get Officer Smith up here!" the man shouts after he figures Tucker's far enough away not to hear him.

"Afternoon Chief, you wanted to see me?"

"You told the Lieutenant Governor of Arkansas you're a detective?"

"No Sir."

"Where did he get that impression?"

"Huh…not sure. I escorted him up here, but we only discussed his son."

"You talked to him about this case. What do you know about this?"

"Nothing really. I only mentioned that I knew Powell from the university and he seemed like a responsible young man."

"You knew his son?"

"Well, I didn't *know* him. We talked a couple of times…while I was on duty at the campus after the riots. That's all."

"Go see Knight and tell him everything you can remember about your conversations with Powell Tucker!"

Chapter 64

In the squad room, Jake Smith pulls a chair up to Knight's desk, "Hey Harrison, what's shaking?"

"What are you doing, Jake?"

Overstreet enters the room carrying two mugs of coffee. He sets his down and the other across his desk on the edge of Knight's. Sitting down, "What's going on here?"

Smith grabs Harrison's mug and takes a swig, "Thanks, Don."

Overstreet's eye's lock Smith's, "What the hell do you think you're doing?"

"Chief Parson sent me over to work with you guys on the Tucker case," a broad smile blankets his face.

Knight intercedes. "Let's hear what he has to say."

"Don, just consider me your personal consultant. Play nice and I'll break this for you...otherwise good luck!" Smith stands but doesn't walk off, only takes a slow loud slurp of his coffee.

"Sit down Jake!" Knight commands.

"Ok partners, what do you want to know?" smirks Smith.

"You're are not a partner!" Overstreet too loud. Now has everyone in the room staring their way.

"You tell me what you know and I'll fill in the gaps for you!" Smith still beaming.

"This is a complete waste of my time," Overstreet returns.

"I'm sure Parson doesn't agree!" Smith adds, "I'll check."

"Enough!" Knight takes charge. "What have you got, Jake?"

"Ok, I'll go first!" Smith starts, "You know Powell was kicked out of Krappa Sigma. I'm sure he must have a few enemies there."

"This is a simple OD case," Overstreet butts in, not willing to admit they've already gone through the postmortem report.

"We've been to the fraternity. What else?" Knight staying on topic.

"Your turn!" the arrogant officer.

"We're just getting started. I'm sure we'll discover all the common knowledge you know. If you don't have anything else, we got work to do!" Overstreet trying to end Smith's nonsense.

"One more treat before I go! Powell was secretly in rehab down in Little Rock."

"Don makes some calls." Turning back to his friend, "Which facility?"

"What did Ethan tell you?" Smith rerouting the conversation.

"Who's Ethan?" Harrison acts dumb.

Smith isn't hooked, "This meeting is over. I have to get on patrol!" Smith gulps the last swallow of coffee and walks out the door.

"Did Smith know Eastman before?" Overstreet reflects, more to himself than his partner.

Not bothering to answer, "Like it or not Don, he might know something!"

Chapter 65

Alexis Dench visits coroner. She would like to secure a photo Powell's body for her latest expose´. She's standing writing notes on a small pad as Officer Smith approaches, "Good Morning, Darling."

Looking up, "Hi, Jake." She glances around and gives him a quick peck on the cheek.

"What did Dr. Kleint tell you?"

"Nothing! He threw me out!"

"Don't take it personally. I'm sure he's up to his elbows," simpering at his little joke.

"This town needs unbiased information on every crime. He shouldn't be so quick to dismiss me!" acting rejected.

"Keith's's just doing his job. Let me see what I can find out. If there's anything shareable, I'll let you know."

"Thanks, Dear."

Smith moves to the morgue, "Hi, Doc."

"Hey there, Jake."

The officer looks over the filleted body. "No other marks?"

"Not a scratch. It's a simple autopsy, he had no organ damage and nothing in his stomach. There are traces of cocaine, but he died of a heroin overdose.

Smith doesn't seem surprised, "We don't see much *H* in Fayetteville."

"Only my second heroin OD. Problem is, there's so much in his system, it's impossible he injected himself!"

"Injected? I thought snorting was the method of choice. How many punctures?"

"Thirty-five…between the toes on both feet!" The coroner continues, "Most people start with snorting and graduate to shooting.

It's a terrible addiction. The more you take the more you need. The interesting point, in this case, is no needle-track history. Constant injecting leaves sores, scabs, and scars. Hard to hide. This guy doesn't have any. It's like it was his first time."

"Let me understand. So you're saying someone else injected him on purpose to murder him?"

"Not necessarily to murder him. It could have been partying that got out of control," and the coroner explains other possible scenarios.

Smith thanks the doctor and leaves, thinking, "Holy crap, he was murdered!" and "those jerks didn't level with me," referring to the pair of detectives.

"Alex, there's nothing to report yet," back outside.

"There's always something to report. Did he at least confirm the cause of death?"

"Well…," thinking it over, "yes and no. It's complicated. All I can say is it's probably a drug overdose."

"What drug?"

"That's the complicated part!"

"How so?"

"Alex is this off the record. And I mean *WAY OFF*!"

"Of course, Dear."

"Powell is a coke-head and I guess, he partied too much. The problem is he died of a heroin overdose. That's all I got!" Smith repeats, "*Off the record.*" He's not about to reveal that he suspects Powell was murdered.

"That's not top secret! A lot of addicts progress to harder drugs."

"There's going to be a lot more as soon as Keith gets to the bottom of it. If I were you I would write a blurb about Powell's known life and how much he'll be missed. The bigger story will have to wait."

Alex smacks Jake on the lips, "I have to get to work. Dinner tonight?"

"I'm on the swing shift, it'll be a midnight gala," smiling at his insinuation of food and sex.

Laughing, "You're a funny one, Mr. Smith."

Back at the office, Alex gets on the horn making call after call to her informants, students she's previously interviewed and every official she knows. She pieces together a complete story up to the time of death. Omitted is the final facts on how and why.

Her banner reads; LIEUTENANT GOVERNOR'S SON DEAD! With the subhead reading, MURDERED BY DRUGS." She doesn't have a clue how accurate she really is.

Her half-pager outlines Powell Tucker's fall from grace at UOA. His escalating cocaine and alcohol addictions, getting kicked out Kappa Sigma, suspended from the university, and culminates with the escape from Pillar Point and return to Fayetteville.

Chapter 66

After a long night shift, Smith changes into his street clothes. As he walks past the detective room he enters. The place is empty and he looks over the board.

The detectives were busy all afternoon and hadn't updated. Smith snatches a notepad off Knight's desk and writes Squirrel and on additional sheets, BAD members, murder by heroin. He walks back to the board and adds the sheets.

Arriving first that morning Don Overstreet studies the board. He sees the unknown handwritten additions.

"Good morning, Don?" Knight surprises his partner.

"Your buddy's been messing with our board!" snaps Overstreet.

"How do you know it was Smith?"

"Who else! He doesn't know anything and we don't need him interfering."

"He's only trying to help," Knight sticks up for his friend.

"Help I don't need. He a nuisance. I'll straighten him out once and for all!"

Three hours later Smith sticks his head in, "Hey guys. Did you see I cooperating now?"

"Is that what you call it? Knight comments.

"Stay out of our investigation! And I'm not asking!" Overstreet addresses the meddler.

"I have informants too, Guys!" Smith overlooking the command.

"What informants? It's time you come clean with us, Jake!" Knight's firm.

Studying his wristwatch, "Jeez, I have to get to work. We'll share later." Smith spins and walks out.

"Smith get in here!" Overstreet barks.

Returning and making himself comfortable in an empty chair, "So what do we have?"

"Nothing for you! Let me make this crystal clear for your pea brain! You are *not* part of this investigation! Stay out of my face or you'll have more trouble than you can handle! Understood?"

Smith walks to the board. He taps his note saying, "Squirrel's your man."

'Who's Squirrel?" questions Knight.

"The drug dealer that murdered Tucker."

"What about Brown? He supplies the county!" Knight asks.

"That's true, but Ken Walker supplied Tucker."

"Who the hell is Ken Walker?" Overstreet asks.

Smith walks to the board removing his pen. He adds a slash behind Squirrel and adds Ken Walker.

"Jake, how do you know about this Walker-Squirrel guy?" Knight questions.

"Ethan. You need to talk to him."

"We're going to pick him up at the club this afternoon."

"You can get him at Madison's now."

"And who is Madison?" Overstreet demands not realizing Smith had just hooked him in.

"The dancer he's staying with."

"Where does Madison live?."

Anything else?" Smith fakes innocence."

"Get the hell out of here!" demands Overstreet.

After Smith strolls out, "Let's pick up Eastman!" Overstreet on his feet. "Smith really, I mean *really* pisses me off!"

Chapter 67

Smith's is on the swing shift and late in the evening stops by Powell's apartment. He needs to talk to Ethan Eastman but wants to recheck the room before he goes looking for him. The door is still sealed with yellow, "CRIME SCENE DO NOT CROSS" police tape. Smith rips down the tape and enters the apartment.

Looking over the scene, nothing new is visible. He checks the phone. The line is dead. There is an answering machine, but no tape present.

Using his flashlight he studies every inch of the apartment, behind the ceiling tiles, under the toilet tank lid, beneath the table top. Nothing. He stands in the small kitchen enclave staring at the old refrigerator.

Smith looks inside. It's all but empty except for some old moldy half eaten unrecognizable pizza. Smith pulls the unit from the wall. He duplicates everything the investigator had done and does not find a single thing new.

It's time to get out of this dead-end roach motel. As he pushes the refrigerator back but the left side of the front kick plate comes loose from the unit. Disgusted he just leaves the appliance sitting cockeyed away from the wall.

Standing at the front door, Jake takes a last look around the room. He looks at the frig and shakes his head. The officer goes back and tries to kick the plate back into place. It doesn't work and he just shoves the unit to its position against the wall. As he does the plate falls completely off and clatters on the floor.

Jake reaches down and tries unsuccessfully to push the panel back onto its mounting nipples. He drops to his knees to figure out what's going on. That's when he notices the shiny tip of a baggie along one inside wall jammed next to the compressor. Smith unclips his flashlight from his belt again and shines the beam inside the compartment. He reaches in and pulls out a baggie of cocaine.

His shift is almost finished and he heads to the police station and the evidence locker. The door's locked up tighter than pirate's booty. "Arrrr!" He goes up to the detective room.

Smith, searches Knight's desk and finds Powell's answering machine tape and pockets it. There's nothing else of interest and he goes to his locker to retrieve his player.

It only contains a couple of older messages from the first month the roomies had a phone before disconnection. One message was from Squirrel and the second from Madison. Ethan mentioned the stripper, and that he was hoping to stay with her until his apartment is released. Smith had never met her and doesn't know where she lives.

Smith changes into street clothes, grabs his baloney sandwich and drives to Kats.

Entering the strip club he sees Ethan isn't working and sits at the bar. He orders a soda and asks for Madison.

"She over there," pointing to a booth where a woman is standing talking to two sitting men.

He walks over. "Madison, can I have a moment?"

The dancer looks him up and down, "Crap! What do you want?" instantly knowing he's a cop.

"Let's sit over there for a minute," pointing at an empty table. Madison follows Smith. The officer sits, the dancer stands.

"Look, Madison, I'm not interested in you. I looking into the Powell Tucker murder."

"I thought Powell overdosed. Now he's murdered?"

"Murder isn't what I meant, I should have said death," backtracking, "Anyway, I'm looking for his roommate to see what happened."

"Ethan? He had nothing to do with it, he wasn't even home. Ethan's not a drug user anyway."

"I know. I talked with him…I just have one more question for him and that should close the case," Smith lies. "Do you know where he is?"

Thinking it over for a few moments, "I don't care. Neither one of us has anything to hide. He staying with me."

"Do you mind if I go over to your place and ask him?"

"If that will keep you off my back, go ahead."

"Thank you, Madison." Oh! Do you know where Powell was buying drugs?"

"I'm not into drugs!"

Smith obtains her address and drives to her apartment. He beats on the door four or five times before a groggy Ethan opens it.

"Hi Ethan, remember me?"

"What are you doing here, man?"

"Just a couple of follow-up questions on Powell's murd…err, overdose." Smith doesn't want to make the same mistake twice. "We're just wrapping this up. Can you tell me where Powell was buying Heroin?"

"Heroin? Powell never used smack!"

"He didn't? How do you know?"

"We were roomies, man. I know everything about Powell."

Smith hands the guy a twenty, "You can really help me get this thing closed. How long did you guys know each other?"

"I met him at Kats, maybe a year ago. He used to meet Squirrel there."

"Does Squirrel hang at Kats?"

"Sure. He's married to Lu. When Lu first started I was interested but she wasn't into me. She met Ken a couple of months later and they got married and had a kid."

Another twenty, "What's Ken's last name?"

"Look, man, I don't like Squirrel, but I won't rat out Lu," realizing he shouldn't have said so much already.

"Ethan, I'm cool and don't want you or Lu involved, but if you want to get on with your life I need to know about Squirrel!"

Ethna looks over the man. He doesn't trust cops though he has nothing to hide. Finally, "Ok man, Squirrel's name is Ken. And that's all I know."

"So where do Ken and Lu live?"

Ethan refuses to say another word. Now is the time to apply the pressure. Smith pulls the baggie of powder from his pocket, "Guess what, I found your drugs in the frig!"

"That's not mine!"

"Funny, it has your fingerprints all over it! Drugs are a felony. You're looking at seven to ten! If you and I are friends this thing goes away!"

"Friends! You're extorting me, man!"

"Don't get all high and mighty on me, I'm trying to help *you*. Just answer a couple more questions."

"Give me a break, man!" he begs, ready to drop to his knees if he has to. "Friends sound good!"

"Friends share," the widest grin possible stretches across Smith's face.

"Ok…Ok, man, Lulu Love is her stage name. Her real name is Liz Walker. They live out in the country. I don't remember how to get there. I only gave Liz a ride home once," he adds, "that was more than a year ago, man."

"Where in the country?"

"Somewhere down by Morrow."

"Thanks, Ethan. I'm going to make this go away for you."

On Smith's way to the door, he turns, "Ethan, where did Liz live before getting married?"

"Here, man."

"Here? In this apartment?"

"Yeah, with Maddi."

Smith starts looking, with more than simple curiosity, around the apartment.

"Hey, man you can't do that without a warrant!"

"I'm going to hold onto this a while," shaking the drug bag. "You know, just so you don't forget who your friends are!"

Smith sits in his car vigorously writing notes. He wonders how he's going to search Madison's apartment.

And now there's two dancer's involved!

Chapter 68

Lulu Love gets to work just before three in the afternoon. Denny has been watching for her and picks up his microphone for the speaker system and calls her to the office.

Seconds later Lulu is knocking on the door. Charlotte walks over and lets her in. "Take a seat Liz!" abruptly.

"Want's up, Charlotte?'

"Sit down, Liz. We need to talk!"

Liz Walker sits across the desk from Denny. His wife remains standing. "Liz, we're missing a lot of money and I know you stole it!"

"Me! What are you talking about!"

"Two thousand dollars! Charlotte tells me you were the only one around…and not working!"

"When was this?"

"Cut the crap! Where the hell is my money!" Denny demands.

Liz's waterworks start. She drops her head, barely squeaking, "I'm sorry. It was only a loan. I'm getting your money back."

"You're damn right you are…*TODAY*!"

Charlotte barely shakes her head at her husband, "Tell me what's going on Liz?"

"I…I can't get you involved. It's my problem."

"Dear, all the girl's problems are my problems too. If you don't tell me I can't help you."

Contemplating, Liz finally comes clean, "I…I murdered Powell Tucker."

"What are you talking about? I read that was a drug overdose!" Denny speaks up.

Liz walks them through the whole story, starting with her rape, then onto the drug buy, and carrying out her murder plan. They are astonished at her tale.

"You have until Saturday to get me my money!" Denny stresses.

"I can't get it that fast. My husband has money, but I can't let him know what happened and how I handled it."

"You should have come to me right away, Dear." Charlotte sympathizes.

"Your problems aren't mine! *Saturday!*"

"Sweetheart, I think we can give her a little more time than that." Charlotte addresses her husband.

"Nobody steals from me!"

"Liz go to work. I need to talk with Denny!"

The husband and wife talk it out. Charlotte tells her husband she'll pay the money back herself and work it out with Liz. Denny's furious. He emphatically states he has to take action so no girl gets the idea that he's soft. *Stealing demands retaliation.* Charlotte convinces him that if Liz hasn't told Ken, she hasn't told anyone. Denny eventually relents and agrees with his wife's solution only for the sake of their marriage.

Mrs. Daniels sets up a repayment plan with Elizabeth.

Chapter 69

The coroner releases the body ten days later and Powell Tucker's funeral is set for March thirtieth.

Officer Smith, wearing his best suit shows up at the cemetery for the graveyard service. He wants to see who is in attendance. And have a serious talk with Newton Tucker. He arrives a little late and the minister is just finishing up.

Smith is shocked at the low turnout. He expected a massive affair, fraught with dignitaries. Instead, it is a tiny, family-only gathering, and not even the whole family. Powell's father is absent. Smith doesn't know a single person, except the officiating minister and Angel.

When finished, Minister Laymann steps aside and lets the family say their final farewells. He approaches Smith, "Let's step over here." Motioning to a large Magnolia tree.

Away from the group, "So how are you, Jake?"

"Fine."

"I hear you and Maggie aren't together?"

"No. She's a wonderful lady, but unfortunately, we didn't have a lot in common."

"Like our Lord and Savior?" Laymann questions.

"Well…" wanting to avoid the trap, "it's really the social-economic differences."

"Money can be the root of all evil, but it's not insurmountable where love comes into play."

Time to change the subject, "I'm surprised Powell's Father couldn't make it?"

"That is unfortunate. I'm afraid he ostracized his son in death. Possibly he's trying to avoid defending Powell's troubled life to the press."

"Who are the people here?"

"You know Angel. Judith Tucker is the lady in black with the veil. Next to her is Nikki and William Hacket with their three children. Nikki is Powell's sister. The other couple is Newton's older brother and his wife. And Dr. Yakiniku is Powell's doctor from Pillar Point Recovery Center. Now is not the time, Jake!"

"I understand," though he can't miss this opportunity.

As the group starts for their rented limousines, Jake approaches Powell's mother, "I just wanted to offer my condolences, Mrs. Tucker."

"Who are you?"

"Jake Smith. I sorry for your loss. I knew your son from school."

"Aren't you a little old to be going to University or are you a professor?"

"Actually neither. I'm a police officer."

"Leave us alone!" interrupts William Hackett.

"It's not like that. I used to patrol the campus and your son and I had many conversations about the state of our country. None were official business, I just liked talking with Powell. He is…was such a bright young man."

"Thank you for coming, Mr. Smith," Judith replies. "But if you'll excuse us."

"Of course. Your husband and I have a couple of chats also. I can see why Powell wanted to follow in his footsteps." Smith tries to keep the interaction alive. "I better let you go now. Again, sorry for your loss." He touches her shoulder and steps back.

"Mr. Smith, we're going back to Mountain House for a bite to eat and a little reminiscing of the good times. Would you care to join us?"

"Mother!" Nikki pipes up.

"It's alright, Dear. Mr. Smith is Powell's friend and can tell us about his campus life." She's just as interested in what Smith and her husband talked about.

"I shouldn't intrude at a time like this."

"Nonsense. This is the time."

"Well if you insist. I'd like that," putting on his saddest face. "I can meet you there."

As they embark the two limousines, Smith looks around for Dr. Yakiniku. He spots her walking off in the opposite direction and hurries after her.

As soon as the others are safely inside their rides, Smith calls out, "Doctor, can I have a word with you?"

The woman stops and turns to see who is beckoning her.

Jake is sprinting and arrives out of breath, "Sorry to hold you up. Jake Smith, I was a friend of Powell," he holds out his hand.

She lightly takes it and gently shakes, "How do you know Powell?" suspicious of the middle-aged man.

"We met while I was patrolling the campus."

"You're a policeman?"

Smith gives the woman the same almost truth as he offered Powell's mother. And asks, "The man I knew wasn't a heroin user?"

"Is this an official interview?"

"Heavens no! I'm more concerned other students might be experimenting."

"I certainly hope not. As you can plainly see, heroin isn't anything to mess with!"

"Doctor. I need to level with you. I am investigating Powell's death and I don't believe it was an accident."

Thinking it over, "How could someone intentionally inject that much into his system without he fighting back? He was an athletic young man."

"That's precisely what I intend to find out. How did he get along with your other patients?"

"I can't discuss him or anyone else.

"I just want to confirm that when he was under your care, you didn't find any drug use except cocaine."

"That's right cocaine, marijuana, and alcohol abuse. Nothing else. Now if you'll excuse me I have a long drive."

"Of course Doctor. Thank you and have a safe trip home."

He watches her continue to her vehicle. "Oh Doctor, if I have any other questions, can I call you?"

"That would be fine."

Smith turns to his Datsun and drives to Mountain House.

Smith and the Tucker family spend three hours discussing the good and bad times spent with the dead boy. Smith learned that Powell's prize sixty-six Mustang is missing coupled with numerous high-value sports memorabilia pieces.

Eventually, Judith is wrung out and decides to retire to her room. Smith hugs her long and hard before leaving himself.

Chapter 70

Even though he took the day off to attend the funeral, late in the afternoon, Smith ends up back at the police station.

The first task is look up Powell's Mustang registration history and find who owns it now and where it is. Smith is on hold with the DMV sitting at an empty desk in the squad room. Knight is walking by to the restroom when he spies Smith. His pee can wait, Harrison edges in and sits down.

Smith holds up his index finger signaling to wait a minute as he continues to write notes. "Ok, thank you." Smith hangs up, "What's going on, Harry?"

"Just passing by and saw you. I thought you were taking a sick day?"

"I went to Tucker's funeral."

"Oh yeah. See anything interesting?"

"Not many people were there, a couple of family members and Dr. Yakiniku."

"Did you talk to anyone?"

"Everyone," Smiling.

"Well?"

"The Pillar Point doctor wouldn't say much…only that Powell wasn't on heroin."

"Overstreet talked to her."

"The interesting part…" clearing his throat, "Powell sold his beloved car and all his belongings and at Christmas, he stole an expensive diamond necklace from Judith. He was going through money like water."

"Judith who?"

"Tucker, his mother. He pawned it for twenty-five hundred. The Little rock cops got it back and Newton didn't press charges, but it strained their relationship. The father didn't even show for the burial."

"Who was on the phone?"

"DMV. I found Powells Mustang. Some guy in Rogers owns it now. Want to go for a ride?"

"Sure. Let me tell Overstreet I'm stepping for the rest of the day."

"I'll meet you in the parking lot."

Harrison informs his partner that since the day is drawing close he's going home a little early to check on Judy, who has a touch of flu. He hurries to the parking lot and finds Smith next to his compact truck.

"Let's take my department car. It's more comfortable and the Chief pays the gas," laughing.

A half-hour later Knight pulls into a gas station and asks directions to the address. They pull onto the dirt strip along E. Pine Street in front of the older home. In the driveway sits Powell's sixty-six Mustang. They glance at each other and get out of the car. As they walk around the vehicle and look in windows a guy yells through the screen door, "Get the hell away from my car. It's not for sale!"

"It's a beauty, Sir. What year is it?" Smith acts friendly.

"Doesn't matter to you! Get off my property before I call the cops!"

Knight holds up his badge, "We are the police, Sir. Can you step out of the house?"

The half-dressed man comes out, "What's going on Officers?"

"When did you acquire this vehicle?"

"About a few months ago, Thanksgiving weekend. What's this about?"

"Who did you buy it from?"

"A friend down in Fayetteville."

"Does your friend have a name?" Smith asks.

"Denny Daniels, he's a businessman."

"That's a familiar name," Knight comments.

"He owns Kats," the car owner states.

"We know," Knight acknowledges.

"It's a legitimate business. Anyway, I paid cash and got a receipt and pink slip."

"Do you visit Kats frequently?"

"Only when I'm in town. Denny and I grew up in the same neighborhood. He's a little younger than me, but our parents were friends."

"How much?" Smith questions.

Hesitantly, "A grand."

"That's not a good deal, that's stealing!" he adds.

"No, Sir! Denny set the price. He just wanted to unload it. Like I said we go way back."

The detectives thank him and drive away. They talk about Denny and Powell on the drive home and conclude Powell must have been desperate for a fix to dump the car. At the station, Harrison drops Smith off at his truck and goes home. Smith goes to Kats.

"Where's Denny?" Officer Smith asks Grace Udal the barmaid.

"He and Charlotte went to dinner. Probably won't be back until nine or ten."

He looks up at the Dj in the corner and walks over, "Hey Ethan, we need to talk!" yelling about the blaring *Never Fall in Love Again*.

"Let me set up an auto-play. I'll be down in five." He screams back.

Minutes later Ethan and Smith are on the front sidewalk smoking a cig. "How's it going, Ethan? Still at Madison's?" Smith asks.

"Yeah, I let the apartment go and am living there."

"I need to know how your boss got Powell's Mustang?"

"I don't know?"

222

"Ethan, Ethan, Ethan! I thought we trusted each other? I got the heat off you in the Powell thing, but I can just as easily put you back in!"

"You know I didn't have anything to do with that!" screams the scared lad.

"I don't know that!"

"I was here at the time. You checked it out!"

"Funny, I don't remember! Let's go down to the station. Overstreet and Knight are waiting."

"What do you want, man?"

"To know why your roommate sold his Mustang to Denny," Smith demands.

"We weren't rooming together then!"

"Look, I have done a lot of checking on you…"

"No man, I'm clean now!"

"I still have your drugs from the scene. You're mine anytime I want."

"Ok, Ok! But you didn't hear it from me, man. Powell attacked Madison one night and Denny beat the crap out of him. The next thing I know Denny has the Mustang. He only had it a couple of days and I never saw it again."

"Did Denny pay for it?"

"Nah, I heard he just stole it, man."

Smith shoves a twenty in Ethan's top shirt pocket, "If you hear anything give me a jingle!"

He counts off on his fingers to himself, "Madison, Ethan, Liz and Squirrel, Denny, and Charlotte." He concludes, "The killer is here! Maybe all of them!" Smith decides to keep the information to himself. "Overstreet can do his own damn legwork!"

Chapter 71

"Operation Waterfall!" Newton Tucker leaves Arthur English a message on his answering service. It's Saturday, April third, just after three in the afternoon.

By nine o'clock Newton's waiting by the falling water in Garvan Woodland Park. He stands shivering in the cold late evening air for more than an hour. Eventually, with English a no-show, he drives home, mad.

Just before midnight, Newton's alone in his study. He's stewed long enough and is trying to calm down with Jonny Carson show. It isn't helping. His private phone-line rings. He stares at the phone. Only a few people have this number. Deciding it must be important and probably Billy, he picks up.

"Come outside in five minutes," a strange altered, barely audible voice states.

"Who is this?"

"Operation waterfall."

"English?"

CLICK. The line goes dead.

Newton dresses and hurries to the front porch. He stands in the dark looking hard around his tree-filled property. Seeing nothing he proceeds down his long driveway. A hundred yards further he stops and turns to head back.

Newton's started by Arthur English stepping from behind a tree. By now he should know English's modus operandi. "Good evening Mr. Tucker. What's going on?"

"Art, what in the hell are you doing here?"

"I got your message."

"That was nine hours ago!"

"I'm busy. You're not my only client," English. "Besides I thought we were finished?"

"How you get my number?"

"What do you need?" ignoring the question.

"Powell's dead!"

"At Pillar Point?"

"No, he snuck out and back to Fayetteville."

"How did he die?"

"Heroin overdose. I want the dealer taken care of!"

"Heroin? Powell was not on heroin when I checked him in!"

"You must have missed it!"

"No. Dr. Yaniniku had all the tests run to see exactly what Powell's problems were. I had her send me the report. *NO HEROIN!*"

"It's irrelevant now. I just want the low-life and anyone else involved eliminated from this planet. Can you do it or do I need someone else?"

"One of my specialties. What do you have in mind?"

"I don't care how…just do it and send me the bill!"

"Operation Gazebo! Are you familiar with Hot Springs National Park?"

"What are you talking about?"

"There's an observation gazebo there. That's our new contact location." English turns and disappears into the trees.

Chapter 72

Arthur English is back in Fayetteville late Sunday afternoon subsequent to the start of Operation Gazebo. He checks into the Dickson Street Inn; a fifteen-minute walk through the business district to the University of Arkansas.

He lazily walks through the old downtown area in search of a dinner house. He enters The Grill and orders a steak. As he sits nursing a gin and tonic while waiting for his meal, Arthur notices a man and woman sitting three tables away. The lady has her back to him, but the man keeps taking frequent glances his way.

Just as his food arrives, he watches the man going towards the restrooms. Arthur leaves his food to get cold and follows the guy into the men's room. He stands in front of the mirror combing his hair while the man takes a leak. Soon they're standing side by side at the sink.

"Eve'n Mate," Arthur speaks first.

"Hi, there? What part of Texas are you from?"

"Texas!" laughing. "Eugene McKenzie, London, England."

"Nice to meet you, Eugene. Jake Smith. You knew in town?"

"Just bumbling through the village. And you, Sir?"

"Naw, I have been here a while…wish I was passing through." Both men laugh at Smith's joke.

"I could not help but noticed your lady friend. You might want to linger a while longer." They continue to kid around for a few minutes before Jake invites his new friend to join them. English thinks it's better to know his enemies and quickly accepts.

Back in the dining room, Eugene moves his drink and plate of food to the couples table.

"Eugene McKenzie, mame," holding out his hand.

226

"Alex Dench. Please have a seat."

"Watch what you say, Alex is a reporter for the Times." kids Smith.

As English sits, "A news reporter! Very good, sounds exciting?"

"It can have its ups and downs." Alex chimes.

The three spend the evening chatting like chipmunks during mating season. They get along very well and form an immediate like for each other.

After an extended dinner, they share drinks for another hour before Eugene makes an excuse, "I should get cracking. Have to get up quite early and get on. Quite a lovely evening, cheers." He leaves. Jake and Alex sit for a while longer joying the moment.

Finally the pair leave for Alex's home and a nightcap.

Chapter 73

Monday morning Arthur English walks back into Kappa Sigma house. He enters, as usual without knocking. Young men are scurrying around tripping over each other getting ready for classes. Arthur stands in the front room looking for Andrew, the frat brother he had previously talked with.

A brother running for the door bumps into English, "Hey, man, sorry." Stopping and scrutinizing the stranger, "Who are you?"

"I am looking for Andrew."

"Which one?"

"How many do you have here?"

"Three, man."

"How many Sams?"

"Samuel, one."

"Flat at the end of the hall?"

"Yeah man, that's him." The student suddenly jerks his arm free and runs out the door.

The PI goes upstairs and down the hall. Opening the door he sees two students still sound asleep. He walks over and kicks a bed hard. The small earthquake startles the man awake, "What the hell, man?"

"Samuel?"

"No man!"

"Take a hike, Mate!"

"This is my room…you get the hell out!"

Arthur grabs the student by the neck and jerks him to his feet, "I asked quite nice. Now it is time for you to bugger off!"

The naked young student runs from the room. Arthur walks to the other bed and kicks it harder, "Time to rise and shine, Sweetheart!"

"What do you want?" the young man suddenly wide awake, responds.

"We need to discuss Powell Tucker."

"I don't know him." And turns over to go back to sleep.

Arthur yanks the kid out of his bed and throws him to the floor, "You need to understand, we *are* going to chat a while."

"I told you I don't know him."

English drops his number ten shoe on the man's head and starts applying pressure.

"Ooow! You're hurting me!" screams the terrified youth.

"Not quite!" calmly and pushing harder.

"S...Stop I'll tell you!"

Silence.

"I said I'll talk, take your foot off!"

"You chose this way. Now we talk first, release second."

"What do you want to know?" he painfully answers.

"You do drugs with Mister Tucker?"

"N..." the pain intensifies. "Once, ok man? One time!" More pressure applies. "Stop, Stop! We did it all the time." cries the boy.

"Did you now! What drugs did you take?"

"Weed...and coke."

"And heroin!"

"No...no. What are you talking about?"

"Heroin!"

"Nobody ever does smack! I don't know where you heard that!"

The interrogator releases the youth, "Does Squirrel sell heroin?"

"I don't know." The foot's back on the head. "I DON'T KNOW, Man!" screams the petrified youth.

"If you are being less than truthful, I *will* find out! And the next chat will not be as pleasant for you." Arthur strolls out of the room and out of the frat house. He checks his watch, it's ten thirty and time to visit Kats.

Before Officer Smith goes to his afternoon shift, he stops by UOA for no particular reason. He just walks around looking over the campus and students while thinking about Powell.

At the edge of the campus, the PI rounds a building and runs into Jake Smith.

"Eugene! What are you doing here?" Jake surprised at seeing the man.

"Thought I might tour the area and campus today."

"You said you had to go to Springfield for a meeting?"

"That is correct, but it is only a couple of hours and my appointment is not until late this afternoon."

"I'll be happy to show you around a little," Smith offers.

"That is not necessary. Quite enjoying stretching my legs, but I should be heading to my room and packing in a few minutes."

"Well, have a good trip. If you're ever in Fayetteville give me a call." Smith hands him his police business card.

Arthur glances at the card. Smith studies his face looking for a reaction. Nothing was telling, though Smith would swear his eyes dilate.

"I look forward to seeing you and Alexis again, Jake," Eugene extends his hand.

They shake and walk off in different directions.

Smith thinks it's strange that the man is still in town when he had told them he had to leave early. And now his story changed.

Chapter 74

Arthur English walks back to Dickson Street Inn. He packs and checks out. As he drives away he notices Smith tailing him a block back.

English pulls into a gas station. Smith drives past and parks on a side street a half mile ahead. He walks to the corner and waits to see which direction his suspect goes.

Arthur moseys around slowly filling his tank and getting a coffee. English pulls out of the station and continues the same way he was traveling. Smith runs to his car and drives around the block, parking midway through, engine running. Moments after English passes, Smith pulls to the main street and resumes his tail.

The lead man turns onto Highway 49 and heads north towards the Missouri border.

A half-hour later they pull into Rogers and English watches Smith, in his rearview mirror, turn off. The PI continues north towards Bentonville and pulls off the highway into a small grove of trees. He sits for a half hour. Smith never passes him and he turns around back towards Fayetteville. When he hits Springdale, English turns west and finds an independent motel and checks in.

He sits in the depressing room and pulls out his files, Spreading them across the chipped and well-used small desk, Arthur finds what he's looking for, the main street name he had pried out of Liz.

He spends the afternoon driving around the Morrow countryside looking for their farmhouse. Art locates what he thinks is their place. There is a blue car with oversized rear tires and a Volkswagon Beetle in the yard. He parks a fair distance down the road and walks back. Inconspicuously, hiding in various spots, he scopes out the layout.

At one point he climbs a large pine tree. Art sees the next farm over through the trees. Climbing down the PI jogs across the fields and through a grove. He stands concealed and watches. A while later an old gentleman emerges from the house and goes to his barn. English quickly runs over to the corner of the barn and waits.

When the owner appears, Art steps out, "Pardon me, Sir!"

The startled man jumps and spins around. He looks past the stranger and inspects his yard and lengthy dirt driveway. "Where did you come from?"

"My car hire is stuck on the road. Possibly you would be kind enough to let me use your blower to call a lorry"

The suspicious man balks, "What's wrong with your car?"

"I am afraid I not much good under the bonnet. I was sightseeing and my car just quit." He then asks the man if he can get a drink from his hose. The farmer assumes anyone who would drink from a hose can't be all bad, even if he does have an English accent.

"Come on in. I'll get you a glass."

While the man, in his kitchen pouring a glass of water from the spigot, he overhears the stranger calling and talking to a tow company.

Art puts his hand over the mouthpiece and yells, "How do I tell him where I am?"

The older resident explains the street and landmarks ending with, "Once he's on the road he should see your car."

Arthur pretends to explain into the unconnected line.

The man brings the water and hands the glass over. Art takes a long drink before, "Thank you. You are a lifesaver," and, "how long you lived around here?"

"My whole life. It was my father's farm before he passed and I got it."

"Quite nice. I assume you know everyone around these parts?"

"Well not everyone, but lots of folks."

"I was considering looking for a place in the area, any suggestions?"

"Well, I can call Jan for you. She goes to my church and is a realtor."

"That would be just jolly. What about the place next door. It looks perfect with some renovation."

"Renovation hell! It needs to be torn down and rebuilt. Anyway, the Walkers have been renting it for a while. Nice young couple."

English finishes the water and hands the glass back, "I better get cracking. Thank you for the refreshment, old Chap. Cheerio." He starts for the door.

"Don't you want to know about Jan?"

"Jan?"

"The realtor."

"Oh quite, slipped my mind. Worried about my hire I imagine."

"That's understandable. Let me get you her information."

The farmer is heard rustling papers in his kitchen while English slips out the door and is gone.

Charlie Stone returns to the living room and can't find the man. "Strange Duck!" he thinks.

Chapter 75

Arthur English drives home to Little Rock. He spends the next four days returning calls, meeting with potential new clients and visiting his lady friend.

On April ninth he returns to Fayetteville. He leaves his office at midnight and makes the four-hour drive in his backup sedan and arrives in Morrow just after four AM. Art parks his light blue Ford LTD with a souped-up V8 a mile from Walker's farmhouse on a dirt field-access road off the main paved road.

He shoves a silenced Smith & Wesson Model 52 twenty-two caliber in his front waistband and a 45 mm German Heckler & Koch P9 beneath his pants in a holster strapped to his right leg. In addition, English slings an Armalite A-18 automatic assault rifle over his shoulder.

He jogs the mile across planted fields and stays off the roads. When a few cars are heard traveling along the main road, English hits the dirt, lying deathly still under the brilliant full-moon-lit night.

Approaching the old farmhouse, Art stands quietly behind a familiar tree scouring the scene. "Crap!" he thinks to himself. "The Volkswagon is not here." Squirrel's Chevelle sits proudly displayed in front of the main door. All the house lights are dark and only a low glow emits from a flickering television set. English rationalizes that the drug dealer is the target anyway and Liz is only a potential identifier, who probably wouldn't think twice about their one short encounter. The location of their baby doesn't enter his mind.

Satisfied, he proceeds stealthy onward to the corner of the home. Peering through the un-curtained front window, he spies the man sitting on a couch with his back to the kitchen.

The assassin sneaks around behind the structure and through the door into an empty pantry room. He slowly steps through the large country kitchen with the doorless opening to the living room. Arthur stands silently for many moments until content that he was unheard.

As rapidly as a pouncing lion, he is directly behind his prey and fires two quick muffled shots into the back of Squirrel's head. The drug dealer slumps forward with blood flowing from his wounds.

Arthur finds the shell casings and pockets them and glances around the room before exiting the premises back the same way he entered.

Reversing the procedure, he picks up the assault rifle from the tree he left it leaning against, returns to his vehicle, and speeds off. This time he drives directly west into Oklahoma. Two hours later just outside of Sallisaw, he stops at a wayside motel and rents a room. English parks his car out of sight behind the building and catches a couple hours sleep.

When he wakes, the PI jumps on Interstate 40 and drives the freeway four hours to Little Rock.

Back at his office, he calls William Masse's private number and states, "Operation Gazebo concluded," and hangs up.

Chapter 76

Liz pulls into her yard in Morrow and parks next to her husband's muscle car. It is almost five AM. The wife would have been home earlier if a couple of girlfriends and she hadn't gone to a Waffle House for breakfast.

The house is dark except for the flickering television set. She flips on the living room light as she walks in. Her husband, Ken, sits on the old worn out vinyl couch; the numerous rips held together with gunmetal gray duct tape. His head slumped over and fresh sticky blood covering his shirt.

She hurries to him and gently pushed his shoulder. He falls over and lay unmoving, his forehead shattered and all but missing. Running to the baby's bedroom crib, her child lay motionless. She cradles the cold lifeless body for a long time before gently laying her back onto the bare crib mattress.

Elizabeth Walker runs to the barn and digs three full flour sacks from the dirt floor. She quickly throws them in the Chevelle and returns to the barn grabbing the spare gas can.

She walks through the dilapidated farmhouse and pours gasoline around every room. At the front door, Liz stands for the longest time looking over the living room and her husband's body.

She torches the house.

Elizabeth retreats to the yard watching the flames spread, with buckets of tears draining from her eyes sockets until the place fully engulfs

She climbs into Ken's car and fires up the thunderous 454 cubic inch engine. The Cherry Bomb Glasspack dual mufflers rumble and shake the vehicle to life. Liz drops the manual four-on-the-floor shifter into first gear and punches the gas. The large back oversized

Wide Oval tires gyrate wildly in the dirt as she spins a doughnut and hauls ass out of the yard and down the dirt lane to the main paved road. Her headlights are off but she is as comfortable with the familiar getaway route as a gopher is maneuvering through its burrow. Her husband and she practiced it many times. She waits until she is a mile down Williams Road before turning on the headlights.

Elizabeth Walker drives Ken's car to his cousin's Fayetteville home. She parks on the dirt in the large yard and goes inside to ask her if she can park in their garage. After juggling cars, Liz sits in the kitchen while the young woman pours a couple cups of coffee.

"Where's Willie? I don't mean to wake him and the kids." Liz asks.

"He's working the early shift and had to be there by five. That's why I'm up and coffee made." Viv goes on, "Why are you here? Where are Ken and Emily?"

"Ken's dead! So is my precious baby!"

Chapter 77

Patrol Officer Jake Smith's radio barks to life, "Car 215 what's your 10-20?"

"Heading east on West North Street."

"State Troopers are requesting immediate assistance at an accident scene on 412 at Highway 49 intersection. Run Code 3."

Smith flicks his lights and siren on and whips a U-turn heading to Highway 49. It's just after one-thirty in the morning on April eleventh, two days after Walker's assassination. He figures some drunk leaving a bar shouldn't have been driving. He hits the junction north and can see the flashing lights at the end of the long straight-a-way in the southbound lanes. He'll be on scene in four minutes.

Officer Smith continues just past the area and pulls through the grass divider and returns to the head of the accident. Both lanes ahead are blocked with cop cars and emergency vehicles and he positions his car kitty-corner between the two lanes to stop all traffic. He turns off the siren and leaves the lights flashing. Grabbing his flashlight, he flags down the lone approaching car and tells the driver to detour, through the grass median into the north traveling lanes. The man starts to protest and Smith points north, "You can get off at the next exit and take the frontage road south or sit here for hours." Turning around is the best option and the man quickly complies.

The officer retrieves a box of flares from his trunk and proceeds to light and lay them in a long pattern shutting down the outside lane and funneling any coming vehicles to the inside lane where he can initiate a turnaround for them as any northbound traffic permits.

Finishing his chores Officer Smith stands just in front of the flare line waving his flashlight back and forth. Traffic is extremely light at this hour and only two cars come in his direction.

A few minutes later another Fayetteville officer pulls in beside his car, "What's up, Smith?"

"Looks like some drunk killed himself. Can you hold down the fort, Jerry, I'll go and see what's up?"

"Sure, you go, Smith, I don't need to spend the rest of my shift writing reports!"

Jake walks down the highway. There's a two-trailer chicken truck sitting cockeyed in the middle of westbound 412 and sixty feet south on 49 is an unrecognizable red vehicle resting at a forty-five-degree angle against the bottom of a tall Southern Short-Leaf Pine.

"What happened?" Smith asks two troopers standing, conversing privately.

"It appears the Vette ran under the back trailer of the chicken truck and hit somewhere high on the tree before crashing to the ground."

The front of the Vette is gone. Its engine is laying in the ditch between the highway and the Pine tree. What fiberglass body parts are still attached to the car are cracked worse than an old master's painting. The ground is littered with the rest of the body and not a piece over a foot square in size.

"Red car?" Smith thinks to himself. He walks over to inspect the area. There's part of a mutilated body still seat-belted in the driver's seat. Everything above the chest is gone. He takes a long hard look at the vehicle. "It can't be!"

He walks to the rear end of the car buried a foot deep into the soft ground and starts scooping away dirt and pine needles from around the center of the bumper.

"What are you doing?" screams the State Trooper in charge.

"Just checking the license plate. I think I know this guy." Smith shines a beam and sees the "SURF'S UP – San Diego, California" license plate frame. "My God, I think it's Detective Harrison Knight of the Fayetteville Department. At least it's his car!"

"Great! Now get back to traffic control!"

Dazed Smith wanders back to his patrol car. He's whiter than a sheeted-kid pretending to be a ghost on Halloween night.

"What happening?" Officer Jones questions.

"It's Knight's car!"

"What the hell is he doing out here at this time of night?"

Smith quietly opens his patrol car door and gently slides into the seat.

"Where do you think you're going?"

His glazed over eyes look up at his peer, "I have to tell Judy."

"You sure it's him? Maybe his car was stolen."

Not answering, Jake starts his car and backs up. He drives down the grass median passed the accident and heads to the Knight home.

Harrison always kept his prized 'sixty-three split-window Corvette Stringray garaged. Arriving, Smith sees Judy's Mustang parked on the street and the driveway empty, as it would have to be if Harrison had taken the Vette out.

He pulls his squad car into the driveway and sits contemplating how to tell his friend's wife. Finally, Jake goes to the front door and rings the bell. After a few rings and five minutes he hears a woman's voice through the door, "Who is it?"

"Judy, it's Jake Smith."

Opening the door, "Jake what are you doing here? What time is it?"

"Is Harry here?"

"No, he left a while ago. Said he needed to go for a drive. What's up?"

"Can I come in?"

Looking at Smith's pale distraught face, Judy bursts into tears, "NO! NO! Not Harrison!"

"Let's sit for a minute."

Officer Smith tells the new widow that Harry's car was involved in an accident but they don't know if he was driving. She responds asking Smith if he can go to the scene and see. He explains he was already there, but nothing is conclusive at this time.

Judy thinks about his statement for many minutes, before, "What are you saying?"

Barely audible, "Judy, it is pretty bad. They'll have to run some tests." He goes on, "Is it possible someone else would be driving his car?"

Through the bucketing tears, she stammers "H…He doesn't let anyone touch his b…baby."

"It's possible he was somewhere and his car was stolen."

"What am I going to do?" not hearing Jake.

"Why would he go out this late? Was he working a case?"

"I…I don't know. He never talks about his job."

After a moment of silence, Judy states, "Sometimes when a case or something is bothering him he takes a drive to think." More silence, "Wa…was he alone?"

"Is there a reason you think someone might have been with him?"

"No…it's just that…that he has been working a lot of hours lately. You know, you always think the worst."

"I know Harry better than anyone. Judy, he is the most faithful man I ever met. He adores you and the kids."

"I know.. it's just…" she doesn't finish, breaking down into bucketing tears.

Her friend asks, "Is there someone you can call to come over and be with you?"

"I need to phone my mother."

Smith sits quietly while Judy retreats to the kitchen to make the call.

She comes back, "My parents are on their way over."

"Good. I wait until they arrive."

Chapter 78

Officer Jake Smith goes back to the death scene of his best friend. He parks behind Alexis Dench's car, which is next to Officer Jones patrol unit.

"Alex?" baffled, "What are you doing here?"

"Good morning, Officer Smith." Even though the whole county knows they're a couple, they still remain nonchalant in public. "I'm a reporter," solemnly.

"I know that, but how did you hear about this so quickly?"

"Everyone has scanners these days. What I don't catch, my office does. They monitor twenty-four hours a day."

"When did you get here?"

"Jake, I'm so sorry about Harrison." To hell with protocol, she throws her arms around her boyfriend. Cheek to cheek they share Alex's tears.

After the long hug, "Jake, let's go somewhere and talk." She suggests.

"I can't leave Harry here alone."

"Jake, he's gone. There isn't anything you can do." Salty drops rolling both their faces.

"I know…it's just…I don't know…let's just go."

Alex follows Smith's squad car to Lou's All Night Diner.

After talking for hours, Smith needs sleep. He drops his unit at the station and drives home. Alex is already there. Without removing their attire, the pair lay on top of Smith's bed embracing until both nods off.

Jake tosses for hours before falling into a deep sleep. He wakes late in the afternoon alone. Before his usual coffee making routine, he calls the station and talks to Lieutenant McGill. Smith apologizes for missing his shift and states he's on his way in. McGill assures him it isn't a problem and to take some time off. As much as he needs. Jake thanks the man telling him he'll be there in the morning.

His next call is to the Times office and Alex. They talk for twenty minutes. Before signing off Alex tells him she'll be there before six with Chinese takeout.

The next morning Jake is up early, dressed in his uniform. He sits at his kitchen table, drinking coffee and chain-smoking as he reads Dench's article on Harrison's accident over and over. It's complete with a formal portrait of his friend and a large photo of the Corvette leaning against the tree.

"How does she do that?" he thinks.

Smith gets in his pickup and drives to the station. Along the way, he stops by a closed Chevrolet dealership and looks over the two Corvettes on the lot. He needs a new car.

Chapter 79

The fallen officer will be buried in police tradition with full honor. Judy Knight's parents made the funeral arrangements with the service to be held at the one hundred and fifty-year-old Fayetteville First Baptist Church. Fairview Memorial Gardens will be Harrison's final resting place.

Jake Smith has once again fallen in discord with his boss. He jumped-the-gun being the first person to contact the family, even before the body was positively identified. Chief Parson's responsibilities include family notifications. It's not a job he relishes but it is *HIS* job. Officer Smith receives a stern talking to but not a formal reprimand inserted into his file.

When Jake arrives at the church a half hour early, Judy's sister is standing on the front steps and introduces herself. After discovering who the officer is and accepting his condolences, she escorts Jake to the second-row right behind where the family will sit and tells him they would like it if he sat close to them. He thanks her and steps outside and around behind the extremely large sanctuary for a smoke.

By ten o'clock Tuesday morning the church is overpacked with standing room only. Smith has already returned to his assigned seat. The minister walks to the podium beside the flag-draped closed casket. You could hear an angel's feather hit the floor in the deadly silence.

The service is well conducted with numerous eulogies from family members. Finally, Chief Parson solemnly walks to the podium. He gives heartfelt condolences on behalf of himself and his force.

At the conclusion, eight pallbearers, including Don Overstreet and Jake Smith, carry Harrison's casket to the waiting hearse.

The twenty-mile precession takes an hour. Four motorcycle State Troopers lead, followed by the hearse and family limousine. Next in line is the mayor's car and other local dignitaries and behind them, friends' personal automobiles. Finishing the line is a hundred police vehicles. Every department for fifty square miles is represented. More than half the official cars display black bunting. Every uniformed officer wears a black shrouded badge.

The graveside ceremony includes a 10-42 last radio call ending with "Gone, but not forgotten." After which guests are invited to speak; Jake Smith goes forward and talks about Harrison's time in San Diego. At the end of the affair, the Color Guard is called on for a three-volley salute.

A post-funeral reception is held at the Knight home for family and close friends. Chief Parson and Lieutenant Williams attend representing the Fayetteville force.

Smith corners Williams in the backyard, "Lieutenant, what has been discovered about the accident?" Smith asks.

"Apparently Harrison pulled up to a red light next to a souped-up blue Chevelle in front of the Waffle House on the corner of 412 and 49 in Springdale. A young male employee, hearing the loud engine noise from the hot rod, was watching. While the light was still red the Chevelle smoked it with wheels spinning and screaming like a banshee. Harrison took off but by the time they turned onto Highway 49 he was way behind and losing ground."

"What's the name of the kid?"

"You're not investigating this. Stay out of it. That's an order!"

"What was determined at the scene?"

"Well, the Chevelle must have been a good half mile or so ahead. A two trailer chicken hauler had just pulled out of Tysons. His back trailer's lights were out. We think the Chevy passed and the truck pulled out not realizing how fast Harrison was traveling. There

245

weren't any skid marks and we don't believe he saw the second trailer until the last minute and raised his arms. His vehicle went under the trailer taking off the top off the car and decapping everything above his chest. His arms and cranial were found along the roadway. The car veered to right off the road and hit the ditch embankment catapulting it sixty feet through the air. It hit the pine tree thirty-five feet up and crashed to the ground. According to the figures on how far he flew and where he hit the tree, he was traveling somewhere above a hundred and ten miles an hour."

"Holy crap! The Chevelle must have been flying. Who owns it?"

"A dead drug dealer. His burnt body was found two days earlier out in Morrow. His wife is missing and we think she had to be driving."

Chapter 80

The day following the funeral Jake Smith gets up after five hours of sleep. He sits in his breakfast nook sucking down coffee. After the second cup, he takes a shower and puts on slacks and a sports coat before driving to the Waffle House on 412 in town.

"Good morning, Sherry, I'll have a large regular black coffee to go please."

When the server hands him the coffee and rings up the sale, Jake asks, "So I heard there was a big race around here last week?"

"That's what the night shift says. I heard some guy in a Vette was killed."

"Wow. What was he racing?"

"Teddy said it was a raked Super Sport."

"Is Teddy around?"

A woman sticks her head into the pass-thru opening, "I was here. Ain't nobody ever going to beat that SS."

"I'd like to give him a run. Where do I find him?"

"Oh yeah! What kind of car do you have?"

"Fifty-five satin-black Bel Air," Smith lies.

"I wouldn't have thought you were a hotrodder?" Sherry pipes up.

"Haven't seen it around here?" the woman in the back mentions.

"My younger brother keeps it in his garage. We just finished it a couple of weeks ago."

"Cool man."

"So where do I find this guy?"

"He hangs at UOA, but I haven't seen him for a while. His lady and her friends come in once in a while. Haven't seen her either."

"How would I recognize this guy?"

"He's a short skinny brown-haired guy. They call him Squirrel. I shouldn't say but he sells weed. Always has a group around him."

"Does the rodent have a real name?"

"Must. I don't know it though. Oh, the misses is named Lulu. She works down at Kats."

"The strip club?"

"That's the place."

"Thanks, Ladies. I'll head over to the school." Nothing new offered that he doesn't already know.

Leaving the establishment, Smith drives to Kats. He wonders if Madison or Ethan has talked to Lulu?

Kats is closed and doesn't open for an hour until eleven. There are a couple cars in the lot and Smith enters through a back door.

"Hey man, we're not open yet!" a guy behind the bar.

"I looking for Lulu," Smith flashes his badge.

"Liz hasn't shown up for work for a while." Madison, stepping from the dressing room. "You know since her husband was murdered."

"Hold up, Handsome…" a girl pipes up recognizing her savior. "I never had a chance to thank you! You know, for what you did here New Year's Eve. You saved my life."

"Just doing my job," the standard cop answer.

Officer Smith leaves and drives over to UOA. He wanders around the campus looking for anyone buying. In the quad, he spies a group of SDS students and goes over.

"Hey guys, remember me?"

"Officer Smith. All's quiet what are you doing here?"

"Looking for a foraging little vermin goes by Squirrel," knowing Walker is dead.

"Don't know any Squirrels." Powell's replacement pipes up.

"Not an animal lover? That's not what I heard."

"Ok, I might know who he is, but I don't know him. Seen him hanging around the frat house a couple of times. Anyway rumors have it that he bit the dust."

"That a fact. Who's taken over his business?"

"What business?"

"Dime bags."

"I'm not into that. Why would you be looking for a dead man?"

"Actually I'm trying to find Lulu Love."

"Who's that?"

"His old lady."

"Didn't know he had one," Kappa Sigma brother, Josh Edwards adds, "How could I, didn't even know him."

"I gotta scamper. We can exchange acorns at the tree later." Smith walks off.

He sits in his car and makes few notes on his pad. And heads to the station. After parking, Jake goes directly to Lieutenant McGill's office.

"Lieutenant, have a minute?"

"What are you doing here this early?" the lieutenant asks. He's suspicious that Smith's dressed like a detective. He never saw the man wear a sports coat before.

"I was just thinking about Harrison and the race you told me about with Liz Walker."

"I never said any names," the lieutenant interrupts. "I told you not to be snooping around!"

"I'm not. Just stopped for a cup of Joe and overheard some talk."

Hesitantly, "Kenneth Walker was executed, two shots to the back of his head. They also found his baby dead, only no known reason. Think it could have been an unfortunate coincidence. Possibly sudden death syndrome or something. Found both bodies after the fire. Liz's wasn't there. Harrison thought she did it, lit the place up, and went on the run."

"Harrison was investigating?"

249

"It was his case. Anyway, it appears he saw her and was chasing her down."

"Yeah, that makes sense. Thanks, Lieutenant, I'll sleep better now."

"Parson wants to see you."

Jake heads upstairs thinking, "That was weird. McGill's never opened up to me before."

"Hi, Margret, Chief wants to see me?"

"Come on in Jake!" Parson calls through the open door.

"Anymore on Harrison yet?"

"Not yet. But our new detective will figure it out!" Without taking a breath, "Because of Knight's untimely death I'm promoting you. You've done an exceptional job in the last year and a half and deserve it."

"Thank you, Chief. I'm already up to speed with Overstreet."

"I know, but McGill is teaming you with Hollis. You're too close to Harrison. Overstreet and Stevens are paired and looking into it. The rookie can learn a lot from you."

"But I know Harrison's case better than his partner does."

"Might be true. All you guys share the same room. I'm sure you'll be involved more than you already are." Chief Parson continues, "I would like you to start today, but it'll take a good week to process all the papers and your pay to catch up."

"Not a problem, Chief. I'm anxious to get started…officially that is." He can't contain the grin on his face. He now knows why McGill was so accommodating.

Detective Jake Smith leaves work late that afternoon and trades his old Datsun in on a brand new Ferrari-red Corvette Stingray.

Chapter 81

Detective Smith visits Judy Knight the week after her husband's funeral. He wants to touch base and see how she's making out and if there is anything he can help with.

They sit in her living room talking about Harrison. Both Judy and Jake miss him terribly. She tells him that the kids are adjusting well except for their oldest, a fourteen-year-old boy.

Judy goes to the kitchen to fix a plate of chocolate chip cookies she made earlier in the day and brew a fresh carafe of coffee.

While she's brewing the coffee, Jake goes to the boy's room and knocks softly. Martin answers the door. He's wiping his face and his eyes are bloodshot from crying.

Jake hugs the boy, "Can I talk to you for a minute?" The teenager doesn't hug back.

Martin doesn't speak but opens the door wide before moving back to his bed and sitting on the edge. Jake finds a small desk. He pulls the chair away and sits on it backward, legs straddling the backrest.

"Martin, your mother tells me you're having a hard time. I just want let you know that I am too. This isn't easy. It's going to take a long time before we feel normal again."

He pauses giving the boy a chance to interact. Martin sits quietly staring at the floor.

"I was thinking maybe this weekend you and I could rent a boat and follow Beaver Lake up to War Eagle. Have you ever been to the old mill?"

Martin shakes his head without looking up.

"Do you like to fish?"

A small mumble, "Yes."

"I'll go to Walmart and pick up some gear so we can fish along the way. How does that sound?"

Another quiet, "Ok."

"I'll pick you up at seven on Saturday morning." Smith stands, "It'll be good for both of us. I'll see then, Martin."

"Ok," meekly.

Jake goes back to the living room. Judy's already sitting. He tells her of his plans and asks if it's alright. Martin's mother is pleased, and tells him she'll find his fishing pole in the garage and have him ready. She just didn't know what to do with the boy. Her two other children are much younger, three and five years old. They really don't understand their father is never coming home.

Jake asks Judy if she's getting some help. She tells him the pastor at their church is consulting her.

"I didn't know you and Harry attended church?"

"Me more than him. It seems he always had full Sundays, but by the time I got home he was worshipping football." They both offer a strained laugh.

"I have to get going. Judy, if you ever need anything at all, I'm here for you and the kids."

"Thank you, Jake."

They hug and Smith's almost out the door, "Jake, do you want Harrison's files?"

"He has files here?" surprised.

"A briefcase full. I'll get it."

Back at the station, Smith is going through every page, notation and a couple of photos.

Overstreet calls from his desk, "What you got there, Smith?"

"A few things I been collecting," not looking up.

"Do they pertain to my Walker case?"

"Naw, mostly old files from San Diego," he lies.

Smith looks long and hard at one scrap of paper, "VRKWCOUZ1139WANEETAHST" trying to decode the cryptic message.

Robert Hollis, Jake's new partner, comes in and sits at the desk adjoining Smith's.

"Where have you been, Jake?"

"I had a small errand to run." Jake isn't sharing that he's really working on the Walker/Knight case.

"Did you talk to Mrs. Watton, again?" inquiring to Hollis on their current burglary investigation.

"She stuck to the story that they were both home all evening and her husband never left her sight."

"That's hogwash! We need to find someone who saw him leave or in the area of the burglary. I'll check the victim's neighbors again and you can do the suspect's."

Smith walks toward the door stuffing the small note deep into his front pocket. He turns back to Hollis, "Now's a good time, Bob."

His partner jumps to his feet, "I'm on my way."

Smith's first stop is the Chevrolet dealer to pick up his new sports car.

He empties his glove box and the junk from behind and under the seat of his Datsun while they pull the Vette around. Smith throws his stuff into the new trunk and places his personal Taurus 357 sidearm in the glove box. The city street map goes on the front seat.

The salesman is vigorously shaking Smith's hand. Smith is trying to break free without making a noticeable move. He asks if he can go to the office and make a phone call before he leaves.

"Of course, Jake." That did the trick and his hand released.

The salesman walks him to his office. He leaves Jake in privacy and goes to relieve himself.

After going through the screening drill, "Hi, Jake," Alex answers.

"Hi, Dear. I'm just picking up my car. Where would you like to drive to after work?"

"Why don't we go to Bentonville for dinner?"

"Perfect. It will let me see what she'll do!"

"Jake, you don't want to make that mistake." They both know what Alex is referring to without saying.

"I'll pick you up at your place..say seven."

"I'll be ready."

"Another thing, do you know what W-A-N-E-E-T-A-H-S-T means?" spelling out what looks like the only word in his note.

"Sure, it's a street name, Waneetah Street. Go north just past seventy-one. What's out there?"

"She's the consummate reporter, always digging for facts," he thinks. "Just a witness to a burglary I have to see."

After he speeds all the way, Smith slowly creeps down Waneetah looking at house numbers. He comes upon a mailbox two numbers off and the next house should be the one he's looking for. The painted numbers are too faded to read. It's an older home and set back from the road by a huge dirt front yard.

Chapter 82

Back in Fayetteville after dinner in Bentonville with Alex, Jake drops her off at her house. He tells his girlfriend that he put in a tough day and needs to get home to bed. Alexis is disappointed Jake isn't spending the night. They hug and share a passionate tongue-kiss before Smith leaves.

Jake doesn't go home as he told her but drives back to Waneetah Street. He parks his new car on the busier E. North Avenue in a Circle K lot and walks the three blocks in the dark. He enjoys an after dinner smoke on his way.

The detective stands in the shadows leaning against a gigantic tree across the street from what he assumes is 1139. The street is as ghostly as a still desert night. After an hour Smith is wishing he had gotten a cup of coffee at the convenience store.

A half-hour later he ambles across the street. A car turns off the main thorofare behind him. As the lights approach he walks casually down the road with his back to it. Closer and closer the vehicle approaches. And at the exact second the car is passing, he turns and waves. Hopefully, whoever's in the vehicle thinks it's just a friendly neighbor taking a night stroll.

The vehicle turns on Oakwood at the end of the block. Smith stops and waits. All clear. He goes back to the house of interest.

He approaches the free-standing street-side mailbox. Pulling out his flashlight he looks to see if there's a name painted on the side. Nothing. Smith glances up and down the street and at the close at hand houses. A few porch lights shine but no sign of life anywhere. He pulls down the box lid and peeks inside. Today's mail sits untouched.

There's a Harp's eight-page advertisement featuring their weekly specials, addressed to current resident. A postcard with a like label and a North West Propane bill. He pockets the bill and walks to his car.

After purchasing a coffee to go, Detective Smith sits in his vehicle and pulls out the bill. It's addressed to W. Rae. Nobody, he's ever heard of. Thinking, "What did Harrison want with this guy?"

Smith pulls his encrypted code paper from his pocket. He decides to examine the bill and rips the envelope's side down. It's too far from the edge and he accidentally tears the three-folded invoice's end off. "Crap, I won't be dropping this back in the box!"

The account name on the invoice is William & Vivian Rae."

Smith walks over to the outside round cement trash receptacle and throws away his empty paper cup and the invoice.

Over the next couple of weeks, Smith is at the address every weeknight for an hour or more. He never sees a human anywhere on the property. The porch and front room lights are always dark. There is a light from some back room, probably the kitchen that shines until eleven or twelve every night. Frustrated and ready to write this lead off, Smith gets an idea.

The next morning he sitting at his spot in an unmarked department van well before sunrise. At four-thirty an early-twenties age man comes out the front door. He dressed in overalls and carrying a black arched top lunch box. He gets into an old beater and drives off. The guy doesn't even let it warm up.

"Well, well," Smith to himself, "the front rooms are dark because this guy must go to bed at eight. Vivian probably stays in the kitchen making his lunch and doing dishes…maybe a little baking." He smiles and drives to work.

That morning after the daily briefing with Lieutenant McGill the detectives are dismissed and walking toward the room's exit. "Hey Overstreet, does your cous still fix outboards?" McGill calls out.

Smith snaps around so fast he almost throws out a hip, "What did you say?" almost screaming.

"Just asked Don if his cousin still repairs motors. Mine's on its final days."

"That's not what you said!"

"Calm down, Smith! Yeah he does, Abe. I'll get you the number." Overstreet.

"Tell me what you said!" Smith not letting it go.

"Relax!" McGill shaking his palms down open hands, at waist height like he's dealing with a lunatic. "I just asked if his cous fixes…"

Smith's didn't hear the rest as he was running top-speed down the hall.

He rips open his desk and pulls out the scrap with code. "Cous. How damn stupid can I be!" out loud.

"Very!" Overstreet enters.

"KWCOUZ. KWCOUZ. KW COUSIN." The light bulb not only goes off in his head but explodes, "Ken Walker's cousin." He screeches, "LIZ IS AT KENS WALKER'S COUSIN'S."

"Liz Walker is at her dead husband's cousin's house?" Overstreet clarifying.

"YES! YES! The cousin's house!"

"Who's the cousin and where do they live is the question?"

"Vivian and William Rae on Waneetah Street! I've been staking them out for weeks."

"What the hell! Smith you were told to work with us on this!" pissed beyond belief.

"I am. There was nothing to share until now."

"Calm down, Gentlemen." Chief Parson and McGill enter the room. "What's going on here?" the Chief demands.

Overstreet stays silent. Smith can hang himself!

"Sorry Chief. We got a little carried away. Don and I just solved the Walker case. We got Liz!" Smith covers.

"Good! When are you picking her up?"

"As soon as I can confirm she's there!" Smith explains.

"You just said she was! You've been staking out the place," Overstreet trying to figure out what's going on.

"Yes, but I haven't actually seen anyone…well, except for William…I think."

"Smith, you better start at the beginning." Mcgill as confused as the rest.

"I'll be in my office. Keep me posted." Parson leaves.

"Here's what I know." Smith tells his story, "Ken Walker and baby Emily are killed and the house burns down. Liz is driving Ken's Chevelle and on the run. She's our suspect. Harry figured it out and found Liz. He was pursuing her when he crashed. Judy Knight gave me Harry's briefcase. There wasn't anything to speak of inside, but for this note." He produces the small wrinkled paper. Everyone passes it around. "Didn't know what it meant, but I staked out the address and discovered Vivian and William Rae lives there. That's the "VR", Vivian Rae."

He gulps a breath and continues, "The place is always dark except for one light in a back room, so I went there early this morning before sunup. That's when I observed William, I presume, going to work at four-thirty."

"He works, so what?"

"Works early, so he must go to bed early. That explains the dark house. The backlit room is probably the kitchen. That's where Vivian and probably Liz hang out! VRKWCOUS1139WANEETAHST…Vivian Rae Ken Walker's Cousin 1139 Waneetah Street!"

"AND you still didn't come to me!" Overstreet is getting madder by the second. "Come on, Gerod!"

"Hold up a sec. What's the game plan?" Smith inquiries.

"My partner and I are going to Rae's. We'll interview Vivian and find out where Liz Walker is and arrest her."

"No! You can't do that! If Walker isn't there, Vivian will alert her and she'll be gone!"

"Alert her? She already knows we're after her!"

"The point is…if Liz is staying there, we have to know first and set up an arrest before alerting everyone we're coming!"

"And your plan is?"

"Let me go back tonight and confirm!"

"Gerod and I are going with you!"

"Too many bodies lurking around. Give me tonight and you can do whatever you need to tomorrow," Smith begs.

McGill back involved, "Don, that's the plan. Smith goes alone tonight and you guys go tomorrow."

Chapter 83

Detective Smith is back at the Rae home by ten that night. He sneaks around the back. The kitchen bare light bulb is illuminating the room and the window over the sink is half open.

Standing beside the window, Smith takes a quick glance inside. A barefooted woman, wearing a faded dull flowered apron is bent over peering into the opened oven door. A second is sitting at the breakfast bar drinking a soda.

The t-shirt and jean sitting woman puts her soda down, "Viv, I think it's time I leave you and Willie."

Smith quickly ducks below the window frame.

Standing and turning, "Nonsense, Liz. Where would you go?"

"That's it!" upon hearing the name he is waiting for.

"I'm not sure. Somewhere nobody knows me...I'm thinking California...maybe San Fransico."

"Oh Cous, that's so far away. Do you need some money?"

"I'm good for a while. Of course, I'll need a job soon."

"Promise me you won't dance."

"I promise," she lies. "I'll get ready tomorrow and leave after dark." She walks to Viv and they hug for the longest time. "Thanks, for all the help, Vivian."

Smith runs all the way back to his Vette.

At the station, he gets on the horn, "Don, we got her! We need to move now!"

"I'm on my way in! Call Stevens and McGill."

"And Hollis.' Smith adds.

Overstreet and Smith listen to McGill outline the arrest plan in the lieutenant's office. It's after midnight by the time a plan is finalized and the additional men arrive. Everyone is standing in the parking lot ready to hit it.

"Just to be clear! Smith you and Hollis are backup in the alley. Overstreet and Stevens at the front door with two officers. I'll be at the back door with Williams and Olsen. And Bakman and Strand in cars on the street." Thinking to make sure it's solid. "That should do it. Let's go, Gentlemen!"

Every team jumps to their vehicles and heads out the lot. Stevens is ahead as Smith saunters behind, deliberating. His partner stops and turns, "Move it, Jake! We don't want to miss this!"

"Take the unmarked and follow the plan. I'll catch up in my car."

"What the hell are you talking about. You heard McGill. Let's go!"

Smith veers off towards the other end of the lot.

Chapter 84

Elizabeth Walker pulls from her cousin's garage a little after midnight. She left a note on the counter for Viv stating she was anxious to hit the road and is leaving early. She places three one-hundred dollar bills under the note.

As soon as she clears the driveway she notices headlights coming towards her. Behind it appears the second car.

Calmly Liz reverses back into the yard. She spins the car around and circumvents the house to the alley. Lights off she slowly inches the nose of the SS out and sees two more cars turn into the lane. Rather than turn towards town as planned, Liz heads in the opposite direction, away from the coming vehicles. At the end of the alley, she turns right on Oakwood.

A block down she flicks her lights on and speeds up. She watches her mirror like a kid watching a cartoon; eyes darting back and forth from the road ahead to the road behind. She's not gone a country block before she sees a car's head lights coming up fast behind her. Elizabeth punches it. The hot rod sparks to life like being pricked with a needle. Her eyes never leaving the glowing orbs getting larger in her mirror.

Liz runs the stop sign on Lakeridge and hits the gas circling Lake Lucille at sixty. The Cherry Bomb pipes guttural moan a constant reminder that she's still in third gear. She slides the corner onto E. North and most of the short block to Mission. The stranger keeps coming.

Liz drops the Hurst shifter into fourth gear and stomps the pedal to the metal. Even at this speed, the Wide Ovals smoke the pavement as the SS bucks and shoots for the horizon. The header pipes break the still air like an exploding late Summer thunderhead.

At the end of the long straightish road, Liz is hitting one-fifteen. In her mirror she sees a single red flashing light come on from the further falling behind vehicle.

She hits her brakes hard. She has no plans of ever stopping but needs to get her speed in check for the downhill twisted road through the forest patch before Bowen Boulevard.

"Think! Think! What would Ken do?" screaming at herself. Liz misses the last corner leaving the woods and hits the dirt shoulder. The Chevelle's back end is coming around fast.

Her drug-dealing husband had taken Elizabeth out to practice get-aways on numerous occasions. They would slide corners, do open dirt slips and spin doughnuts until both were covered from head to toe in the dust. Only their peering eyes hinted at their humanity.

The practice enclosed her like the shell of a robot. Everything became automatic. Liz shoves the shifter down into third, pops the clutch and cranks the wheels into the slide. The belching monster responds, fishtailing back onto the pavement. Rubber catching, Liz throws it back into fourth gear and screams down the road.

"I can't get to the Goshen post office stop. They'll be waiting for me," she reasons. The only road heading south, before is Round Mountain. "Those bastards probably think I going to hide in National Forest and will have that blocked off too." Talking to herself, "The only option is to take the 359 loop north back to Mission and head west. Hopefully, they have set the trap ahead of time and will be waiting verses following."

Liz creeps, lights off, just past the stop sign. She was right. Mission Boulevard is quiet. She cranks right towards town and turns on the headlights. Liz never gets close to her starting point before turning south and taking back roads to the highway miles south of Fayetteville.

Smith lost sight of the runaway. He's gunning the Vette at just over a hundred miles an hour by the time he slides to a stop in the dirt at the Goshen Post Office. He screams into his walkie-talkie but far out of range. Smith pulls back onto the road and heads back to the Rae location. He never sees the Chevelle again.

Liz turns south on state Highway 71. It takes her, driving the mountainous edge of the Ozark National Forest, more than four and a half hours to make Fort Smith. She stays within the speed limit and only passes a couple of late nighters going in the opposite direction.

After another four-hour drive, around nine in the morning, Liz finds a small motel outside of Texarkana and rents a room. She parks the highly visible vehicle out of sight behind the end of the building and walks back to her room.

She is an emotional wreck and exhausted from driving all night. Liz flops, fully clothed, on top of the covers and crashes for twelve hours.

The young fugitive wakes late evening. She walks outside and lights a cigarette. While standing in the cool night air she notices Burger Delight across the road and walks over for a burger and shake.

She returns to her room, grabs the three flour sacks stuffed with hundred dollar bills before heading to her car and driving south to Corpus Christi. It takes Liz fourteen hours choreographing off-beaten country roads.

She plans to make her way to Laredo and across the border into the safety of Mexico.

Chapter 85

A cluster of hot rodders meets on the beach in Corpus Christi. The last to arrive is an older thirties something man. His '32 deuce is followed into the dirt lot by a Texas State Trooper.

After parking the souped-up car in line with his compadres, the patrol car blocks him in. The officer walks to the driver's open window, "Sir, can you step out of your vehicle?"

"What's wrong officer?"

"I just wanted to admire your car, but I can see you have many violations." He goes on inspecting the Angus beef-black hot rod. It's chopped and channeled with bright yellow flames jetting from the hoodless firewall along the door panels. The wheels are matching yellow with centered bright chrome baby moons. "First your back tires are too large. They must be fully under the fenders." He carries on but soon interrupted.

"Excuse me, Officer." The hot rodder hasn't been paying attention with his eyes focused on the new muscle car at the far end of the beach. "That blue Chevelle looks familiar."

The trooper turns to see where the rodder is looking.

"I know cars and I'm sure I saw that one on the news."

"What are you talking about?"

"Some woman out of Arkansas killed her husband and baby. She's on the run. I'm sure that's her car!"

"Stay here!" The trooper goes to his vehicle on gets on the radio. A few moments later he exits and walks down the beach. As he approaches the Chevelle he draws his pistol and sneaks up to the driver's door from behind. He inspects into the back seat as he passes and looks into the empty front compartment. He scours the beach in both directions before heading back to his car.

"It's your lucky day. I won't be citing you anytime soon." He compliments the hot rodder, "You have a good eye for cars, thank you for your help." And he adds, "I wish I had a vehicle like yours," beaming.

Within minutes two more patrol cars pull into the lot. The four officers split up with two going one direction up the sandy beach and the other two heading the opposite way.

The first trooper and his buddy spot a lumpy blanket under a group of bushes off the sand. They look at each other and pull their weapons. Quietly and careful not to break any twigs the men approach the unmoving cotton lump.

"Put your hands where we can see them!" screams a trooper.

Shocked the woman rolls over on looks at the intruders.

"Raise your hands!"

Slowly both hands appear, "What's the matter, Officers?"

"Are you Elizabeth Marie Walker?"

"No. Who's that? My name is Madison."

"Is that your Chevy in the parking area?"

"I don't have a car. I'm homeless and walked here for the night."

"Come out from under the blanket and show us some ID!" The girl doesn't have any.

After she stands one of the troops holsters his gun and searches the blanket. Nothing is there. He walks over and places her in cuffs.

"I didn't do anything!" yelps the young woman.

The second man puts his gun away and searches the woman finding car keys, "Let's take a look at your phantom car."

"Look, Officer, I'm driving that car but a lady picked me up hitchhiking in Odem. She said she had to get rid of the car and gave me the keys."

The three walk to the Chevelle meeting the other two officers there. They search the vehicle and find a purse with Liz's pictured Arkansas driver's license and the three money stuffed flour sacks. Liz is arrested and taken downtown.

At the station, detectives question her for hours before getting on the horn to Fayetteville. The next day detectives Donald Overstreet and Jake Smith drive to Corpus Christi to transport Elizabeth Walker back to Arkansas.

Chapter 86

Overstreet and Smith arrive in Corpus Christi at five AM after a twelve-hour drive from Northwest Arkansas. Overstreet's partner, Stevens, had taken a personal week off and Lieutenant McGill assigned Smith to accompany Overstreet. They had minimal conversations on the road. Smith kept trying to befriend the man while Overstreet answered with brevity or not at all. They checked into a hotel for a couple hours sleep and head to the police headquarters a little after nine the same morning.

The Texas detectives tell them Elizabeth hasn't said a word, except to tell them they have the wrong person. It takes an hour and several coffees each before the paperwork is complete and they're ready for the long drive home.

The threesome arrives at the Fayetteville station well after midnight on Sunday, May ninth. Liz spent most the journey sleeping on the back bench seat. Overstreet lightened up and actually had a conversion with Smith. He asked about Jake's career in San Diego and what went wrong and how he ended up in Arkansas. Smith opened up with honest answers and told of the cases he and Alan Jones, his murdered partner, worked on.

Overstreet gains respect for the disgraced man and his tenacity. By the end out their trip, they both got along well and planned to have a beer together. Overstreet went as far as inviting Jake over to meet his family and have a barbeque.

In the station, Overstreet handcuffs Liz to a table in the interrogation room. He grabs a mug coffee and goes to his desk.

Detective Smith goes into the men's locker room and takes a refreshing shower. Redressing in a clean white shirt and slacks sans the sports coat he walks the deserted halls to the break room. He steps in and pours himself a coffee in the largest cup he can find. He maneuvers the halls to the detective room and sits at Stevens' desk across from Overstreet.

Overstreet thanks Smith for accompanying him on the drive.

"McGill didn't ask!" Smith grins.

"I'm going to speak to Abe and request you as my partner."

"What about Stevens?"

"He can work with Hollis. I want the "A" team." Smith believes he observes a slight smile cross Overstreet's face.

Finishing the coffees, "Ready?" Overstreet stands.

They shake hands with the detective putting his left hand on the Smith's bicep. Neither utter a word but their pleased expressions say it all.

Overstreet turns on the recorder, "Elizabeth, we are going to record this conversation." He Merandizes her again and asks if she wants a lawyer present.

She shakes her head, "I haven't done anything."

"Could you state your name for the record?"

After the formalities finish, Detective Overstreet asks, "Can you tell us what happen the morning of April ninth of this year?"

Both detectives are surprised by her tearless emotion-free tale, "I got off work around three in the morning. Maddi and I and another girl went to the Waffle House for breakfast…"

Smith starts to clarify the first statement with, "Who was with you?"

"We'll ask questions after her statement, Detective." Overstreet breaks in glaring at the other man. He doesn't want to muddy the waters as long as Elizabeth is spilling.

"We went for breakfast and I drove home. The house was dark except for the TV. I walked in and turned on the light. Ken was slumped down on the far edge of the couch. I walked over to wake him and he fell over. That's when I saw all the blood and bullet hole in the back of his head. I ran to Emily's room. Her lifeless body just laid there."

"Was she…uh, your child shot also?"

"No, just dead. I don't know how."

Overstreet looks at his notes, "Where were you working?"

"Kats."

"That's a strip club is it not?"

"Yes."

"Which Waffle House did you go to?"

"The one on North Street. It's on my way home."

"And who was with you?"

"Maddi and Kitty."

"What are their full names?"

"Madison Kespar and Kathy…er, Kathleen George."

The clarifying questions go on. Eventually, Overstreet gets to the main subject; the murder of her husband and baby. "So you found Ken shot and Emily passed away from an unknown reason?"

"Yes."

"Who would do this?"

"I don't know."

"We know, Liz. You did it!" Smith blurts out.

"No, I love Ken and my little girl!"

"You promised to come clean. We know you killed Ken. If it was an accident, that's understandable." Overstreet back engineering the locomotive.

"He was shot in the back of the head!" Liz blankly states.

"If, as you say, didn't murder your husband who did?" Smith asks.

"Ken had some enemies."

"Name them."

"Powell Tucker for one!"

Smith almost wets his pants. This is what he is waiting for. His scribbling more pages of notes than *War and Peace* and faster than a court recorder.

"Powell Tucker died of an overdose in March," Overstreet states as though it is impossible for Powell to be the culprit.

"Yes. That, was after this guy came to the club and threatened me. He wanted to know about Ken and his business." Liz remembers and adds, "He mentioned Tucker by name."

"What man is that?" Smith asks.

"Some English son-of-a-bitch. He sticks a knife in my throat and questions me about where we live and all."

"When was that?"

"I don't know, a few months back. He was a real scary bastard!"

"What did you tell him?"

"Anything he wanted. I thought he was going to kill me."

Overstreet dismisses the incident in his mind, rationalizing a crazed druggie trying to score. He asks about Randal Brown.

After Liz tells about Ken's supplier and other drug dealers trying to take over her husband's business, she ends the suspect list with four names; Randal Brown, Powell Tucker, Ethan Eastman, and Denny Daniels.

"We just covered Brown. According to you, he doesn't have a motive unless you're keeping something from us, Liz?"

"No!"

"And Tucker's been dead for a month. Do you think his ghost came back and killed your husband?"

"No."

Looking at the next written name, "Tells us about Ethan Eastman."

"He likes me. A little too much." She adds. "Also he and Tucker are roommates. Maybe they decided to do it together. You know get rid of my husband."

"What about your boss?"

271

"Denny? He and Ken did not get along. After Denny beat up Powell and stole his car, he tried to rip off Ken's sports stuff. Ken refused to give him anything. Denny threatened to kill him and banned him from Kats."

"Was the sports stuff gone when you found Ken?"

"I don't know. I didn't think to look around."

"I have a problem with your story, Liz." Overstreet states. "You didn't walk into a burning house and find your husband shot."

"No."

"So you think the murderer was still lingering around and lit the place up after you left?"

"No."

"How did the house catch fire, Liz?"

"I did it."

Overstreet acts calm over the earth-shattering admission. Smith goes ballistic. "Detective, can I see you outside?"

"Not now!"

"That doesn't make sense! Elizabeth, if you didn't kill your husband, why didn't you call the police? And why would you light your own house on fire?" Overstreet addresses the suspect.

"I wanted to die too." Moments of silence, "I lit the fire and laid on the floor beside Emily's crib. It started getting so smokey. I could feel the heat. My chest was burning and I couldn't stop coughing." Quietly head down, "I'm such a chicken-shit, I just got up and ran from death." A single tear slowly drips from one eye.

Chapter 87

HELP! HELP! The guard shrieks could be heard throughout the Washington County Jail's second floor.

It's six o'clock in the morning and the guard is walking the cell hall waking up the overnight drunks and longer termers. All jump off their built-in cots and stand at the bars straining to see the action. "What happened? What's going on? Who is it?" the floor is thick with futile unanswered questions.

The uniformed man quickly unlocks the cell door. He enters the small cell and stares at the lifeless woman hanging by the neck. A bed sheet suspends the small dangling body from the steel caged ceiling light fixture.

Within moments the cell and hallway filled with guards. The finding man runs to the outer room and grabs a chair, quickly dragging it to the scene. The screeching metal legs across the cement floor worse than fingernails on a chalkboard.

The overseeing sergeant jumps onto the chair. He struggles to lift the body and untie the knot around her neck. The pale carcass drops to the floor with a muffled thump.

Jumping from the chair, he puts two fingers against her carotid artery. No pumping blood felt. He stands and looks around the room shaking his head, "Call the coroner!" He adds, "And Warden Marks."

Shortly Marks comes down the cell ward. Coroner Keith Kleint is wide steps behind.

"What happened?" the warden questions.

"Elizabeth Walker hung herself."

"How could you let this happen, Sergeant?" blaming the man in charge.

"I just came on duty, Sir."

"Call Price and get him back here now!"

While the coroner gets to work, Marks takes the duty officer and sergeant to his office. He needs to get to the bottom of this sooner than later. Traumatised night charge officer, Price quietly slips into the room.

The volume of indignation escalates beyond any reasonable level. By the time reporter Alexis Dench gets wind it's essential the warden has all his ducks in a row. It only ends when Price agrees to accept full responsibility. He's immediately put on suspended duty.

The female bulldog has been with the Times for years. She won't be easy to deal with and certainly won't let this go for weeks or even months. Warden Marks can only pray a bigger story comes along quickly.

By eight-ten the body is gone, taken to the morgue for autopsy and Alex Dench is marching into the jail's reception portal, "I need to see Warded Marks!"

"He's a little busy this morning, Ms. Dench," the desk officer stops her.

"I imagine he is, Stan. But the fact remains we need to talk *now*!"

"I see if he's available, Ma'am. Please have a seat."

Dench remains standing.

Twenty minutes later the warden appears "Alexis, it's nice to see you. Too bad it's under these unfortunate circumstances."

"Circumstances! Is that what we're calling your screw up?"

"Let's step outside for a minute, Ms. Dench."

On the front landing Marks and Alex go back and forth. The man has his excuses and puts full blame on Price's shoulders, letting Alex know it's already handled by the suspension.

Dench is demanding he take responsibility by personal resignation. At an impasse Warden Marks excuses himself. He has an investigation to do.

274

Dench takes a couple steps down. With her back to Marks, she removes her camera from the oversized purse she carries. Turning around, "Warden, one more thing!"

Marks leans out the still open door and spies the camera up and ready. "Click! Click! She snaps two quickies of his dumbfounded face.

Marks' wide hollow eyes set deep below his hard-lined forehead will make a perfect quarter page lead photo.

Alex heads to the morgue hoping to secure a secret photo of Liz's dead body filleted open on the stainless autopsy table. That would certainly outweigh Marks' photograph!

Alex visualizes the front page story; above the fold; a four-column photo of the dead girl on the left and the warden's shock face spread across, maybe two or three, right-hand columns. In between the pics, bold copy subheadings will highlight the full-page story. The top extra large banner will read, "JAIL SUICIDE! WARDEN MARKS AT FAULT!"

Chapter 88

Outside the coroner's building, Alex calls Jake and tells him of Elizabeth Walker's suicide.

She glimpses through the double glass doors. The hallway is empty as is behind the glass of the reception window. The day shift hasn't started yet. The reporter boldly enters and proceeds down the hall.

Over the next thirteen minutes, she stands to watch Klein, through the small glass window in the morgue door, working on Walker's body. Her cocked camera is hanging at her side.

The doctor walks to the coffee pot. With his back to Dench, she runs in and snaps two quick pictures. Started by the clicks in the dead quiet room, Kleint spins, "What are you doing?"

"I have a couple of questions, Keith."

"You can't be in here. I need you to relinquish that film!"

"I can't do that...you know freedom of the press and all that."

"There's no freedom of the press in this cloistered room without prior authorization. Hand it over!" stretching out his palm.

Trading on her good looks, Alex gives her best seductive smile and lays her hand on his, "Keith, we've been friends for a long time. I like you a lot and have always admired your character. You know I would never do anything to hurt you", blinking rapidly and producing watery eyes while looking up into his from her lowered submissive head.

Melting into her irresistible charm, "Alex, I would never do anything to hurt you either. You better get out of here before someone else shows up."

She stands on her tiptoes and pecks his cheek, "Thank you, Keith".

Approaching the door and almost reaching freedom, "Alexis, write a positive story of this poor young lady. With good words, you don't need a degrading picture."

"I'll heed you're your insight, Keith."

Resting in her car, guilt consuming her body, she misses seeing a car pull in next to hers. Surprised by a knock on her window, Alex looks up at Jake's grinning face. He is motioning to roll it down.

"Hi, Jake," sully voiced Alexis.

"Honey, what's wrong? You look like a lost spirit."

"Oh, Jake," sorrowfully looking at her lover with a tear rolling down her cheek. "I hate my job."

"What are you saying? You love your job. You're the best reporter in the state."

"The price is too high. I need to be a better person!"

"That's ridiculous. What's really going on?"

"I can't take lying to people anymore just to get a story." Alex puddles up. She looks at Jake threw the teary eyes, "I grew up in this town. These are my friends!"

"Can you wait here? I have to see Kleint, then, we can go somewhere and talk."

"I can't talk right now. I'll see you tonight." Alex starts her car.

Smith doesn't give up; nonetheless, she misses his words and drives away. He stands in wonderment watching until she's out of sight.

Entering the morgue, "Klein, was Alexis Dench in here?"

"Just left."

"What happened?"

"Nothing, she was her usual charismatic self."

"That's not what I saw. Anyway, tell me about this," pointing at the corpse.

"I haven't dug deep yet, but there's no question she hung herself. No other visible bruises or inclusions suggesting someone else did it to her. I should have this wrapped up in an hour or so and have it sent over."

Smith thanks him. He needs to get to work. Alex will have to wait.

Chapter 89

Smith sits at his new desk, slurping scorching coffee, watching his new partner write on a yellow legal pad. Finally, Overstreet acknowledges him.

"What is so intense?" Smith clipped voice over his burnt tongue.

"Just making notes for our report. This Walker thing looks wrapped up. You heard about Elizabeth?"

"Sure, but I have been thinking…she didn't do it!"

"What do you mean… she admits being there and burning the place. If she didn't do it, why not call it in instead of fleeing?" Before Smith can retaliate, "We got lucky she was picked up. A few miles from Mexico, I might add."

"I don't disagree she was in the wind, but where's her motive?"

"There are hundreds of motives. She was married to a drug dealer for one. They were probably high and fighting daily," Overstreet theorizes.

"If they had problems that is one thing, but she loved her baby. And we know she was out with friends that morning."

"But she didn't murder the child! Ken could have killed Emily or the baby died of natural causes. The autopsy couldn't confirm how she died. Burnt too bad. Maybe Liz came home and found the child and assume her husband did it and finished him off."

"Everyone I ever interviewed told me they were happy and wished they had a relationship so good."

Next Smith suggests Randal Brown, SOD, someone at Kats or a drug client. Overstreet demands a motive for each suggestion.

Smith's turn to offer flimsy theories. "Could easily have been a deal gone bad. We both know Randal Brown is quite capable of shooting someone who he thinks wronged him!" rubbing his previous shot shoulder.

"That was never proven to be Brown! The Dagger Society's be dissolved and there's no connection there anyway."

"It's a secret society. The key word being *secret*. We don't have any idea if they're still active or not."

"So why would they kill Walker?"

"Same reason, over drugs or money. Or revenging Powell's murder!"

"Nonsense. Nobody robs and leaves the money, which incidentally Liz had in *her* possession. And Tucker wasn't on their radar after getting kicked out of Krappa," using Smith's nickname for the fraternity.

"What I truly believe is it has to be someone from Kats. Denny or Charlotte Daniels, Madison, Ethan, or Grace. Hell, almost anyone from that rathole," Smith confesses.

"Big question again, why?"

"We know…err suspect Denny beat and stole Tucker's Mustang and Walker was next. He's not a nice guy. We have to find out if he got Squirrel's sports collection. Or maybe Squirrel and he got into in over drugs…or Squirrel did something to one of the girls or Charlotte. And of course, there's Eastman. We know he was in love with Liz! With her husband out of the way…well, who knows?"

"How the hell would I know all that. More to the point, how the hell do you know that and why haven't you ever told me any of this crap?"

"If you remember, you weren't always the easiest person to talk to! Harrison and I found Powell's car up in Bentonville and discovered the circumstances surrounding that fiasco."

"*ME*?" referring to Smith's first statement. "Never mind, get your notes, I want to know everything you have!"

"I'm trying to tell you," defensively. "What about Madison?" back to Kats employees, "She would do anything for Ethan. I think there's more to that story. And Liz and Grace Udal never got along. The whole place is a powder keg."

"Anything else?"

"As a matter of fact, Eugene Mckinize is a person of interest."

Disgust oozes from Overstreet's face, "AND who is that?"

"I'll grab a couple of coffees. Why don't you update the board?"

Smith meanders around the halls talking to all he sees. He steps into the washroom and takes a leak. Finally, he thinks Overstreet has had enough time to cool off and grabs two mugs full and back to the detective room. His partner hasn't moved; the board hasn't changed.

"All right, *James Bond,* twenty questions is over. Start at the beginning!"

"Let's discuss Mckinize first." Smith relates his story meeting the guy and having dinner and the following day trailing him north.

"Some traveling salesman passes through town and now *he's* our murderer, unbelievable!"

"Yeh…I never thought twice about it until Liz mentioned an Englishman. McKenzie is English and I mean straight from London! My run-in with the salesman was a few days before Walker's assassination. He could have been casing the place and returned later."

"And the motive is?"

"Don't know. I just don't believe in coincidences."

"Well…maybe we looking at this all wrong…what if Liz was the target?" Overstreet grasping.

"What did she ever do?"

"Your Sherlock Holmes, you tell me!" after a moment of silence, "Maybe we should ask, who did she do?"

Smith finally pulls out his notes and starts at the beginning. This goes on for two hours.

Overstreet offers numerous theories; Smith keeps to what he knows. Neither concedes one iota. Finally, at an impasse, Smith thinks it's more likely something to do with drugs. "I'll look for disgruntled clients; someone Squirrel cheated."

"I'll review everything we have on Kats."

Overstreet and Smith silently concede to work as a team.

Chapter 90

"Hi, Pumpkin." Alex and Jake are meeting for lunch after the morning episode in the coroner's parking lot.

"It's a long way to Halloween. Are you all right, Dear?"

Alex offers a small giggle, "Halloween has nothing to do with a term of endearment. I'm fine. Just a minute of silly guilt."

There's no doubt in Smith's mind that Alex's story is going to carve up Warden Marks from a pumpkin into a jack-o-lantern.

"I guess you're closing out the Walker case today?"

"Ahh…not exactly."

"Show and tell!"

"It's just a hunch. You'll be the first to know," he fakes counting his fingers, "well, the tenth for sure."

Laughing, Alex whisper's, "I love you, Jake Smith."

Looking around the room, "Me too."

After an hour with her boyfriend, Reporter Dench is deep into her articles. Elizabeth Walker's death is finished and she's onto slicing up Marks."

Smith's thoughts were right on. She writes a scathing story of the jail's lackadaisical oversight and failure of Marks' abilities. It includes Marks trying to shift all the blame onto Sergeant Price's incompetence.

The last paragraph, "*Warden Warren Marks' unfit capacity as the person in charge of other human being's lives should result in his firing. I for one, as a citizen of Washington County, have already written Sheriff Johnson in regards to this matter and suggest every citizen do the same. If Mr. Marks was a man of greater stature, undoubtedly, he would resign on his own immediately!*"

Alexis reads and rewrites her story on Warden Marks all afternoon. Each time her anger thermometer rises until off the scale. The story gets more and more scathing until the last redo. When she has gratified it is finally right, Alex turns it into her editor and phones Jake. It's after six and she's hoping he's free for the evening.

Chapter 91

Late Friday afternoon Overstreet and Smith sit at their desks silently discouraged. They reinterviewed everyone ever connected to Kenneth and Elizabeth Walker. No one remembers anything different or willing to disclose new information on Ken's murder.

"What now?" asks Overstreet at a loss on their next move.

"We have to be missing something," responds Smith.

"I think it's time to go public. Someone knows what happened," sadly hinting at defeat.

"What exactly are you suggesting, Don?"

"Let's leak some information to your girlfriend. She can write a story and solicit the public's help. Maybe a witness will come forward."

"Which facts should we let out?"

"So far everything points at Liz. Let's stir the pot. We don't have to list all our suspects by name, but why don't we say Liz appears to be a victim too and we looking at two people with strong motives and an arrest is imminent. Something along the line of, if anyone has information on the drug trade in town related to a popular strip club and their connection to certain students at the University of Arkansas please call your local police department," Overstreet suggests. "I don't know the wording but you get the idea."

Rationalizing it over, "Yeah, maybe. Alex will know what to say and how."

"It's getting late, take the weekend and put some thought into it. Monday morning, if we can't come up with a better plan of action, we'll make a decision," Overstreet proposes.

"My mind is numb. I think you're right, a couple of days out of here it is the ticket."

Both men shuffle around their desks at various papers and stare at the corkboard. Before Overstreet eventually stands, "I'm going home and pray for a miracle. See you Monday, Buddy."

Smith spends another futile hour thinking and writing possibilities. He looks at the wall clock glaring six-fifty. Jake rummages through his desk and finds an empty bottle of aspirin, "Crap!" he throws it at his trash can. Missing, he doesn't bother to pick it. "That's why we have a janitor," he rationalizes out loud.

Jake picks up the phone and calls Alex, "Hi honey, I'm just getting out of here. I need to make a stop at the drug store and head home."

"Are you alright?"

"Just a little headache. Can I bow out tonight?"

"Of course, Dear. Would you like me to come over and make you something to eat?"

"No need. I just have to take my mind of this case, but you always welcome."

"I can guarantee to get your mind free! I certainly don't have to stay long."

"Sounds wonderful. I'll tell you what, I'll stop at the QuicMart and pick up some aspirin and Chinese next door and meet you at my place."

"You're on."

"I love you!"

"I love you too, Jake. See you soon."

Shortly they're sitting at Smith's kitchen table sharing Kung Po chicken and egg rolls. Alex refrains from asking about his work. Finishing, Jake asks her if she would like to watch a movie. At the market, he picked up *Butch Cassidy and The Sundance Kid.* Jake pops in the VCR tape and they snuggle on the couch through the show. Alex enjoys the movie. Jake sleeps through most of it.

The next morning Alexis wakes early. She lays watching the sun come up through the window, after which she decides to make coffee. As soon as her lover wakes she'll prepare him a special breakfast. She rolls over to give him a gentle kiss before raising. The bed's empty. She glances at the bathroom. The doors open and the light's on.

Alex gets up and slides on one of Jake's t-shirts. He's not in the bathroom and she flicks off the lights and heads to the kitchen. Coffee is already made. She pours herself a cup and wanders the house. Jake's nowhere to be found. The back porch is empty. She glances around and sees a puff of smoke billow over the small rise. Alexis walks down the path to the lake's edge

The reporter stands quietly behind him watching as he stares over the water smoking and drinking from his favorite mug. After many content minutes, she sits beside him, "Good morning, Honey!"

He snaps his head around, "Oh Alex, you startled me."

"Sorry, I should have said something."

"It's alright," he leans over and kisses her cheek. "How did you sleep?"

"Like a cow in tall grass."

Jake laughs, "Me too."

Withdrawn in their thoughts they watch small ripples on the still lake for the longest time.

Jake breaks the silence, "Alex, can we talk?"

"Always," She answers, waiting to hear what's on his mind.

"Don and I are at an impasse on the Walker case. I need your advice." For the next three hours, Jake walks Alex through everything he knows about the murder. He leaves nothing out, not the facts, not the theories, and certainly not the long list of suspects and motives.

Alexis absorbs every word. "Jake, I had no idea this was so complicated. I thought Liz did it and it was over."

"That's the consensus but certainly not the case. Any thoughts?"

It'll take me time to process everything you said." After a few moments, "I'll make you brunch and we can revisit this later."

"Sounds good. I didn't mean to burden you with my troubles."

"I like being involved in your life, Jake. I love you!"

They spend the rest of the day enjoying each other's company. Walking hand in hand along the lakeshore, driving into Springdale to pick up steaks for an evening BBQ and sharing a little afternoon delight. The Walker case is never brought up. Smith actually didn't think about it until later that evening after Alex retired.

The next morning it is Alex's turn to be up before dawn. Jake sleeps late. When he finally rolls out, Jake finds her at the kitchen table with a full legal pad of notes and still writing.

Jake grabs a cup of Java and sits watching her. Alex, deep in her task, never acknowledges his presence and keeps working.

A half-hour later, Jake goes to the back porch for a smoke. Another half hour and Alex joins him. He sits and waits for her to speak first.

Eventually, he can't stand it, "What do you think?"

"I don't know, Jake."

It isn't what he expects. Stillness encompasses them again.

Smith stands, "Would you like another cup. I'm going in to make a pot."

Alex doesn't hear him and continues in thought. He leaves her alone and goes to make the coffee.

The pot finishes percolating and he grabs two clean mugs from the cabinet just as Alex enters and takes a seat at the table. Jake joins her.

"Honey. here's what I think," she rips all her pages from the pad and proceeds to lay them across the table arranging in different stacks. Alex seizes one pile and moves it in front of her. She picks up her pen and goes through the papers circling different items. The pages with circles are placed in a new pile. When she finishes, she places the unmarked pile aside and moves the marked pile directly in front of her. Again she proceeds through arranging the papers in some kind of order.

Alex looks into Jake's eyes before starting. "First, you guys compiled a mountain of information. From what I see, Ethan appears guilty, but as I kept digging, he really doesn't have a known reason. There's not any collaborating evidence on any, one suspect." Pausing, "What if the Powell Tucker and Kenneth Walker's murders are connected? I mean more than a supplier-user connection."

"We thought that too, but Tucker was killed first and couldn't have done Walker. Powell didn't have any friends to speak of except his roommate."

"Friends no, family yes!"

"You think his parents murdered Squirrel? Or his sister or uncle?"

"His sister has a family and lives down in Austin…not too much motivation. Aunt and Uncle? Don't see a motive. Now his parents…that's a different story."

"I don't think Judith is up to it. I met her for breakfast. She's remorseful, not revengeful. And Newton Tucker didn't even care enough to even show up at the funeral."

"Which could be a cover. I like the English fellow as the triggerman. The father could be the employer."

"Talk about too much to lose." Smith states.

"In my experience, people don't generally consider consequences when committing a crime, only outcome of the actual event."

"Now you're sounding like a cop," enjoying himself.

"Jake, police, and reporters have a lot in common. We both research and investigate people and facts. You write reports, I write Pulitzer Prize-winning articles."

"You have a Pulitzer?" shocked at the revelation.

"Not yet, but I certainly working on it!"

After five minutes of hysterical laughter, Alex continues, "In a nutshell, you have two avenues of pursuit, Ethan Eastman, and

Newton Tucker. Ethan has the opportunity but not a real motive. Tucker has both!"

Smith reflects in silence, before answering, "You're a sharp gal. I'm going to look into it!"

"Gal!"

Chapter 92

Monday morning Newton Tucker's involvement is ensounched in Smith's mind. He places a call to Maggie's son Adam Harvey in Little Rock. Adam is an Assistant State Attorney. Not getting past the truculent secretary, he's forced to leave a message.

He tells his partner he's going to lunch. In reality, he's going looking for Randal Brown. That man will know any street rumblings. First, stop the College Club. It's where Knight and he arrested Clarke receiving the protection payoff from Brown.

He enters the bar. Looking around, Brown's not present. Smith approaches a table of students scarfing down tacos and beer. A young man with a large golden-yellow peace sign on his chest looks him over. He asks through a mouthful of ground beef and cheese with red sauce dripping from his lips, "What do you want?'

"How's the food here?" Smith didn't have to ask the rhetorical question.

"Not bad," hardly understandable. The guy wipes his mouth with a well used stained napkin and chugs a little beer.

"That's better," observes the detective. "Have you seen Randal Brown?"

The kid shoves in the last half a taco. Cheeks puffed out like a blowfish he shakes his head.

"Anyone," scanning the remaining of students.

"We don't even know who he is!" a defensive girl.

"Is that a required freshman class!"

"What do you mean, Officer?"

"Know Nothing101."

"Look, Buddy, go hassle a criminal!" the kid wearing a two-spread fingered fist on his tye-dye.

291

"I'd like that. Just tell me where to find him!"

Another girl, "Did you try the Waffle House?"

"It's hard to vision Brown enjoying Waffle House ambiance."

"He likes waffles and fried chicken."

Smith thinks better of asking how she knows, "Thanks, I'll give it a try."

Amazed that she was right, Smith finds Brown, sitting behind two plates of waffles and a basket of fried chicken.

He takes a seat without waiting for the invite.

"Po po man, wassup, Homie?" all blinged out and grinning.

"Back at you Brown," Smith responds, not even close to fluent in Ebonics or Southern dialect for that matter.

"I'm game for hook-up. I be at College Club later. It's da bomb, fo sho. Stop by, I've a little skrilla for ya."

"All I want from you is an alibi!"

"Yous not still upsets ov'r that li'l misunderstandin'?"

"Shooting me is not a misunderstanding!"

"Wees up after New Year's poppin. Man, you da shit that night."

"Where were you the night of April ninth?" Smith trying to force the conversation back on track.

"Apra ninth? Hows I knows?"

"You better. That was the night your little rodent was murdered."

"Rodant? Ohs yous means Squirrely?" He pulls out wads of paper from three pockets and starts shuffling through them. "Ahs, here theys are."

He hands Smith a dozen torn tickets subs. Jake shuffles through them. They are from Baldknobbers' Theater in Missouri for the nights of Friday, April ninth, and Saturday, April tenth. "You're telling me you were in Branson?"

"Iss like countys music. Took da fellas."

"You don't have to be in town to kill someone."

Laughing hysterically, "Iss not a violents man, Mister Smith."

"You think I, of all people, believe that?"

292

"Heys, I takes care of those gangsta fools. Theys never bes backs here."

"You just keep stubs handy for alibis?"

"Iss haven't sees my taxes lady. She makes me keep alls receipts," proudly smiling like he's a tax paying citizen.

"What's the word on the street regarding Walker's murder?"

"No words. Everyone's tighter than a fugly ho, fo sho."

"Like you said you owe me big time, Friend. Now I'm collecting. Tell me about Liz Walker and Powell Tucker!"

"Some fool pops that scrub and wallin Boo does herself.

"Tell me something I don't know!"

After figuring it doesn't matter now with Liz gone, "Shes buy smack." Quickly adding, "It's not my gig, but Iss hook her up."

"You sold her H?"

"I just tolds ya that."

"How much?"

"Un fitty Benjamins."

"Fifty hundred…five thousand dollars worth?"

"No! un fitty…uno cinco."

"Fifteen! How many ounces?"

Laughing, "Hunred gram."

"Crap, a hundred grams. Was she dealing?"

"No, figures she's fiending, though not her flava. Afters reading the papers, I knows shes flip out with that Tucker dude."

"Let's be clear! You're saying you sold Elizabeth Walker one hundred grams of heroin and she and Powell Tucker shared it?"

"Thas not whats I say." Thinking it over, "True dat, fo sho."

"Did Liz and Tucker have a thing going on?"

Brown's putting it together, but only voices, "Words is hes bin runnin da mouth about thems sharing pussy, only she not game."

"You're saying Powell Tucker raped Elizabeth Walker?" Smith realizes to himself, "That's the connection we were looking for."

"Makes sense, uh Homie? Tucker dude dos her and hers dos him."

"Then who killed Ken Walker?"

"Hows I knowns?"

"Why do you think someone would want to kill him?"

"Don'ts know."

"What about Ethan Eastman?"

"Maybes a years ago, befores he and dats Madson cracker hooks up."

"Ethan and Madison?"

"Dat whats I says. Words theys havin a baby and weddin'."

"Thanks, Brown, We're almost even!"

"Ya stops tis afternoon an' have a forty an' wees talk biz."

Smith heads for the door. He yells back, "Next time we chat, drop the phony speech!"

"Sure thing, Detective Smith," Brown whispers to himself.

Smith enters the office foyer and the duty officer hands him a folded message. He missed Adam's call.

At his desk, he picks up the phone and dials, "Detective Smith returning Mr. Harvey's call. He's put on hold and a few minutes later Attorney Adam Harvey picks up.

"Officer Smith, what can I do for you?" not knowing Jake has been promoted.

"A couple of questions about Newton Tucker."

"That's was extremely offensive the way you broke off with my Mother!"

"I'm sorry, Adam. It's just that I felt it was unfair uh…you know underachieving I guess. She's such a great woman, she deserves more than I have to offer." Smith satisfied he's out of the limelight and ready to get down to business.

Unfortunately not. "Jake, love isn't about money or position. She never *judged* you, but accepted you unconditionally, good and bad, rich or poor! You were the first man she ever invited home since my father's death. My mother took a chance on you and you broke her heart!"

"Crap, what now?" he thinks fast. "Adam it really wasn't about money…well partly, but the reason…is…" he blurts out, "I'm not a religious man. I couldn't justify lying to her about God." That should do it.

No! Adam's persists. "Jake, God isn't going to church every Sunday and studying the Bible. God is in the heart and soul of good people. It's how you live your life and how you treat your brothers. Don't you think you qualify?" Maggie taught her children well. Jake recognizes the trial close and needs to get off subject before the sale's pitch continues.

"I'll call Maggie and talk to her. Thanks for your help Adam." Changing the subject, "Listen about Tucker, I'm investigating his son's death."

"That was sad, though not unpredictable from what I understand."

"I'm also working on another case, Kenneth Walker's murder. He was Powell's dealer."

"Is that the guy I read about in the paper? Wasn't his wife arrested and then committed suicide? Isn't the case closed?"

"Almost. Do you know how Newton and his son got along?"

"Only what I read." Thinking back, "Oh and one item that never made the papers. Last Christmas, you know when you hurt my mom, Powell stole a very expensive necklace from *his* mother. It was recovered at a pawn shop and Newton refused to press charges. I assume he didn't want the publicity."

"How do you know?" overlooking the jab and thinking Judith's secret is really common knowledge in the right circles.

"I'm friends with Tony Nolan. He was the investigating detective."

"I'll give him a call. It was good talking with you, Adam. I'll try and get a hold of Maggie."

295

"Smith, don't hurt her again!" Adam warns.

Chapter 93

Jake tells Don he's sure Liz murdered Powell from what he learned and that leaves Tucker murdering Walker. Smith's investigation of Newton Tucker strains every cognitive ability he possesses.

First, he calls Tony Nolan at the Little Rock PD. Nolan is forthcoming and tells Smith the story as he knows it. Jake asks him about Newton's attitude towards his son and is told of the father's disgust and visible disappointment.

Jake makes a note, "Father and son strained relationship," and added it along with other updates to the cork board. He stands to stare at the board for a long time.

"What are you thinking?" Overstreet questions Smith.

"We have got to find who Newton knows and trusts!"

"Hell, he's the Lieutenant Governor! He knows everybody!"

"Yeah, that's a problem." Minutes later, "We need his phone records."

"What's going on, Jake?"

No response from Smith. He goes to the break room and returns with two foam cups of coffee. Setting one in front of Overstreet he sits at his desk. Picking up the phone Smith calls his girlfriend at the Times. He asks Alex if she has any friends at AT&T.

"Jake, I've told you, I know everyone! What do you need?"

"Newton Tucker's phone records for the last six months."

"Whoo, that's a tall order! I'm guessing our talk is on the table now?" not wanting prying ears to understand what's happening.

"Yes! Can you get them?"

"I'll see what I can do. It might take a while."

"How long?"

"A couple of days…maybe longer."

"Just let me know. Thanks, Honey, I'll see you tonight."

Dench knows it's going to be a huge exclusive. She grabs the phone and calls a telephone company supervisor she's acquainted with from church. She's told that request isn't possible. She racks her brain for someone else. She picks up the receiver and calls a lifelong girlfriend.

"Hey Rhonda, do you remember that guy at our twentieth reunion we're talking with. I think he was a lineman for the phone company?"

"Garrison Gregory?"

"Yeah, that might be it. You wouldn't happen to know his number?"

"No, he married Sue Billings, but I heard they divorced."

"Great. I have her's, I'll give her a jingle."

She pulls out her address book and dials Sue.

There's no answer and Alex calls Rhonda back to see where Sue works. She looks up the Boutique Basket in the Yellow Pages and gets ahold of Sue. The woman tells her that the bum is working on a pole just down the street from her shop.

Alex rushes over. She parks across the street from the easily recognizable phone truck and walks to the bottom of the pole. A man is hanging by a Staked D lineman's belt thirty feet up the stanchion.

She yells, "Hello up there!"

"The surprised man looks down, "Well hello yourself. I'll be down in a minute."

The lineman hurries to finish and descends the pole.

Sporting a broad smile at the attractive woman while causally tensing his biceps, "What can I do for you, Gorgeous?"

That's the right question, only this guy isn't who Alex remembers, "Are you, Garrison?"

"I'll change my name?" smirking.

"I really need to talk to Garrison!"

"There is nothing he can do that I can't do better, Darlin'!" puffing out his chest.

"I'm sure that's true?" returning the flirt.

"Now we're talking. I'm off at four, Darlin'." visibly excited.

"Tell you what, let me know how to find Garrison and I'll meet you at Lou's at four."

"Garrison just left. He's headed over to Mountain House to fix their system."

"Thanks. Four at Lou's!"

At the hotel, Alex tells the desk clerk that she's with the phone company and checking on their man working there. She directed to the basement phone room.

Dench finds a man working on the panel and confirms it is who's she is seeking. They tease back and forth for a few minutes before she asks a favor.

"Garrison, I'm told you're the man that can work miracles?"

"I'm not God, but for you, I can get awful close!" chuckling at his joke.

Alex joins him giggling, "I need Powell Tuckers last six month's phone records!" getting to the mission.

"Is he cheating on you too!" smirking uncontrollably.

Dench contemplates her answer, "That's exactly what I what to know."

"It's doable at a price!"

"How much!"

"Money isn't the currency, Darlin'!"

Sue was right about this bum! "If you can get me the info, I'm sure we can work out payment."

"Meet me at Denny's in two days. Say six o'clock."

"Until then, Handsome."

Alex never asked the first lineman's name. He was only a backup plan anyway. And now with Gregory's commitment, she's a no-show at Lou's.

Chapter 94

Friday evening two days later Alex sits in Denny's highway restaurant waiting for her date. She assumes Garrison picked this spot because he's cheap. When she saw that the restaurant sits on the corner of a hotel parking lot, Alex knows the real reason.

She arrives a half hour early and picks a booth close to the front door which has constant foot traffic. Alexis Dench sips sweet tea while she waits.

She notices him walking across the lot. He cleans up well. Garrison's wearing a light cream shirt under his blazer. The two top buttons are undone showing a tuft of chest hair.

He enters and stands in front of Alex glancing around the place. "There's an empty booth near the back that looks more comfortable."

"I'm fine here and we have the best waitress in the house," trying to dissuade him.

He doesn't appear pleased as he sits. They kid around with small teasing after ordering. Eventually, Alex asks if he got the items. He repudiates her question with, "Don't you trust me, Honey?" and continues joking on a different subject.

Alex demands, "Do you or don't you have the information!"

"Calm down, I have it!" and he pulls a stack of papers from his inside coat pocket.

"I'll take those!" a man appears at tableside.

"Who the hell are you?"

"Detective Jake Smith, Mr. Gregory," displaying his badge.

"YOU BITCH!" Garrison bolts from the establishment.

Jake sits down in the vacant spot.

"I hope you like cheeseburgers," Alex laughs as the waitress sets down two meals.

Chapter 95

"We're in the chips, partner," Smith to Overstreet the morning after the Denny's sting.

"What do you have?"

"Newton's phone records. I tried for six but only got four months," setting down a stack of papers.

"How'd you manage that?"

"Don't ask," smirking like a kid with a pocketful of jellybeans.

Smith looks the lists over, "Jeez, this guy talks a lot!" He roughly splits the stack in half, handing Overstreet a share. "We'll be at this a couple of days! You start at the bottom and I'll start at the top."

"You know this time could be spent on the streets collecting real evidence." Overstreet is second-guessing their decision on Tucker.

They each start making call after call. "Good morning, is this the Gray residence?" is the standard opening.

Some people answer, "No, you have reached the Jones residence." or whomever. Most just hang up. The detectives write down every name they receive.

Not dissuaded by hang-ups, they keep dialing. The dialog continues with the ones that answer. "I'm calling on behalf of Newton Tucker and doing a short survey. If you can help me with four quick questions?" Those that stay on the line are barraged with more than four. The scam starts out with a couple of job performance inquiries then proceeds with what they expect from his office and other related questions. In the mix are numerous personal and family information requests. Very few last the whole interrogation.

Starting with the January record, Smith dials William Masse's private line. The phone picks up immediately and Smith starts his spiel.

Halfway through the first sentence the phone slams down. Jake just sits quietly still holding the handset.

"What's wrong?" Overstreet questions.

"There was a man talking in the background. I think it's Newton Tucker."

"Give me the number!" Overstreet calls back. "Good morning, I need to talk with Newt."

"He just stepped out. I'm Bill Masse, his Chief of Staff. You can tell me!"

"It's personal. I'll wait a few minutes and try his number again. Thanks."

Overstreet doesn't hang up. He sits quietly.

Inconceivable, "Is this Operation Waterfall?"

"I can't divulge. I'll try his line again," once more sitting silently.

"CLICK." Masse hangs up.

Overstreet looks white-faced at Smith, "Operation Waterfall!"

"What's that?"

"Don't have a clue. We need to find out!"

They return to calling. The next one is a private investigation firm. Smith hangs up without a word. He tries the next number, "English Investigations, Art of Secrecy." Another written note.

"Here's a strange one. A ten-second incoming call from a gas station down the street from the Tucker resident at midnight." Overstreet voices. Tucker's address listed on top of each invoice.

"How do you know?"

"Some girl, a teenager I think, answered and told me it was a pay phone at an Atlantic Richfield station and its location."

Looking at the wall clock, "We need a break. Let's get some lunch?" Smith suggests.

303

They go to the close at hand deli for a couple of sandwiches. At a sidewalk table, "So what's your take?"

Smith answers, "Not sure. What's Newton calling PIs for?"

"Operation Waterfall could be anything…a cheating wife or girlfriend. Even digging up dirt on another politician."

"I don't think the latter, Masse would handle that. It has to be closer to home!"

"Next step?"

"Unsure."

Each is quiet and thinking during the remainder of lunch. Walking back, Smith voices, "I'm calling back both the PIs."

The first call is answered by the same woman as his previous.

"Operation Waterfall," is all Smith states.

"Excuse me, Sir?"

"Operation Waterfall," he repeats.

"I'm sorry, Sir, I don't know what you're talking about."

"Is your boss available?"

"He's still at lunch."

"Any other investigators around?"

"Not at this time," she states. CLICK, the line goes dead.

"Couldn't get past the gatekeeper?" Overstreet observes.

"I'll try them later. Maybe I can get someone who knows more."

Smith dials the next company, "English Investigations, Art of Secrecy."

"Operation Waterfall."

"Who is this?"

"A friend of the family," trying to bait the answerer.

"What family would that be?"

"Newton Tucker's."

Silent on the other end, ultimately, "Is this Masse?"

"Yes, call me William."

"Wrong answer!" The line goes dead.

"BINGO!" Smith yells gleefully.

Chapter 96

Two days later, Smith and Overstreet are no further along on Tucker's investigation. They've called and recalled every number on Newton's records. Everyone has clammed up tighter than a Steelwater gun safe.

"We need to take a trip," Smith suggests to Overstreet.

"Little Rock?"

"The vacation spot of the world!" tilting his head sarcastically.

"I think you're right. I'll clear it with McGill and we'll leave this afternoon."

After Overstreet and his lieutenant concur, "Smith, we're clear to go!"

"I'll head home and pack an overnight bag."

"Me too. Meet you in the parking lot in two hours."

Looking at the wall clock, "Make it noon." Smith has to drive east of Springdale and back.

Once home, Smith makes an instant coffee and toast with peanut butter and honey. After the quick lunch, he packs and phones his girlfriend. Alex is out of the office. The phone answerer doesn't know where she went or when coming back. Smith leaves a message with the girl that he'll be out of town for a couple of days.

By three-thirty the same afternoon, the pair checked into the downtown Sam Peck Hotel in the Arkansas capital. It's a hundred-year-old building that was modernized during the sixties urban renewal project.

In their shared two-bedroom, Overstreet carefully places some folded clothes into a dresser drawer and hangs a couple of shirts and coats in the closet.

Smith throws his bag of wrinkled-wear on the floor. The only blazer he brought is on his back. He sits on the bed and lights up a cigarette, thinking, "It would be nice to have a wife for folding and packing."

"Jake, please smoke on the balcony." Overstreet replicating a light cough.

"Don, let's find English Investigations first?" taking another puff.

Overstreet pulls the phone book from the desk drawer and looks up English Investigations. "Only a number." He calls and receives a message recorder. Don next dials information and told they don't have a listed address.

"Give me the phone, I'll call Nolan!" Smith strides over. Tony Nolan tells him he's never heard of the agency.

"What now?" asks his partner.

Pondering over another smoke, "Let's look up his business license at the Development and Planning Department."

Overstreet finds the address and pulls out the city map he got when he filled up the car. "It's over on Markham Street. Too far to walk."

After driving over, the detectives find the information they need from public records. They thank the clerk for his help and leave.

In ten minutes, they sit in their vehicle staring at an old smaller two-story manufacturing building across Markham Street, two miles from office they just left.

"You sure this is the address, Jake? It looks abandon!" unable to read the faded hand-painted sign spread across the wooden slats over the main doors.

Smith double checks his scribbled note. "Maybe it's 913, we're at 713." They drive two blocks to a vacate lot. The pair walks around looking at adjacent buildings, before returning the original location. They restudy the building. Looking at each other Jake shrugs, "Let's give it a shot," and gets out of the car. Don follows.

On the other side of the side of the street, they walk in opposite directions around the structure checking doors and trying to peer through boarded up windows. Meeting at a roll-up door on a ground level cement loading dock, "This is a bust! Let's get out of here!" Smith exclaims.

"Not so fast!" Overstreet produces a small black kit from his inside coat pocket. Removing a couple odd shaped stainless steel tools, he picks the padlock. "Ready?"

"You amaze me. What, were you a burglar in your former life?" more a snide remark than a question.

Overstreet just smiles and pushes the heavy door up a few feet. They duck under and enter a dark warehouse. Both pull flashlights from their pockets. The room is littered with trash and broken rusted shelving. Old destroyed tables sit around the eastern portion of the warehouse. They stay close to one another maneuvering their way past piles of debris to the open area at the other end. The floor is heavily stained from where numerous large oil-leaking machines once stood.

A light is leaking from below a closed door. The men glance at each other and move to the access barrier. There is a doorknob that turns, but the door doesn't budge. Unknown to them a thick flat steel bar on the other side is slid into wall-mounted end brackets preventing entry.

Smith bangs on the door many times. Not receiving a response, "What now?"

Overstreet walks away, his beam searching the floor while he kicks trash to the side. Close to their starting point, "Ahh, here we go." He finds an oily old crowbar under a splintering ancient plywood shelf.

Detective Smith follows him outside, where they roll down the door and relock it. With Smith still on his heels, Overstreet stops at a boarded window just before a large second roll-up door near the other corner of the building. This door has combination locks on both ends.

The panes of the window are broken the same as the rest around the structure. Don drags a rickety old saw horse from beside a mound of rotting wood and positions it under the window. He climbs on it using the wall as a steady with the wooden frame shaking uncontrollably. "Hand me the crowbar."

Overstreet knocks out a few remaining slivers, of what appears to be white painted glass, and shoves the crowbar between the inside plywood cover and the pane holding structure. In the end, with Smith trying to steady the swaying menace while his partner pushes and pulls on the steel bar with everything he has, the wood slowly separates from the window frame.

Overstreet shines his light inside, "This is it!"

"What's in there?" Smith questions.

A van, a sedan, and an old sports car."

"So he's home?"

"Doesn't appear to be. There's an empty spot right behind the door."

"Four vehicles...I should be a PI." Smith with a small laugh.

"We can't squeeze in without breaking out the grill and mullion. He'll know someone was here."

"Mullion. How many lives have you had?"

"Common knowledge when you work on your own place." As Overstreet jumps off. The sawhorse jeers quickly to the right and his feet hit the concrete at an odd angle. Unable to keep balance he ends up colliding with the ground, flat on his side.

Smith, overlooks the accident and shakily mounts the frame. "Let me take a look-see at that sports car!" the car enthusiast states.

"Jeez, looks like a fifty-five MG TD" First a low creak before a loud crack and the frame collapses. Smith is left dangling by his elbows from the bottom of the window ledge. He cranes his head back and turns it slightly eyeing Overstreet, who is still trying to brush dirt from his trousers, "Can you move the pile of wood over a bit?" after which Jakes releases and lands next to his partner.

Both men look up at the opening. "He's going to know we were here." Overstreet comments.

"Maybe it'll be dark and he won't notice." Both men laugh at the silly notion.

On the street, around the building corner, a Cadillac drives slowly past. "Did you see the way that guy looked at us?" Smith pulls off his dark aviator sunglasses and wipes off the dirt.

"Hard to miss," Overstreet responds. "After a bite to eat, we'll come back!"

By six-thirty, the detectives are again walking around the building. It's completely dark. Not a seep of light anywhere. Smith stops to tie his shoe and Overstreet arrives at their vehicle alone.

A man steps from the shadows, "Can I help you?"

Smith comes around the corner of the building and recognizes McKenzie. He immediately ducks back.

"Mr. English?" Overstreet questions.

"Sorry, can not help you there."

"I want to hire you. My wife is acting funny and I want her followed."

"Sorry, I only do insurance investigations," a rare slip up acknowledging his profession.

"That's not what my friend told me," trying to test the man.

Art looks suspiciously around for the stranger's partner, "Who would that be?"

"Newton Tucker," the detective takes a chance.

"I do not know anyone by that name." Not missing a beat. "If you'll excuse me."

"Operation Waterfall!" trying again.

"Still don't know him," shaking his head coupled with a mystified raised eyebrow look and hand jester. Arthur English walks off across the street and away from his building.

309

Chapter 97

The next morning Overstreet and Smith head to the capitol. On the drive over they discuss whether to see Newton Tucker or William Masse first.

Overstreet want's to start at the top, while Smith's thinks Masse first so they hopefully have something more concrete to discuss with the Lieutenant Governor. Smith's logic wins out.

Each shows a badge to Masse's secretary saying that it's imperative they speak to the Chief of Staff. Twenty-nine minutes later they're led into his office. Undoubtedly he alerted his boss of their presence.

Without standing, "Gentlemen, I only have five minutes. Can you make this quick?" Masse takes charge.

Overstreet starts as lead, " Mr. Masse, thank you for seeing us. We looking at Arthur English and have a couple of quick questions."

"Who's that?"

"He owns a private investigation firm and one of his clients, up in Fayetteville, contacted us. The client claims Mr. English bilked him out of a lot of money."

"How so?" Masse is hooked.

"I can't go into details, but it's a kind of a Ponzi scheme."

"I don't know any English. Sorry I couldn't help you." He stands, Overstreet and Smith remain in their seats.

Smith's turn, "He calls the scheme Operation Waterfall!"

Masse goes white and sits back down, "Operation Waterfall?"

"You've obviously heard of it. I hope you didn't fall for his trap?" Smith again.

"No. No…I can't say I ever heard of that term," thinking his best buddy got scammed.

"Glad to hear that. I'm afraid your boss wasn't so lucky!" Overstreet adds.

"Newt's a sharp guy. I can't imagine he's involved."

"Involved?" back to Smith. "We were thinking he might have been taken!"

"Tha…that's what I meant."

"So just to be clear, you're not privy to Mr. English or any schemes?"

"No!" But he then adds, "Come to think of it we used a couple of investigators during the last campaign. I wasn't personally included, my assistant took care of it. I think English could have been one of the firms used."

"What's his name?" Smith.

"Janice Jackman. Unfortunately, she's moved on. Phoenix, I believe."

"You must have files," Overstreet teams up.

"No…no not on those types of opera…err, background checks…err, it's common practice to shred everything after a campaign," Masse bumbles along.

"Mr. Masse, nobody destroys information files on anyone. We need to see them now!" Smith turns up the heat.

"I'll have my secretary see if she can locate anything, but I sincerely don't believe they're still around," sounding more like a politician. "Call me this afternoon and I'll let you know if she finds anything."

"Should we use…" and Overstreet rattles off Masse's private number.

Not showing surprise, "You're the guys that called yesterday! Had that bogus survey story."

"One and the same." Smith's on a roll.

"What are you guy really investigating?"

"Newton Tucker's involvement in killing the drug dealer that murdered his son," Smith plays his ace.

Masse rubs his forehead for the longest time trying to put his head around what Detective Smith just laid on him. Looking up, "Powell was murdered? I thought it was a drug overdose."

"Intentionally administered by someone else!" Overstreet plays another ace.

"Shit! Newt never told me that!"

"You're in jeopardy of taking the fall for your good buddy. At the very least conspiracy after the fact. Have you ever spent time in jail, William?" hinting at his participation.

"No! I haven't done anything wrong or have any knowledge of a crime…before or after the fact!"

"You know Arthur English and talked with him on Tucker's behalf," Overstreet fishes.

"No, I haven't. Some man called a couple of times. He didn't identify himself and I didn't ask. All he said was Operation Waterfall and hung up and I told Newt. Nothing more!"

"Tells us about Operation Waterfall!" Smith asks.

"I don't know what it is!" Masse responds.

"And you didn't ask?"

"I did but wasn't told anything. Only to let him know when I receive a message."

"Ok, *Bill*." Overstreet stands. "Keep this conversation to yourself if you want to be divorced from this investigation. Do I make myself clear?"

"Yes, Sir!"

"Good, I hope, for your sake, you mean it!"

Alone with his door closed, Masse reviews their discussion. As habit he writes *PRO* and *CON* on a sheet of paper and below makes a list under each heading. He studies the sheet before picking up the phone, "Newt, get out of your office now!"

Chapter 98

Showing their badges, "Is Mr. Tucker available?"

"Sorry Officers, he's out for the rest of the week." Can someone else assist you?"

"Thank you. We'll check back."

Overstreet and Smith power-walk to their vehicle. They race to English's building hoping to catch an emergency meeting between Tucker and the PI. The street has a spattering of cars. None look new enough to be Tuckers. They pull into the rear yard and block the ground level car door with their vehicle.

Overstreet pounds the door with his fist but doesn't get a response. "I have qualms about them meeting here."

"Let's find out." Smith moves a couple of old wooden crates to the window and climbs up to the loose sheet of plywood they had previously pried open. He pushes it off the two final nails holding it up. It crashes to the floor. "Don, do you have your light?"

"Hold on." Overstreet retrieves his and his partner's flashlights from their car and hands Smith one.

"The van and sedan are here. No Caddy and the MG is gone," shining a beam inside.

Smith pushes away from the window. Overstreet has one door lock open and laying on the ground. He is picking the second.

"Got it!" he discards the security device on the concrete and pushes the door up to the top. Jake turns off his unneeded light and both agents enter.

The room, like the warehouse they were previously in, has one level with twenty-foot high ceilings. Though along the inside length of the outer long wall is a two-story set of office suites with multiple windows, but only one entry door.

Smith follows Overstreet to the office door. It's locked and Don gets to work. Smith looks around the large room finding nothing more than the two vehicles.

Overstreet turns the door handle without opening the door. He slowly twists it back into position and backs up.

"What's wrong, Don."

"The knob made a funny click. I don't like it!"

"They're not here! Let's vamoose!"

"Hold on, I have an idea. There's roll of masking tape in the trunk. Can you get it?"

Smith complies while Overstreet goes to the far wall. He removes the steel bar securing the door and enters the warehouse they had inspected the day before. Smith returns with the tape and doesn't find his partner.

"Don!" He whispers loudly.

Overstreet re-enters carrying a ball of brown packaging twine, and a brick "These should do it. Hand me the tape." He approaches the door. Smith observes as his partner lay the brick on the floor and carefully push it with his foot against the bottom.

"What's that for?"

"Don't want the door accidentally opening before I'm ready." Don sets the twine on the floor and puts his shoulder into the door for extra security. Carefully he turns the knob and tries to tape it in the open position. It takes him a few tries before the knob is secure. "Hand me the string and get behind the van, Jake!"

Jake complies and walks past the sedan and squats behind the van, peeking out.

Don watches him, before nodding and getting on with his task. He makes a slip-knot loop in the twine end and places over the knob slowly, very slowly tightening it around the neck. He checks the brick with his foot. It's snug. Satisfied he leans away, separating his shoulder from the door. Nothing moves. Very gently Overstreet starts unwinding the ball of twine while he backs towards the van.

314

It's more than five minutes before he securely crouches next to Smith. "Ready?"

Smith nods.

Overstreet tugs gently on the line. The brick starts to slide as the door moves outward. Two inches open, BLAM-BLOOM! The van violently rocks!

The thunderous noise and giant fireball rip the door off its hinges. The oak door flies twenty-feet crumpling the front quarter panel of the sedan and splintering into pieces. The detectives start to stand when explosion number two engulfs the inner office in flames. A second later another explosion bigger and louder than the first, occurs upstairs blowing out the walls. It's snowing flaming wood around the room.

Smith and Overstreet ran faster than either man ever ran before and dive out the roll-up onto the concrete driveway, one on each side of their car. Two more blasts disintegrate each inside vehicles. They jump to their feet and are running down the street when the last series of explosions occur around the warehouse. Every building wall is crumbling with flames shooting towards the heavens.

A block away they stop gasping for breath. They barely made it out alive. They turn and look at the violent scene. Their department vehicle has caught fire and the destruction behind, a massive wall of flames. Within minutes sirens are wailing from every direction.

Overstreet turns to Smith, "Let's get out of here!"

"We have nothing to hide."

"Our bodies! It can only help us if English and Tucker think we're dead!"

Chapter 99

Six blocks away Overstreet flags down a cab. They take it across the river to North Little Rock. Smith asks the driver where a cheap hotel is. Minutes later they're dropped off at the Rose Motel in a scattered business-residential mixed area.

Smith waits in a laundromat across the street while Overstreet checks in. Don pays cash for a single for three nights.

Meeting up with Smith, the pair walk three blocks to the closest gas station. Using the outside payphone, Overstreet calls their headquarters. He lays a handkerchief over the receiver and asks to speak to Chief Parson.

"Sorry Sir, I can hardly hear you. Who are you looking for?"

"Chief Parson!" trying a little louder.

"This is Sergeant Williams. I can help you, Sir."

"No, you can't give me the Chief." Pissed and a little too loud. "Overstreet?"

"Crap!" covering the mouthpiece with his hand. "My name is Robert. He knows me. This is personal," again a loud whisper.

"Yes, Sir. I'll see if he's available."

"Chief Parson here."

"Chief, this is Overstreet."

"What's going on, Who's Robert?"

"Nobody needs to know we're alive. There…"

Interrupting, "What do you mean alive. I'm talking to you!"

"I know. Let me explain." He goes on to tell his boss the situation; they're hot on a trail and walked into a trap. The car's gone, the building destroyed. And the rest of the sorted details. He ends with, "Don't believe what you see on the news tonight. This is working for our advantage. Can you send Stevens and Hollis down here with another car, money and clean clothes for Smith and me?"

"What about your family and friends? They shouldn't have the trauma of thinking you guys are dead!"

"I was only thinking of the case. You're right. I'll call my wife and tell her and Smith can tell Alex, but nobody else must know!"

"Better do it quick before the story breaks. I'll get Stevens and Hollis on the road. Where do they find you?"

Meeting arrangements are made. Overstreet calls his wife.

After hanging up, "I thought *mum's* the word?" Smith asks.

"We can't have family thinking we're dead. You need to call Alex. Just stress not to let the word out. It's easy for my wife staying at home, but Alex will have to put on the act of her life!"

Smith makes the call. Alex is rightfully concerned for Jake and his future safety. He assures her it's alright and he can take care of himself.

And she assures him she'll take care of things on her end.

Chapter 100

Overstreet heads back to the Rose Motel after talking with Chief Parson. Smith waits across the street smoking a cigarette. He watches the motel closely. After his smoke, Smith walks to the intersection and down the adjacent street. Just past the corner church, he cuts through an open field and behind the back row of motel rooms. At the corner of the building, Smith peeks around. Not seeing any movement, he walks rapidly to number 120. Overstreet had left the door cracked and Smith glances around one more time before entering.

His partner has pulled the mattress to the floor beside the box springs. "Your choice!" Overstreet, fanning his arm, tells Jake.

"Doesn't matter to me. I'm hitting the shower."

Don is laying on top of the springs lost in thought when Smith emerges. "Figured out a plan?" he asks.

"Just thinking how lucky we were today. If you're finished, I'm jumping in."

Overstreet goes to the bathroom and Smith turns the television set is on with its sound off and lays on the mattress.

When is partner rejoins him, Smith starts, "We need to find where Tucker stays in town and pay him a visit. I'll call Nolan and have him to find the address."

"And what are we going to tell Tucker?"

"Something along the lines that we got to English and he ratted out the operation."

"And if he's heard about the fire and he asks why our car was still at the warehouse if we already had English? The times don't fit."

"We picked Arthur before he escaped and went back to search his office."

"What if English called him after the fact?"

"I figure Tucker talked to English immediately, probably while we were still at the capitol. English rushed over to save his MG and wire the building before splitting. He wouldn't have reason to call Tucker back. It's just the chance we have to take."

"English can't drive two cars! Where's the other one?"

"That bothered me too. His MG is a classic. He obviously wasn't prepared to lose it so he had to hide it…maybe a storage unit or a friend's place. Then he had to get a ride back for the Caddy. After that much time, I doubt he wanted to keep driving. I'm betting we find the Caddy abandoned at the airport."

"Why wouldn't he just get a ride straight to the airport if he's losing the Cadillac anyway?"

"Because he didn't want *anyone* to know he was leaving town."

Thinking hard, "You might have something there. The timeline fits and it explains why both cars are missing."

Smith monitoring the TV jumps up and turns the sound to hearable volume. The flashing "Breaking News" banner turns in to a film of the burning warehouse. A newscaster's voice comes over the air, "This just in; A massive explosion and fire in the nine-hundred block of West Markham Street! The empty building of the defunct LR Manufacturing caught fire earlier this afternoon. Witness say they heard numerous explosions, as many as ten or more as the fire quickly spread and engulfed propane tanks and gas lines. One man stated many vehicles were stored inside. It appears each one contributed to additional explosions."

"A black Ford LTD was burnt to a total loss in the parking area. Little Rock Police Detective Tony Nolan states that the car belonged to the Fayetteville Police department. The two Fayetteville Detectives can't be located and presumed dead inside the structure."

The screen fades to a picture of Overstreet and Smith. "Detective Donald Overstreet and Detective Jake Smith are the missing Fayetteville Officers. If you see either one of these men please notify LRPD immediately." A blinking telephone number appears across the bottom of the screen. "It's possible they were not in the building at the time of the explosion but haven't come forward at this time. The building won't be able to be searched for hours…"

The report and pictures continue as Smith turns down the volume to zero again.

"There you have it, reporters reporting what they don't know! You've got to love them!" Overstreet observes.

"Stevens and Hollis should be here soon. I'll head down to the gas station now," Smith looking at his watch.

The detective is standing next to the outside door to the men's restroom having a coffee when two cars pull in and park. Hollis gets out of one and Stevens the other. Smith walks over, "Gentlemen, it's good to see you."

"Jeez Smith, you look like you're homeless," observing the man's filthy clothes and the ripped out knees of his trousers."

Grinning, "It's been a *bang-up* day."

Looking around, "Where's your partner?"

"He's waiting at the motel, didn't want to be seen standing around together. Why did you bring two cars?"

"Chief's idea. Thought we should mix the teams and each have a vehicle. We got a double at the Travelodge by the highway. You and I'll stay there, and Stevens and Overstreet can bunk where you rented," Hollis offers.

Thinking it over, "Sounds good. Overstreet is a few blocks down at the Rose, room one-twenty. Why don't you pick him up?" talking to Stevens, "and meet us at the Travelodge." Smith goes on, "You'll have to get a second room at the Rose. We only have a single." As soon as the words leave his mouth, he knows they'll never live that down.

When Overstreet and Stevens walk into the Travelodge room, they're carrying bags of fast food burgers and fries. Don and Jake have only had a candy bar each all day and scarf down the food as fast as they can.

The four men sit around. Overstreet briefs the newcomers on what happened since they arrived.

Stevens speaks up, "You're assuming the bombs were meant for you just because you happened to be there. What if they weren't? Just suppose this English guy was splitting and set everything on timers. You know, to cover his operation. And you guys just happened to set it off early."

"What difference…"

"Wait a minute, Jake. Let me finish. So he's got it ready to blow and hasn't left yet. Then he sees your pictures on TV. Now there's no rush to split. He could still be in town!"

Chapter 101

Later that evening. "Detective Tony Nolan, please," Smith on the phone to the Little Rock police station.

"He'll be in tomorrow," comes the answer.

"This is Chief Parson in Fayetteville. It's imperative I speak with the detective ASAP!" Smith lies.

"Yes, Sir! I'm sorry about your two detectives," the desk man offers. "If you can hold, I'll see if I can locate him?"

Seven minutes later, "Chief, are you still there?"

"I am."

"I'll patch you through to Nolan. Hold on."

"Hello Chief, this is Detective Nolan."

"Tony, Smith here."

There's a little silence, "Where the hell are you?"

"We're both alive and well, but that has to stay between us."

"The hell it does! When no bodies were found, we have every man looking for you guys. We thought you might be hurt wandering the streets in a daze or kidnapped, or bodies moved. What are you guys trying to pull?"

"Can we meet, Tony? And I'll explain everything. Please don't let it out that we're still alive, just not yet anyway."

"Where?"

Smith tells him to meet him at the North River Landing as soon as possible.

"I'll see you guys in a few," the line goes to a constant buzz.

Smith takes one of the cars and drives off.

After a long chastizing from Nolan, Smith explains what happened and their current plan. He asks for Nolan's assistant in finding Tucker's whereabouts and gives him English's Caddy's description and license plate number, which he memorized from English's first drive by. Nolan tells him he'll do what he can for the next couple of hours, after that he compelled to let his lieutenant in and he's sure the situation will go public.

Back at the motel, Smith tells his companions that Nolan's onboard and will radio over Tucker's address. Also, he put out a BOLO on English's Cadillac.

"What do we do?" asks Stevens.

"Hollis and me are going to the airport. One of you should monitor your car radio in case Nolan gets back to us quickly."

Stevens says he needs a smoke and will sit in the car. Hollis and Smith drive off to the airport.

The detectives cruise the parking areas, but can't locate the Caddy. Hollis is ready to leave, but Smith asks to be dropped off at the terminal and waited for.

Inside Jake finds the lost baggage claim office and goes in. "Hello, I'm Detective Nolan," he fabricates, quickly flashing his badge. "Can you check outgoing manifests for yesterday and today?"

"Sure, who are you looking for?"

"Arthur English."

Smith stands to wait for many minutes. "Sorry Sir, nothing listed for that name."

Smith thanks him and walks out. He stands watching luggage going around a carousel. Turning back into the office, "What about Eugene McKenzie?"

Shorty, "Here he is. Scheduled for an Air Canada flight to Montreal. That was at five-ten this afternoon." Putting his chin in his hand, "It doesn't appear he showed. You might check at the Air Canada ticket counter."

Smith goes to ticketing. Along the way, he's thinking, "English is screwing with me using that name."

On the way back to the motel their radio crackles, "Nolan here. Anyone there?"

"What did you find out, Tony?" purposely not identifying himself over the air.

"Tucker lives in Hot Springs. But he also has an apartment here at Jesse Powell Towers on Battery Street."

"We'll check out the apartment. Can you get us his vehicle make and number?"

"All ready did." Nolan lists the four cars registered in Tucker's name and their license plate nomenclature.

Smith gets on the radio and calls Stevens still sitting in the car waiting for the information on Tucker. Smith tells him Tucker's apartment location. The four meet in the Tower's parking lot.

"None of Tucker's car's are here!" Smith leads off.

Hollis jumps in, "But it's only three blocks from the Capitol, he could have walked."

"I doubt he ever walks anywhere!" Smith remembering when he met the man.

"Smith and I'll go upstairs. You guys wait here," Overstreet commands.

They show their badges to the doorman and are let in. At the security counter, they explain to the private guard that they need an escort up to Newton Tucker's apartment. The young man is only too eager to get involved. At the top floor, the guard is told to go back to his station. He closes the elevator door but doesn't push the down button.

Overstreet pounds on Tucker's apartment door, "POLICE OPEN UP!"

Chapter 102

After several poundings, a voice is heard through the door, "Who is it!"

"Police, open up!"

The door cracks a couple of inches. Newton sees Overstreet and Smith holding their badges in plain view.

"How can I assist you, Officers," acting as friendly as he can.

"We need to talk, may we come in!"

"It's late officers, come by my office in the morning."

"We were there today and you ran! We either talk here or downtown!"

Looking at each stern face, "Certainly. What's this all about?"

"The murder of Kenneth Walker!"

Acting like he's racking his brain, "Sorry. I don't believe I know that name."

"Arthur English says different!"

Staying cool, "Well come in Gentlemen. I'm sure we can straighten out this misunderstanding."

Newton opens the door wide. He stands in a dark blue, almost black satin bathrobe and black slippers. His top bald head reflecting the room lamp with the side hair in disarray. The men are shown to an overpriced VIP Chesterfield Sofa featuring a soft rich-brown exotic leather overstuffed tuck design.

"Would you gentlemen like a drink?"

"No."

"I'll have scotch if you don't mind?" While Newton pours himself a no-ice triple, Smith notices an antique long rifle on the wall above a low walnut bookshelf. "I see you have a squirrel gun," grinning at Newton.

"My daddy used to take me hunting as a young lad," as he slides into a couch-matching chair. "Now, what's on your minds, Boys?" patronizing the detectives.

"Back to Arthur English," Smith again.

"It's my understanding Mr. English isn't even in the country?"

"Sorry to disappoint you, but we picked him up at the Air Canada gate this afternoon. I guess after the little bang, he was planning on vacationing in Montreal. His Holiday will have to wait...forty to life."

"I don't follow you!" Newton is as cool as a popsicle on a hot summer day.

"He made a deal to save his skin," Overstreet joins in.

"I don't know Mr. English personally. From my understanding, he did a small job for the campaign last year. What I've been told, Mr. English is very discreet and secretive."

"Englishmen are extremely loyal to God and country, not so much to Americans. I think they might hold a little grudge over that spanking back in the seventeen-sixties," smirks Smith.

Newton still holds it together visually but is starting to question whether Smith could be right. "I have never even talked to Mr. English. Sorry I can't help you, Gentlemen." Newton stands to cut the interview short.

Catching the Lieutenant Governor in a lie, "We have your phone records. You received at least one call from him." Overstreet pulls out his notepad, "Let's see...April third, eleven-twenty-six PM." Overstreet glares in Newton's eyes, "That is six days before Kenneth Walker was murdered!"

Acting like he's deep in thought, "I remember, now. He called me by mistake. As soon as he realized it he hung up. We didn't have a discussion about anything."

"How did he get your number?"

"Have no idea. You know these investigators. Once on a case, they store every number they can get their hands on. If I remember, he was trying to reach Billy."

"Mr. Masse told us that he only took *Operation Waterfall* messages from English for *you*!"

"Operation Waterfall?" laughing, "this is all too cloak and dagger for me."

Overstreet takes over and gives Smith a break. Newton's as cagey as a boy sneaking in after curfew.

Smith stands not being able to come up with anything new, "Call your lawyer! We'll be back." He heads for the door with Overstreet following. When he suddenly swings the door open, the security guard falls into the room.

Looking up embarrassed, "I'm sorry Mr. Tucker…just thought you might need some help."

"Everything's fine, Gene. Please let these men pass."

Overstreet and Smith stand silently in the elevator. The cop wanna-be running down the hall, "Hold the door! Hold the door!" He sticks his hand in at the last second and the door reopens. Disgusted that he made it, Overstreet steps to the back leaving him room to enter.

The door closes and the chamber starts down. "You know I saw him earlier today!"

"Who?" not really paying attention.

"Mr. Tucker. He was walking across the parking lot when I came to work," the security man trying to get involved. "He got into a white Cadillac. When I got into the building I watched through the window. He and another guy sat talking for a while. It kind of looked like they were arguing."

"And," both detectives on full alert.

"Mr. Tucker came in and went upstairs. He hasn't left all day."

"The other guy?"

"He drove away."

"Would you recognize him?"

"Sure, he's been here a couple times before. I talked to him once. He had an accent."

"English?"

"No…I think it was British," the guard's brow scrunched.

Overstreet makes a note and writes down Gene's full name, address, and phone number. The elevator hits bottom. Don and Gene shake hands with Overstreet telling him they'll be in touch.

Chapter 103

"Smith are you there!" the radio is blaring as they enter their vehicle outside of Tucker's building.

Keying the mike, "What's up, Nolan?"

"Where have you guys been, I've been trying to get a hold of you for an hour!"

"Talking to Tucker. What's up?" he repeats.

"We found English's Cadillac!"

"Where?"

"It's on the dead end of Edgewood Road up in the Prospect Terrace section."

"We're on our way!"

"If you find anything, give me a call," Nolan breaks off.

Smith is scouring their city road map. Eight minutes later, "Here we go. West on Markham and north on University."

Hollis yells out the window to Overstreet, "We got the Cadillac! Follow us!"

They turn the wrong way on Edgewood and have to make a U-turn, finally locating the car.

After examining and finding absolutely nothing of interest, "Let's check the neighborhood," Overstreet to his team.

"Looking for the sports car?" Stevens questions.

"A British racing-green MG TD," Smith interjects.

"What's that?"

"A mid-fifties sports car. It small with outside swept-fenders and running boards, kind of squarish. But more importantly, it's a right-hand drive. The steering wheel is huge, you can't-miss it!" the car enthusiast fills them in.

"He won't have it parked in the open! We'll need to check garages," Overstreet states.

"How do you propose we do that?" Hollis chimes in.

"Spread out and sneak up and look in windows. If a garage doesn't have any write down the address and I'll have a look," Overstreet giving the order.

Smith knows all too well how his partner will look, "You brought your kit, huh?"

"Never leave home without it."

"You're going to have to teach me!"

The other two don't have clue what they're talking about and start sneaking up driveways. Smith and his partner walk to the next block and get started.

An hour later Stevens and Hollis catch up with Smith on Centerwood Road. "We got nothing but a long list for Overstreet to personally inspect."

"Yeah, I couldn't find many windows either," Smith responds. "Where's Don?"

Smith points down the block as he notices Overstreet jogging towards them.

Excited and out of breath, "I found it! Third house from the end of the street on left. The garage is in the back and entered off the next street over."

"We better call Nolan and get some backup!" Smith declares. "You guys watch the place and I'll go to the car and make the call."

More than an hour and a half later, Nolan and the posse shows up, search warrant in hand. The local detective takes charge and gives out position assignments. As soon as every officer has checked in, Nolan, the two Fayetteville detectives, and two officers head to the front door.

Nolan nods to the man carrying a battering ram. "POLICE! SEARCH WARRANT!" and the door crashes open, splinters flying from the destroyed door frame. The three detectives go straight up

330

the staircase. Flashlight carrying men are running through the lower floor yelling, "Clear!"

A petite woman wearing a light sea-foam green sheer nightgown emerges from a door. Her petite arms crossed over the lace decorated front hiding her small breasts, "What's going on!" she demands.

"Get on the floor!" screams the three in unison.

"Why?" confused at the early morning chaos.

"Police, get on the floor now!" Nolan screams.

She not even fully down before Smith pushes past followed by Overstreet. They run around checking the closet, bathroom, under the bed and in the giant Walnut French Armoire. Overstreet shrugs at Smith.

The diaphanous curtains flutter in a gentle spring breeze. Overstreet bolts to the window and sticks his head out. Stevens is below with his knee stuffed into the back of a handcuffed man.

Hollis looks up, "We got him!"

Chapter 104

Both Arthur English and his friend, Millie Lafarge are hauled down to the Little Rock Police Station.

Overstreet and Smith take on English leaving Stevens and Hollis to interview Lafarge in a separate interrogation room. Nolan broadcasts the detective's miraculous reincarnation from the dead and calls off both BOLOS, the one on the detectives and the second for Arthur English and his Cadillac.

"Well, well Eugene McKinzie is it?" Smith starts.

"I want a lawyer!" Arthur calmly states, arms crossed in defiance.

"We haven't arrested you, just want a little chat, Arthur."

"If I am not under arrest, I am leaving."

"Well, not quite yet. We *are* holding you."

"On what grounds?"

"No grounds. We have a legal right to hold you for up to seventy-two hours," Overstreet now in the conversation.

English smiles, thinking that seventy-two hours is a walk-in-the-park for him.

"It's your right to have an attorney present." Overstreet stands and steps towards the door. Smith stands but doesn't move.

Whirling back, "This is your chance to come clean, Arthur. You know Tucker will squeal louder than a newborn baby!"

Overstreet exits while Smith alludes, "Arthur, you know he's right. I can't picture Newton frying for you." He walks out.

A half-hour later the detectives return.

"What do you want?" English asks.

"Are you waiving your right to an attorney?"

Glowering hard, "Ask your damn questions!"

"Without your attorney?"

The scowling man concedes, "For now!"

Overstreet re-enters and sits, this time he turns on the recorder. The first order of business is Mirandizing the suspect.

When the PI nods. "We'll need verbal answers."

"Yes."

"State your name and address for the record." Continuing.

When English states the warehouse address, Overstreet asks if that is his resident and business address. English acknowledges it is. The detective question about the destruction of the building and are told he wasn't aware of the incident.

"You know the arson and bomb investigators are there as we speak? How are you ever going to pin it on someone else?" Smith's turn.

English remains quiet.

Going on, "There is no way you're getting out of planting those bombs!"

Following some thought, "I had a small flash bang set up as my security system. I'm as surprised as you that it spread beyond control."

"Arthur, Arthur, you underestimate the scope of their abilities." Smith talks to his partner but doesn't take his eyes off the suspect, "Why don't we move on, Don, we can come back to this later."

"What's your relationship with Newton Tucker?" Overstreet not really understanding Smith's logic, but going forward.

"I don't know him."

"Didn't you do work for him last year during his campaign?"

"Yes and no. I did a small investigation for the campaign committee but not the candidate personally."

"So you don't know him, but know *of* him?"

"That's correct!"

"Do you often talk to strangers in your vehicle?" Overstreet pushes.

"I don't understand your question?" English plays at confusion.

"You've been to Mr. Tucker's apartment on at least three occasions. The last time was yesterday when the two of you met in your Cadillac for twenty minutes. We have eyewitnesses willing to testify to those incidents. How do you explain talking to a stranger in your car for twenty minutes?"

"I'm not saying another word!" in his mind trying to figure out how he had been followed without knowing.

"Suit yourself. Smith, can you check if Tucker's ready to deal?"

"I'll be right back, Boss."

Overstreet sits staring at English without a word for more than ten minutes. The suspects mind is racing.

After a cup of coffee with Nolan, Smith returns. He opens the door and regains his seat, staring at English sporting a huge grin of satisfaction.

Before a word can be spoken, "What kind of deal are we talking about?" English asks.

"Well, that depends on how forthcoming you are, Arthur," Overstreet states, a matter of factly.

English quickly decides his spy and torture training isn't going to be wasted on that fat old squealer's freedom, though he sits silent.

"Here's what we're willing to do for you Arthur," Smith back in the game. "You admit that Newton Tucker hired you to kill Kenneth Walker and when we get to Fayetteville, we'll tell the DA how co-operative you were. Your attorney can negotiate a deal. I can't speculate on what that would be, but I'm almost sure the death penalty will be taken off the table and you might even have an opportunity at parole in a few years."

Overstreet has his head in his hands thinking how can Smith even make up such a fairy tale.

"I want to talk to my attorney now!" English recites the phone number.

Smith and Overstreet leave the room. In the hall, Overstreet bedevils his partner, "You can't promise a deal like that! What the hell are you thinking!"

"I thinking Tucker needs to go down and we don't have a thing unless English flips! Besides I didn't make any promises."

"Come on Smith. You can't be that dumb!" Overstreet tramps passed the hall spectators.

Smith runs after him, grabbing his arm and spinning him around, "Don, just give it a chance. You call English's attorney and I'm getting on the horn to Kevin Rogers. We'll just see what he's willing to do."

Stevens sticks his head out of a room to see what all the commotion is about.

"What has that women told you!" barks Overstreet."

"Not a whole lot. Just willing to confirm time and dates when she was with English. I don't think she really knows anything."

"Let her cool for an hour and give it another shot."

Shortly English's lawyer is bounding down the hall, "Which room is my client in?"

"Who are you?" an officer asks.

"Emma Hendricks representing Arthur English."

Bursting into the shown room, "Arthur, you haven't said anything have you?"

"Nothing to do with a crime!"

"What are the charges?"

"Murder, I believe. They haven't booked me yet."

"We're leaving!"

"Overstreet and Nolan walk in, "Arthur English you're under arrest for Attempted Murder with an explosive device, Arson, and Malicious Destruction of Property. Stand up and turn around." Nolan locks on handcuffs as tight as he can.

"I need to talk to my client," Hendricks responds.

"Wait here, I'll bring him back after booking," Nolan assures.

As two officers process Arthur English, Overstreet goes in search of Smith. Finding him pouring a coffee, "Did you get ahold of Rogers?"

"Yes, he non-committal, but will consider lowering charges. He figures even on lower charges he can keep English locked up the rest of his life."

Overstreet lays his hand on his partner's shoulder, "Good job, Jake. I shouldn't have gone off on you."

Smith, "We need to have transfer papers drawn up and get English back to Fayetteville."

"Can't do that now, Nolan just arrested English for the bombs."

Chapter 105

The four detectives arrive back in Fayetteville empty-handed. They brief Parson and McGill on their adventure.

"At least English is off the streets. We'll get a crack at him when Little Rock's finished," their Chief confirms.

"I doubt it," Overstreet speaks up. "If he gets out on bail he'll be in the wind in minutes."

"That guy probably has multiple passports in an array of names!" Smith adds.

"Little Rock promised to hold him for us," Parson speaks up.

"Unless some liberal judge cuts him loose!"

"Do you guys have a plan B?" again Parson.

"We'll have to keep digging on Tucker," Overstreet. "William Masse might be our only hope."

"First thing this morning I'll subpoena Tucker's bank accounts. We'll follow the money," Smith's back up.

"You have done a good job so far Officers. I have every confidence you'll wrap this up."

"Thanks, Chief. We better get to it."

Back at their desks. "It's getting late. I'll call Rogers and get the bank records." Smith states.

"Let me update the board and see what we're missing." Overstreet pulls out his notes and starts making new board slips.

It's after six and the men are looking over their planogram and discussing each name in depth. They decide to start at the beginning with Powell's murder and work every path through Walker's murder to English's arrest. It's as if they are starting their investigation from scratch. Both men are beyond exhaustion and resolve to get a fresh start in the morning.

Overstreet goes home to see his wife and kids. Smith drives to Alexis' home.

Jake stands at the door knocking. He too tired to even look for his key. Alex opens the door and throws herself at her man.

"Jake, I so glad you alive. I just don't know what I would have done."

He sits on the sofa while she runs to make him a sandwich. When she returns to him, he is sound asleep. Alex sets his food on the coffee table and covers him with a blanket. She sits looking at him for hours, before nodding off in a chair.

Chapter 106

The bright sun wakes her just after six o'clock. Alexis rubs the sleep from her eyes. She hears the noise of coffee being made in the kitchen and walks in. Jake's standing at the stove wearing his wrinkled clothes with wet unbrushed hair.

"Good morning, Dear. How long have you been up? Looks like you've already had a shower."

"Not long. After a cup of coffee, I have to run home and change and get to work," Jake explains. "How did you sleep?"

"Like a baby, knowing your home and safe." Alexis stretches the kinks out of her taut back.

Jake pours two mugs. She hugs him long and hard spilling coffee.

"Have a seat. I'll top off your cup and wipe up the floor," as giddy as a school girl.

Smith gulps the hot liquid as fast as possible, "I better hit it. I'll tell you everything tonight, Honey."

Another long embrace and loving kiss, he skedaddles.

When Smith gets to work, Overstreet is already hard at it. They discuss their day's plan of attack. It is decided Smith will go to Morrow and talk to Walker's neighbors. On his way back, he will swing over to Kats. Overstreet is heading to UOA to reinterview some and look for new witnesses to anything. They plan to meet back around noon. Tucker's bank records should be there by then.

Detective Jake Smith is parked in front of the Walker ruins trying to visualize how it could have happened. He's startled by an old pickup rumbling up the dirt road. Looking in his mirror all he sees is the nose of the truck protruding through a cloud of dust.

The vehicle stops next to him and both cars are blanketed with dirt. The older man stretches across the wide bench seat and rolls down his passenger side window, "Howdy Neighbor. You looking to buy?"

"Hi there," returning the greeting. "Nah, just curious. Any idea what happened here?"

The men exit their vehicles and meet at the edge of the blackened patch.

"Charlie Stone, I live down the road a piece," pointing. "Saw the blaze that morning and called the fire department. Sad thing, they were a nice young couple. Had a baby too."

"How well did you know the Walker's," the detective questions.

"Not real well. I'd bring'em some of my vegetables once in a while and we'd sit and jaw for a minute." Thinking it over, "How'd ya know their name? You a relative?"

"Jake Smith," extending a hand. "I'm a detective."

"Funny thing, the cops never came around…only that fellow interested in buying the place."

"Clean this mess up it could be a nice spot!" Smith observes.

"That was before it burnt! I told'em the building needed demolishing and a new one made."

"Charlie, you're telling me a stranger was poking around before the fire."

"I just said that. Some foreigner. Funny thing though, when I went to get Jan's card he disappeared."

"Foreigner? As in English?"

"Yeah, How'd ya know?"

"Who's Jan?"

"A friend from church. She sells houses."

"I really need to get to church more," Smith reflects silently to himself.

"Did Jan ever tell you if she talked to the Englishman?"

"She asked me a few times if he was ever gonna call. I guess he didn't."

"Do you remember what the man told you?"

"Sure. His car was broke down and he needed to use my phone. When he left suddenly, I walked down to the road. I move a little slower these days…a touch of arthritis, you see. Anyway, by the time I got to the end of my drive, I couldn't see him or his car. I figure he got it running and left. I waited a while for Bob to show up, but he never did."

"Bob?"

"He owns the only tow service around these parts. See him at church every Sunday."

"You think you'd recognize the Englishman if I show you a picture?"

"Sure, my legs are bad not my head."

Smith shows him English's mug shot and Stone is positive it's the same man.

"Thanks, Charlie. It was a pleasure talking." Smith sits in his car and writes a note, "English cased the Walker home before the murder - witness: Charles Stone - closest neighbor."

He waves goodbye to the farmer and drives back to town.

Smith walks into Kats. It's early and the only one there is a woman wiping down the bar area. "Good morning."

Startled, she looks up, "Sorry, Sir, we don't open for an hour."

"Detective Smith. Can I ask you a couple of questions?"

"Who are you guys hassling now?"

"Same people!" Smith grins. "Did you read the Times this morning?"

"Don't have time for that trash." She hasn't stopped wiping though it looks like the dirty rag is putting more down than picking up.

"There is a story about an arrest of a man suspected of murdering Kenneth Walker." Receiving a blank look, "Squirrel, Liz…Lulu's husband?"

"I know who Ken is!"

"Good. I'm trying to find out if this guy was ever in here?" Smith pulls the mug shot from his pocket. He tries to hand it the woman. When she doesn't accept it, Smith lays it on the bar and spins it right side up to her.

"Don't remember him," not even looking.

"You don't want to help your friend and her husband?"

"Lu and Ken were no friends of mine!"

Contemplating, "What about Madison and Ethan, are they friends?"

"Sure, Madison got me this job." All of sudden, "I thought I recognized you! The boss has your newspaper picture framed on his office wall. You're the Hero!"

"I would hardly say that. There were a ton of people involved," feeling a blush coming on.

"Grace Udal. It's a pleasure to meet you. Want a free drink?"

"No thanks, I'm on duty. So you don't remember a stranger asking about Liz and Squirrel?"

"Damn!" She decides since she has nothing to hide and this officer saved her friends and her job, "A fellow came in a while back asking about scoring a little weed and I told him about Squirrel."

"Do you remember the conversation?" Thinking it over Smith adds, "With all the men coming and going in here, why would you remember this fellow?"

"He was funny. And left big tips!"

"Did he mention why he was in Fayetteville?"

"Don't really remember…I think he was a salesman."

"Do you know if he scored?"

"Lu came into work and I hooked them up. She wasn't happy about it if I remember. He snuck back to the dressing room when he thought I wasn't looking. Later that night he was back and sat with Squirrel. Then he left."

"Would you be willing to testify if it ever gets that far?"

"I don't think so."

Smith hands her his card, "If you remember anything else can you call me?"

"About Liz and Squirrel or the Englishman?"

"You never mentioned he was English."

"Yeah, had an accent and all. A friend of Tucker's father, I think. You know the kid that OD'd. He used to come in here and cause trouble until Denny eighty-sixed him."

"Will you look at my picture?"

Grace picks up the mug shot, "That's him!"

"Thanks, Grace. I really appreciate your help."

"Yea. Come back later. I get you that drink." She mentions she gets off at six.

Ignoring the invite, "You never said if you were here or not that night."

"Lucky I work the day shift. Missed the whole thing!"

"That's good, Grace. Maybe I will stop by for that drink sometime."

Smith rushes back to the station.

Overstreet's already back looking through papers as Smith enters the detective room.

Jake calls Alex, "Hi Alexis, busy tonight?"

"I hope so! What do you have in mind?"

"I thought I'd pick up a couple of ribeyes. I'm barbequing, interested?"

"You know I am!" excited, "I shouldn't tell you, but I'm throwing away that old rusted Hibachi. I've already bought you a real grill for Christmas."

"Why don't we celebrate Christmas in June this year?"

"I'll bring it with me," still laughing.

Getting to work Smith lays out the two eyewitness he found identifying Arther English's mug shot and their stories connecting to the Walkers.

Overstreet tells him that he found Donna Pearl, who also met an Englishman named Steven George. And identified English as such.

"Did we get the bank records?" Smith asks.

"I just going through them right now!" Overstreet taps the papers in front of him.

"I'm calling Dr. Yakiniku," Jake dialing.

Off the phone, "The doctor told me an English man named George checked Powell in on December thirtieth. I'm going have Nolan take the mug shot over for identification."

"December thirtieth? Tucker withdrew six thousand on the thirty-first. Could be a payment!"

Smith redials Bill Masse's private line and questions him in length about Operation Waterfall and his boss withdrawing cash right after Powell's incarceration at Pillar Point. Masse doesn't offer anything new.

"Let me ask you this, William, after the first of the year, how many Operation Waterfall communique did you receive?"

"None, that I recall. Only Operation Gazebo!"

"What the hell is that?" not being able to contain professionalism.

"New code word I image, the same messenger."

"Do you know the date you first heard that phrase?"

After shuffling through what must be phone message slips, "April tenth...Operation Gazebo concluded. Looks like this is the only time."

Off the phone to his partner, "What withdrawals did you find after Walker's murder...specifically on or after the tenth."

"I'm not into April yet." Overstreet thumbs through his pages and pulls out April's statement. "Holy crap...he withdrew thirty thou!" He goes to another stack, "And forty from savings." Another pile, "And here's eighty from an IRA! That's…" adding with his pencil, "One hundred and fifty thousand dollars in CASH!"

"I'm calling Rogers."

After forty minutes explaining everything they have.

"You guys put everything together like a string of box cars! I'll have warrants ready in a half hour!" Roger's as excited as the detectives.

"Let's make a road trip!" Smith almost falls jumping to his feet.

Hours on the road, just outside of Little Rock, "There's Pillar Point, turn around and we'll get the doctor's ID." Smith points as they drive past.

"I thought Nolan was getting it."

"I didn't have time to call him."

Chapter 107

The Fayetteville pair walks into the Little Rock Police station.
"Good evening, Sergeant. Detectives Overstreet and Smith to see
Detective Nolan."

"Good afternoon Detectives. I'm surprised to see you again so
soon. I'll see if Nolan's still here."

Hanging up the phone, "Go on back, Detectives."

They see Nolan at his desk, relaxing back his hands locked
behind his head, talking with a couple other men. Nolan spots them
entering, "Come on in, Gentlemen. What's up?"

"We're going to arrest Newton Tucker for the murder of Kenneth
Walker and thought you might join us." Overstreet holds up his
arrest and search warrants.

"That was fast. Did you even leave town?"

"Just got back." Smith uncontrollably happy.

"You know it's Friday. Tucker's probably in Hot Springs."
Nolan offers.

"Crap, I didn't think of that!" Smith's smile disappearing." We
were just through there!"

"It's only an hour back." Nolan's turn to laugh. "Check in with
their department. I'll call and see who's on and radio you."

"Thanks, Tony. We'll talk." Smith and Overstreet head back to
their car.

At the edge of town, they pull through McDonald's for a couple
of burgers on the way.

Late evening the detectives are sitting in Hot Spring's Police
Headquarters and explain everything to a detective named Davidson.

The three detectives and two uniforms convoy to the Tucker
mansion. It's almost ten o'clock at night.

Overstreet rings the bell and Mrs. Tucker answers the door, "Mr. Smith, what's going on? surprised at the gang of men.

"Judith, is your husband here?" Smith asks.

"Why are you looking for Newton?"

"Is your husband here?" repeating without explaining.

"I'll get him." She tries to close the door.

Overstreet rapidly stops it with a foot, "We're coming with you!" showing her the arrest warrant.

The woman displays a look of discontent, "He's in his study. Follow me."

As soon as she reaches for the door latch, Davidson grabs her arm, "We'll take in from here, please step back!"

Overstreet tries the door. It's locked, "Police open up!" screams Overstreet.

"Just a minute!"

They hear voices click off and a little shuffling around, as Newton ejects and hides his favorite porn VHS. The unlocking noise is heard and the detectives slam open the door and burst into the room knocking Tucker back off his feet.

"Newton Tucker you are under arrest for the murder of Kenneth Walker! Stay down!" Smith straddles the overweight man and puts on the cuffs.

"Get him off me! You guys made a grievous mistake! I'll have all your badges!" squirming under Smith's weight.

Judith is standing at the open door in disbelieve, her hand covering her gaping mouth.

Overstreet and Smith struggle to get Newton on his feet. In the end, it takes four of them to lift him.

"You finished!" screams Tucker. "I'm suing you for everything you have or ever will have! Judith get all their names and badge numbers!"

Overstreet pushes the fat man into a chair, and throws the search warrant in his lap, "We're searching the house!"

347

"Call Pinneli!" screaming at his wife. "What the hell are you looking for?" to anyone listening.

Two hours later, Overstreet's car trunk contains five cardboard boxes of papers and files. They thank Davidson and the officers for their assistance and tell Attorney Pinneli they are transporting Tucker to Fayetteville.

Pinneli advises, "Newton, do not say a word! I have to get some things from my office and will be there as soon as I can."

Chapter 108

Newton Tucker stays ballistic with threats and filthy language insults for the entire three and a half hour drive. Overstreet and Smith are silent. An hour in, Smith's head is thumping to the constant beat of a marching band. "Doesn't this guy ever shut up?"

Overstreet is concentrating and doesn't answer the rhetorical question.

Once inside their station, they take Tucker's mug shot. After all the screaming and resisting, finally, Tucker exhausts and gives in. The officers get him standing on the floor marks. Refusing to take the handcuffs off, Smith has to reach in and hold the identification plaque. The simple task took a half-hour manhandling the large restrained man.

"If you want to make this easier on yourself, we can take your fingerprints and sit for a chat," Overstreet tries a little diplomacy

"I'm saying a ******* word without Pinneli. You two bastards can go **** yourselves!"

Overstreet tries to Mirandized the suspect over his shouting. Smith walks away and returns with a small piece of cloth.

Tucker's in mid-sentence when Smith shoves in the rag.

Overstreet repeats the Mirandize over the muffled incomprehensible reverberations.

"What the hell are you guys doing?" yells Pinneli as he runs to his client.

"We just Mirandized him," smiling Smith. The band has stopped in his head.

Pinneli pulls out the rag. "You ******* bastards!" Newton continues, never missing a word.

"Calm down Newton," Pinneli resting his hand on his client's shoulder, "we'll get this straightened out."

Newton Tucker continues screaming profanity at the detectives until hoarse. Finally quiet, "Ok detectives, please remove the cuffs," the attorney submits.

Overstreet moves behind and as soon as the first hand is free, Tucker throws a roundhouse into Smith's mouth. He reels backward in the counter. Blood instantly flowing from his upper lip.

Four uniforms jump on the lunatic and throw him to the floor. It takes every present officer wrestling with Tucker before he's re-cuffed.

Smith retreats to the washroom. Pinneli steps back from the far side of the room. The rest try to regain their composer and calm their nerves while sucking in volumes of air. Newton struggles to stand and Overstreet rams his shoe into Tucker's back, "You're not moving!"

Eventually, Tucker is all but carried to an interview room and chained to the table.

"How are you fairing, Jake?" concerned Overstreet at Jake's swelling jaw.

"Just give me five minutes with that asshole."

"You know that's not happening."

"Two minutes!"

"Let's go talk to Tucker."

Pinneli trails Overstreet and Smith to the waiting suspect.

Pinnelli, "This really isn't necessary. I'm sure Mr. Tucker will control himself. Please take the cuffs off."

The detectives ignore the lawyer's request and try to extract information from Tucker for two hours. Nearly every question is answered by Pinneli with, "Don't answer that or Mr. Tucker invokes his Fifth Amendment rights."

The detectives finally retreat to their desks. The sun has just risen. Not five minutes later McGill enters.

After Overstreet delivers a short hypothesis, the detectives agree to meet with the DA later that day.

McGill tells them to go home and get some sleep.

Chapter 109

Pinneli stays to talk to his client after Overstreet and Smith leave the room.

"Why are we here, Newton?" wanting the unabridged version.

"Because those ******* bastards are trying to railroad me!"

"How's that?"

"Apparently they arrested some guy I never met, and he told them I murdered some drug dealer I never met! If these idiots buy this bunkum I'm going down and the real criminal is going free! I can't believe this bullshit!"

"Can you give me the names of these two?" though he already knows from the attempted interview by the detectives.

"How the hell do I know?"

"Newton, how long have we worked together?"

"Shit, five years?"

"Nine. I've always been on your side. This time isn't any different. I'm here for you no matter what!" The attorney pauses for effect, then, "If you can't trust me and tell me in a calm rational dialogue exactly what is going on, there isn't much I can do for you! Do you understand?"

Tucker's demure response, "Of course, Rudy. I'm sorry. They just make me so ******* mad."

"I know, but let's try, Ok?"

"All I know is my son was murdered with heroin that came from this Walker guy…"

"Who is Walker?"

"The drug dealer I was supposed to have murdered!"

"I thought you didn't know his name?"

"What ******* difference does it make?"

Pinneli adds another note. "I thought your son overdosed?"

"The police figured it out. They arrested Walker's wife. *She did it*!" Newton's blood pressure's on the rise. "Then the slut commits suicide rather than face the death penalty."

I'm confused. Walker's wife was arrested for murdering Powell?"

"NO! Her husband!"

"Who murdered Powell?"

"Walker! He sold my son the heroin! Understand?"

"Just about. You're trying to say Powell overdosed on heroin and it's the drug dealer fault for selling it to him?"

"And *the fact* that he murdered Powell by deliberately over injecting him!" Tucker trying to clear it up.

"Who told you that?"

"The police."

Pinneli sits rubbing his forehead. "Was Walker, *the husband*, arrested?" Before receiving an answer, and thinking aloud, "And why would a supplier want to eliminate a customer?"

"That's the million dollar question. I lay awake at night trying to figure out the ******* motive."

"Ok. So just to be clear, Walker, the husband, kills Powell..." looking down, stroking his nose, "then he is murdered..." pointing his left index finger to the side and watching it bounce up and down, "and Walker, the wife..." now pointing his right-hand finger, "did it..." taking his right pointed finger in an arch touching his left hand, which he closes to a fist "and it is solved, so she kills herself..." curling his right finger into his fist. Staring at the two closed fists, "Why would she kill her husband?" more questioning himself.

"Because he's a ******* drug dealer!"

Finally, Pinneli looks up and recaps again for clarity, "Walker, *the husband*, kills Powell; Walker *the wife* kills him; she's caught and kills herself. Two murders, both solved and the final killer dead. What's all this have to do with you and some other guy?"

"I don't have a ******* idea!"

"Please, Newton, stop the language. It doesn't help." Pinneli asks, "Do you know the name of the other guy they arrested?"

"Mr. English or something. I think it's the name of a country."

"All right Newton. That's enough for tonight." Pinneli stands, "Don't say a word to anyone!"

"You don't have to ******* tell me that! Are you getting me out of this ******* place?"

"Not right now. Try to rest and I'll see you a little later." Pinneli knocks on the door and is let out. He walks down the hall mumbling to himself. He makes his way past the front desk and takes a seat.

Rudy is sitting alone trying to make sense of what Newton Tucker is really saying. He glances at the counter, "Excuse me, Officer, what cell is Mr. English in?"

The officer looks up, "Don't have an English in custody."

Pinneli stands, "Are you sure?"

"Of course."

"Can you please double check?"

After a couple minutes, "No English."

Pinneli walks out into the cold air. This night is over.

Chapter 110

Smith has been ringing Alexis' bell for five minutes. He wants to catch a couple hours shut-eye at her place rather than driving all the way home and back. Knowing she keeps a loaded gun in the top drawer of her nightstand, he thinks better of walking in on her. Tired, he just departs for home.

Halfway to Springdale Smith pulls into a gas station. He tries to phone her. She doesn't answer and the machine is off. He is beat but wrestles with whether to go home or back. He decides he needs to check on her well-being.

He drives back to Alex's home. This time he uses his key and enters. Jake pulls his gun and sneaks through the house checking rooms. Going down the hall he takes a quick glance into her dark office and continues past the spare bedroom to her room. He is quietly turning the knob when the distinct sound of a cocking gun breaks the silence. He spins and squats, while raising his gun, in one smooth motion. Smith is staring down the barrel of a .357 Magnum.

"Jake, what are you doing?" Alex lowers her weapon.

"You scared the crap out of me!" Smith doing likewise and standing. "Where did you come from?"

"I was sleeping on the office couch. And heard the floor squeak."

Smith laughing, "I glad you're alright, I was pretty worried."

"You were worried! Where the hell have you've been?"

"It's a long story. Overstreet and I went to Little Rock to arrest Newton Tucker. He wasn't there and we had to go back to Hot Springs, where we got him! It's been a circus ever since." Rubbing his swollen jaw for a little sympathy.

"We had a date tonight! You couldn't call?"

"I'm sorry Alexis, the time got away from me?"

"How much time does it take to let me know you're alive and well?"

"You're right…I'm such a prick!"

"Don't tease me when I'm mad at you!"

Laughing they entwine, "You make me so happy," Smith whispers in her ear."

"And you make me so mad!" She pulls back and looks him in the eyes, "Honey, I worry about you. It's important that you let me know…" stopping when she notices his swollen face, "What happened. Are you alright? Come into the bathroom where I can look at you."

Smith enjoys her soft touch as she closely inspects his jaw and cut lips. "What happened, Pumpkin?"

"Tucker cold-cocked me."

"You have to be careful when your arresting criminals!"

Unable to control his laughter, he barely squeaks out, "This was at the station, hours after his arrest."

"I need a drink of water. Let's go to the kitchen and you can tell me all about it." Alexis suggests.

An hour later, after Smith's Reader's Digest version, while cuddling on the back porch swing under a blanket, Alex's asks, "Do you have to work today?"

"Overstreet and I have to go through all Tucker's paperwork, and meet with Rogers." Alex stretches up and plants a long passionate gentle kiss on his sore mouth.

"I'll call Don and leave a message that I would be there until eleven or so." Getting a second wind, "Hey, let's get some donuts!"

Chapter 111

Saturday morning, just after ten o'clock, Pinneli is back at the police station. "Is Detective Smith or Overstreet in?" he asks the front desk.

"What's your name?" The officer calls up to the detective room.

"Detective Overstreet's coming down. Have a seat."

Five minutes later, "Mr. Pinneli?"

"Detective. You don't have English in custody! What's going on here?"

"English *is* in custody!"

Before the detective can explain, "I must have been misinformed. What cell is he in?"

"Not sure. He's in Little Rock."

Pinneli thinks about it, "When is he being transferred up?"

"Don't know. A few months probably. He was arrested in a separate case down there," Overstreet not in the mood to go into detail.

Pinneli thanks him and asks the desk sergeant to see his client.

"What's English saying?" demands Pinneli to Tucker.

"How would…"

"Newton, let me make this perfectly clear; Monday tells whether you spend the next two years in jail or not."

"Two years? I think I can handle that." Tucker perking up.

"That's just *before* a trial starts! If English flipped on you, you *will die* in prison! DO YOU UNDERSTAND?"

"What do we do?"

"Tell me about Arthur English and your relationship! Did you hire him and how much did you pay him?"

"Six thousand dollars, but that was just to scare the drug dealer. I certainly didn't want him killed! That's the God's honest truth, Rudy."

"Newton, let's start at the beginning and tell me everything up to this minute. No lies! No omissions! The whole truth!"

Newton Tucker, the Lieutenant Governor of Arkansas, spends the next two hours confessing to his attorney. By the end of his story, he is a broken man. Crying! Ashamed! Scared!

Pinneli has no words. After sitting for a long time in silent, he stands, "Newton, I have got my work cut out for me. I'll see you in court Monday morning."

"What are you going to do?" Tucker questions.

"Phone *my* private investigator to find out what's really going on."

Chapter 112

Monday morning at eighty-thirty, Smith downs his last swallow of coffee and turns to his partner, "Let's mosey over to the courthouse. Rogers might be there early and have a couple last minute questions."

Overstreet squints at the clock and watches it painfully click seconds away, slower with each tick. The detectives started before sunup and reviewed their entire investigation. The last hour more torturous than waiting for a late bride.

"All right. Let's go!"

The clock doesn't click another second before Smith is up and walking.

In the courthouse hallway, Judith Tucker and Nikki Hacket are sitting with Pinneli looking worried as he talks softly to them. The rest of the benches are empty. The detectives sit as far from the trio as possible.

At five minutes to nine, Kevin Rogers enters the passageway carrying a huge scuffed brown-leather briefcase in his left hand. It's larger than salesman's product tote. His right arm juggling a mountain of additional papers. He struggles past the Detectives smiling and offers a nod of confidence.

By straight up nine o'clock the packed corridor is empty. A guard softly closes the felicitous double Cherrywood doors as the bailiff commands, "All rise! The State of Arkansas versus Newton Tucker. The Honorable Judge Goodwin presiding."

The court recorder thumping her stenotype machine.

Jake is frantically searching the room for Reporter Dench. He can't pick her out in the packed room."

359

"Please be seated." As the judge takes the elevated bench in front of perfectly hung American and Arkansas flags.

Jake's cranes his neck, his searching eyes continue to scan the room for Dench.

"Good morning, Mr. Rogers," Goodwin acknowledges the district attorney.

He turns his attention to the defense table. Pinneli jumps to his feet, buttoning his suit jacket, "Rudolf Pinneli for the defense, Your Honor."

"Good morning, Mr. Pinneli."

"Is the state and defense ready?" Goodwin asks.

Pinneli back in his chair. Both attorney's answer, "Yes, Your Honor," in unison.

Smith's reporter slips through the back ingress. The courtroom overfull with spectators, she takes a place along the back wall between other standers. Jake beams a look of relief at Alex. She doesn't see it.

Judge Goodwin looks over the crowd, "This is an evidentiary hearing solely to determine evidence. Hearsay will be allowed at this time." Looking at the defense table, "Mr. Pinneli, how does the defendant plead?"

Returning to his feet, "Not guilty, Your Honor."

"Very well, Mr. Rogers, you're up!"

The DA stands and goes through his list of evidence one point at a time and expounding on each item. At various intervals, he walks around the front of the room, staring at Tucker, and adding emphasis to certain points hoping for a visible reaction. None received. Pinneli did a good job prepping his client. Twice Rogers checks notes to make sure of facts before verbalizing. An hour and a half later, he stands at the edge of the bench and points at the defendant, "There is absolutely no doubt Newton Tucker conspired to murder Kenneth Walker in cold blood!" After seconds of glaring he walks, shoulders back in perfect posture, to his chair and sits.

360

"Counselor, your turn," Goodwin addresses Pinneli.

"Your Honor, I request a short recess to confer with my client?"

Goodwin glimpses at the clock, "Court is in recess for fifteen minutes." He bangs his gavel and leaves the room.

Not a peep from the audience, hoping to overhear every word. Pinneli turns around scanning the horde. He turns back to Tucker, "Come with me." They strut down the aisle, two guards in tow.

As the pair exit the courtroom they're barraged with shouting questions from the press. In the hallway, it continues coupled with three national network cameras rolling and countless flashbulbs exploding. Tucker smiles defiantly trudging through the deep battalion. He follows his lawyer to an off hallway room.

Before Tucker can sit, Pinneli starts yelling, "YOU LIED TO ME! YOU SAID YOU TOLD ME EVERYTHING. YOU TOLD ME YOU PAID ENGLISH SIX THOUSAND DOLLARS. DIDN'T YOU THINK THEY WOULD CHECK!"

They go back and forth for the allocated time. Finally exasperated the attorney announces, "We have to get back!"

Pinneli stands and offers a few feeble retorts on minor accusations. There is no doubt in his mind it's going to trial. In less than twenty minutes he concludes and sits.

Goodwin bangs his gavel several times, "If I can't get silence, this room will be emptied!" After many more bangs, the reporters and audience still. "I find there is enough evidence to hold the defendant over for trial. Bailiff, can you check the calendar for the earliest available date for the arrangement?"

The judge announces a date for the following week, bangs his gavel again and stands, "Consolers in my chambers!" He stomps off.

After a verbal lashing, Goodwin sets rules the attorneys are expected to strictly adhere to. Ending, "This is not going to be a carnival sideshow! Are we clear?"

"Yes, Your Honor!" together.

In the corridor, Pinneli tells Rogers he'll file an Information Release immediately and to get all his files together.

Chapter 113

Pinneli disregards Newton and walks out of the court. The squawking reporters and camera don't phase the fuming man as he clumps past. He doesn't even acknowledge Judith and Nikki's presence. He goes straight to his car and drives to Little Rock.

It's more than two hours on the road before he relaxes and starts contemplating his next move.

At his office desk, he looks up the Attorney of Record for Arthur English and calls the unfamiliar woman. Getting past the receptionist, "Hello, Mr. Pinneli."

"Ms. Hindrick, I'm Newton Tucker's attorney," pausing for a response.

"What can I help you with?"

"I understand you represent Arthur English?"

"That's correct."

"I would like to ask him a few questions…in your presence of course."

"You're welcome to if you can find him."

"Isn't he still in jail?"

"No. With no charges filed pertaining to your case, I managed to make a deal and get his charges reduced. He was released on a quarter million last Friday. I've been trying to reach him since and he doesn't answer."

"English wasn't charged with conspiracy?" stunned.

"Not at that time, I suspect that would happen following Tucker's prelim. I foresee receiving notification any moment."

"Thank you, Ms. Hindrick. Can you keep me posted if you hear from English?"

She promises to and they conclude the call.

Pinneli thinks to himself, "Boy, she moved quick! That's one smart woman."

Rudy next phones Zackery Warak, a veteran criminal defense lawyer.

"Hey there Rudy, how'd the Tucker preliminary go?"

"Not good, Zack. He needs more than I have to offer. I was wondering about you being co-counsel?"

"I would be interested. When can we meet?"

"How about the Capital Grill, say five-thirty?"

"I'll see you there."

They both show up five minutes late for their meeting. The grill is a particularly expensive upscale establishment, but at this early hour, they get a table despite lacking reservations.They haven't run into each other for a few months and spend time catching up over drinks. They ultimately order. Pinneli goes for the prime rib and Warak has the grilled salmon with lemon and basil. Waiting to eat they get down to business.

Warak delights in high-profile cases and demands first-chair. Pinneli doesn't have to think twice about his losing case and relinquishes, though he acts hurt and undervalued.

They end their meal with Crème Brulee and brandy. Pinneli promises to send the files over first thing in the morning.

Chapter 114

Two Fridays later, at nine AM the courthouse is again packed with the surfeit crammed in the hallway.

After an all-encompassing disquisition from DA Rogers. Judge Goodwin breaks for lunch.

Zackery Warak puts on just as a compelling defense, which takes the rest of the day and set to be continued the next.

After the first day's late conclusion at five-thirty, the courtroom is humming with conjecture. Not a single person, barring reporters, vacate the room. The number of Tucker's supporters grows a couple of points, inconsequential, but nevertheless an increase.

Pinneli congregates papers and files oblivious to the brouhaha behind him. Warak is consulting Tucker at the time a woman elbows her way down the aisle. She approaches Tucker and Warak, "Excuse me. Mr. Tucker?" Before Warak can address the woman she serves Newton Tucker divorce papers.

Later in his cell, Tucker reads and rereads Judith's divorce summons and complaint. He lays the documents on the thin mattress, they call a bed and stares blankly at his untouched dinner for an hour.

A guard appears at the barred window above the pass through to retrieve the compartmental steel dinner tray. "Tucker, are you going to eat?"

The prisoners glazed over eyes does not acknowledge intruder.

"Tucker!" a short loud retort trying to snap the man back into the present.

Newton suddenly grasps his orange jumpsuit's upper-left chest with both hands, his eyeballs roll up into their cavities and he collapses to the cement floor.

The guard screams, "Help! Help emergency! Prisoner down!" as he fumbles at his keyring.

Not many minutes later paramedics are defibrillating Tucker's chest with a thousand volts of electricity. The lifeless body muscles react with a violent jolt. The electrocardiography display exhibits a few intermittent spikes emphasized with audible beeps before returning to a continuous straight lime-green line. "Again! Clear!" After the third shock, they get a low but steady beat. Tucker is thrown on a gurney and rushed to Washington Regional.

The ER Doctor immediately starts a Catheter-direct thrombolysis procedure while a surgeon prepares for coronary artery bypass surgery. After more than an hour of thrombolytic drugs, Tucker stabilizes and breathing on his own. The bypass surgery is delayed for the time being.

They wheel Tucker into a recovery room for observation throughout the night. A guard is on duty in front of the closed curtain.

Jake and Alexis are sharing a late celebratory dinner with Don and Martha Overstreet at Mountain House's upscale restaurant. A little after nine o'clock the maître d approaches their table, "Excuse me, Mr. Smith you have a phone call. If you'll follow me, please."

In the alcove off the bar, "Thanks, Chief." Smith leans into the faux Oak wallboard to steady himself. The handset slips from his hand and dangles at the end of a thin-steel coil-wrapped cord. Many minutes later he snaps up and looks around to make sure no one's watching. Jake reaches down for the handset and hangs it back in its cradle.

He weaves slowly back towards their table. His face as big and whiter than Antartica's Polar Plateau. Alex springs to her feet and runs to him, "Honey, are you alright?" she screams. Everyone in the room instantly stares.

The Overstreets are quickly at his side. Don latches on to Smith's arm, "Talk to me, Buddy!"

Jake turns his head to Don, "Newton Tucker's dead!"

"What? How?" stammers his partner.

"Suicide…they found a silenced Smith & Wesson Model 52 on the sheet next to him.

About the Author

David Whalen was born in Northern British Columbia, Canada. At the age of two, his family moved to Vancouver Island off the southern coast of the province. He spent his early spent his early childhood romping the forests surrounding the small logging and mill town.

At age eleven, his family again relocated, this time to Southern California. Mr. Whalen continued his schooling through college, where he earned a multiple degree in marketing/retailing, from Grossmont College in the East County area of San Diego.

During his college years, he married and started a family.

Upon graduation, he promoted into management for a major drug store chain in their eastern California desert location. After an eleven-year career, he left his position, moved back to San Diego, and started a national Christmas Décor manufacturing company.

Mr. Whalen soon became a serial entrepreneur. Through thirty-four years of self-employment, he grew many companies and sold three. While on this journey, he invented and licensed numerous products.

After selling his last enterprise, Mr. Whalen retired and is now pursuing a writing career.

I really appreciate you reading my book!

Connect with H David Whalen

More Books: hdwhalen.com/books.htm

Friend Me on Facebook: facebook.com/hdwhalen

Linkedin: linkedin.com/in/david-whalen-96408a32

Visit my Website: www.hdwhalen.com

Email Me: hdwhalen@outlook.com